Pokémon®

Pokémon Ranger and the Temple of the Sea

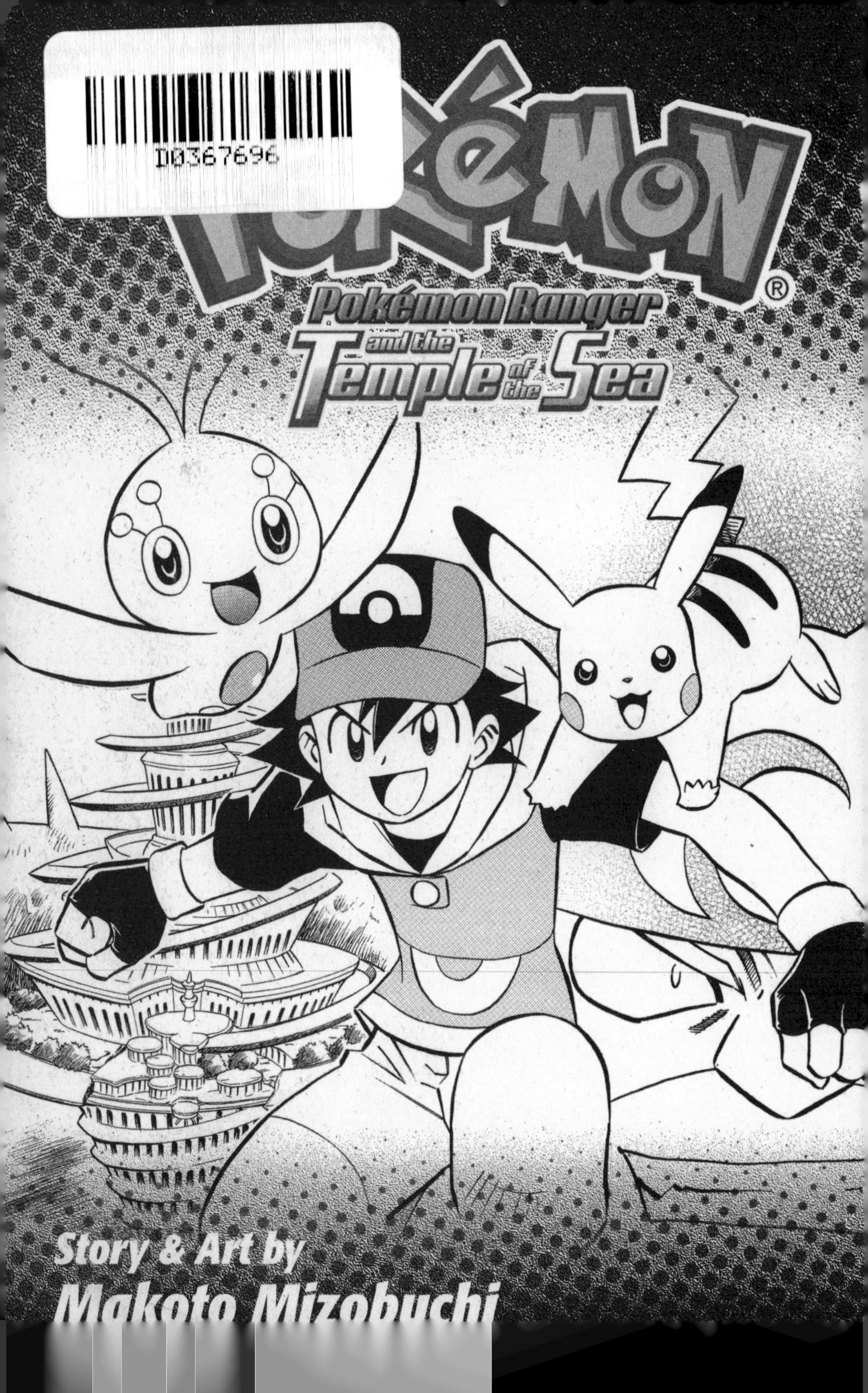

Story & Art by

Makoto Mizobuchi

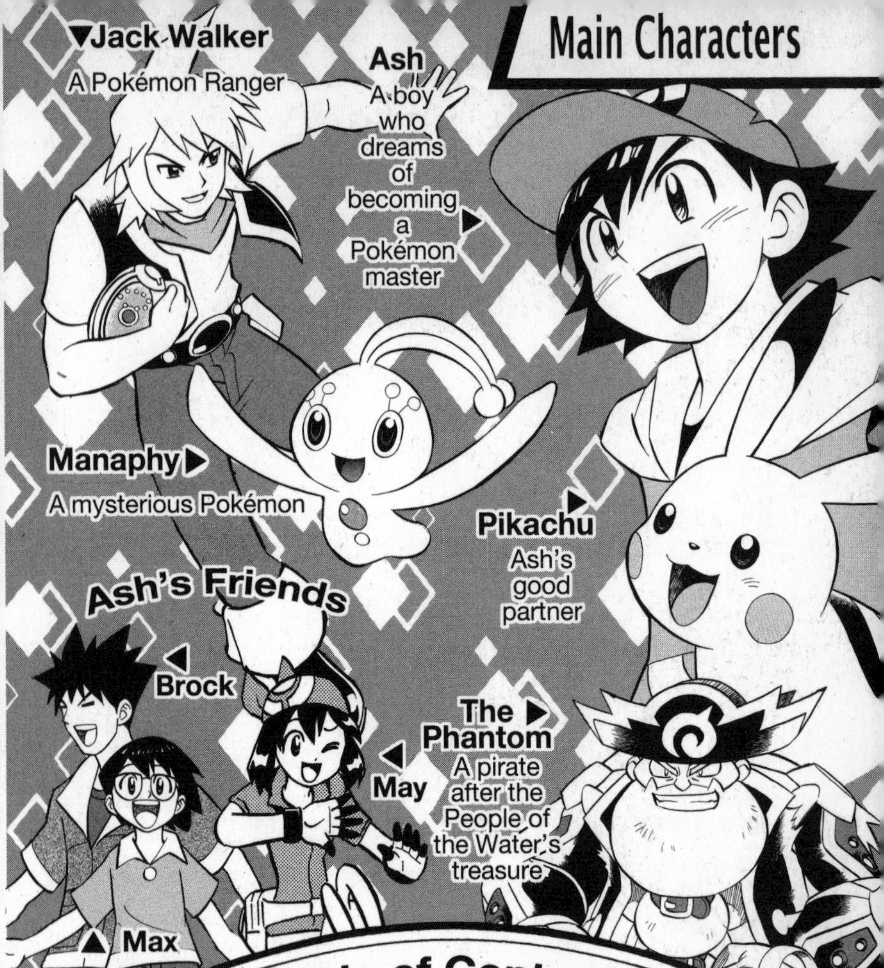
Main Characters
Ash
A boy who dreams of becoming a Pokémon master
Jack Walker
A Pokémon Ranger
Manaphy
A mysterious Pokémon
Pikachu
Ash's good partner
Ash's Friends
Brock
The Phantom
A pirate after the People of the Water's treasure
May
Max

Table of Contents

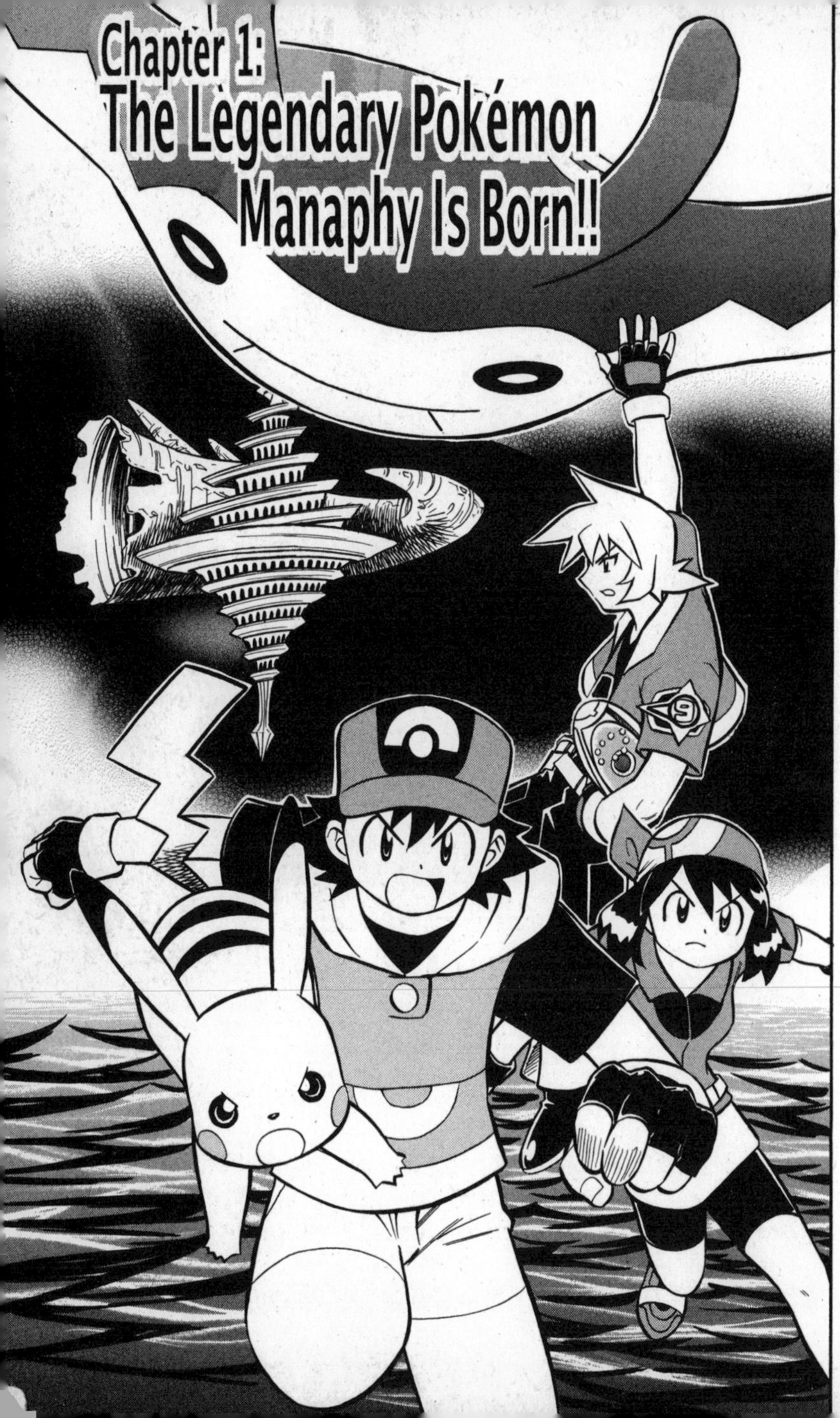
Chapter 1:
The Legendary Pokémon
Manaphy Is Born!!

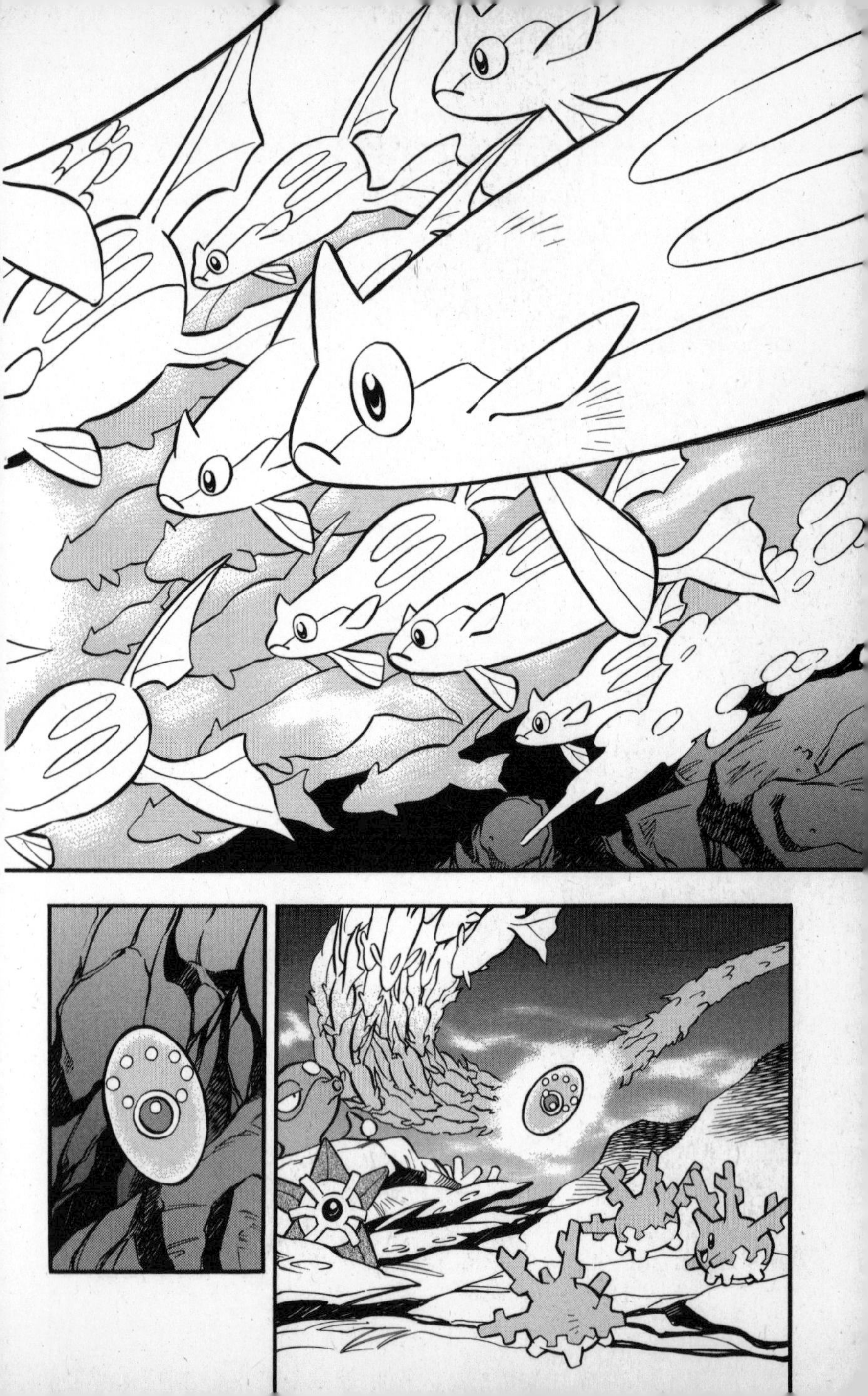

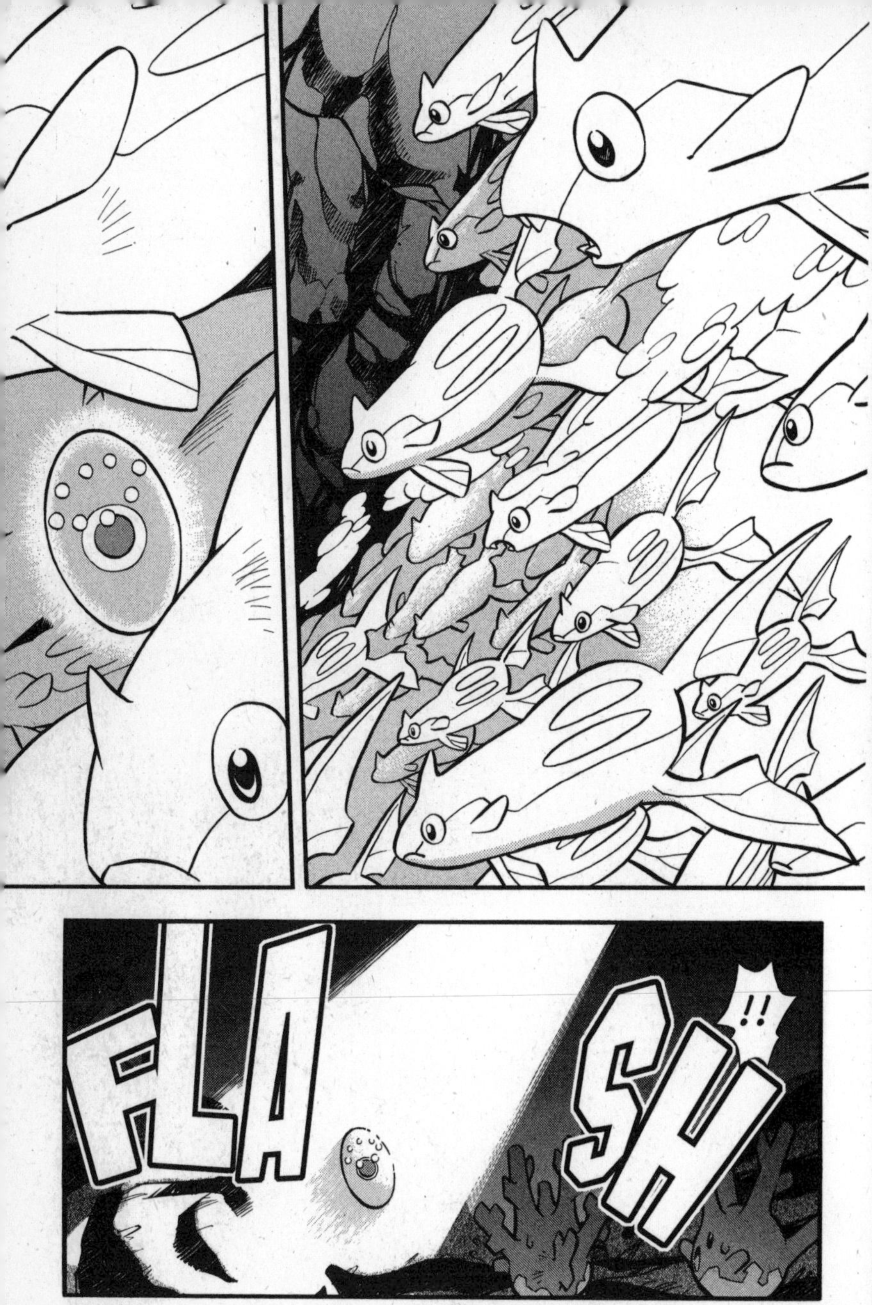
FLASH
!!

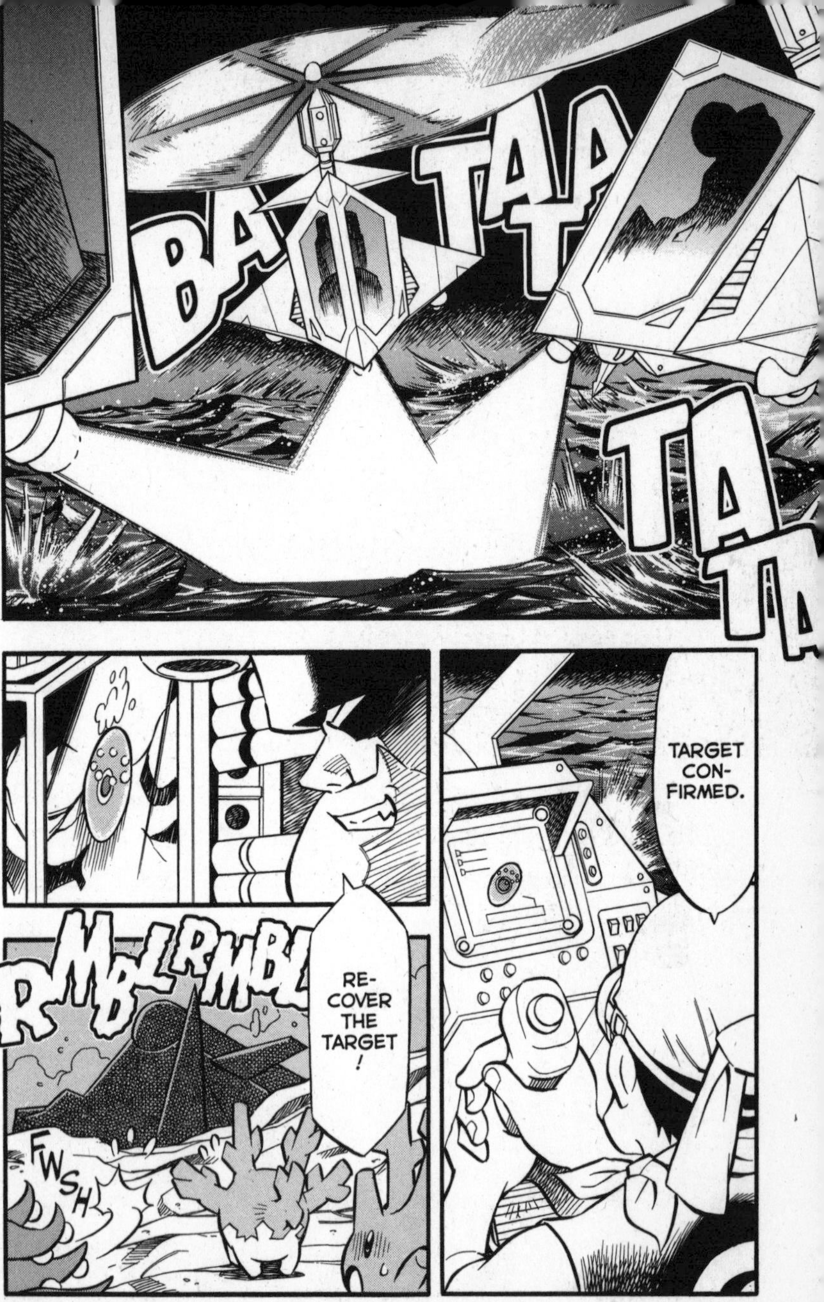
BA TA
TA
TA
TARGET CONFIRMED.
RMBLRMBL
RECOVER THE TARGET!
FWSH

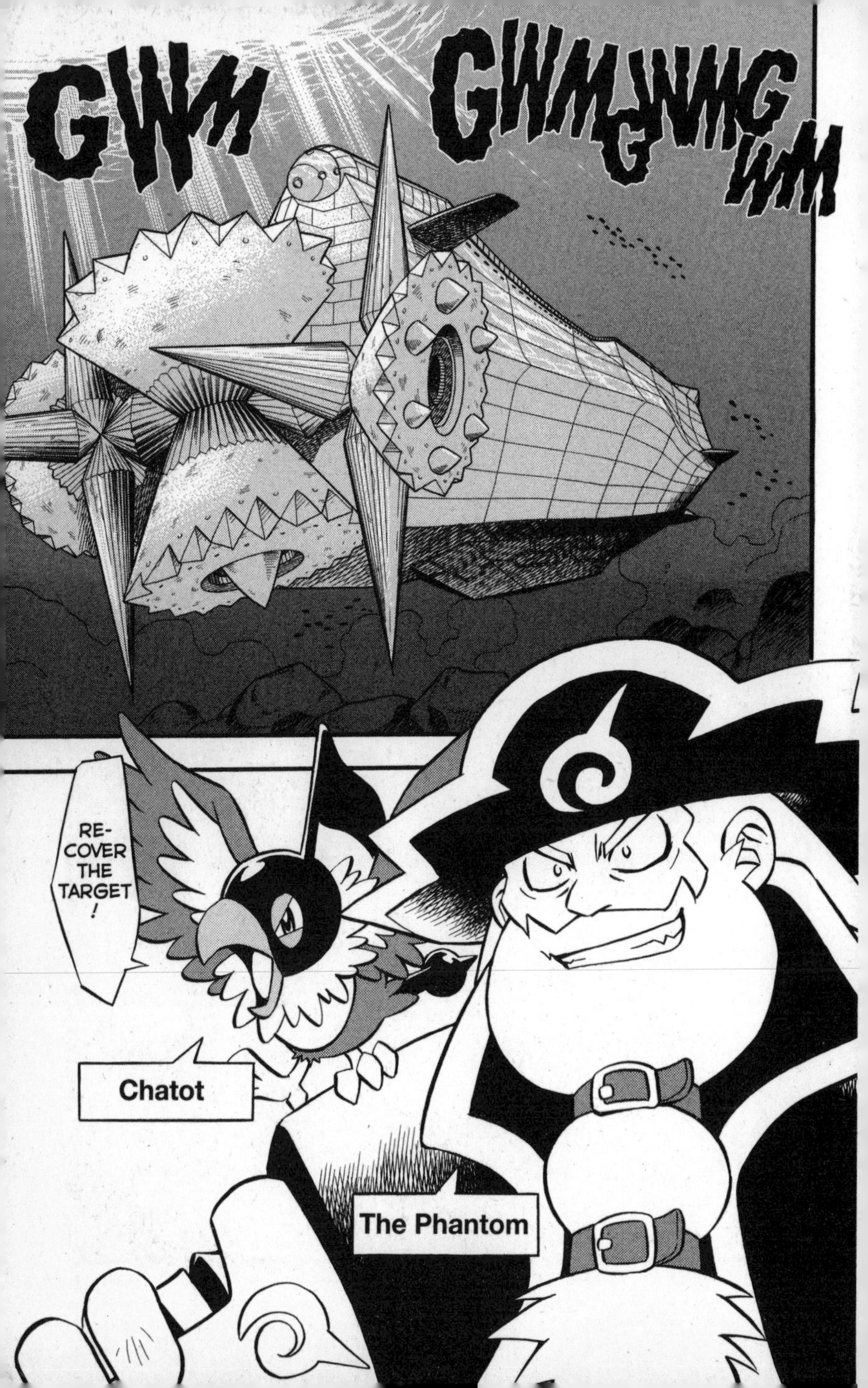
GWM
GWMGWMGWM
RE-COVER THE TARGET!
Chatot
The Phantom

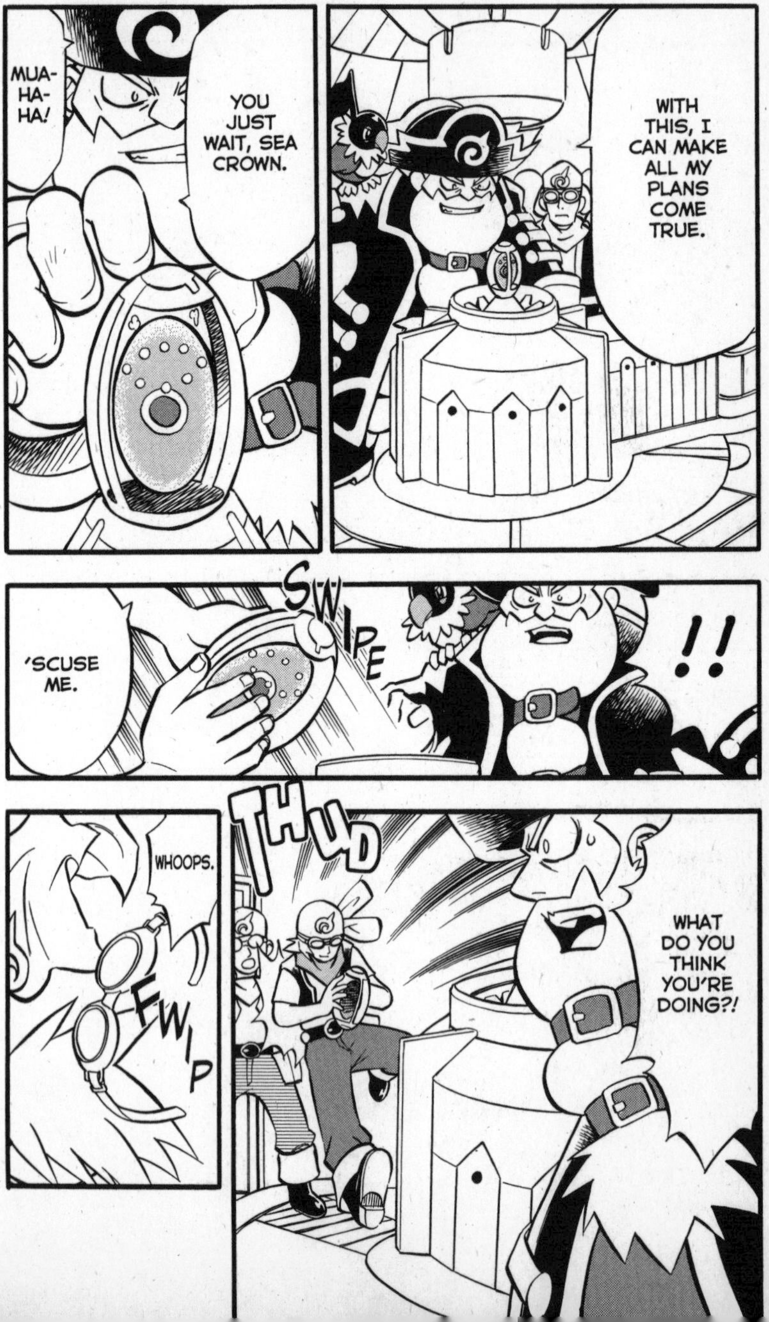
WITH THIS, I CAN MAKE ALL MY PLANS COME TRUE.
YOU JUST WAIT, SEA CROWN.
MUA-HA-HA!
SWIPE
!!
'SCUSE ME.
THUD
WHAT DO YOU THINK YOU'RE DOING?!
WHOOPS.
FWIP

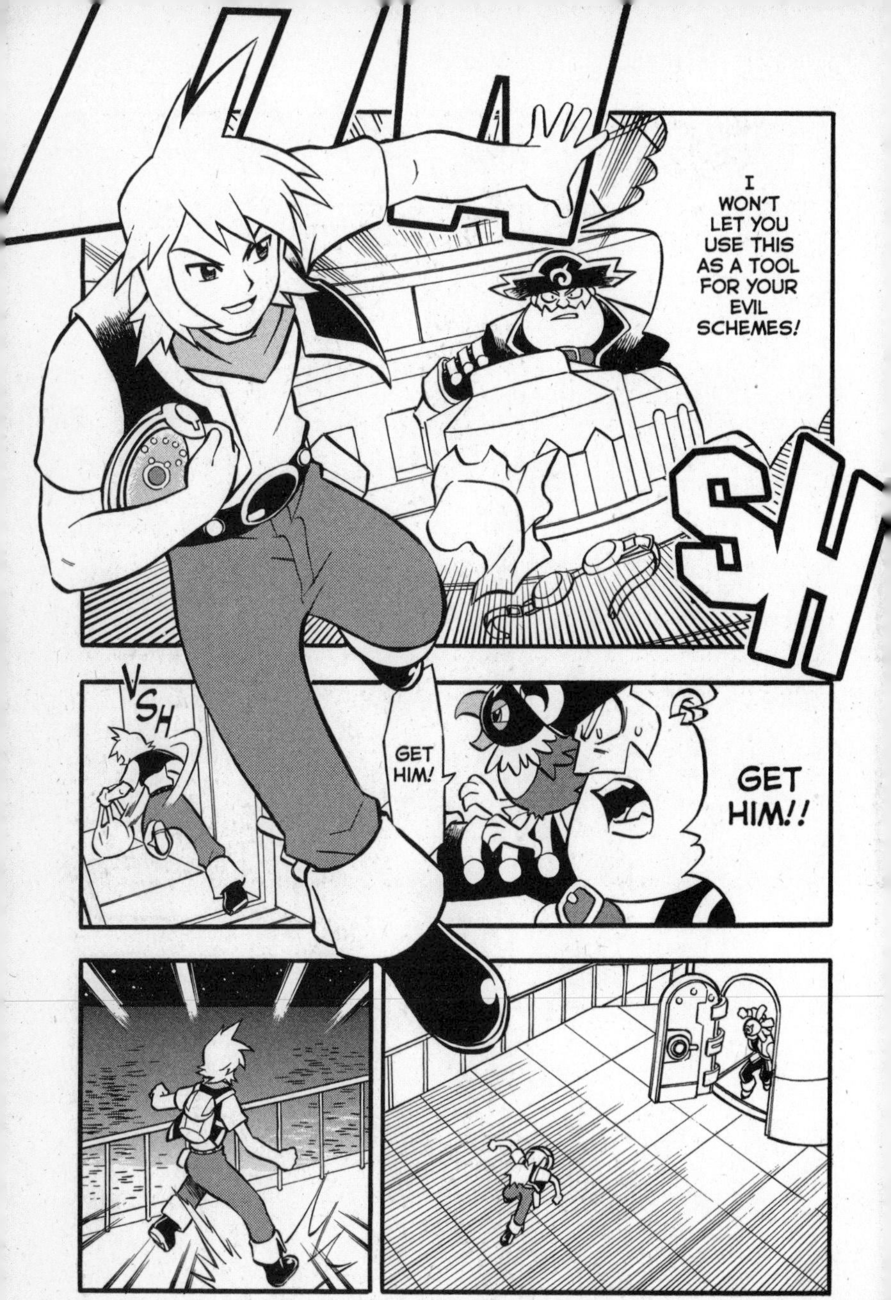
I WON'T LET YOU USE THIS AS A TOOL FOR YOUR EVIL SCHEMES!
SH
GET HIM!!
GET HIM!
VSH

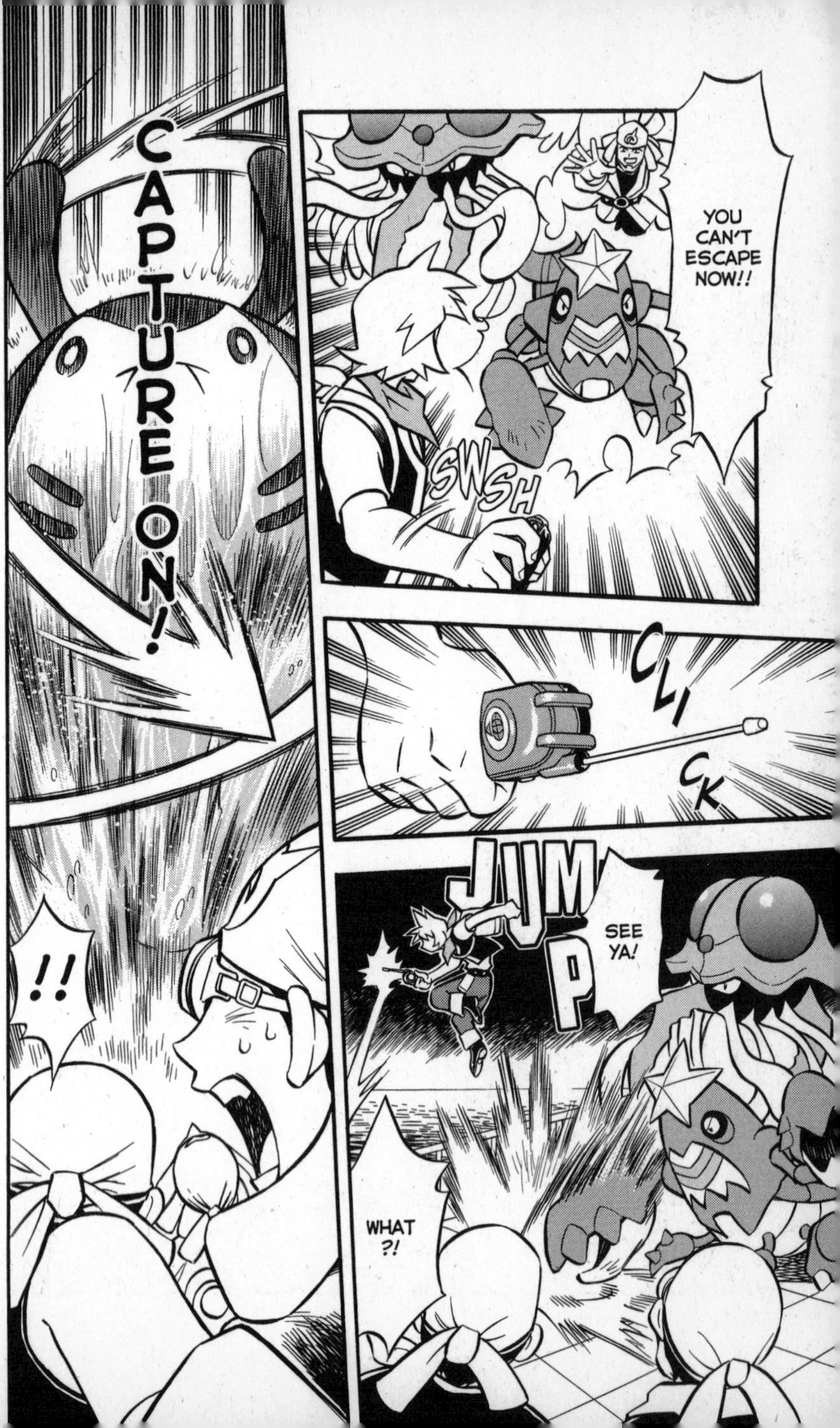
YOU CAN'T ESCAPE NOW!!
SWSH
CLICK
JUMP
SEE YA!
WHAT?!
CAPTURE ON!
!!

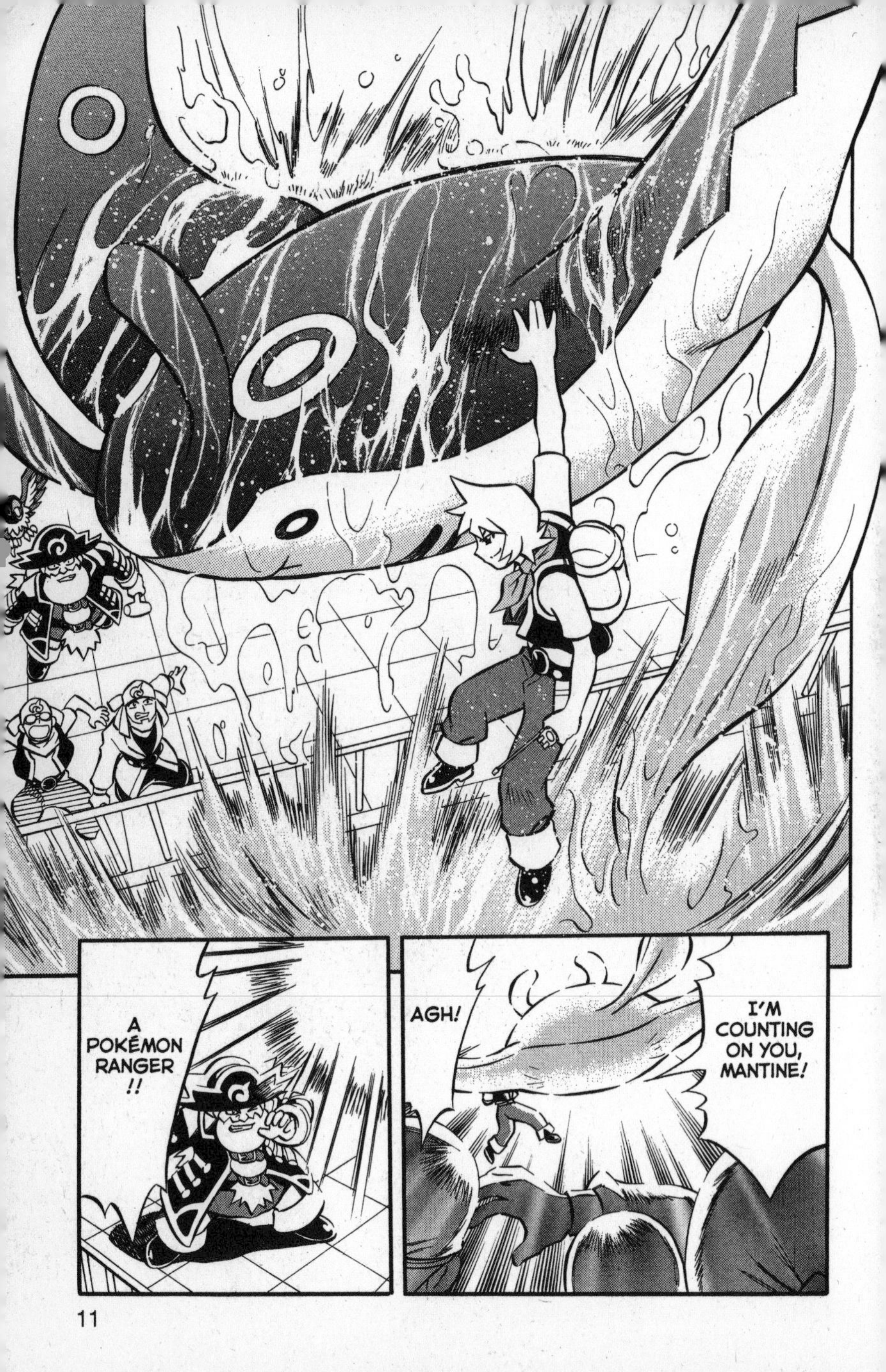
I'M COUNTING ON YOU, MANTINE!
AGH!
A POKÉMON RANGER !!

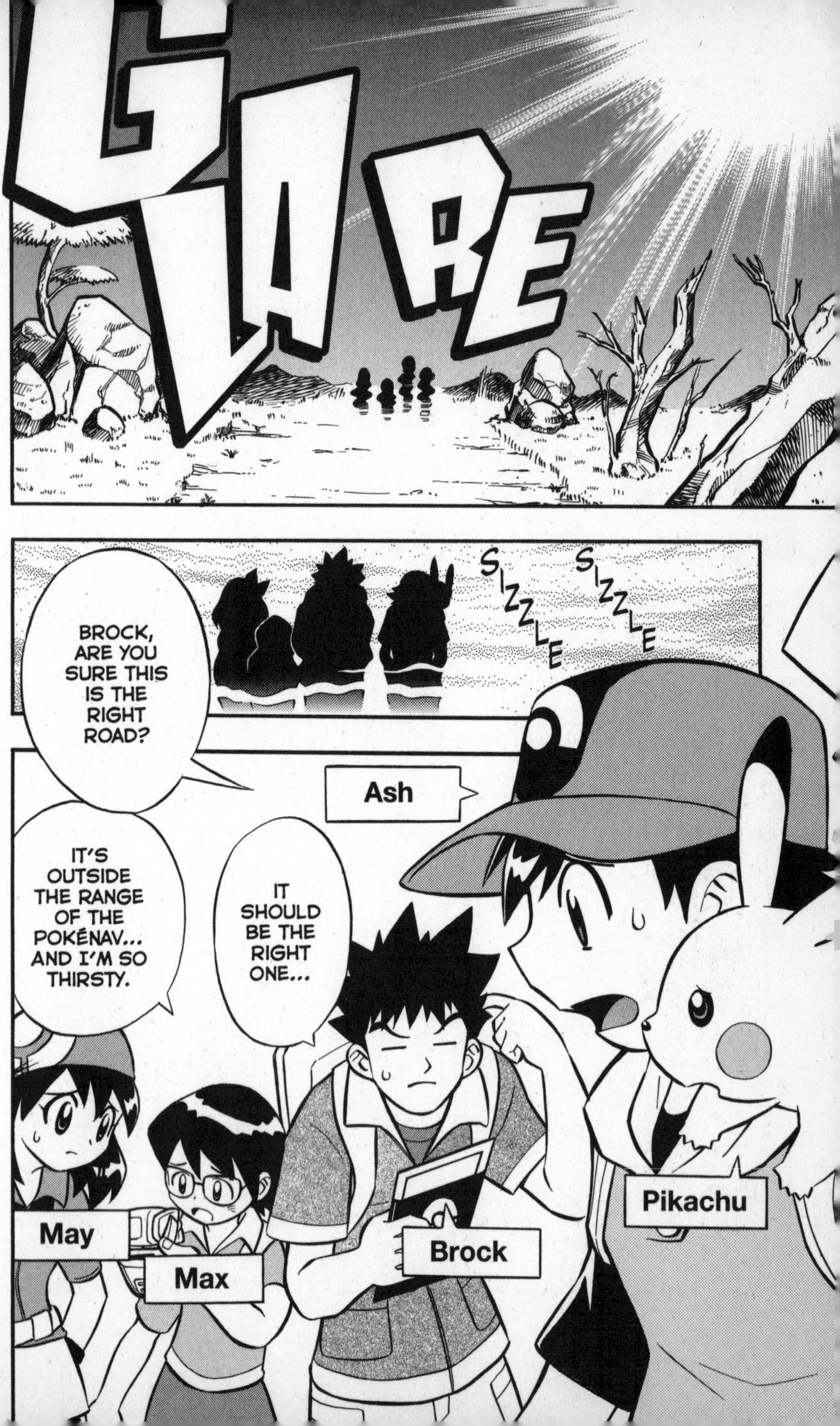
SIZZLE
SIZZLE
BROCK, ARE YOU SURE THIS IS THE RIGHT ROAD?
Ash
IT SHOULD BE THE RIGHT ONE...
IT'S OUTSIDE THE RANGE OF THE POKÉNAV... AND I'M SO THIRSTY.
Pikachu
Brock
Max
May

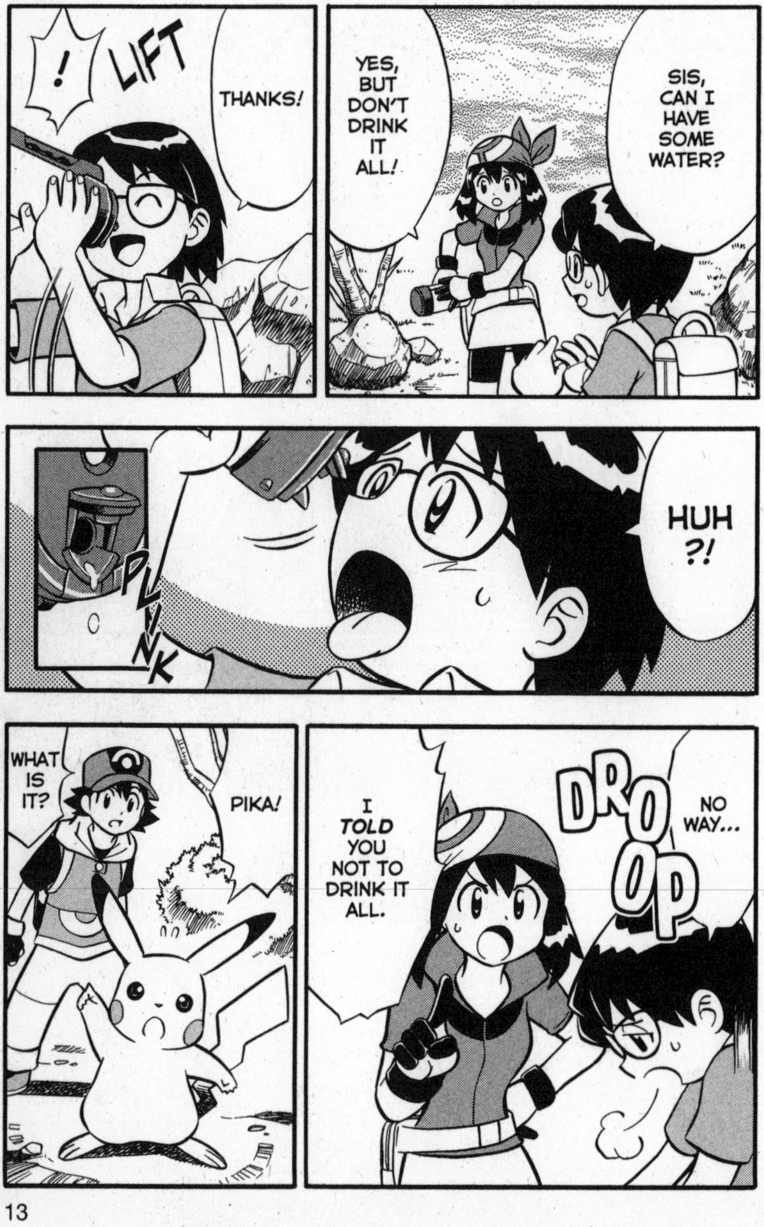
SIS, CAN I HAVE SOME WATER?
YES, BUT DON'T DRINK IT ALL!
THANKS!
LIFT
!
HUH ?!
PLINK
NO WAY...
DROOP
I *TOLD* YOU NOT TO DRINK IT ALL.
PIKA!
WHAT IS IT?

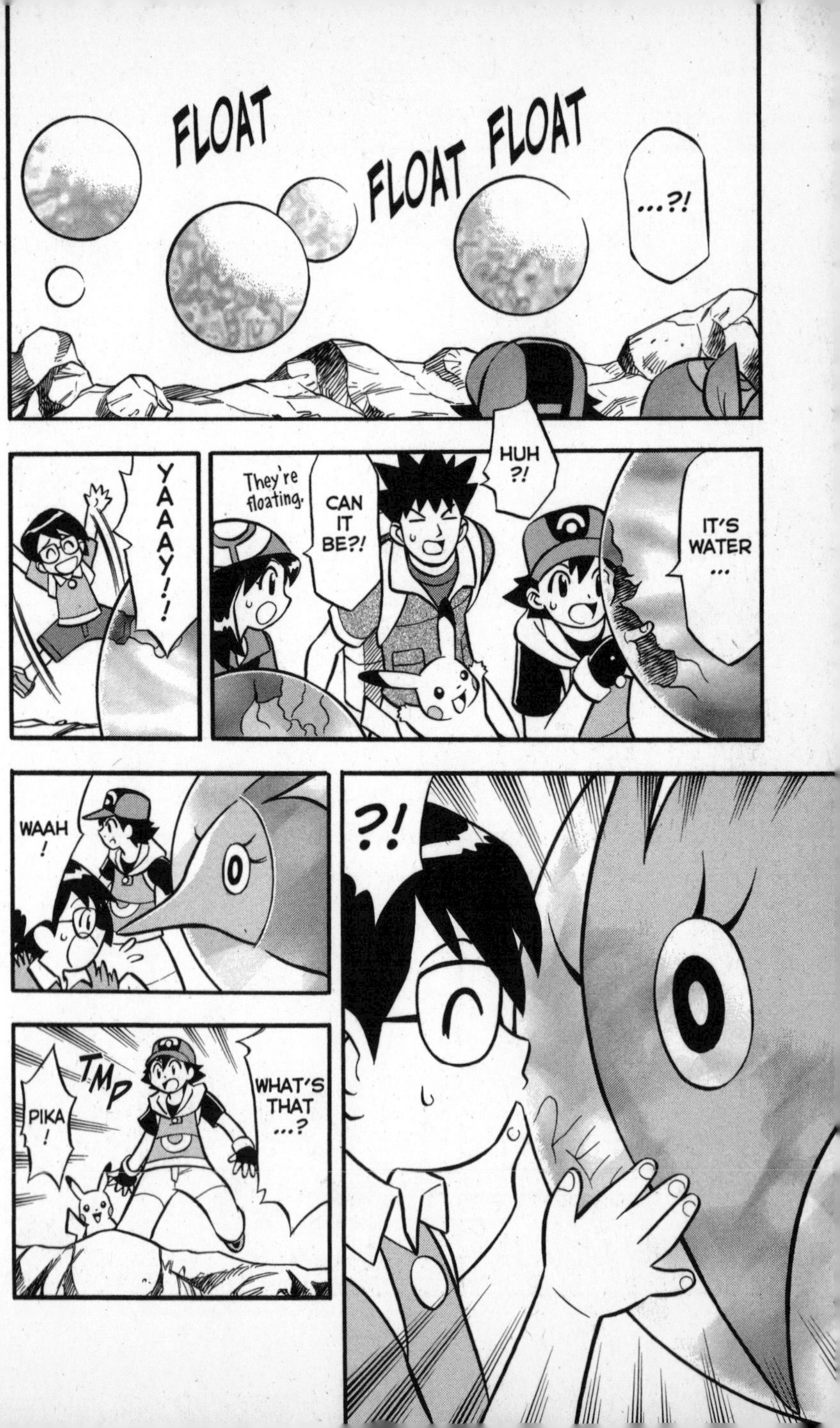
...?!
FLOAT FLOAT
FLOAT
HUH ?!
IT'S WATER ...
CAN IT BE?!
They're floating.
YAAAAY!!!
?!
WAAH !
WHAT'S THAT ...?
TMP
PIKA !

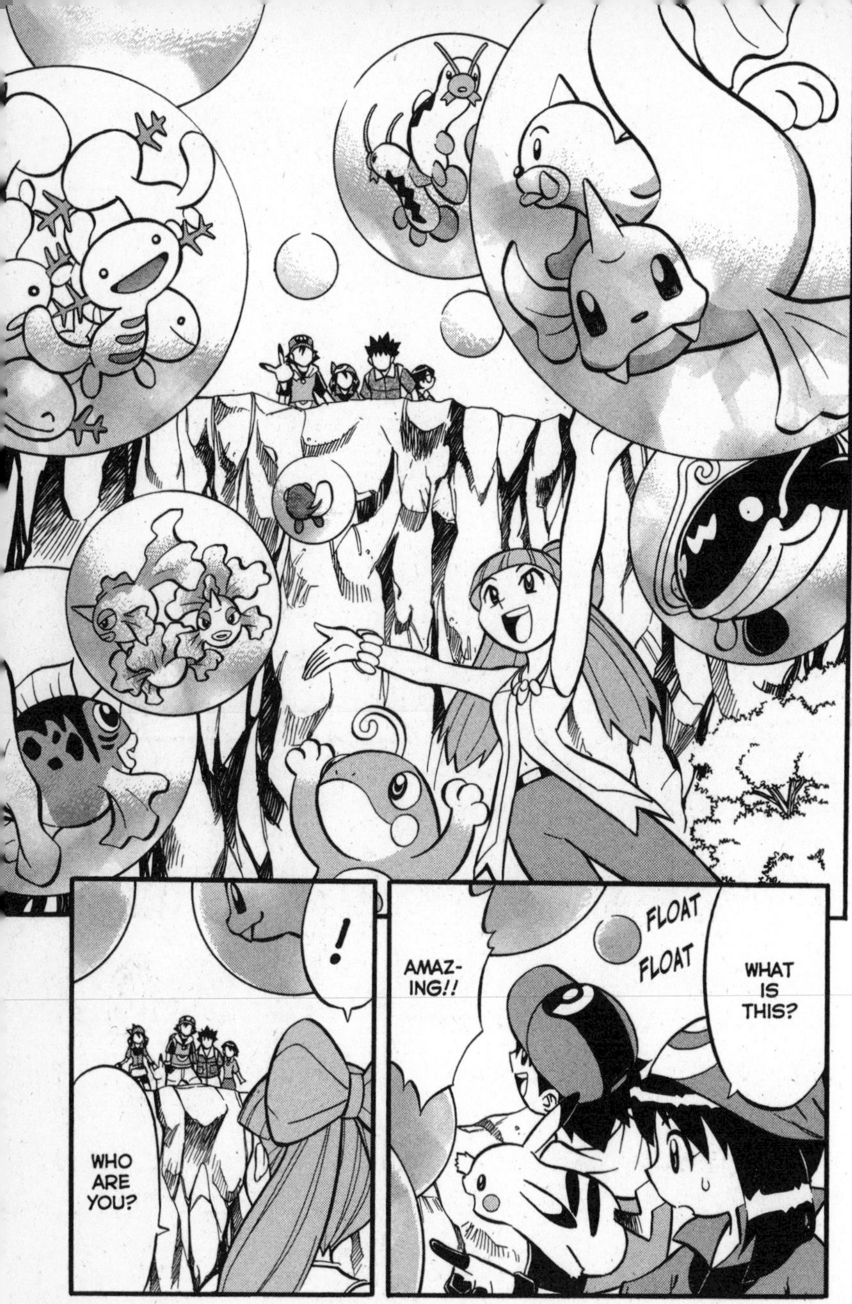
WHAT IS THIS?
FLOAT
FLOAT
AMAZ-ING!!
!
WHO ARE YOU?

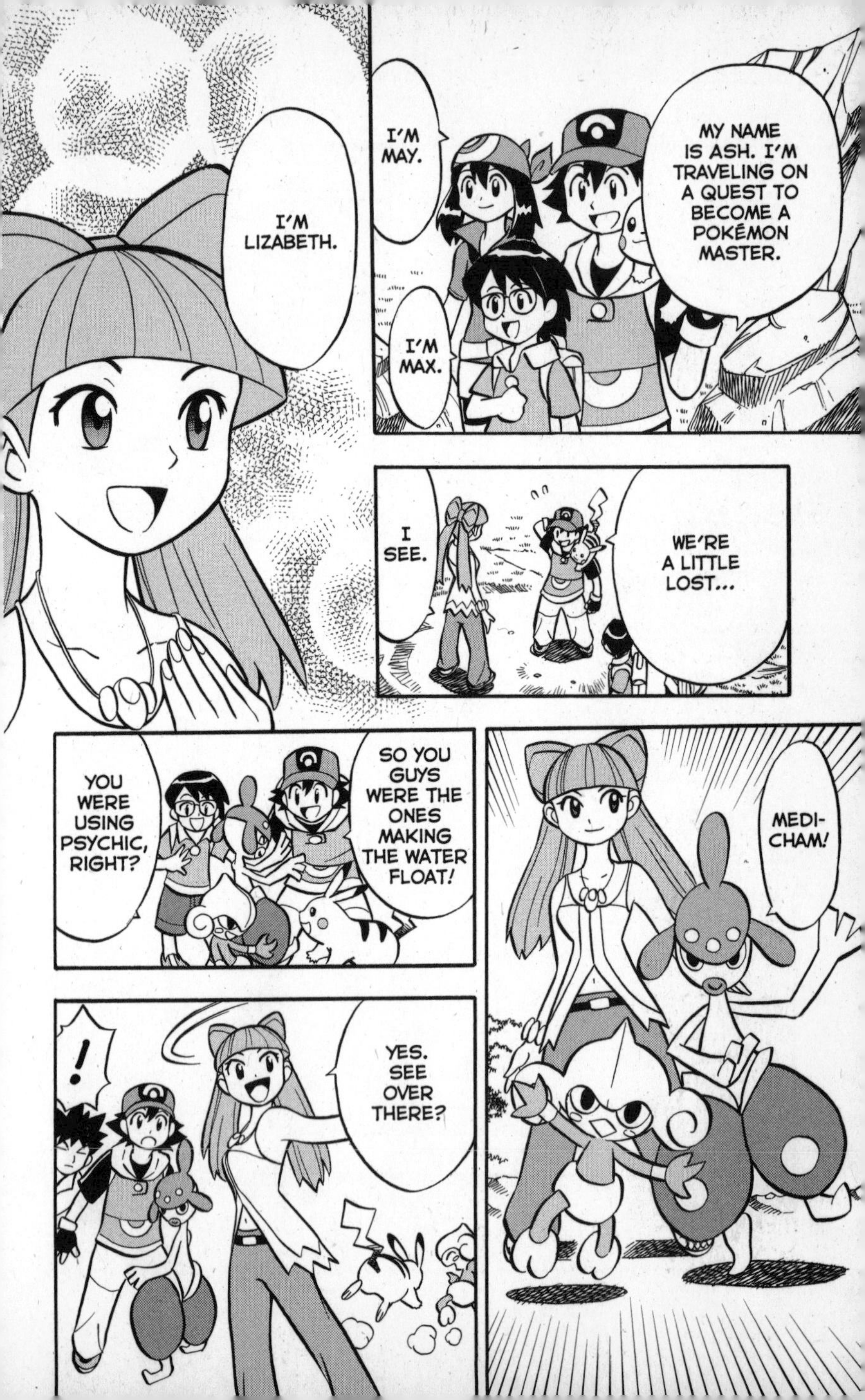
MY NAME IS ASH. I'M TRAVELING ON A QUEST TO BECOME A POKÉMON MASTER.
I'M MAY.
I'M MAX.
WE'RE A LITTLE LOST...
I SEE.
I'M LIZABETH.
MEDI-CHAM!
SO YOU GUYS WERE THE ONES MAKING THE WATER FLOAT!
YOU WERE USING PSYCHIC, RIGHT?
YES. SEE OVER THERE?
!

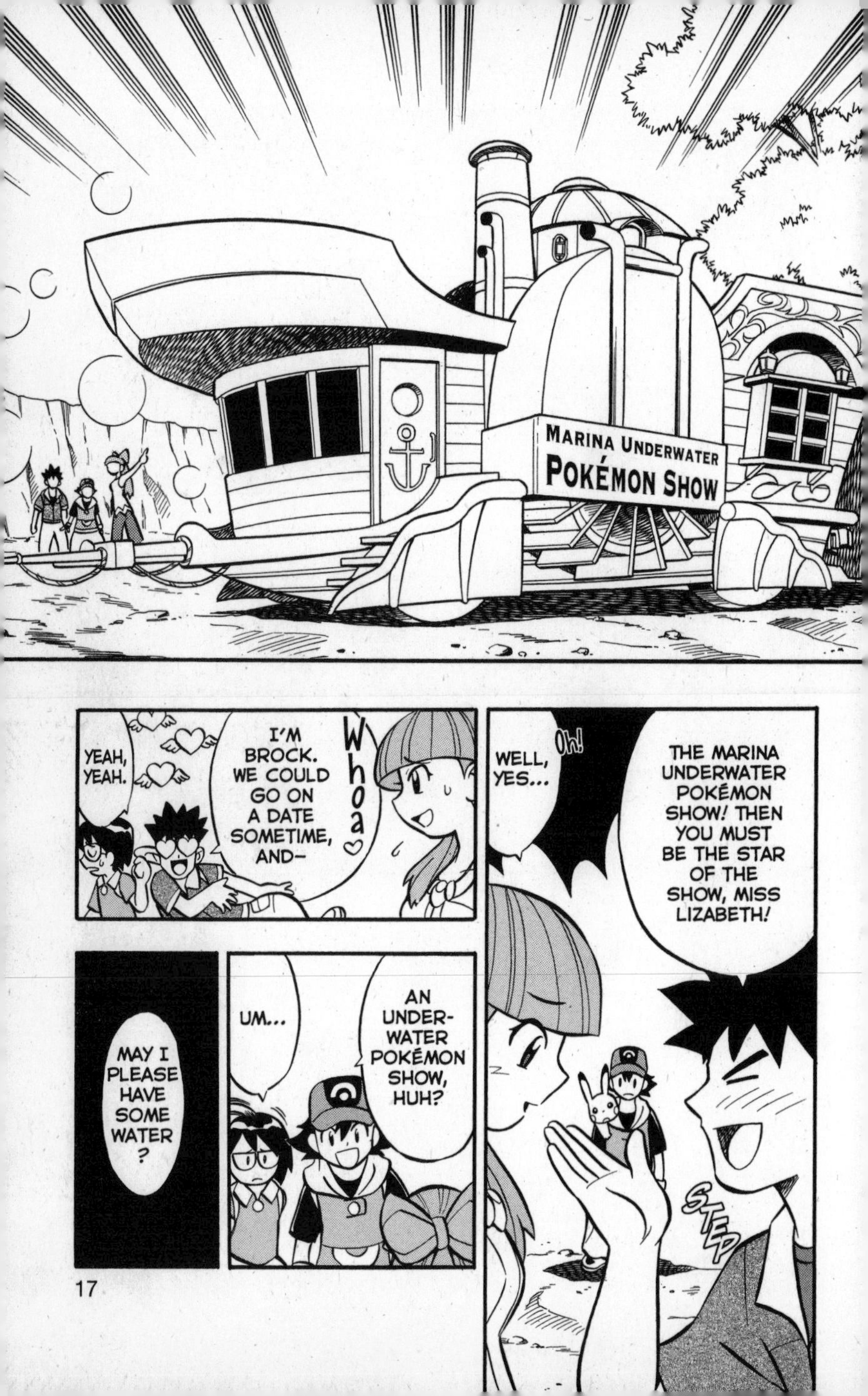
MARINA UNDERWATER
POKÉMON SHOW
THE MARINA UNDERWATER POKÉMON SHOW! THEN YOU MUST BE THE STAR OF THE SHOW, MISS LIZABETH!
Oh!
WELL, YES...
STEP
Whoa ♡
I'M BROCK. WE COULD GO ON A DATE SOMETIME, AND–
YEAH, YEAH.
AN UNDER-WATER POKÉMON SHOW, HUH?
UM...
MAY I PLEASE HAVE SOME WATER?

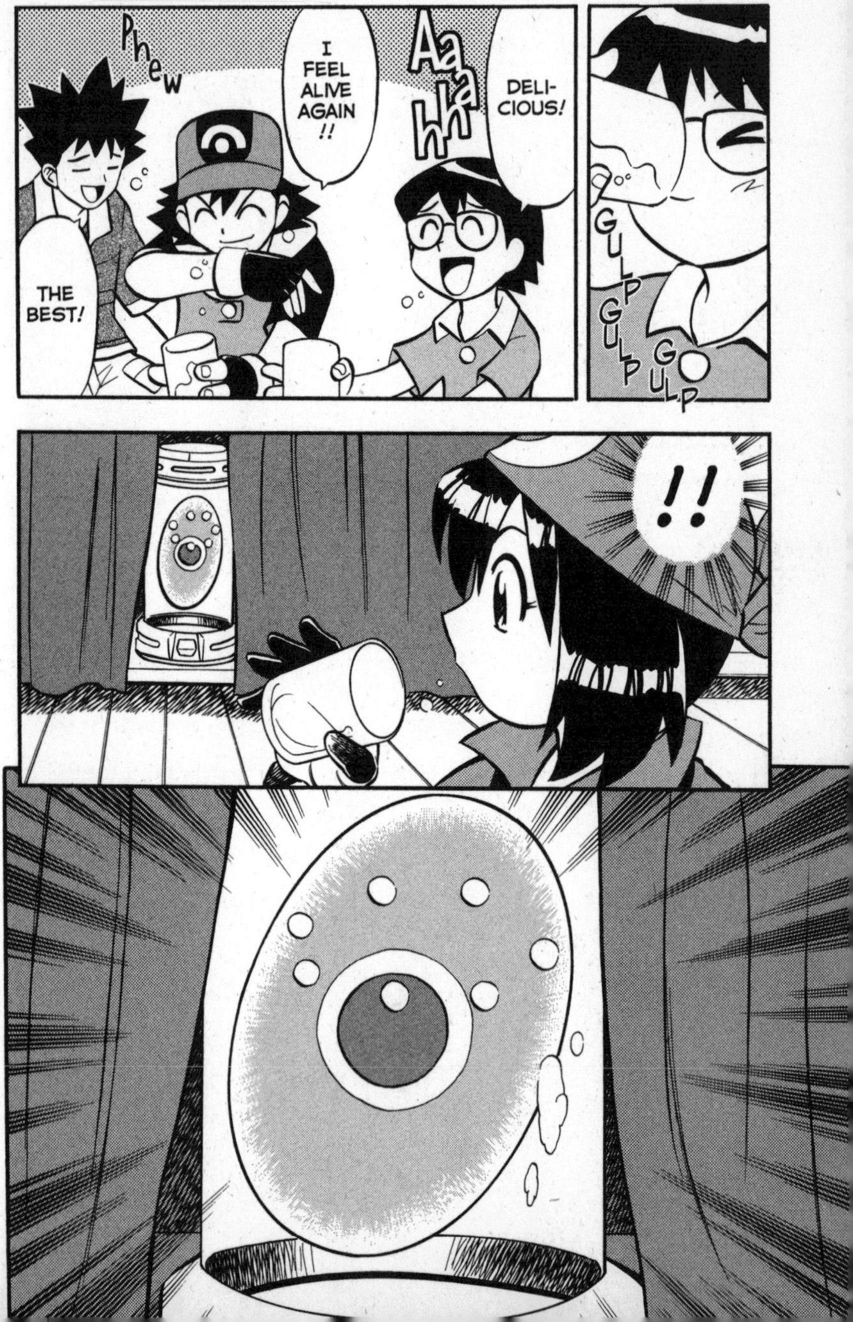
GULP GULP GULP
DELI-CIOUS!
Aaahh
I FEEL ALIVE AGAIN!!
Phew
THE BEST!
!!

READ THIS WAY

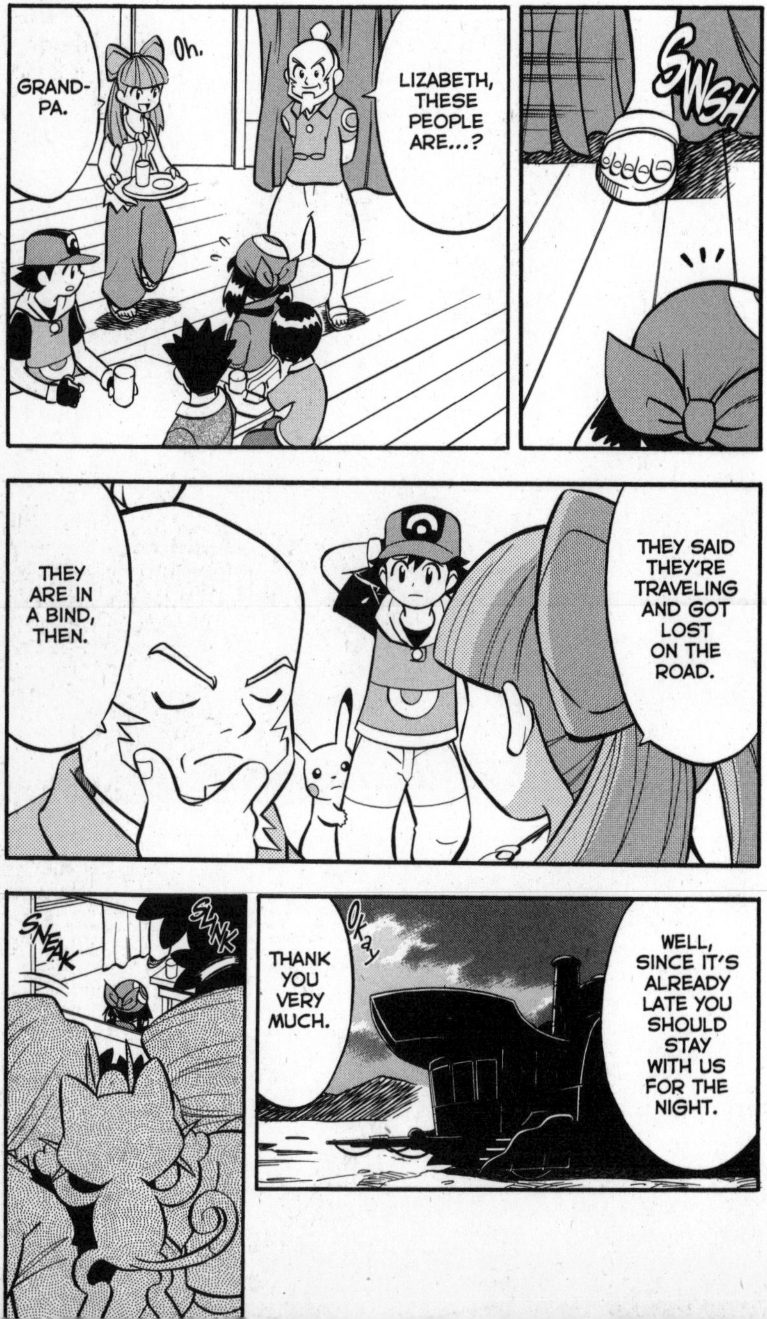
SWSH
LIZABETH, THESE PEOPLE ARE...?
Oh.
GRAND-PA.
THEY SAID THEY'RE TRAVELING AND GOT LOST ON THE ROAD.
THEY ARE IN A BIND, THEN.
WELL, SINCE IT'S ALREADY LATE YOU SHOULD STAY WITH US FOR THE NIGHT.
Okay
THANK YOU VERY MUCH.
SLINK
SNEAK

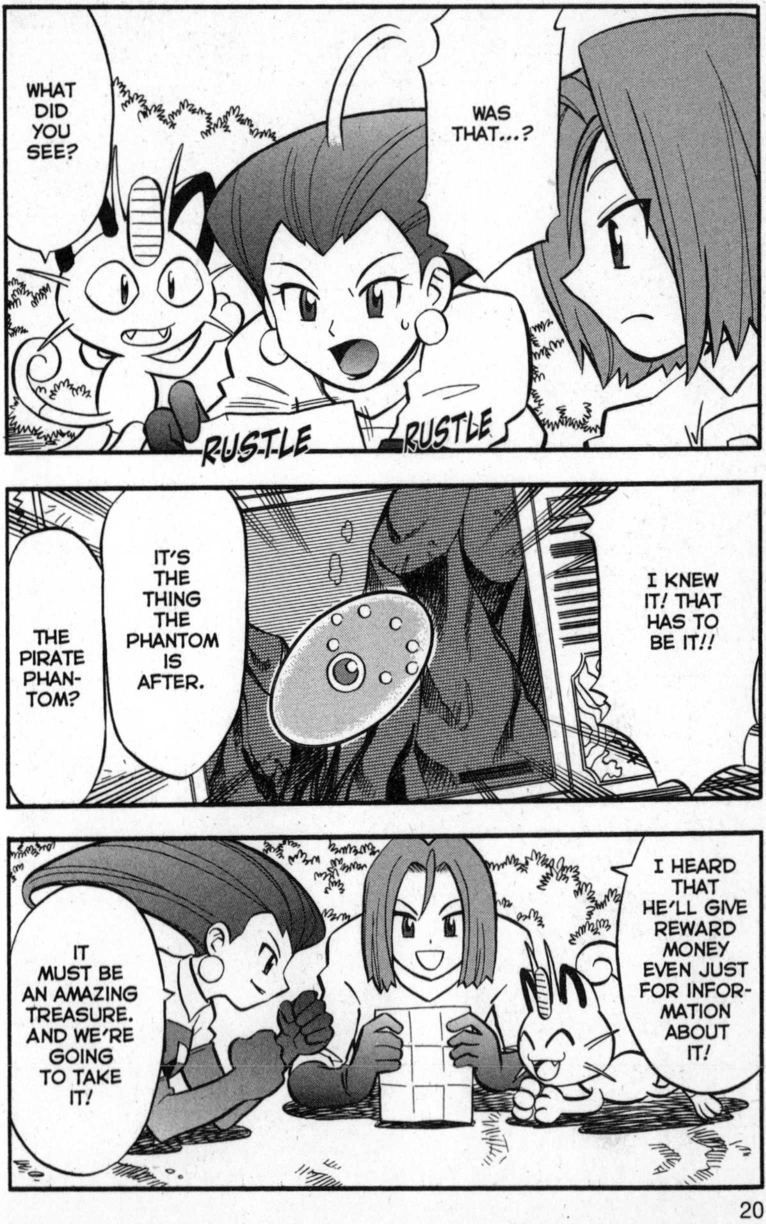
WAS THAT...?
WHAT DID YOU SEE?
RUSTLE
RUSTLE
I KNEW IT! THAT HAS TO BE IT!!
IT'S THE THING THE PHANTOM IS AFTER.
THE PIRATE PHANTOM?
I HEARD THAT HE'LL GIVE REWARD MONEY EVEN JUST FOR INFORMATION ABOUT IT!
IT MUST BE AN AMAZING TREASURE. AND WE'RE GOING TO TAKE IT!

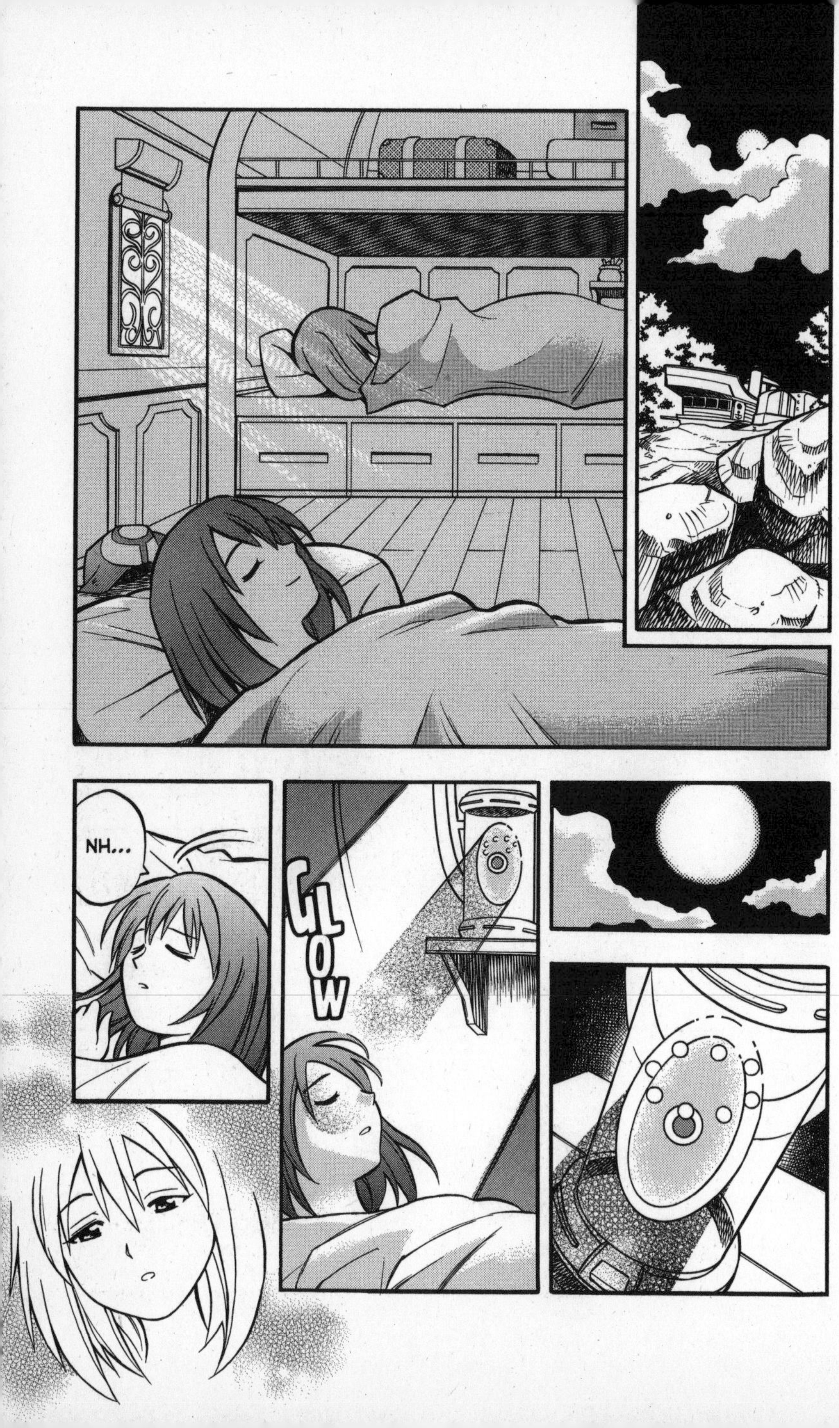
NH...
GLOW

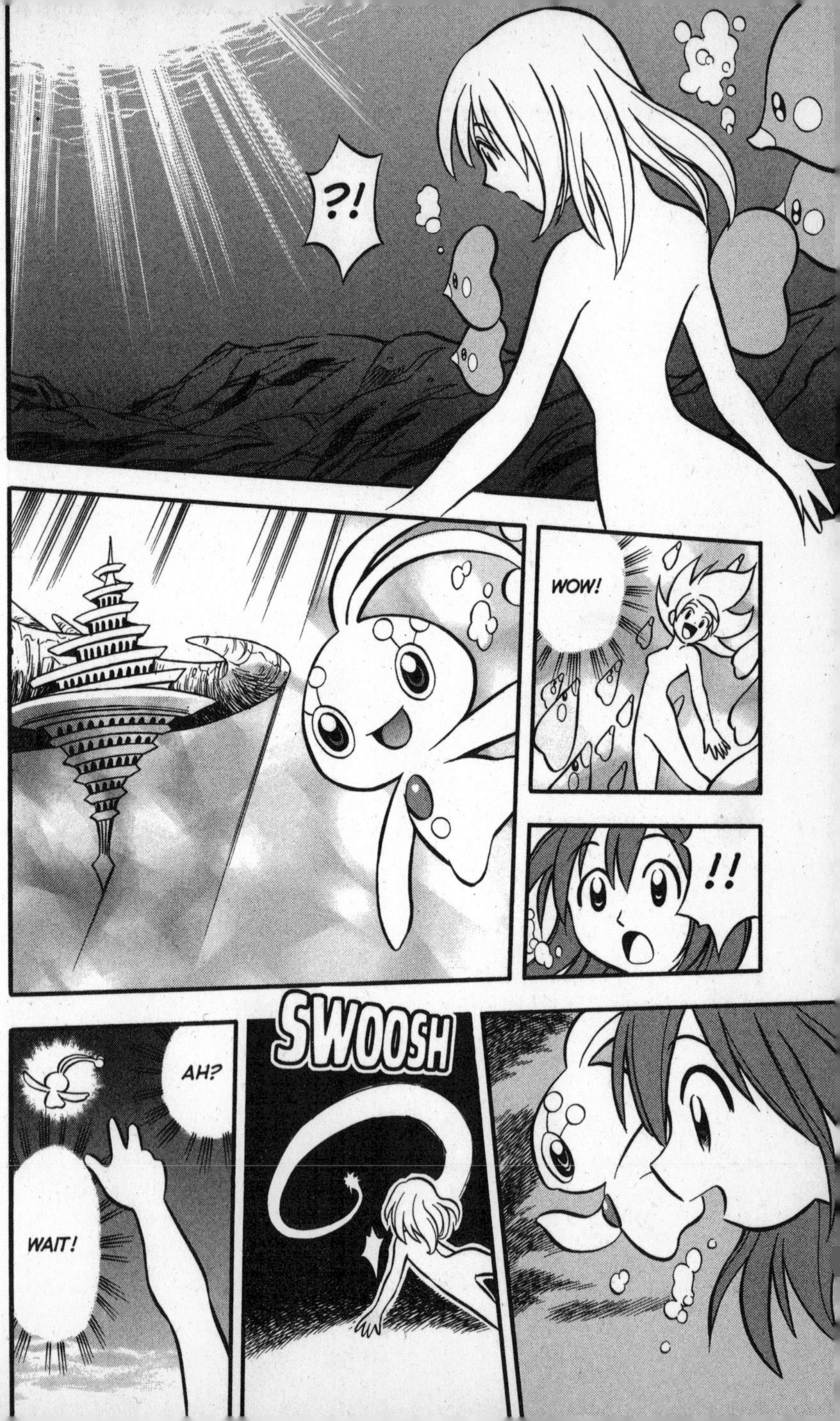
?!
WOW!
!!
SWOOSH
AH?
WAIT!

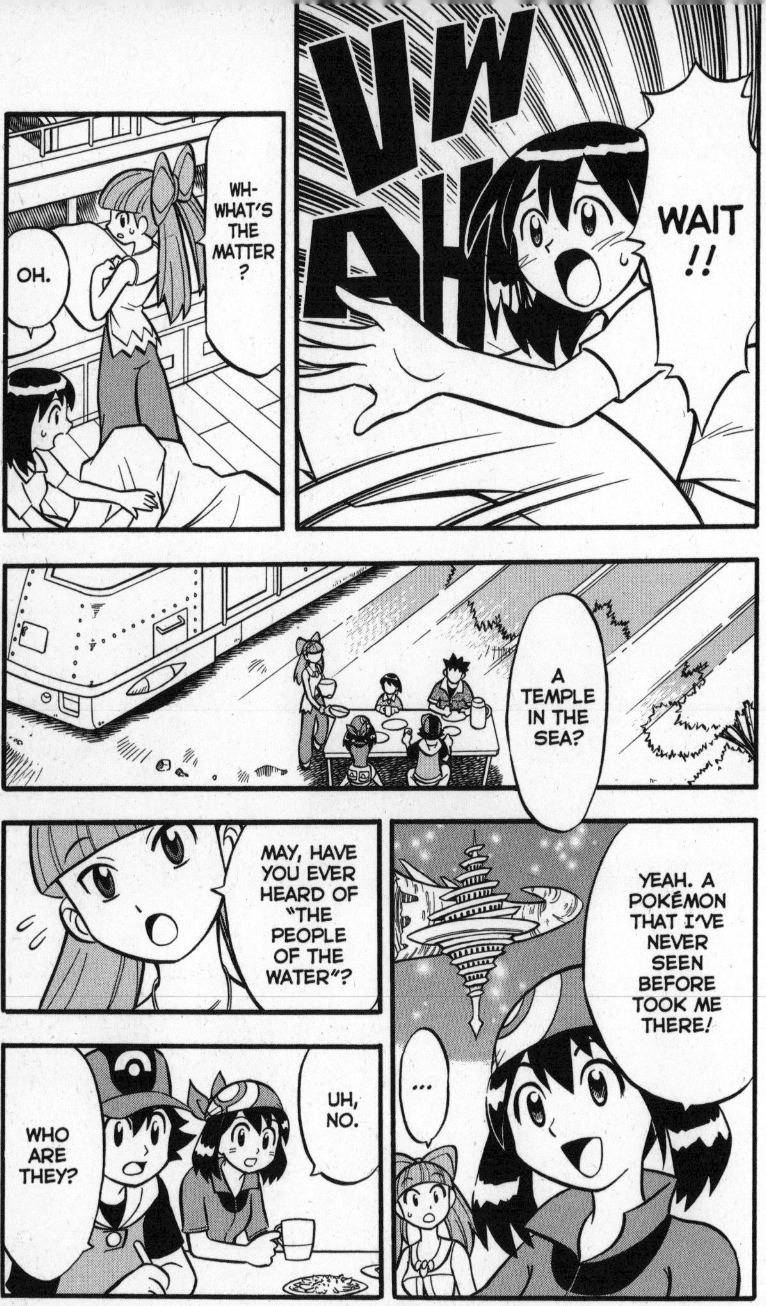
VWAH
WAIT!!
WH-WHAT'S THE MATTER?
OH.
A TEMPLE IN THE SEA?
YEAH. A POKÉMON THAT I'VE NEVER SEEN BEFORE TOOK ME THERE!
...
MAY, HAVE YOU EVER HEARD OF "THE PEOPLE OF THE WATER"?
UH, NO.
WHO ARE THEY?

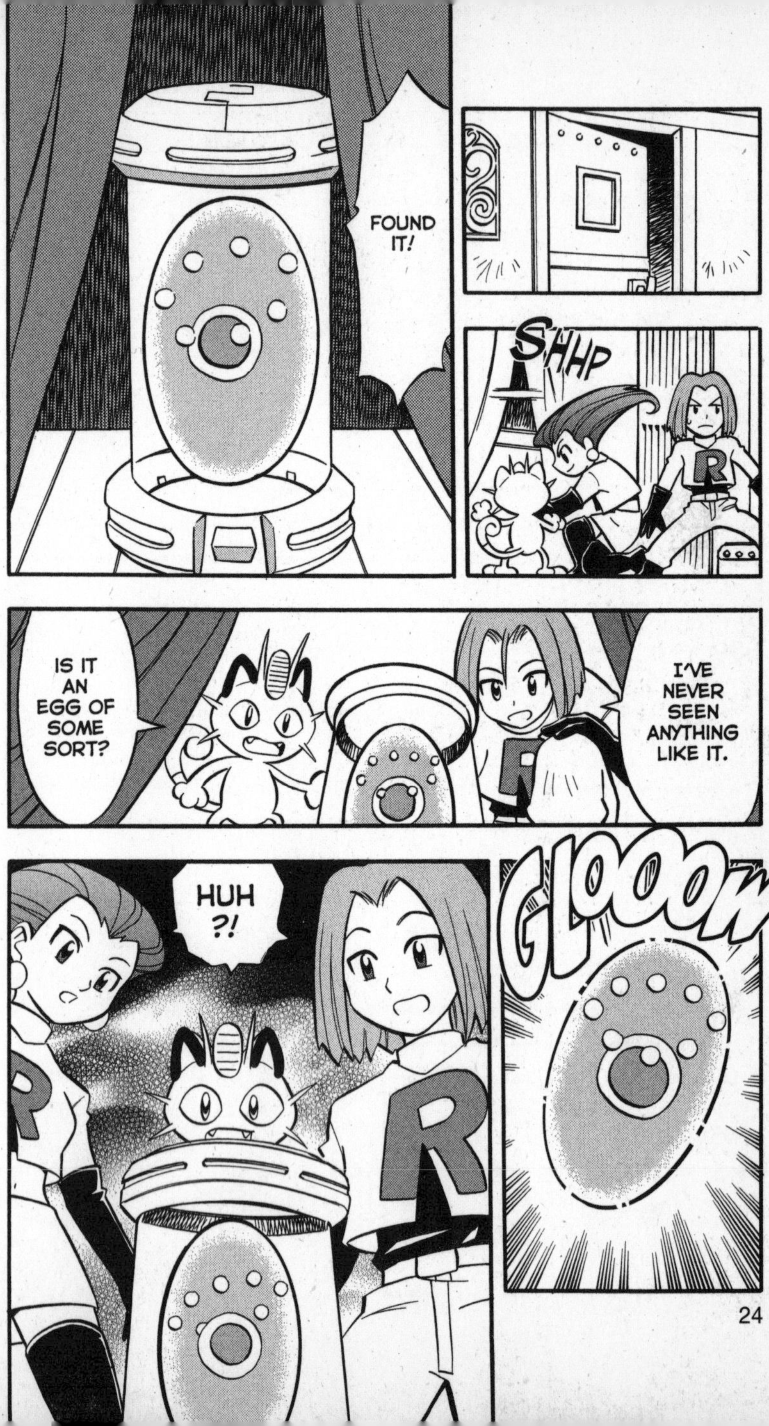
SHHP
FOUND IT!
I'VE NEVER SEEN ANYTHING LIKE IT.
IS IT AN EGG OF SOME SORT?
GLOOOW
HUH ?!

READ THIS WAY

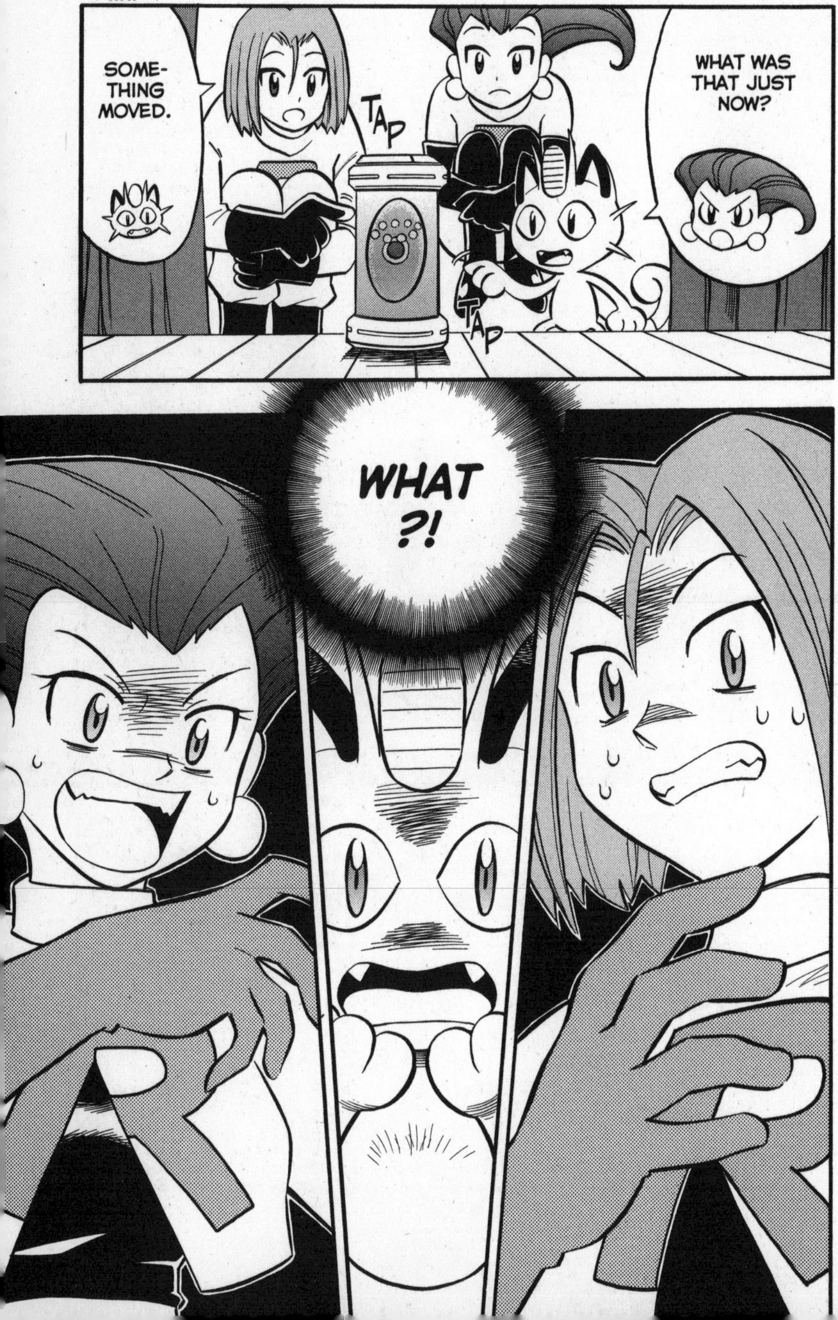
WHAT WAS THAT JUST NOW?
TAP
SOME-THING MOVED.
TAP
WHAT ?!

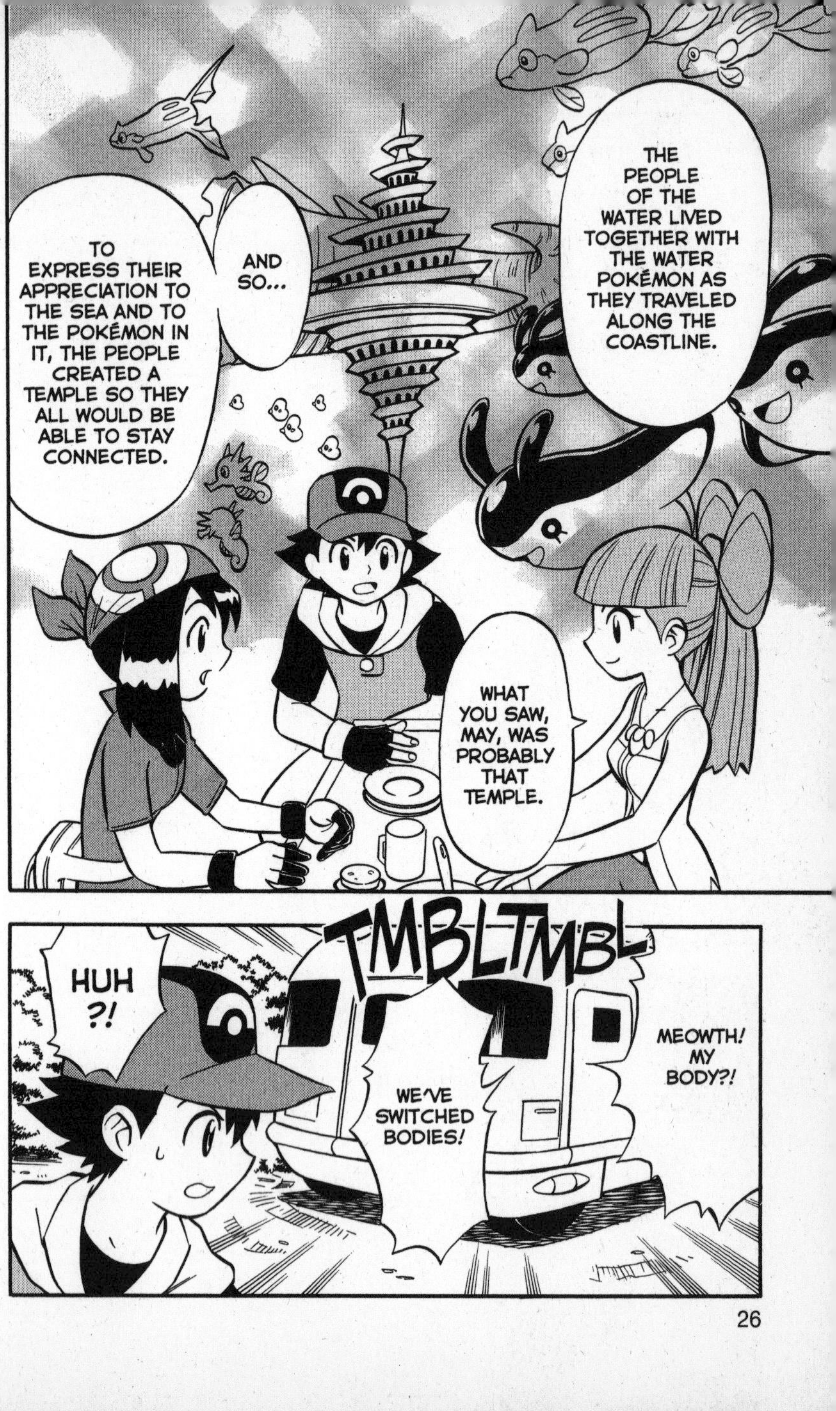
THE PEOPLE OF THE WATER LIVED TOGETHER WITH THE WATER POKÉMON AS THEY TRAVELED ALONG THE COASTLINE.
AND SO...
TO EXPRESS THEIR APPRECIATION TO THE SEA AND TO THE POKÉMON IN IT, THE PEOPLE CREATED A TEMPLE SO THEY ALL WOULD BE ABLE TO STAY CONNECTED.
WHAT YOU SAW, MAY, WAS PROBABLY THAT TEMPLE.
MEOWTH! MY BODY?!
TMBLTMBL
WE'VE SWITCHED BODIES!
HUH ?!

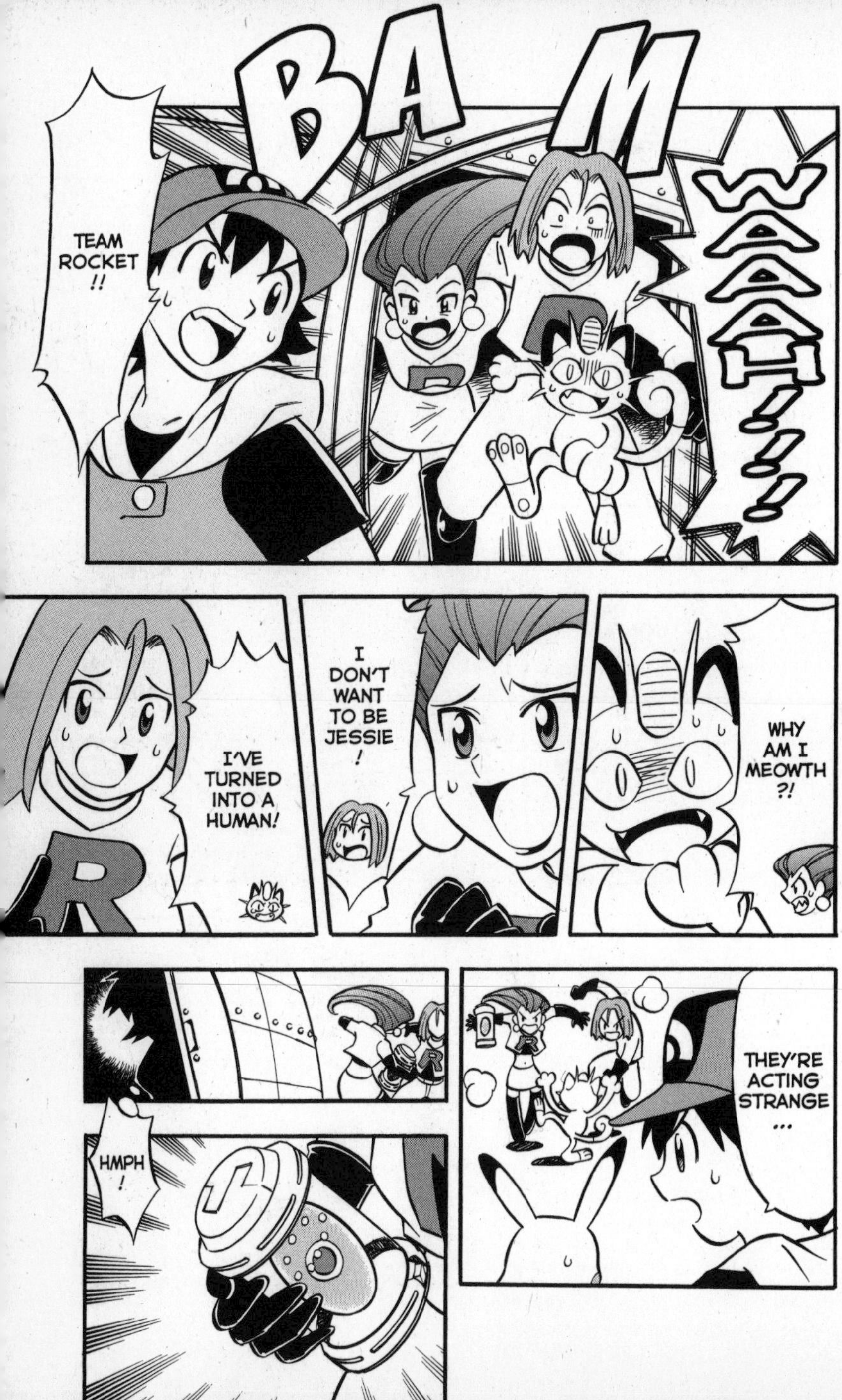
BAM
WAAAH!!!!
TEAM ROCKET!!
WHY AM I MEOWTH?!
I DON'T WANT TO BE JESSIE!
I'VE TURNED INTO A HUMAN!
THEY'RE ACTING STRANGE...
HMPH!

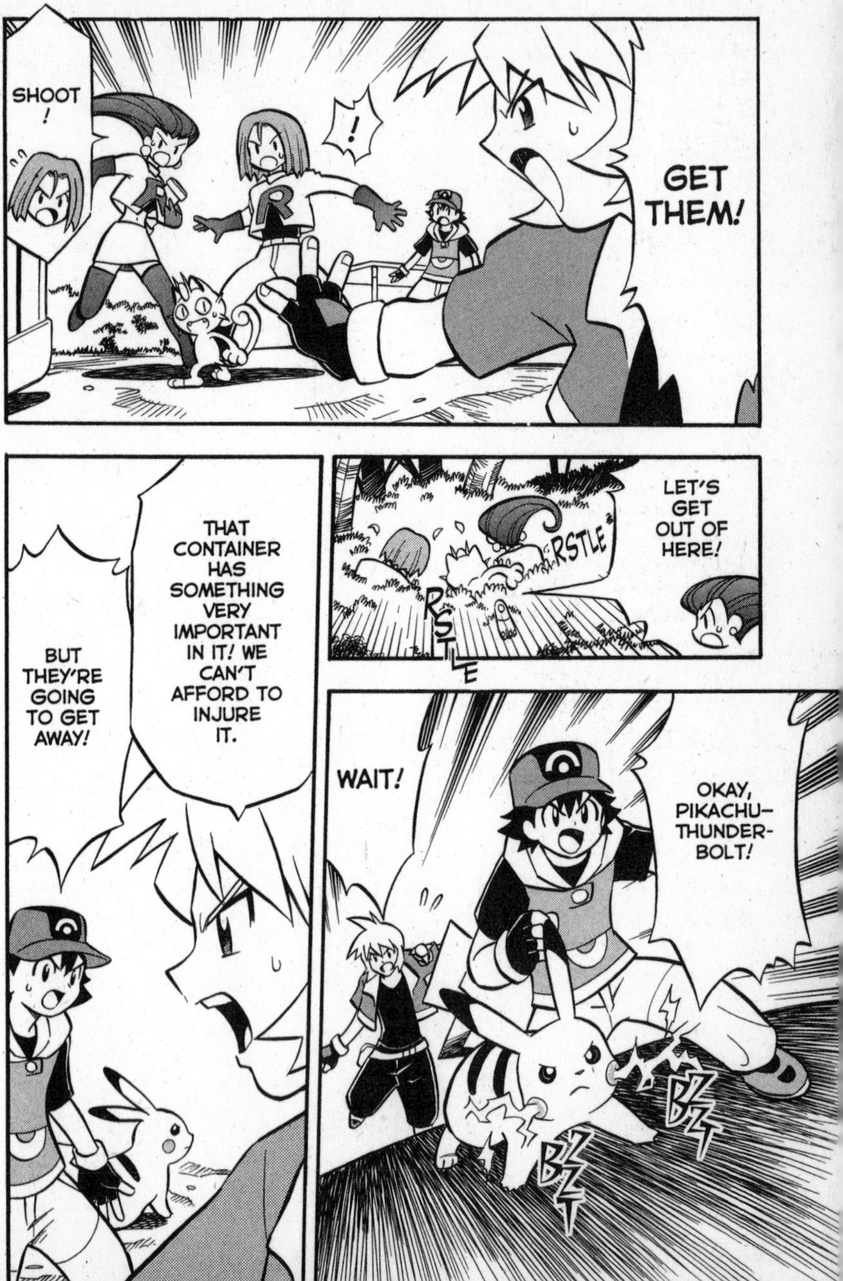
GET THEM!
!
SHOOT !
LET'S GET OUT OF HERE!
RSTLE
RSTLE
OKAY, PIKACHU—THUNDERBOLT!
WAIT!
BZZT
BZZT
THAT CONTAINER HAS SOMETHING VERY IMPORTANT IN IT! WE CAN'T AFFORD TO INJURE IT.
BUT THEY'RE GOING TO GET AWAY!

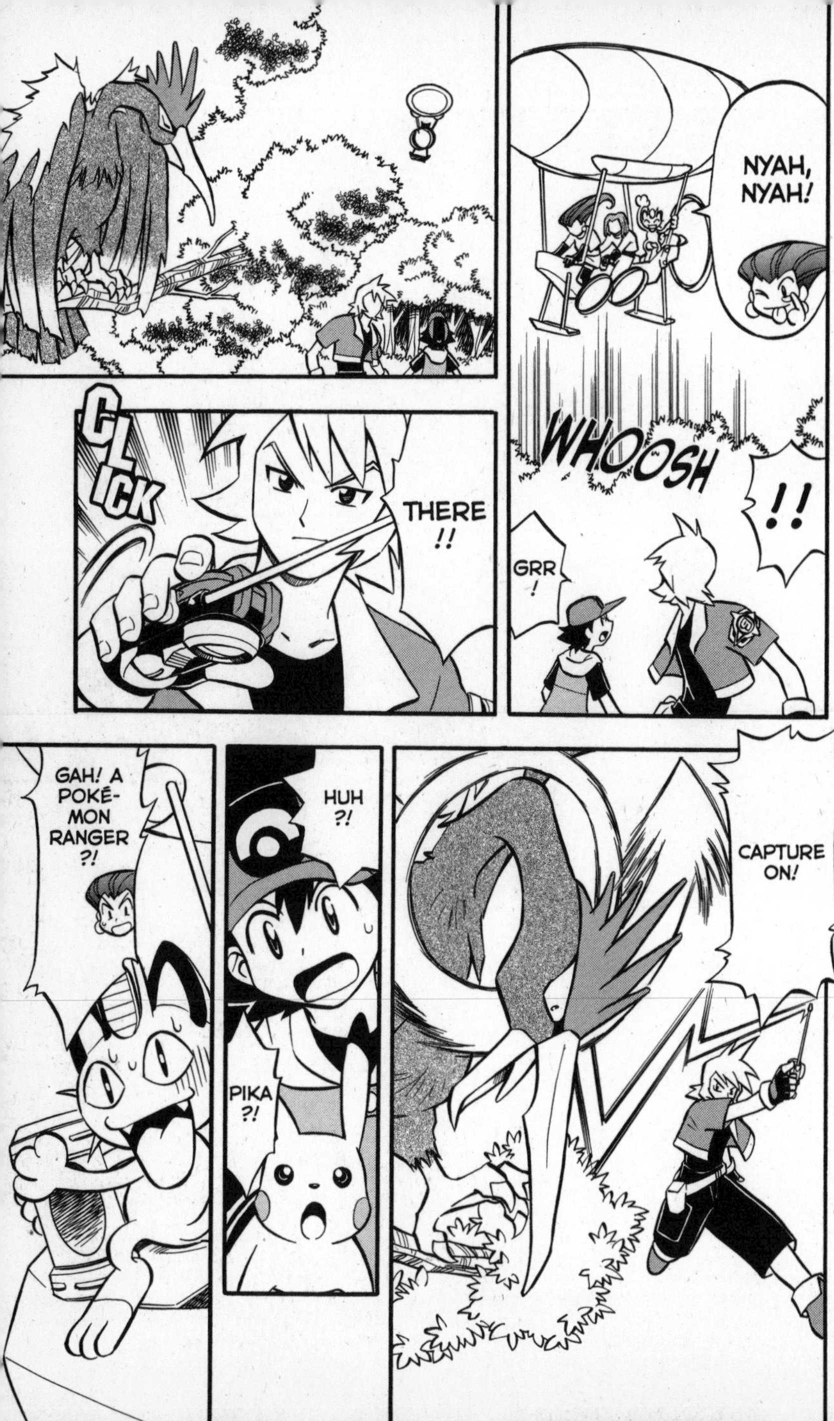
NYAH, NYAH!
WHOOSH
!!
GRR !
CLICK
THERE !!
CAPTURE ON!
HUH ?!
PIKA ?!
GAH! A POKÉ-MON RANGER ?!

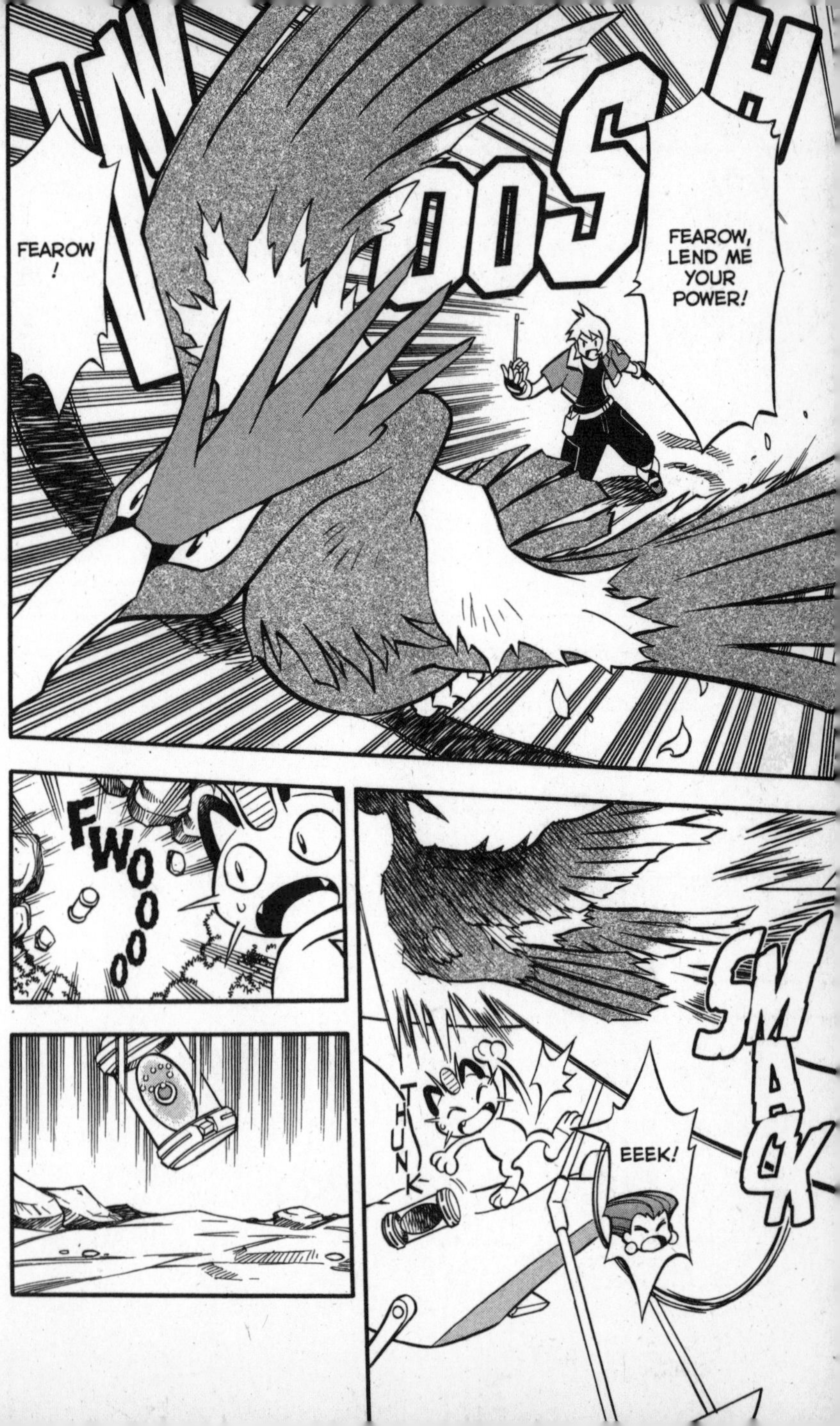
FEAROW, LEND ME YOUR POWER!
FEAROW!
SMACK
EEEK!
THUNK
FWOOOOO

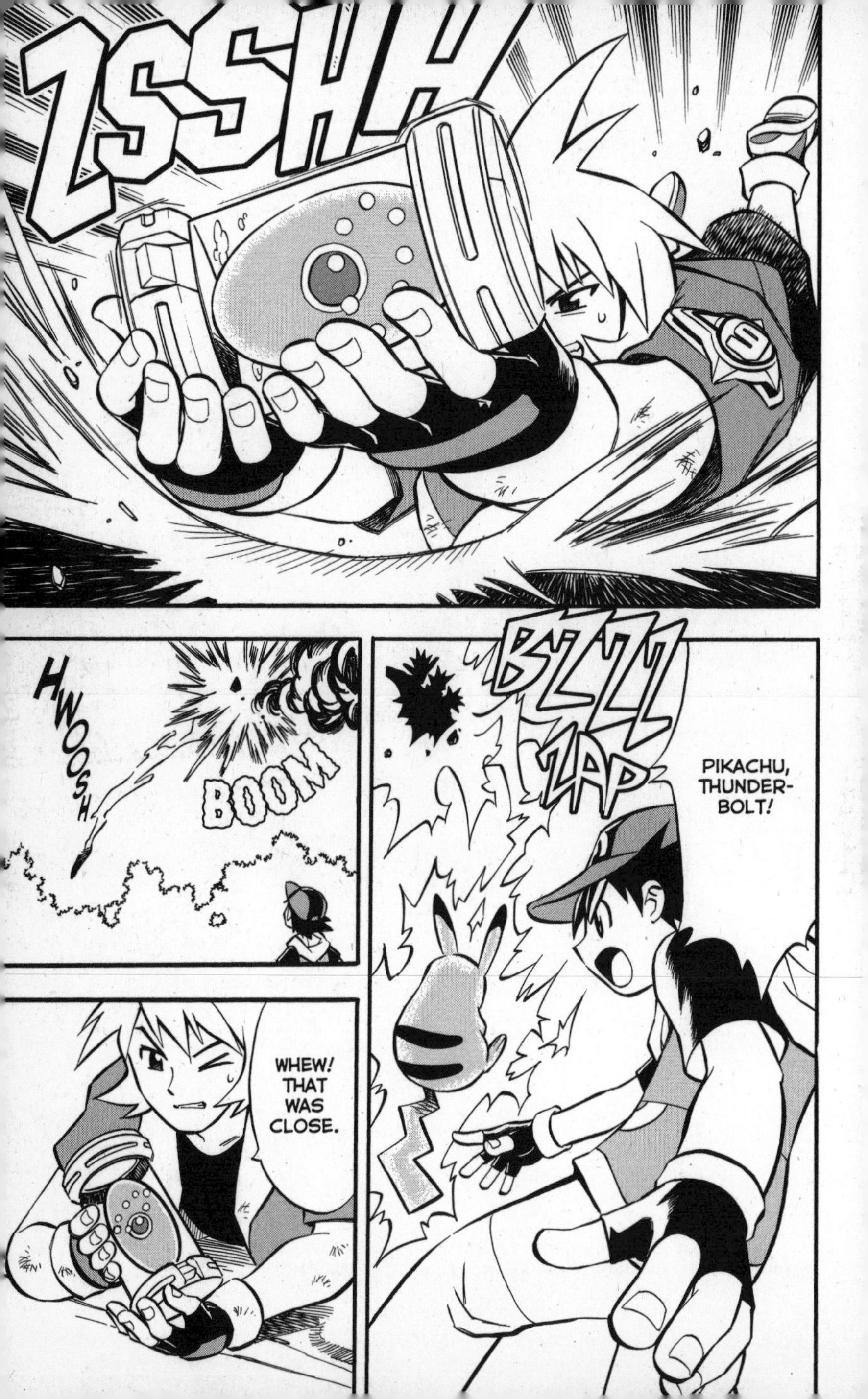
ZSSHH
BZZZ
ZAP
PIKACHU, THUNDER-BOLT!
HWOOSH
BOOM
WHEW! THAT WAS CLOSE.

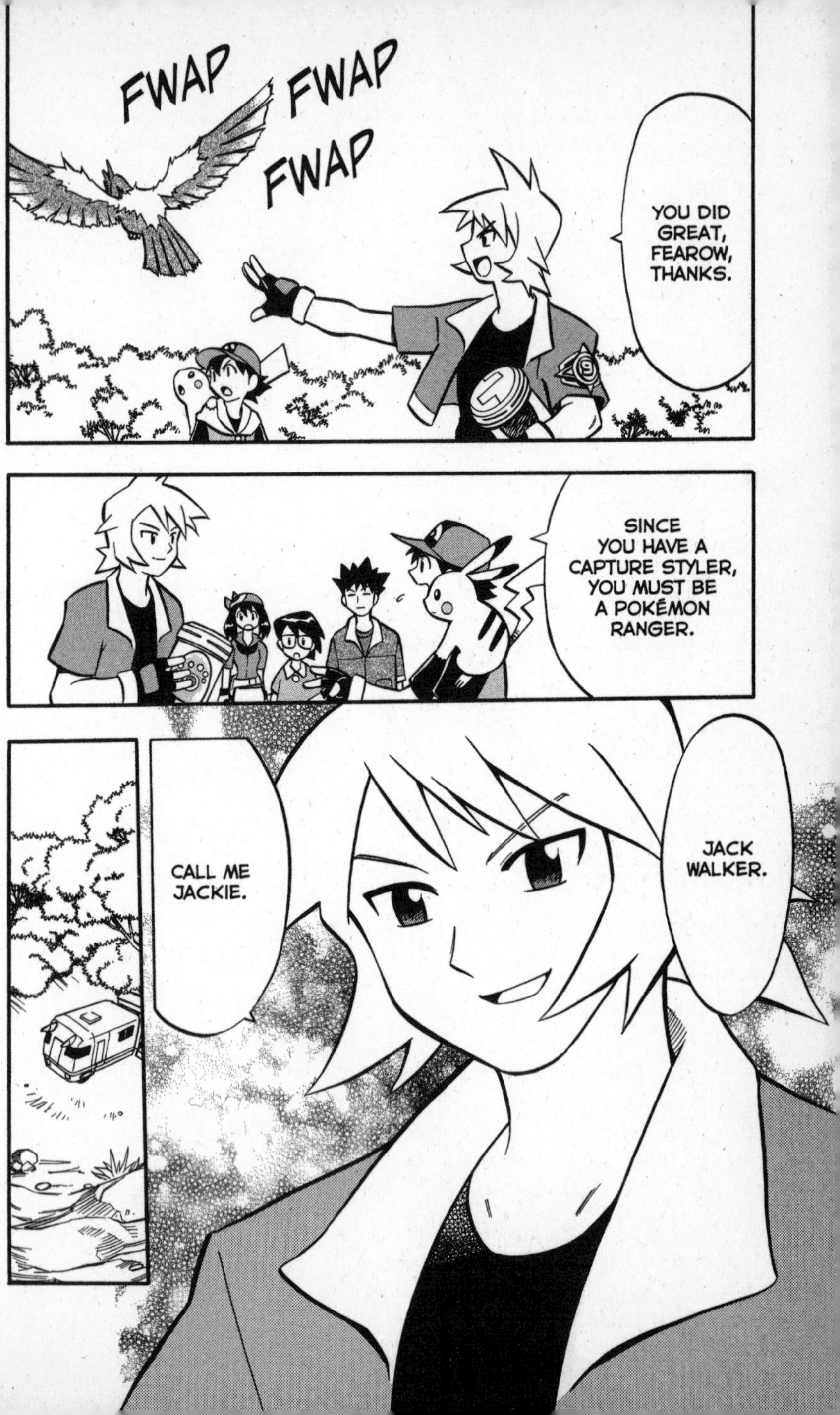
FWAP FWAP FWAP
YOU DID GREAT, FEAROW, THANKS.
SINCE YOU HAVE A CAPTURE STYLER, YOU MUST BE A POKÉMON RANGER.
JACK WALKER.
CALL ME JACKIE.

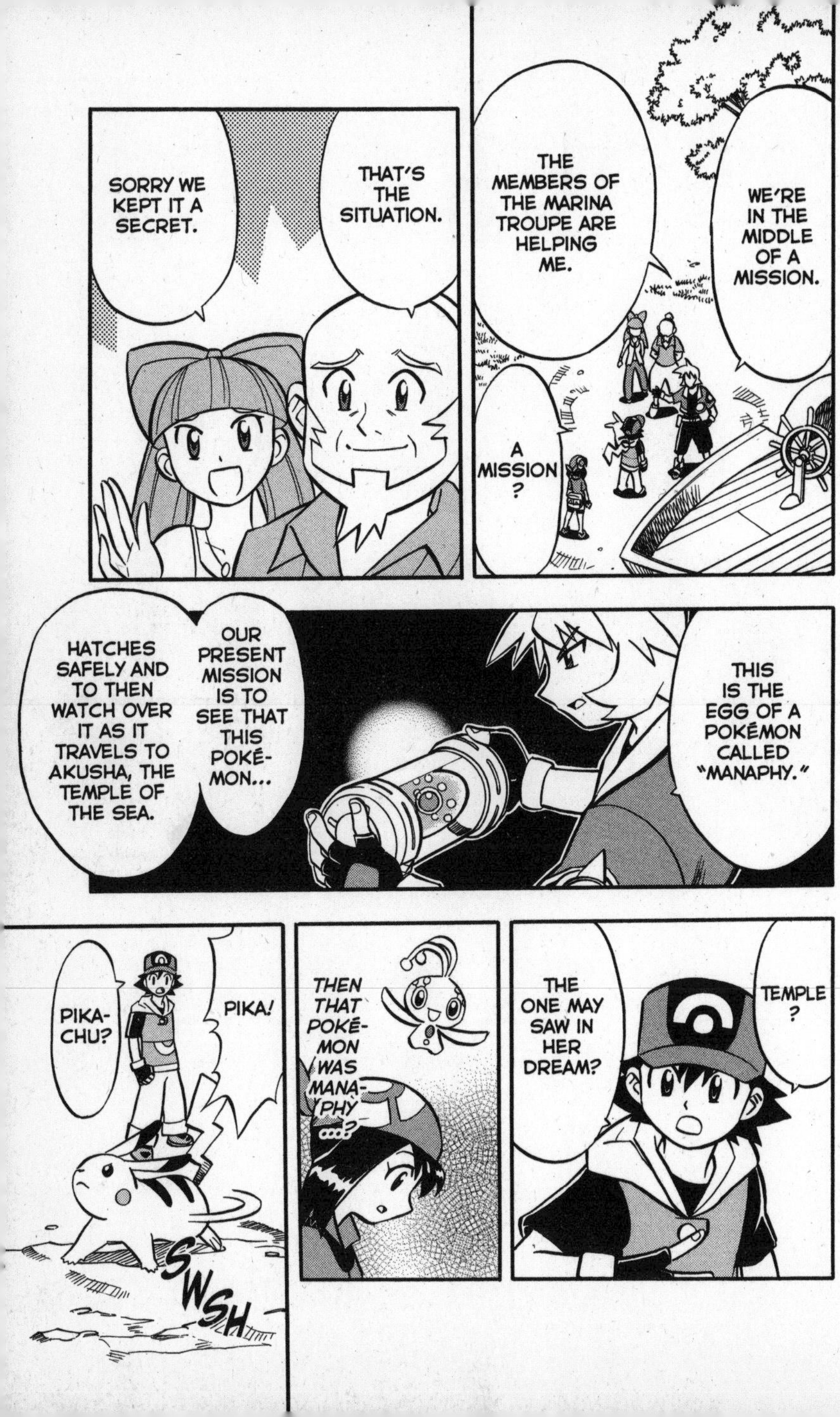
WE'RE IN THE MIDDLE OF A MISSION.
THE MEMBERS OF THE MARINA TROUPE ARE HELPING ME.
A MISSION?
THAT'S THE SITUATION.
SORRY WE KEPT IT A SECRET.
THIS IS THE EGG OF A POKÉMON CALLED "MANAPHY."
OUR PRESENT MISSION IS TO SEE THAT THIS POKÉ-MON...
HATCHES SAFELY AND TO THEN WATCH OVER IT AS IT TRAVELS TO AKUSHA, THE TEMPLE OF THE SEA.
TEMPLE?
THE ONE MAY SAW IN HER DREAM?
THEN THAT POKÉ-MON WAS MANA-PHY...?
PIKA!
PIKA-CHU?
SWSH

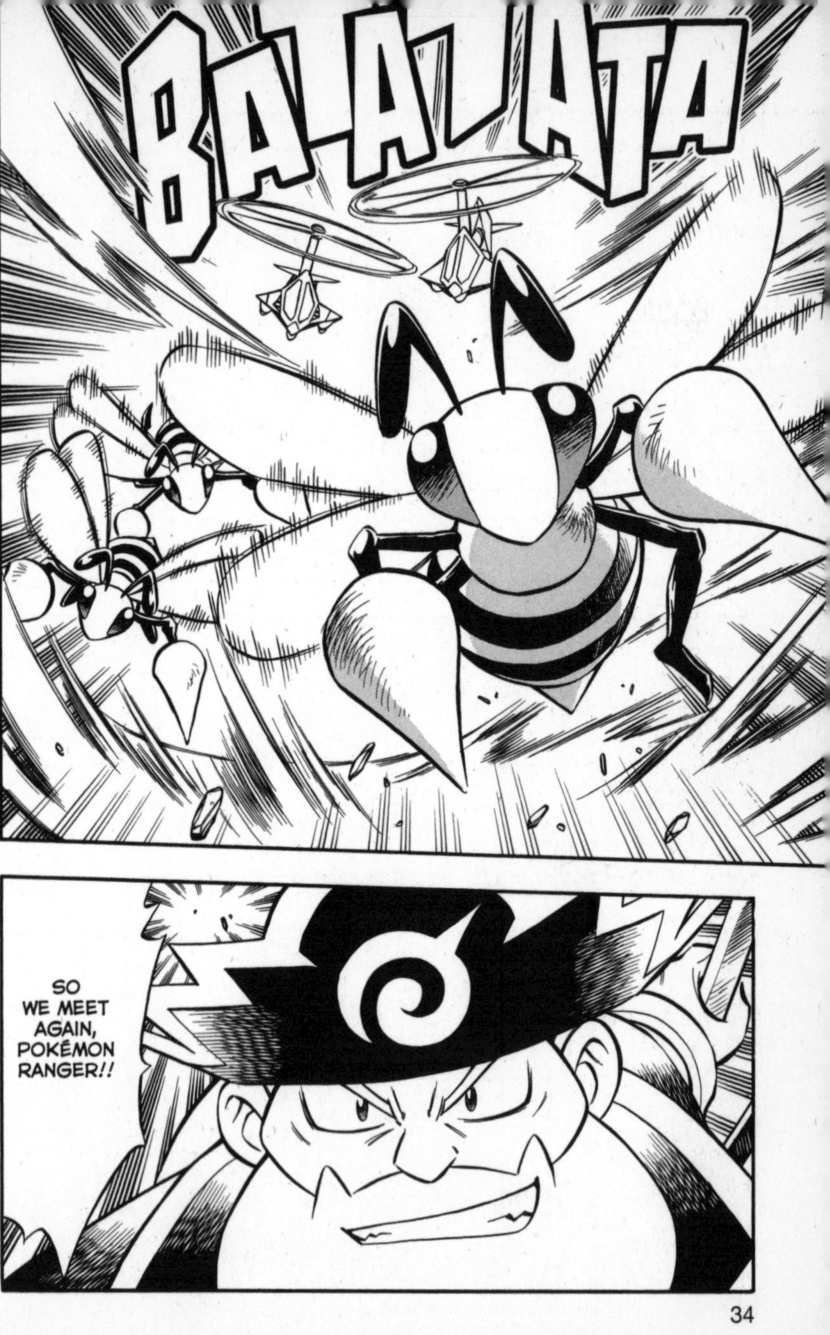
BA-A-A-A
SO WE MEET AGAIN, POKÉMON RANGER!!

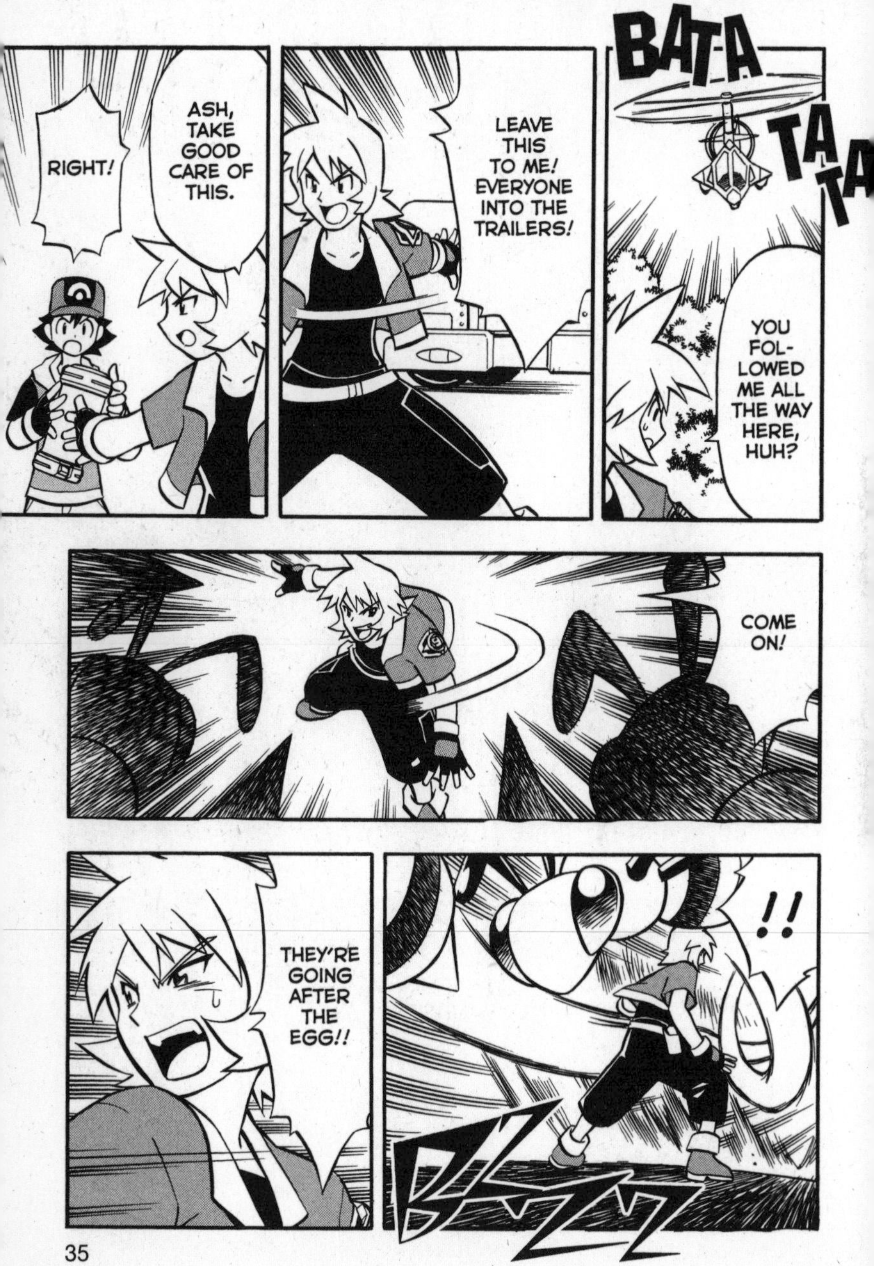
BAT-A
TA
TA
YOU FOL-LOWED ME ALL THE WAY HERE, HUH?
LEAVE THIS TO ME! EVERYONE INTO THE TRAILERS!
ASH, TAKE GOOD CARE OF THIS.
RIGHT!
COME ON!
!!
BZZZ
THEY'RE GOING AFTER THE EGG!!

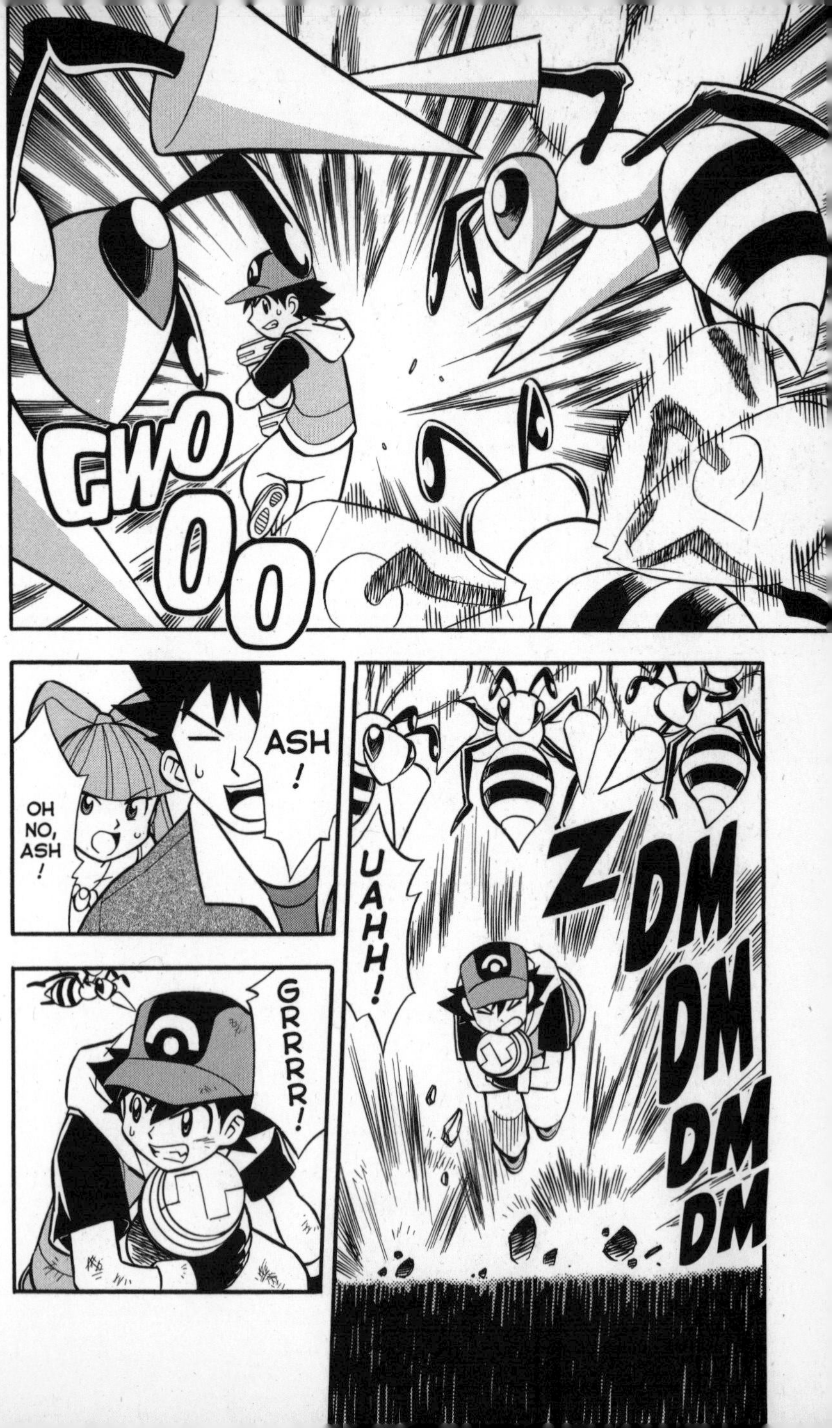
GWOOO
UAHH!
ZDM DM DM DM DM
ASH!
OH NO, ASH!
GRRRR!

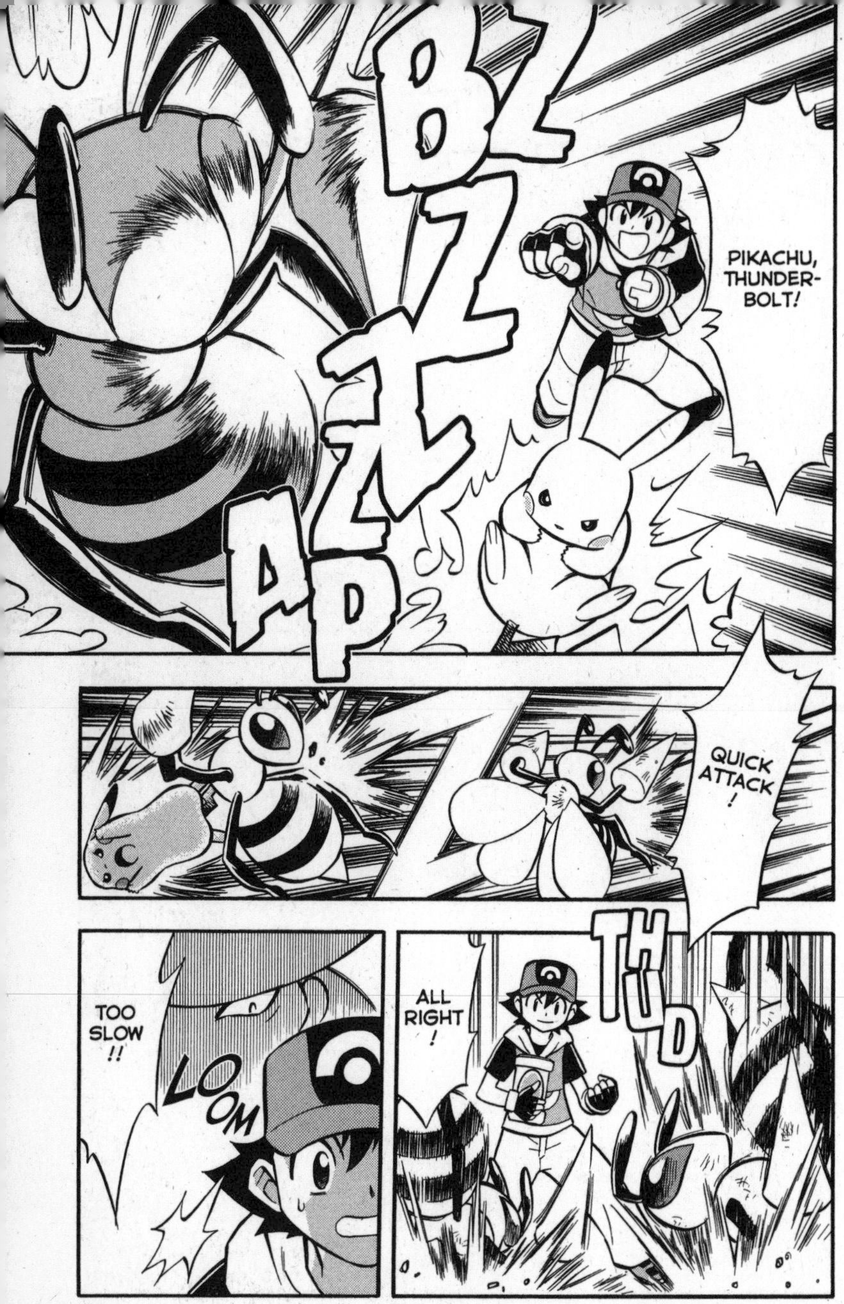
PIKACHU, THUNDER-BOLT!
BZZZAP
QUICK ATTACK!
THUD
ALL RIGHT!
TOO SLOW!!
LOOM

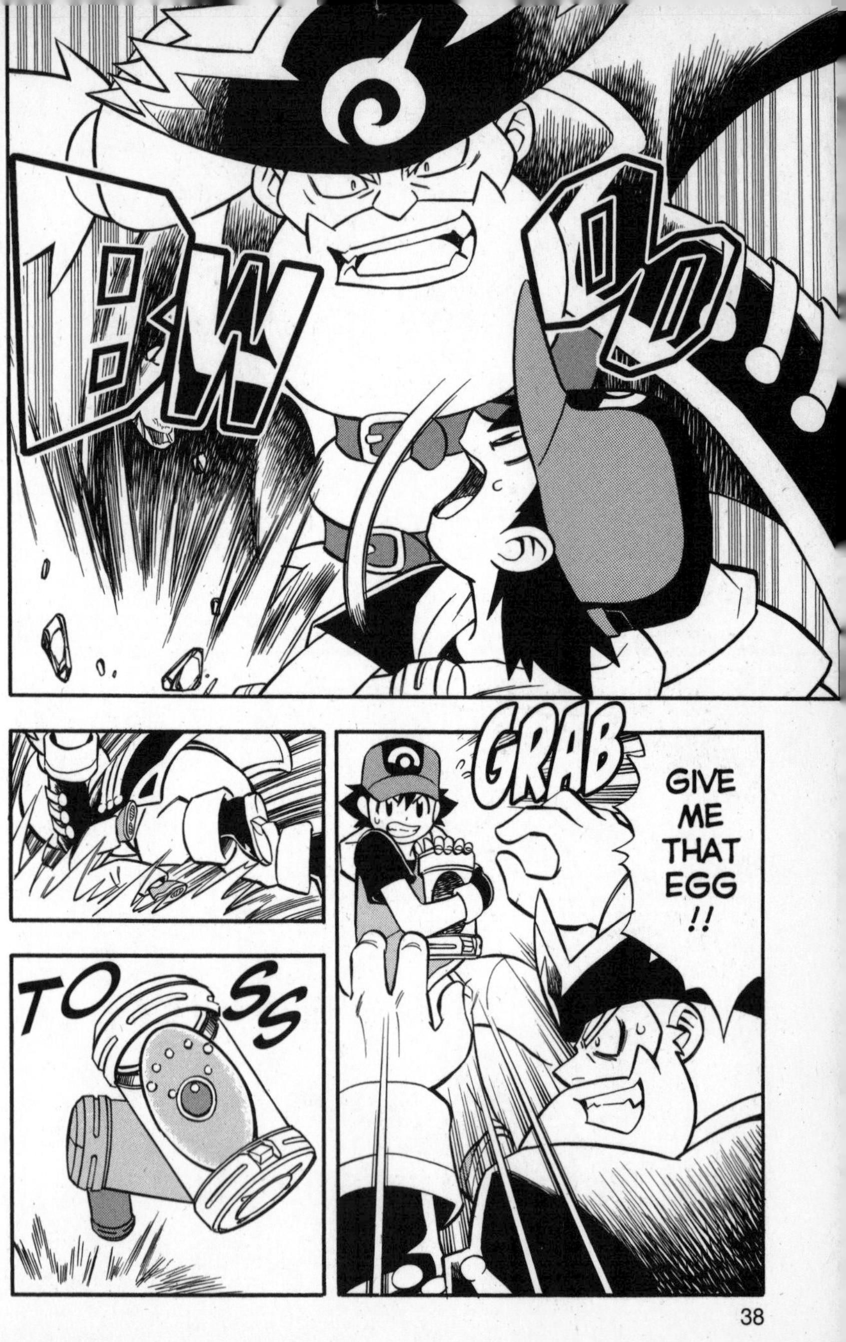
BWOOO!!
GRAB
GIVE ME THAT EGG!!
TOSS

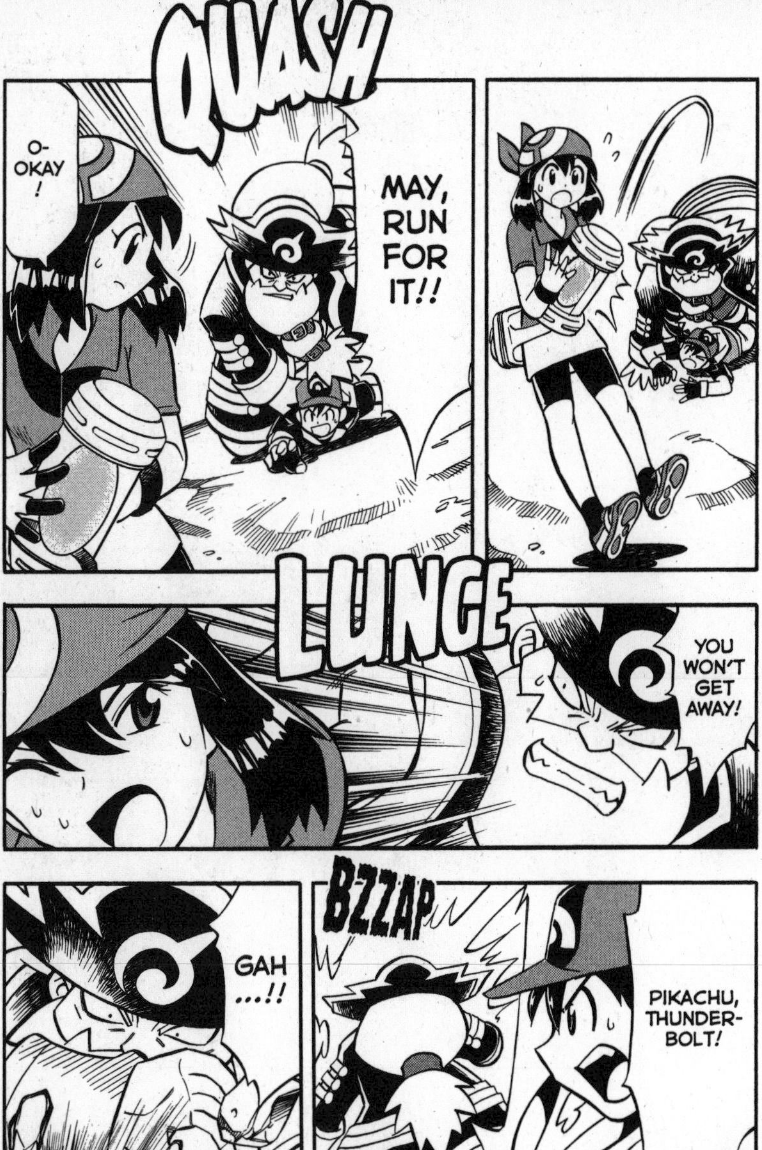
QUASH
MAY, RUN FOR IT!!
O-OKAY!
LUNGE
YOU WON'T GET AWAY!
BZZAP
PIKACHU, THUNDER-BOLT!
GAH...!!

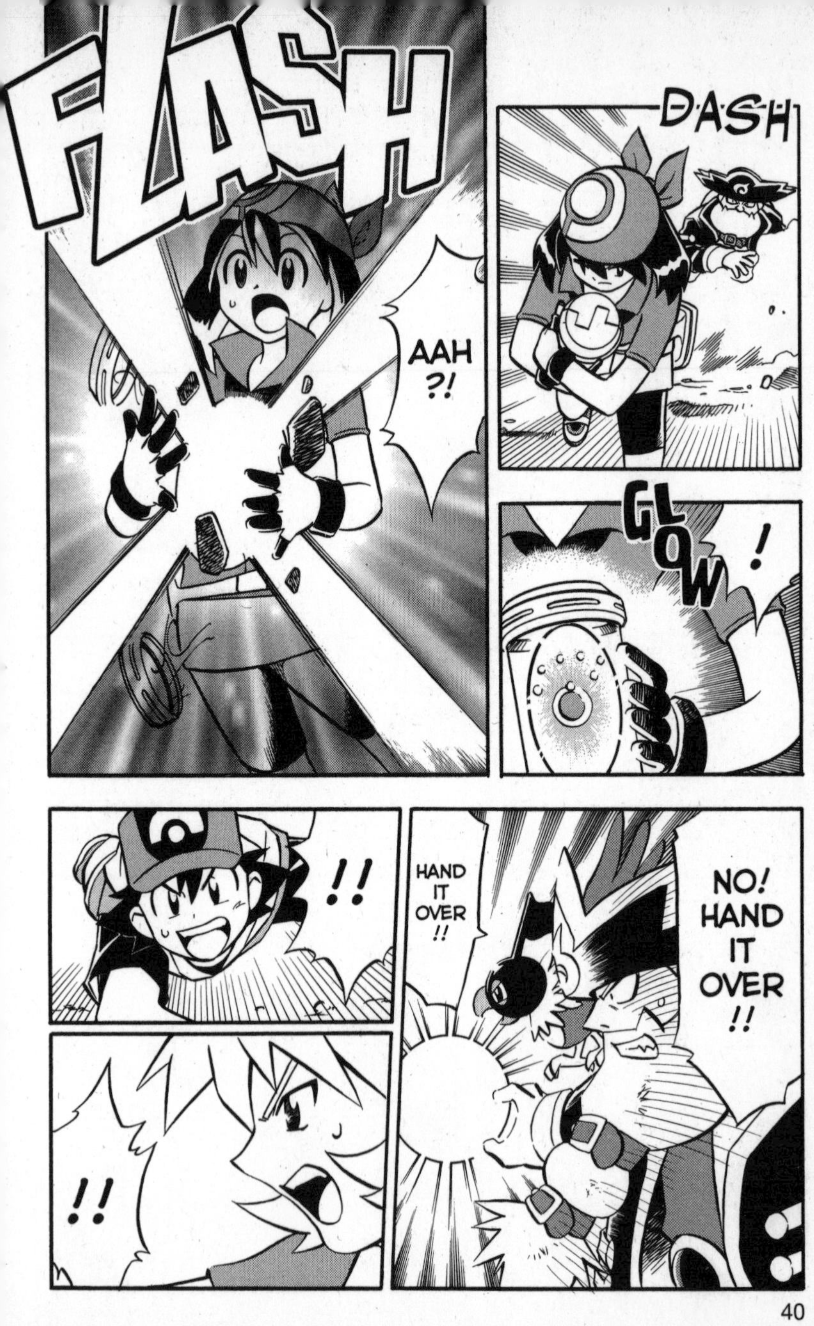
DASH
GLOW!
FLASH
AAH?!
NO! HAND IT OVER!!
HAND IT OVER!!
!!
!!

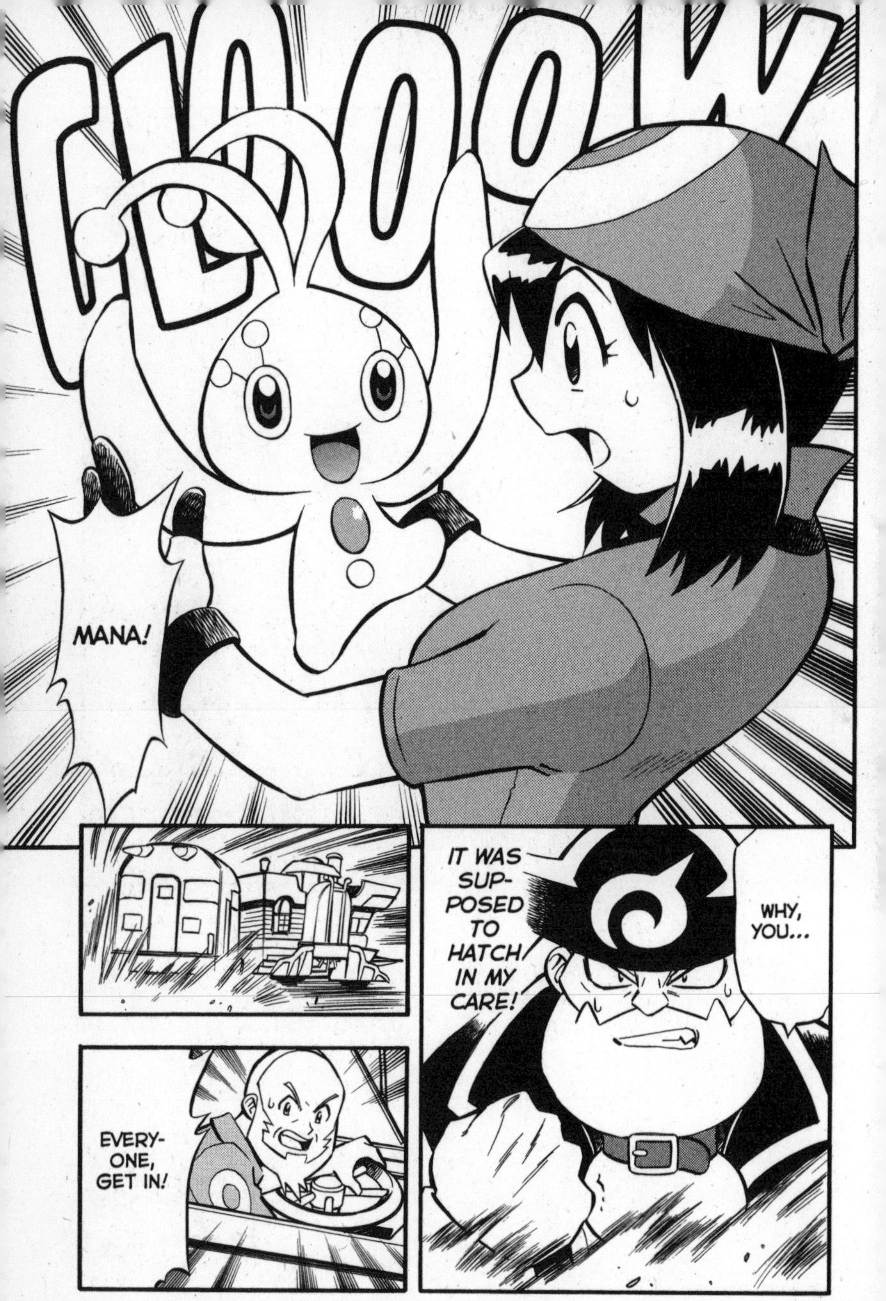
GLOOOW
MANA!
IT WAS SUP-POSED TO HATCH IN MY CARE!
WHY, YOU...
EVERY-ONE, GET IN!

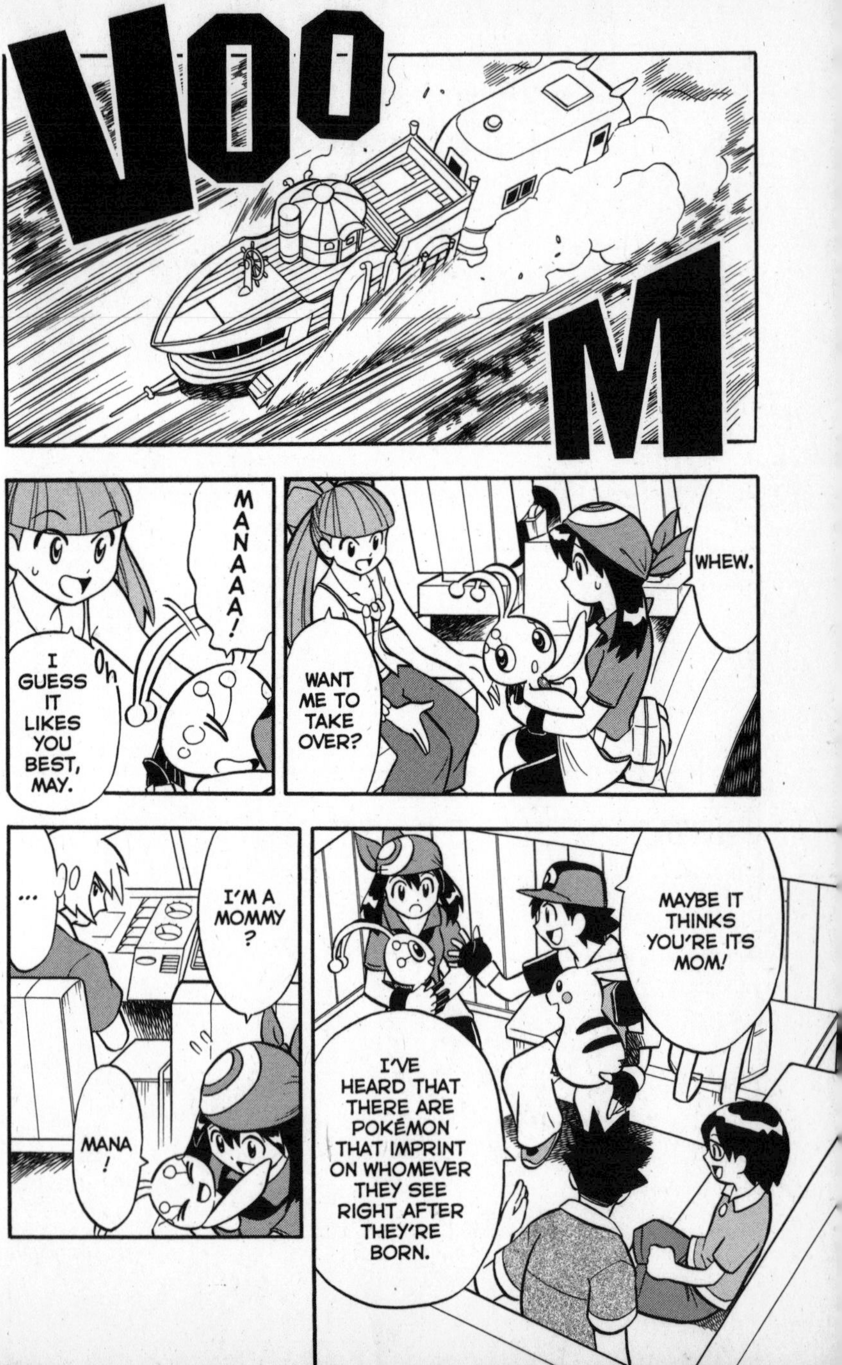
VOOM
WHEW.
WANT ME TO TAKE OVER?
MANAAAA!
Oh
I GUESS IT LIKES YOU BEST, MAY.
MAYBE IT THINKS YOU'RE ITS MOM!
I'VE HEARD THAT THERE ARE POKÉMON THAT IMPRINT ON WHOMEVER THEY SEE RIGHT AFTER THEY'RE BORN.
I'M A MOMMY?
...
MANA!

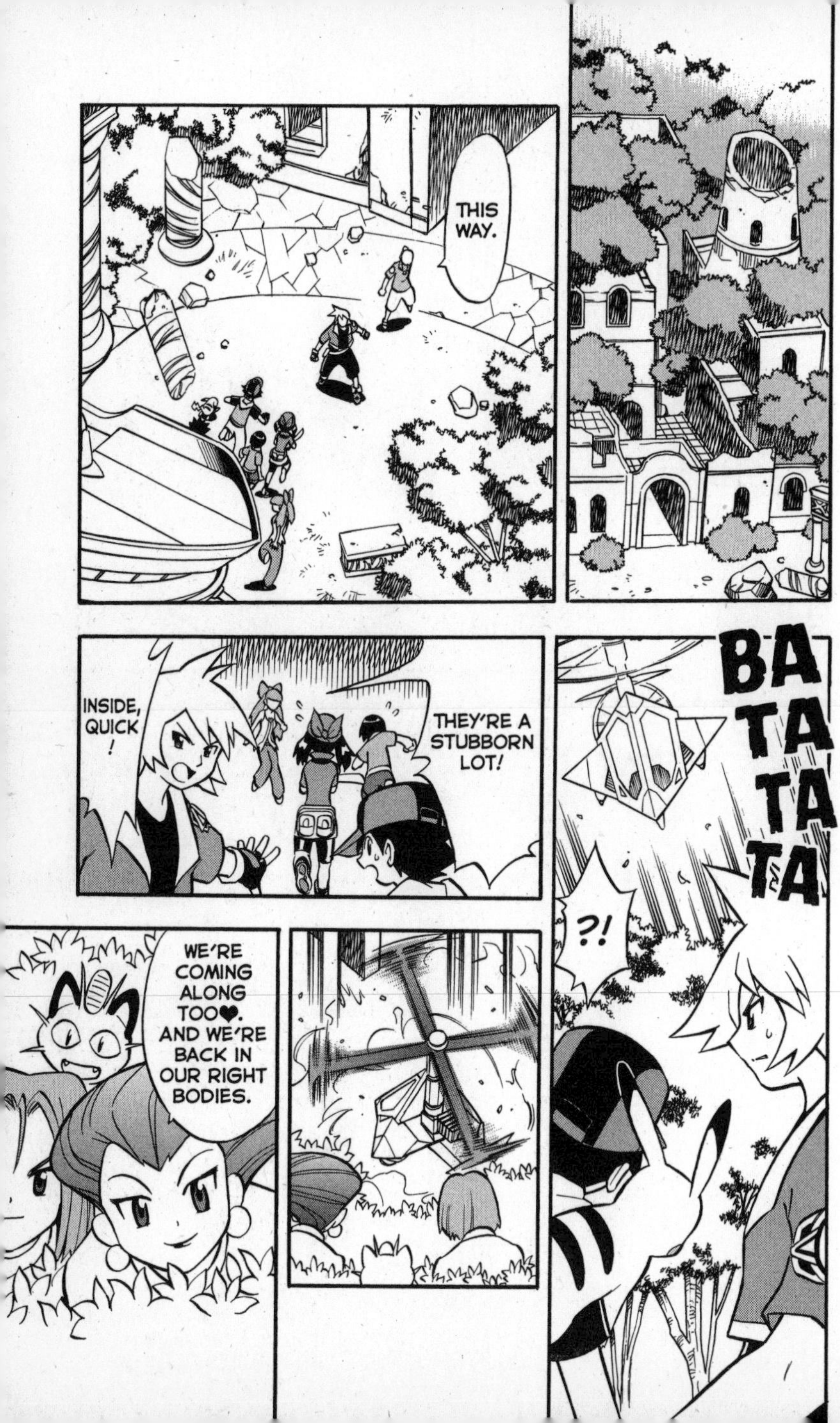
THIS WAY.
BATATATA
?!
THEY'RE A STUBBORN LOT!
INSIDE, QUICK!
WE'RE COMING ALONG TOO♥. AND WE'RE BACK IN OUR RIGHT BODIES.

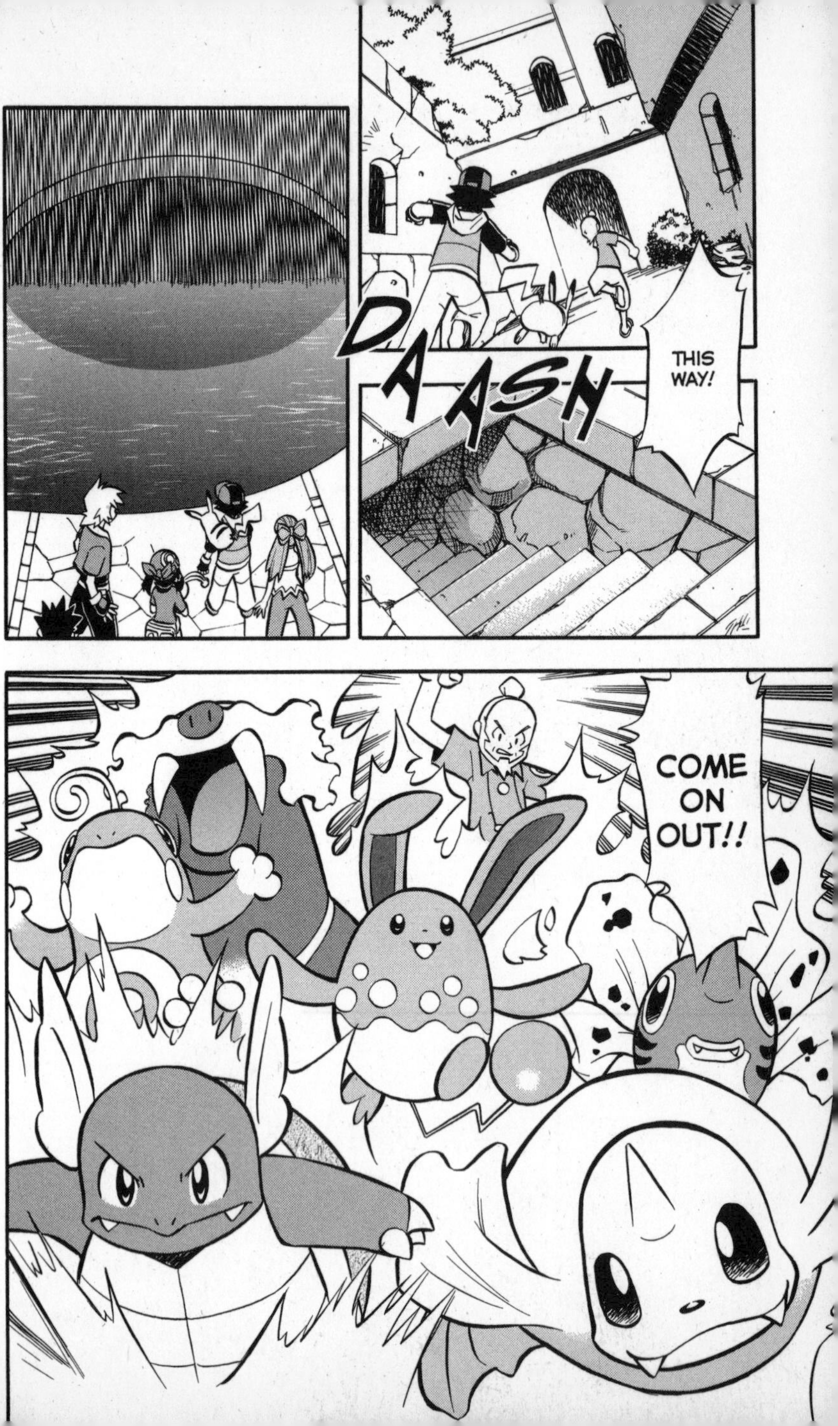
THIS WAY!
DAASH
COME ON OUT!!

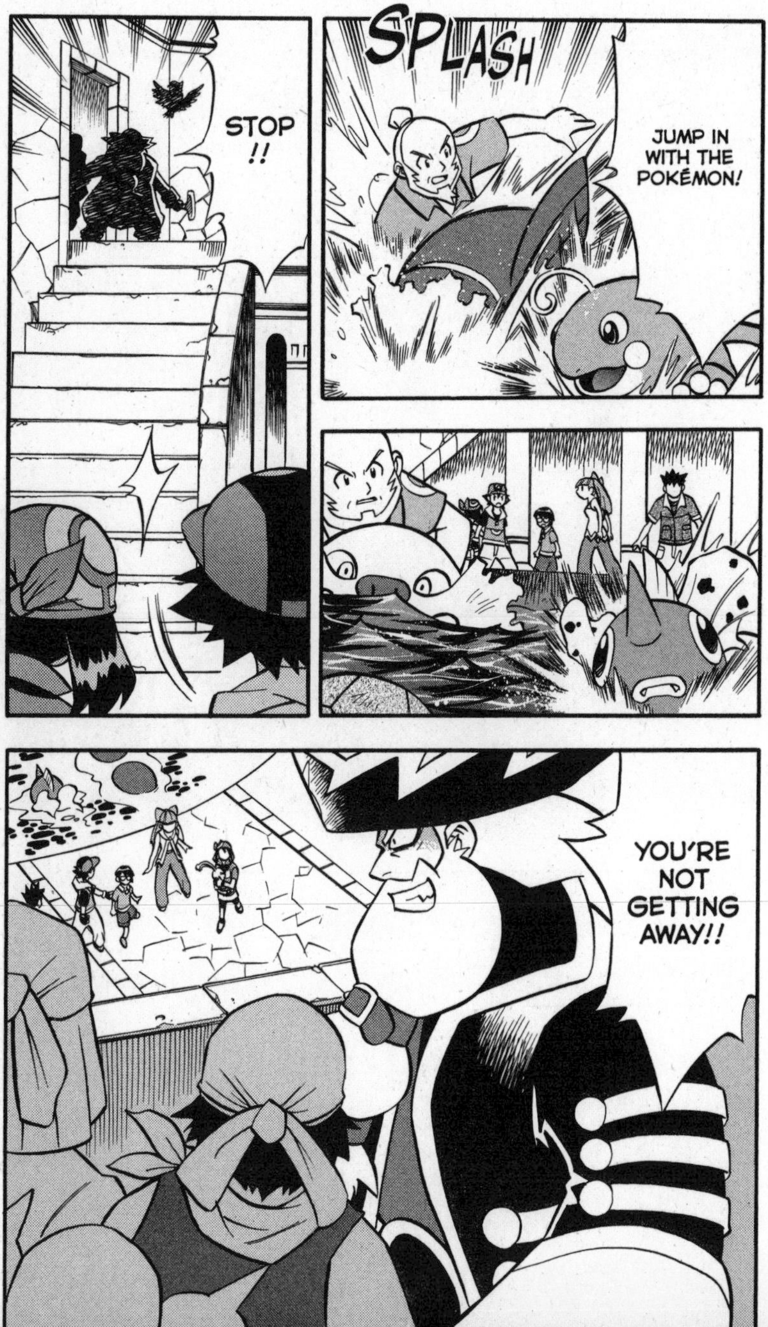
SPLASH
JUMP IN WITH THE POKÉMON!
STOP!!
YOU'RE NOT GETTING AWAY!!

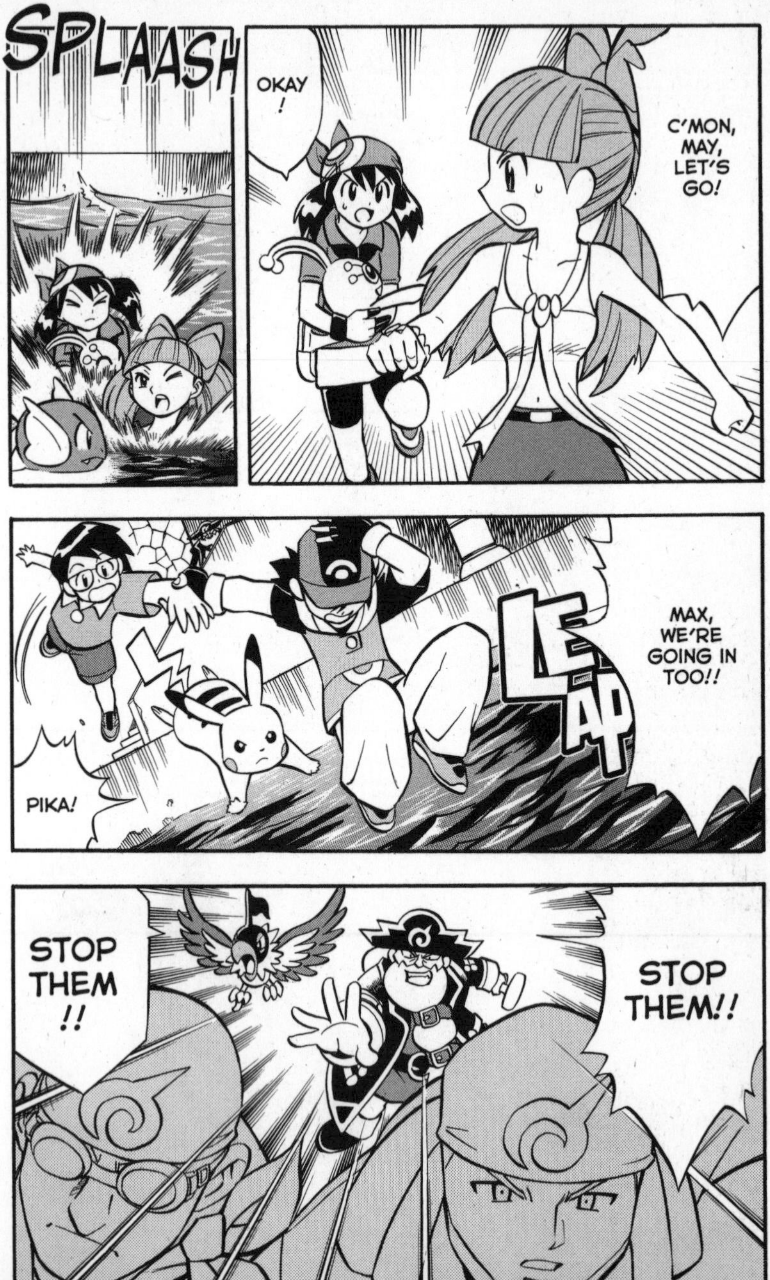
C'MON, MAY, LET'S GO!
OKAY!
SPLAASH
MAX, WE'RE GOING IN TOO!!
LEAP
PIKA!
STOP THEM!!
STOP THEM!!

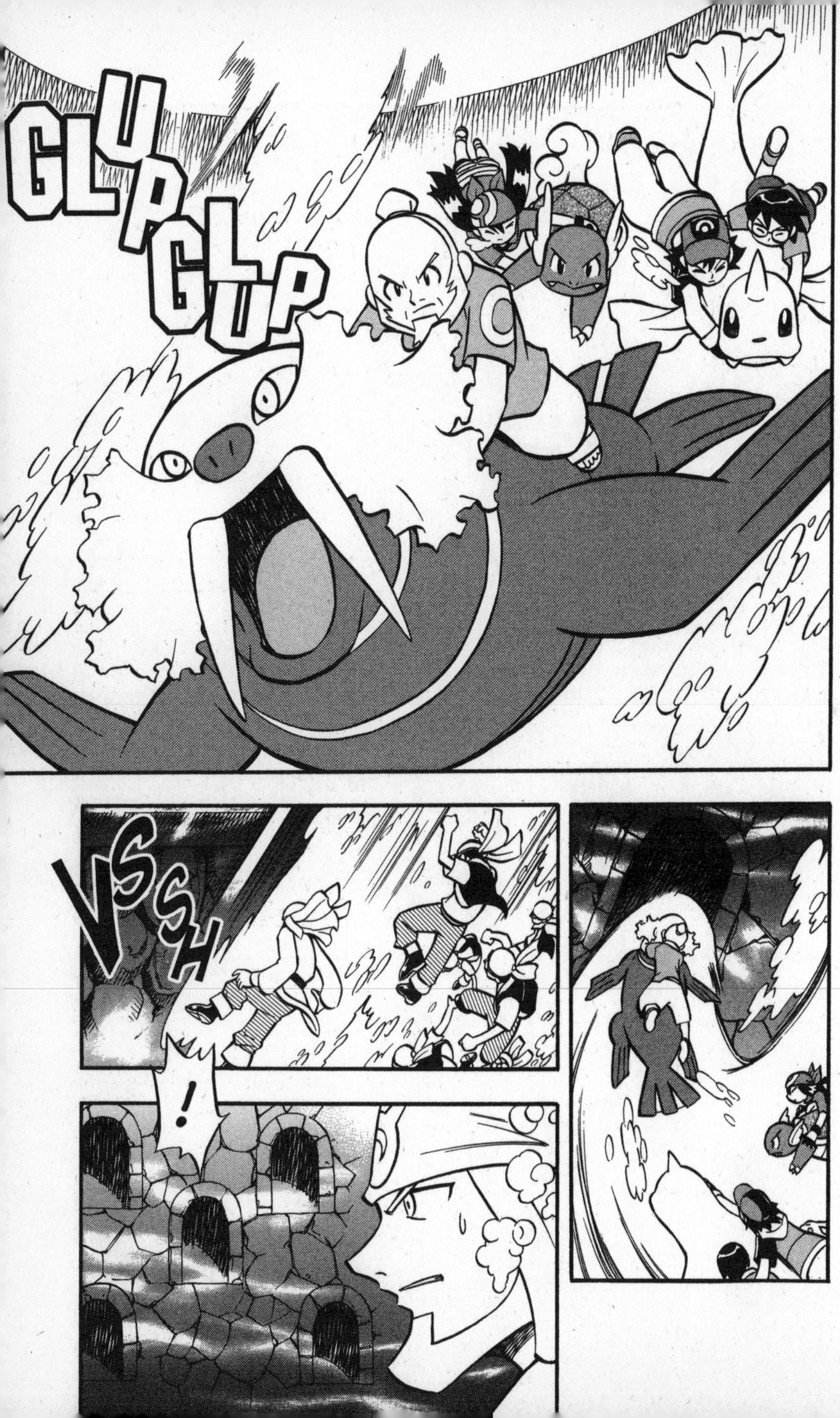
GLUP GLUP
VSSH
!

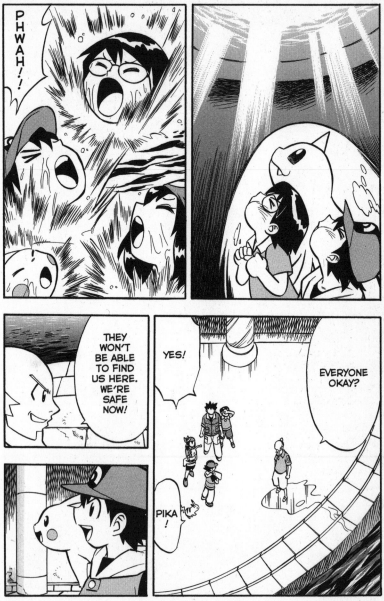

PHWAH!!
EVERYONE OKAY?
YES!
PIKA!
THEY WON'T BE ABLE TO FIND US HERE. WE'RE SAFE NOW!

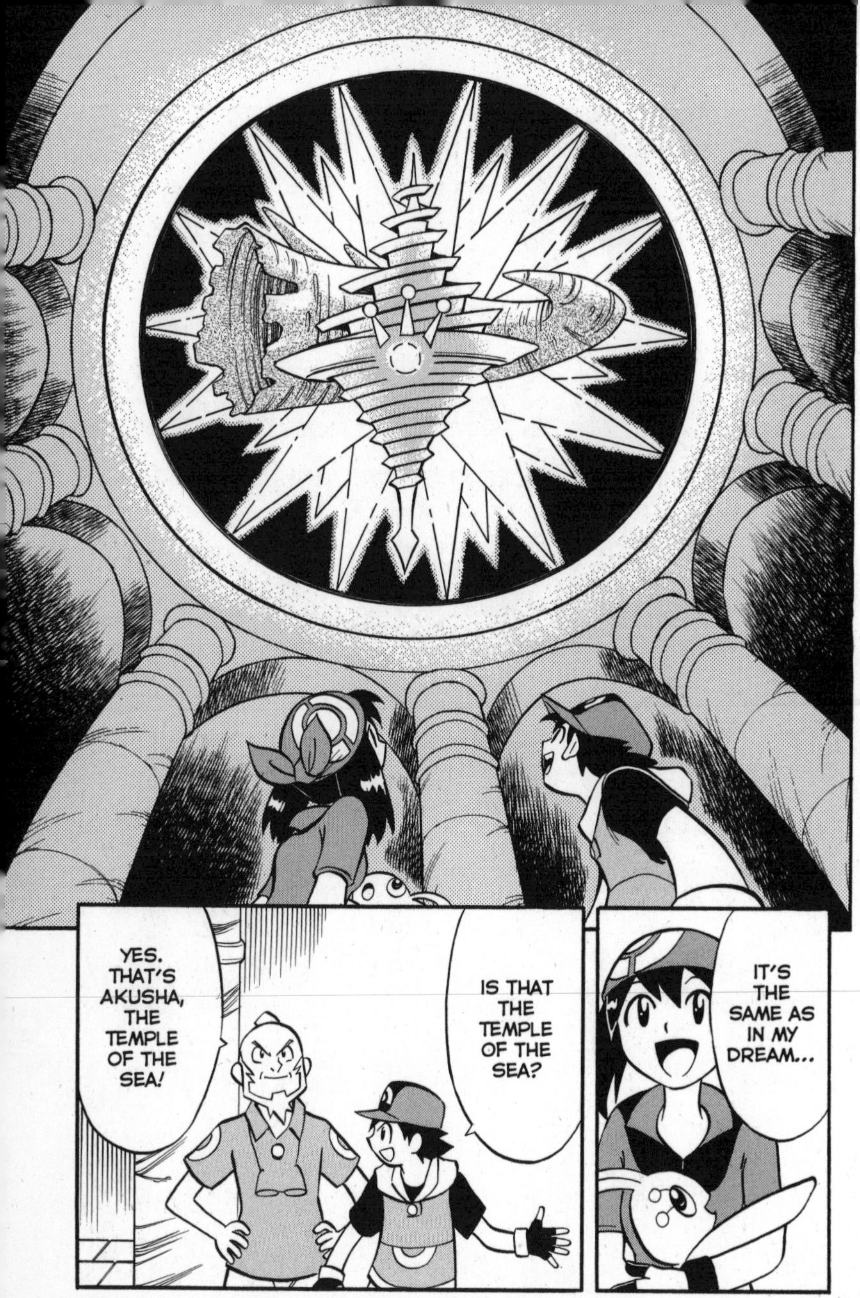
IT'S THE SAME AS IN MY DREAM...
IS THAT THE TEMPLE OF THE SEA?
YES. THAT'S AKUSHA, THE TEMPLE OF THE SEA!

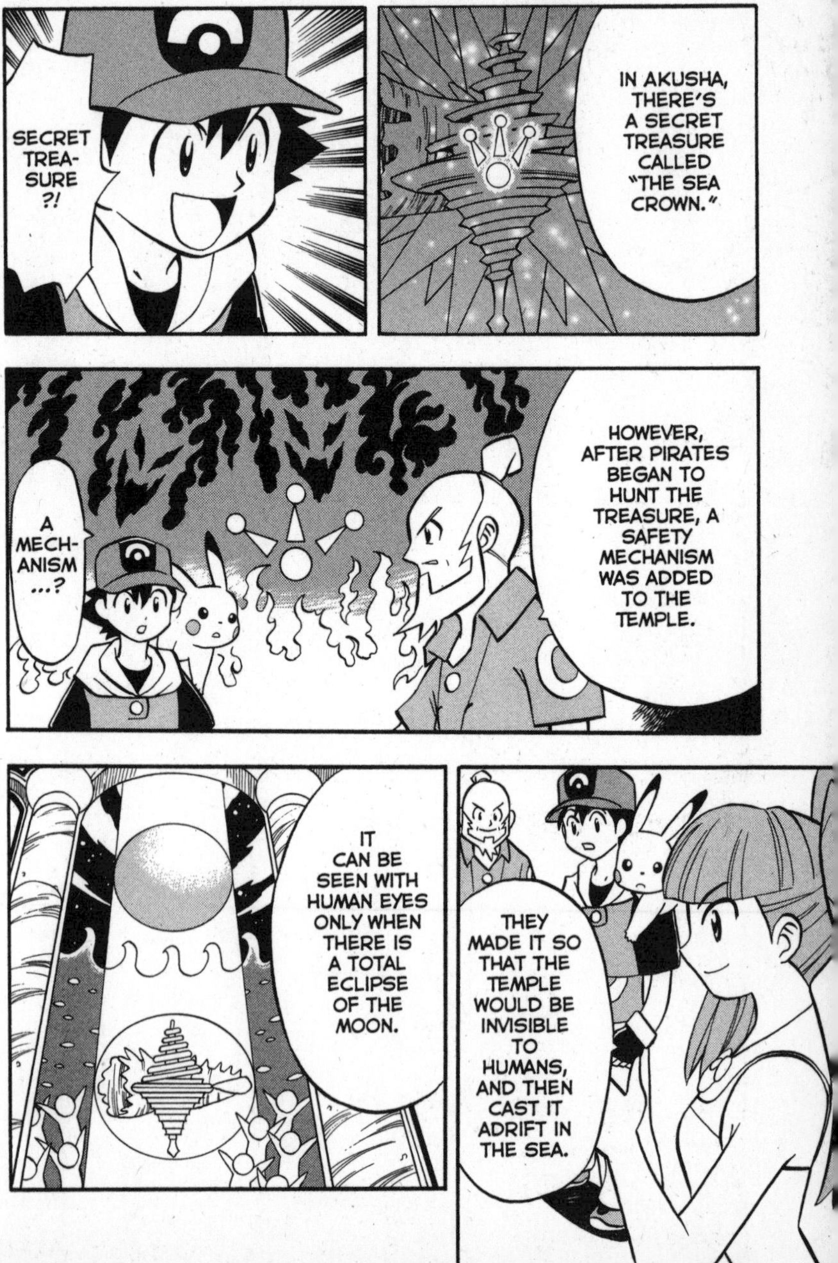
IN AKUSHA, THERE'S A SECRET TREASURE CALLED "THE SEA CROWN."
SECRET TREA-SURE ?!
HOWEVER, AFTER PIRATES BEGAN TO HUNT THE TREASURE, A SAFETY MECHANISM WAS ADDED TO THE TEMPLE.
A MECH-ANISM ...?
THEY MADE IT SO THAT THE TEMPLE WOULD BE INVISIBLE TO HUMANS, AND THEN CAST IT ADRIFT IN THE SEA.
IT CAN BE SEEN WITH HUMAN EYES ONLY WHEN THERE IS A TOTAL ECLIPSE OF THE MOON.

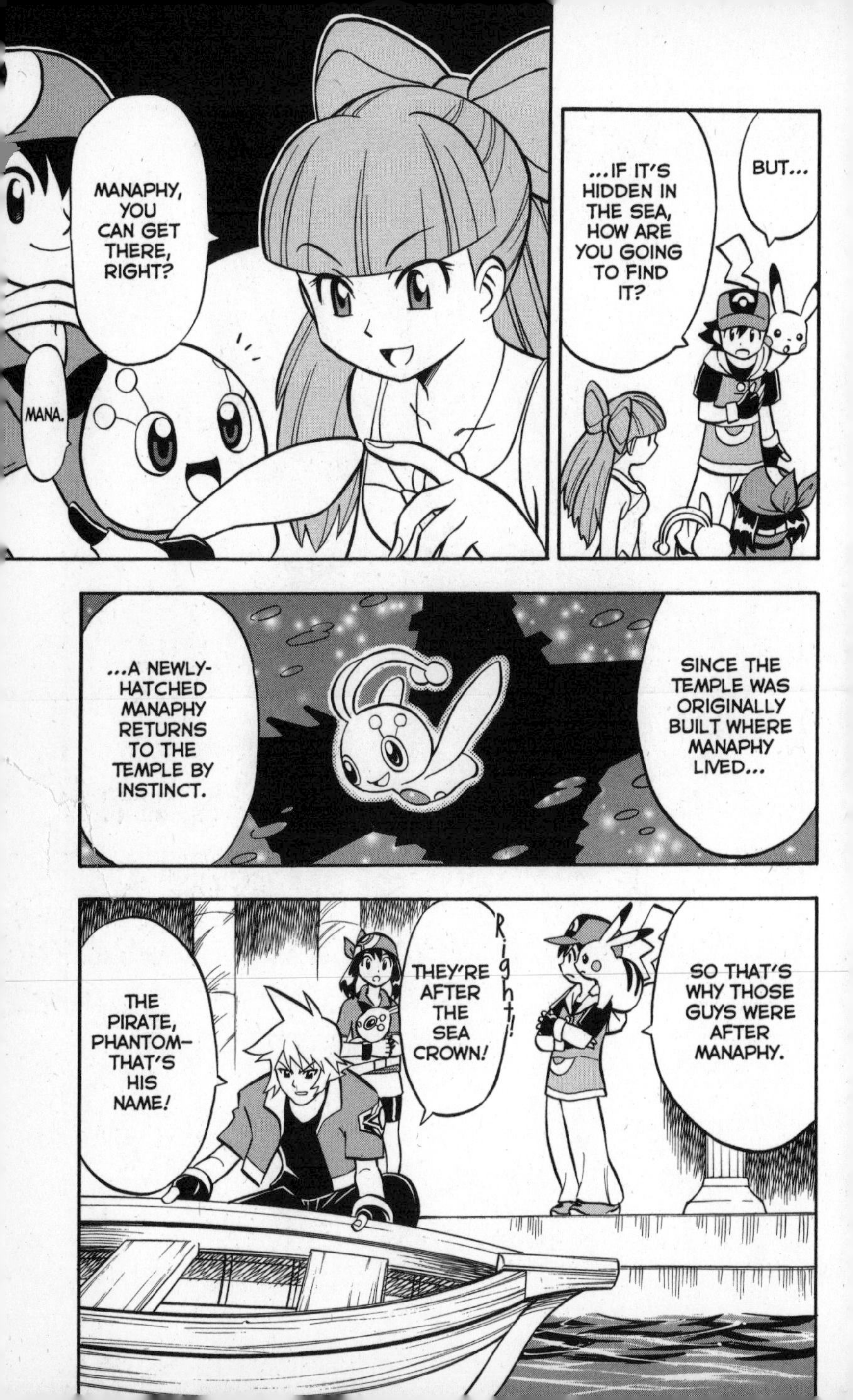
BUT...
...IF IT'S HIDDEN IN THE SEA, HOW ARE YOU GOING TO FIND IT?
MANAPHY, YOU CAN GET THERE, RIGHT?
MANA.
SINCE THE TEMPLE WAS ORIGINALLY BUILT WHERE MANAPHY LIVED...
...A NEWLY-HATCHED MANAPHY RETURNS TO THE TEMPLE BY INSTINCT.
SO THAT'S WHY THOSE GUYS WERE AFTER MANAPHY.
Right!
THEY'RE AFTER THE SEA CROWN!
THE PIRATE, PHANTOM—THAT'S HIS NAME!

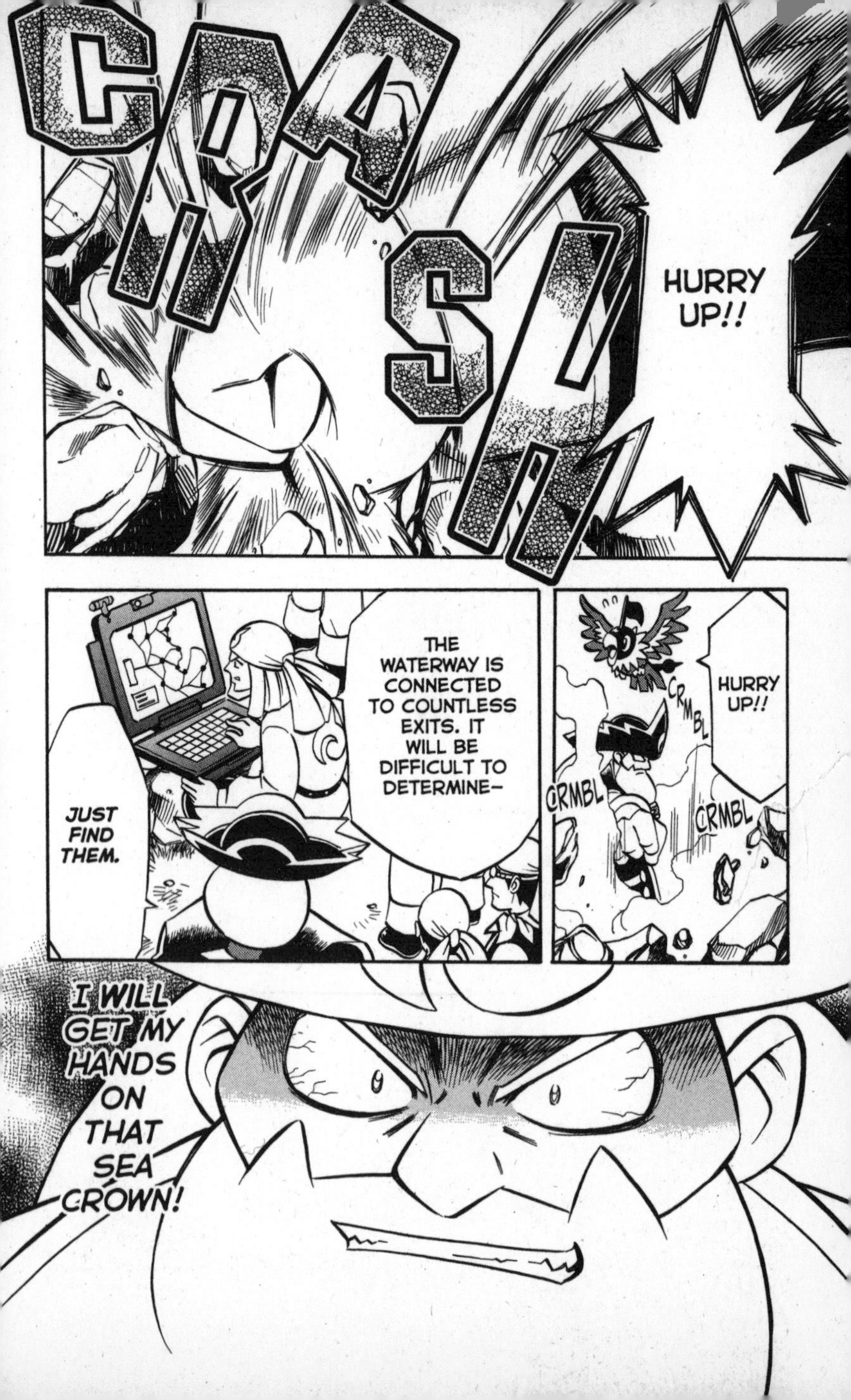
CRASH
HURRY UP!!
HURRY UP!!
CRMBL
CRMBL
CRMBL
THE WATERWAY IS CONNECTED TO COUNTLESS EXITS. IT WILL BE DIFFICULT TO DETERMINE–
JUST FIND THEM.
I WILL GET MY HANDS ON THAT SEA CROWN!

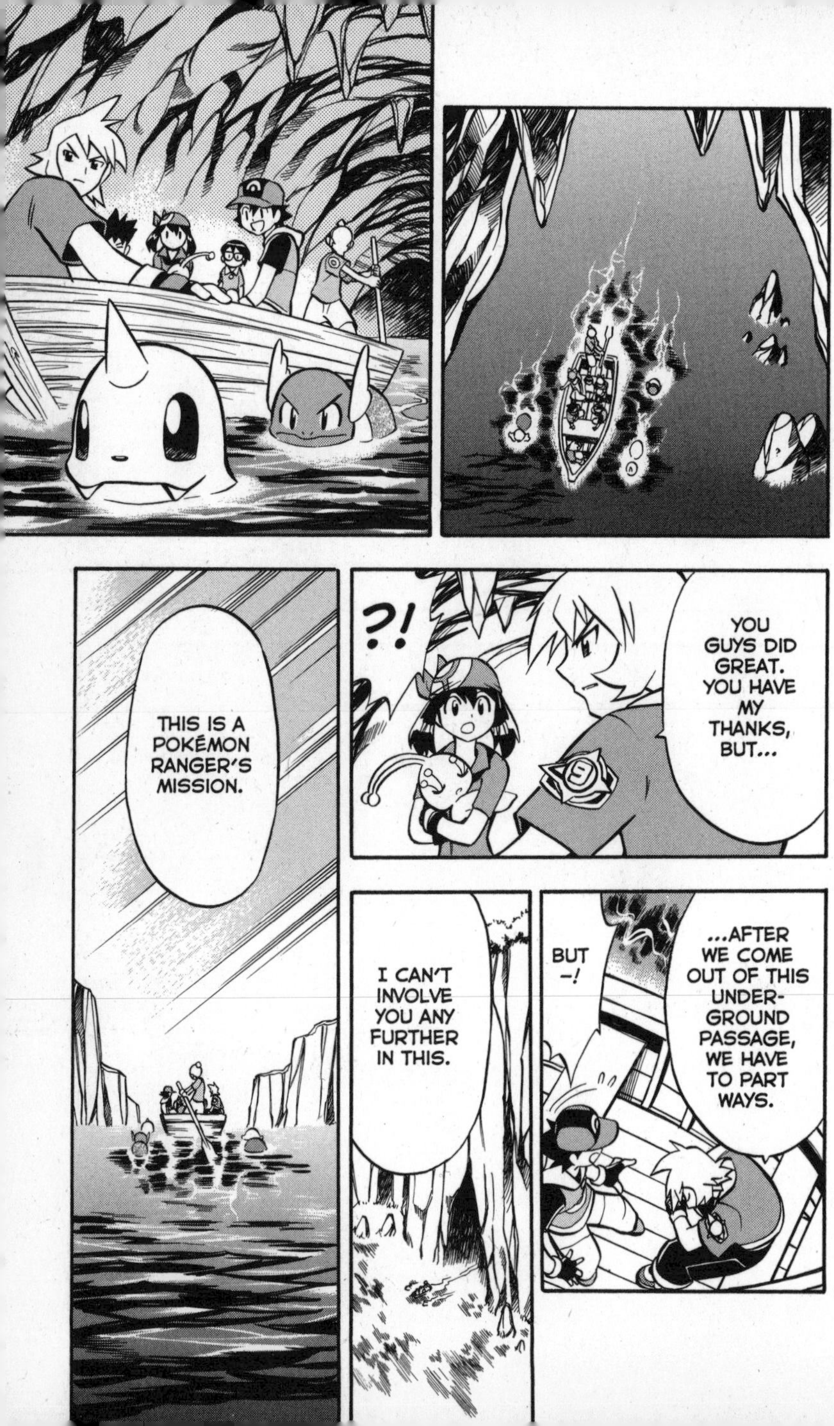
YOU GUYS DID GREAT. YOU HAVE MY THANKS, BUT...
?!
...AFTER WE COME OUT OF THIS UNDERGROUND PASSAGE, WE HAVE TO PART WAYS.
BUT —!
I CAN'T INVOLVE YOU ANY FURTHER IN THIS.
THIS IS A POKÉMON RANGER'S MISSION.

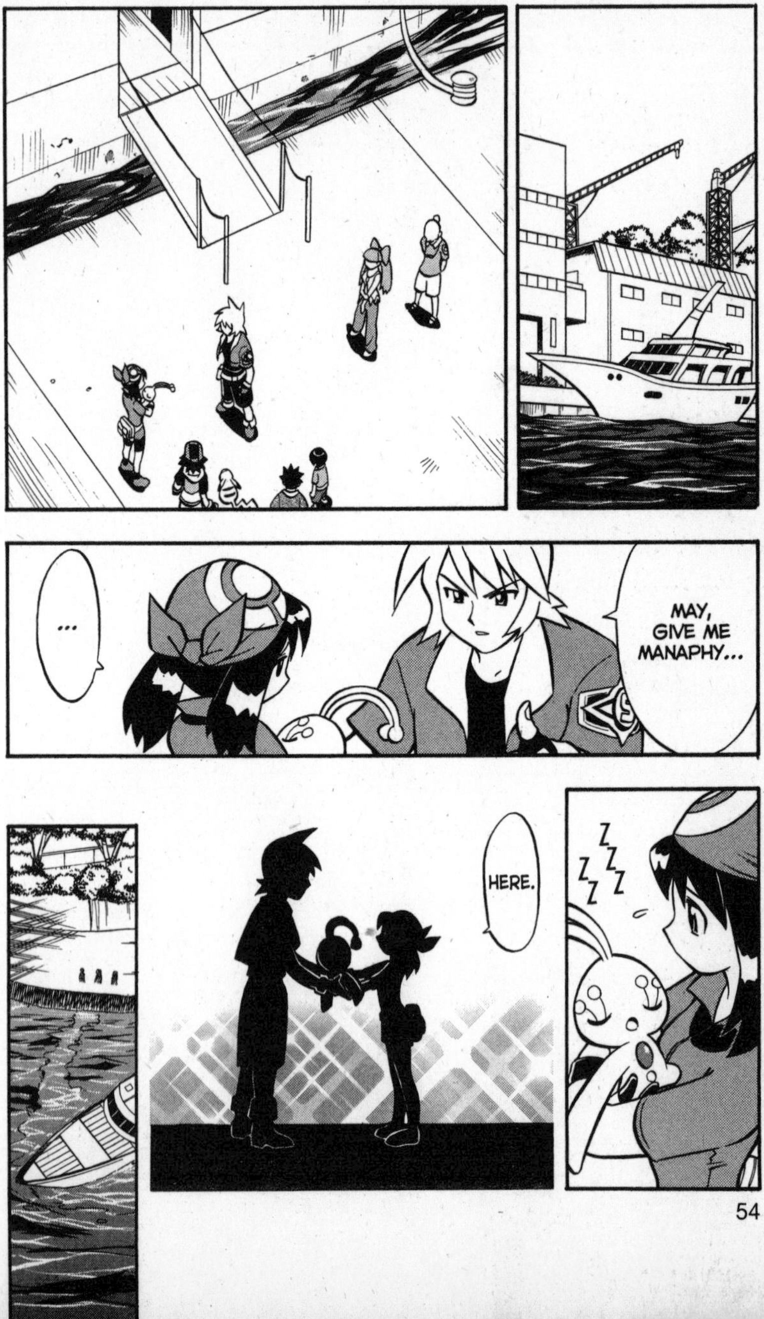
MAY, GIVE ME MANAPHY...
...
ZZZZ
HERE.

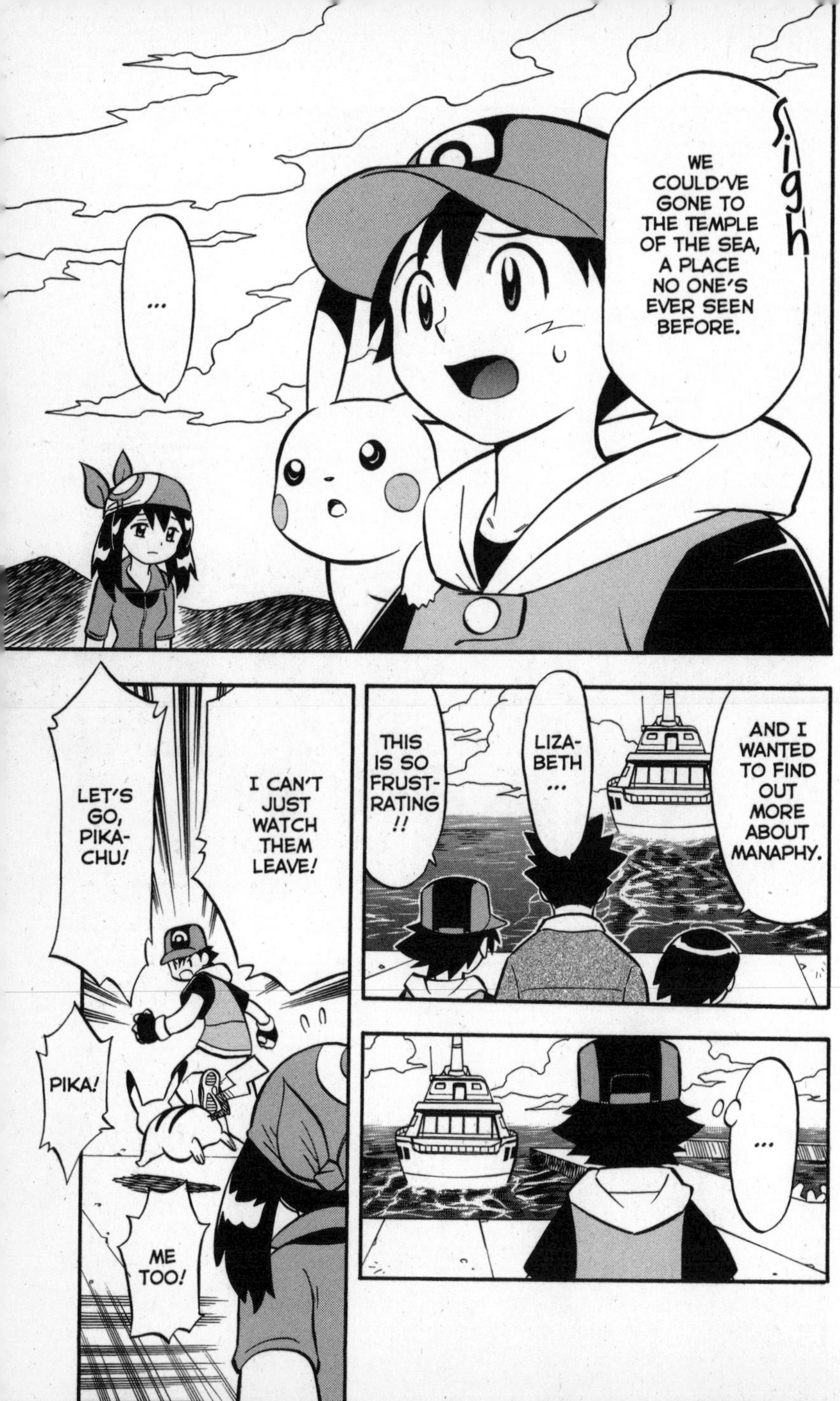
sigh
WE COULD'VE GONE TO THE TEMPLE OF THE SEA, A PLACE NO ONE'S EVER SEEN BEFORE.
...
AND I WANTED TO FIND OUT MORE ABOUT MANAPHY.
LIZA-BETH ...
THIS IS SO FRUST-RATING !!
...
I CAN'T JUST WATCH THEM LEAVE!
LET'S GO, PIKA-CHU!
PIKA!
ME TOO!

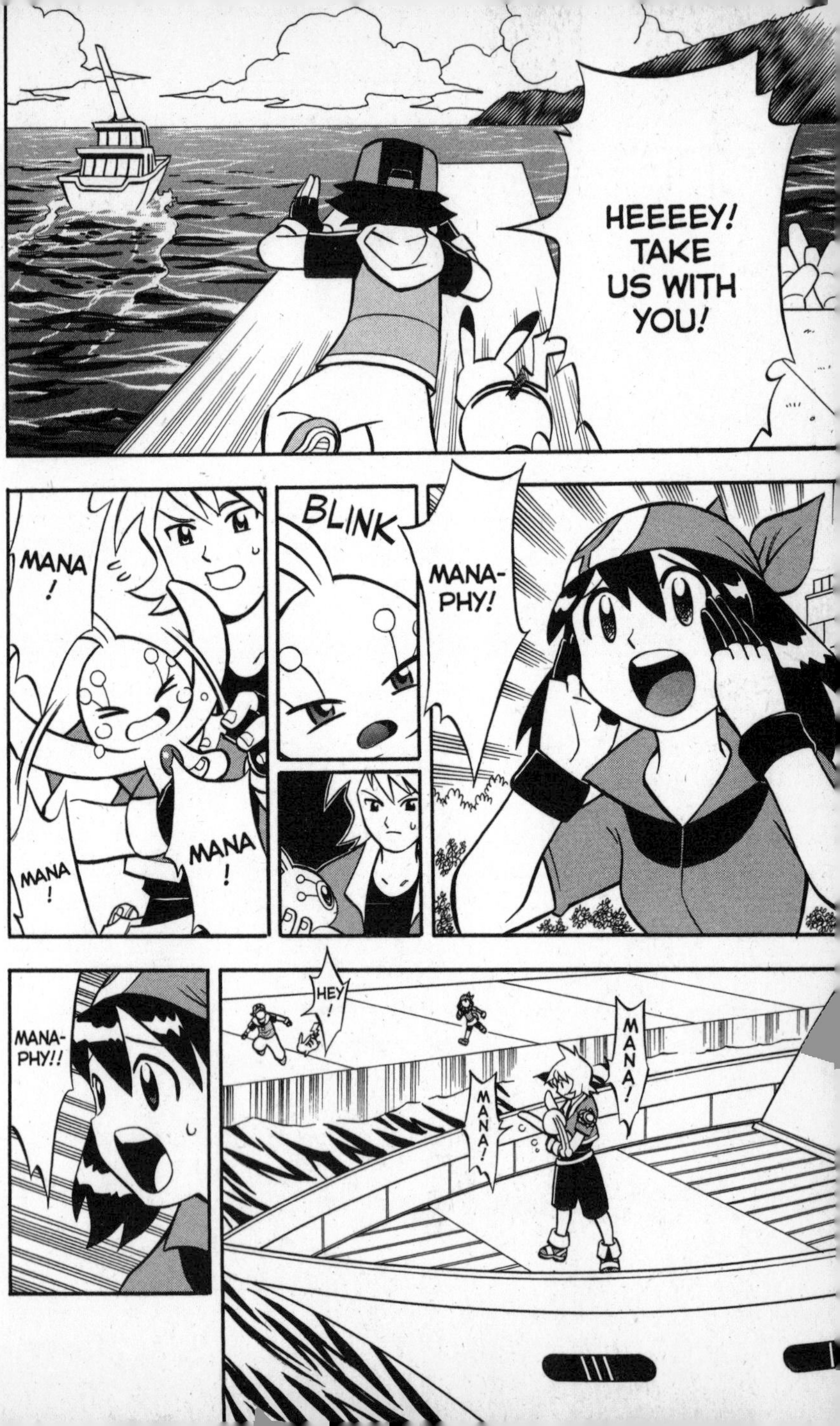
HEEEEY! TAKE US WITH YOU!
MANA-PHY!
BLINK
MANA!
MANA!
MANA!
MANA!
HEY!
MANA!
MANA-PHY!!

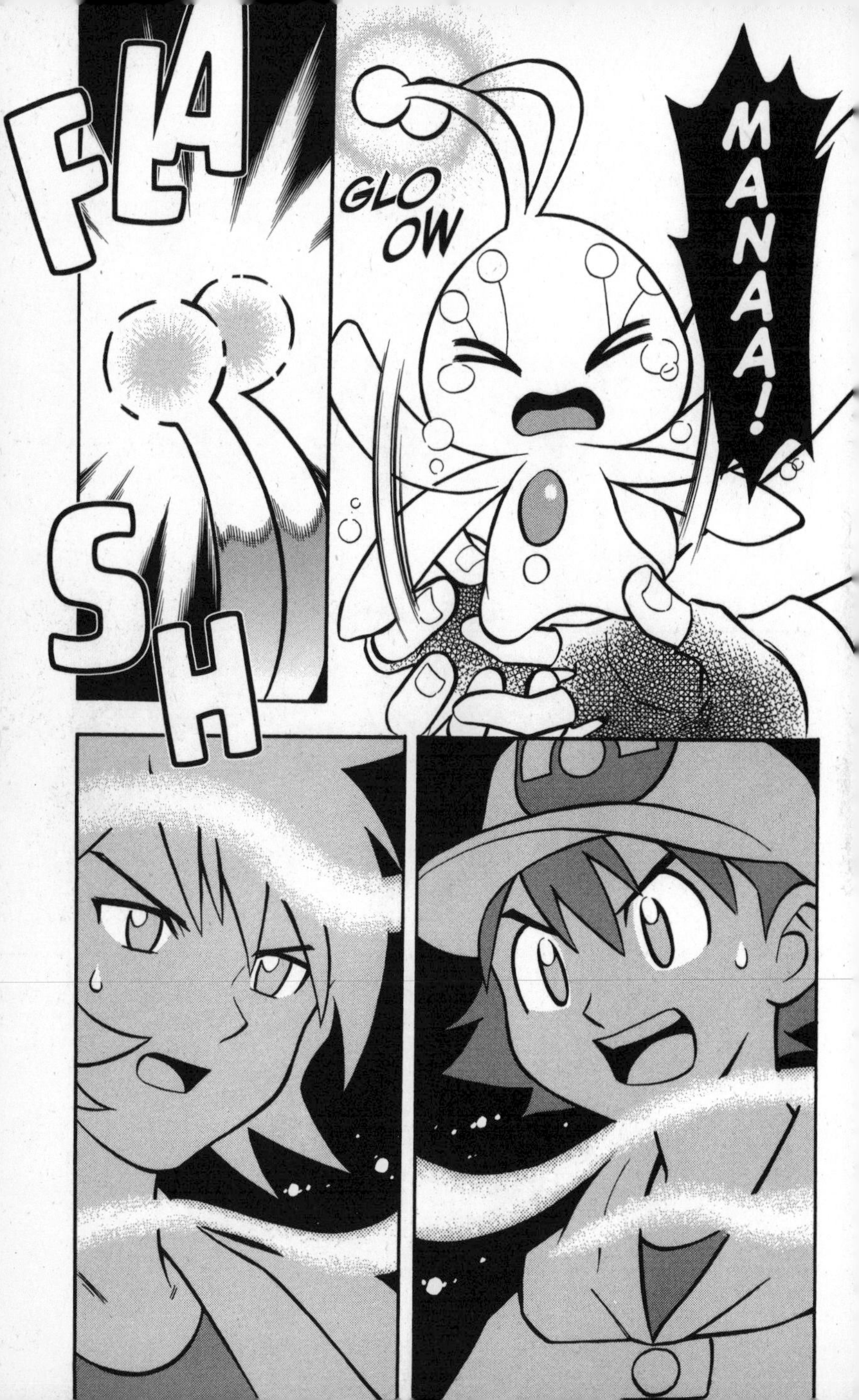
MANAAA!
GLOOW
FLASH

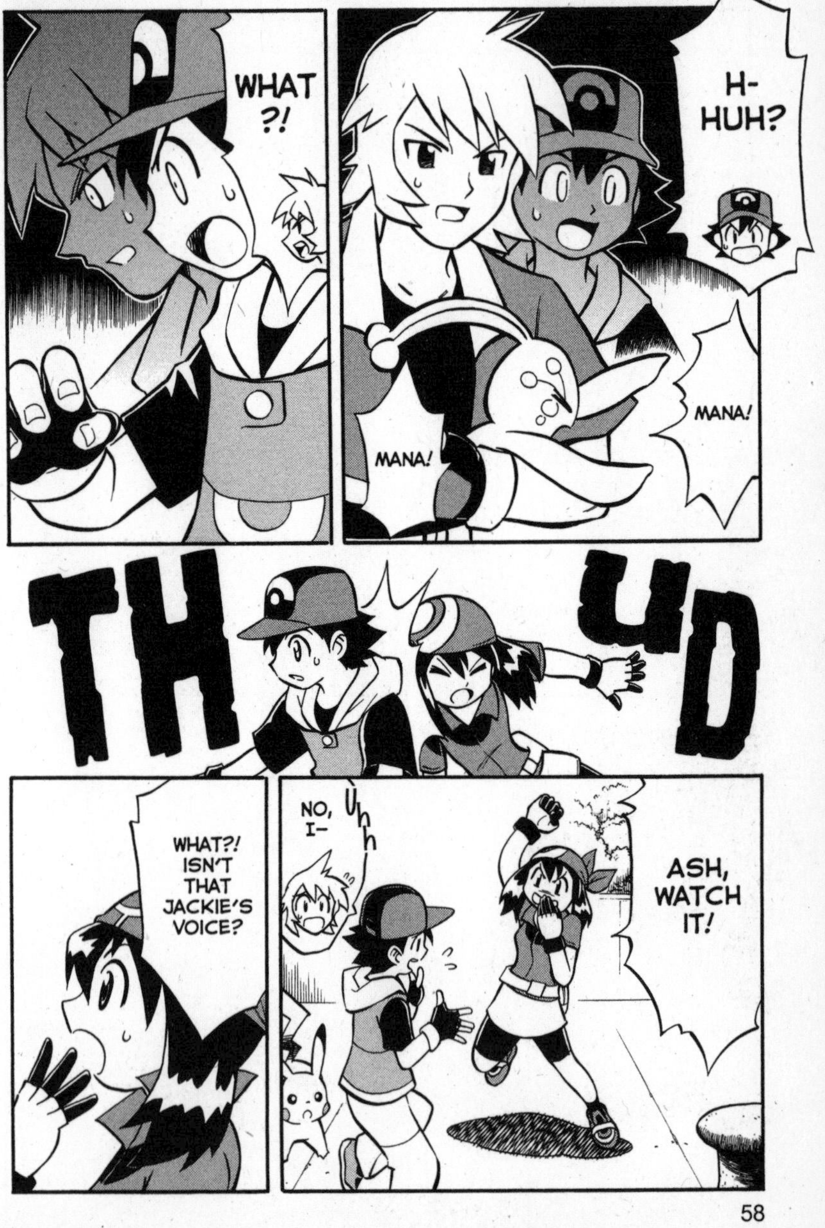
H-
HUH?
MANA!
MANA!
WHAT
?!
THUD
ASH, WATCH IT!
NO, I—
Uhh
WHAT?! ISN'T THAT JACKIE'S VOICE?

READ THIS WAY

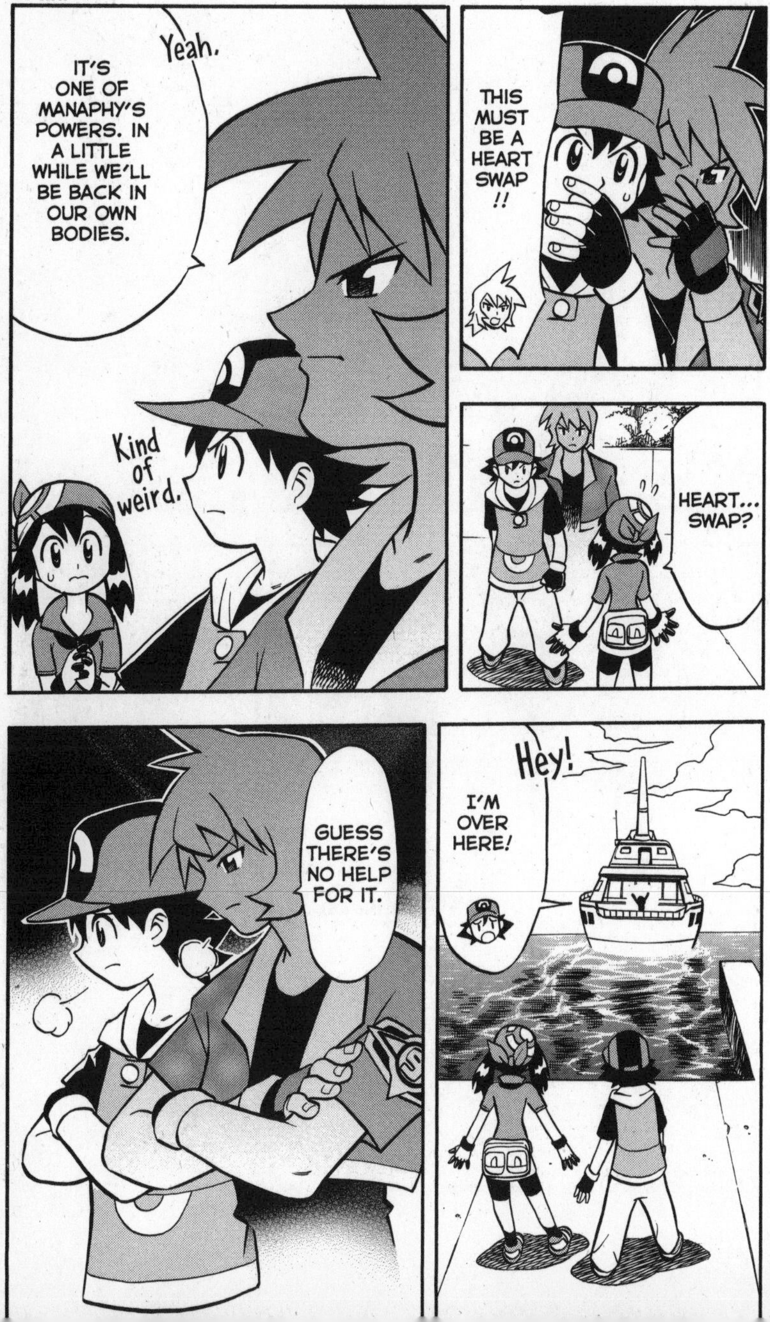
THIS MUST BE A HEART SWAP!!
HEART... SWAP?
Yeah.
IT'S ONE OF MANAPHY'S POWERS. IN A LITTLE WHILE WE'LL BE BACK IN OUR OWN BODIES.
Kind of weird.
Hey!
I'M OVER HERE!
GUESS THERE'S NO HELP FOR IT.

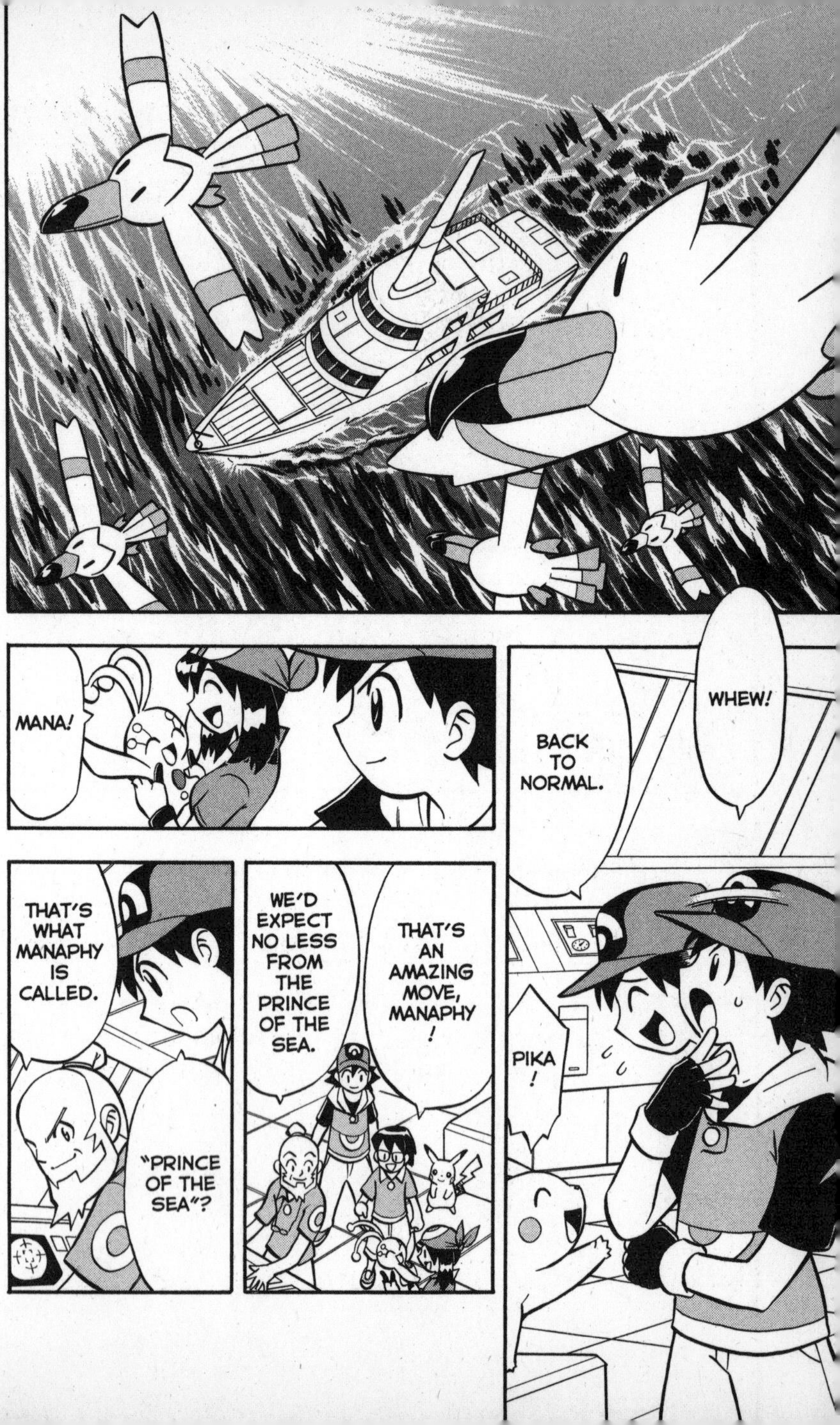
WHEW!
BACK TO NORMAL.
PIKA!
MANA!
THAT'S AN AMAZING MOVE, MANAPHY!
WE'D EXPECT NO LESS FROM THE PRINCE OF THE SEA.
"PRINCE OF THE SEA"?
THAT'S WHAT MANAPHY IS CALLED.

READ THIS WAY

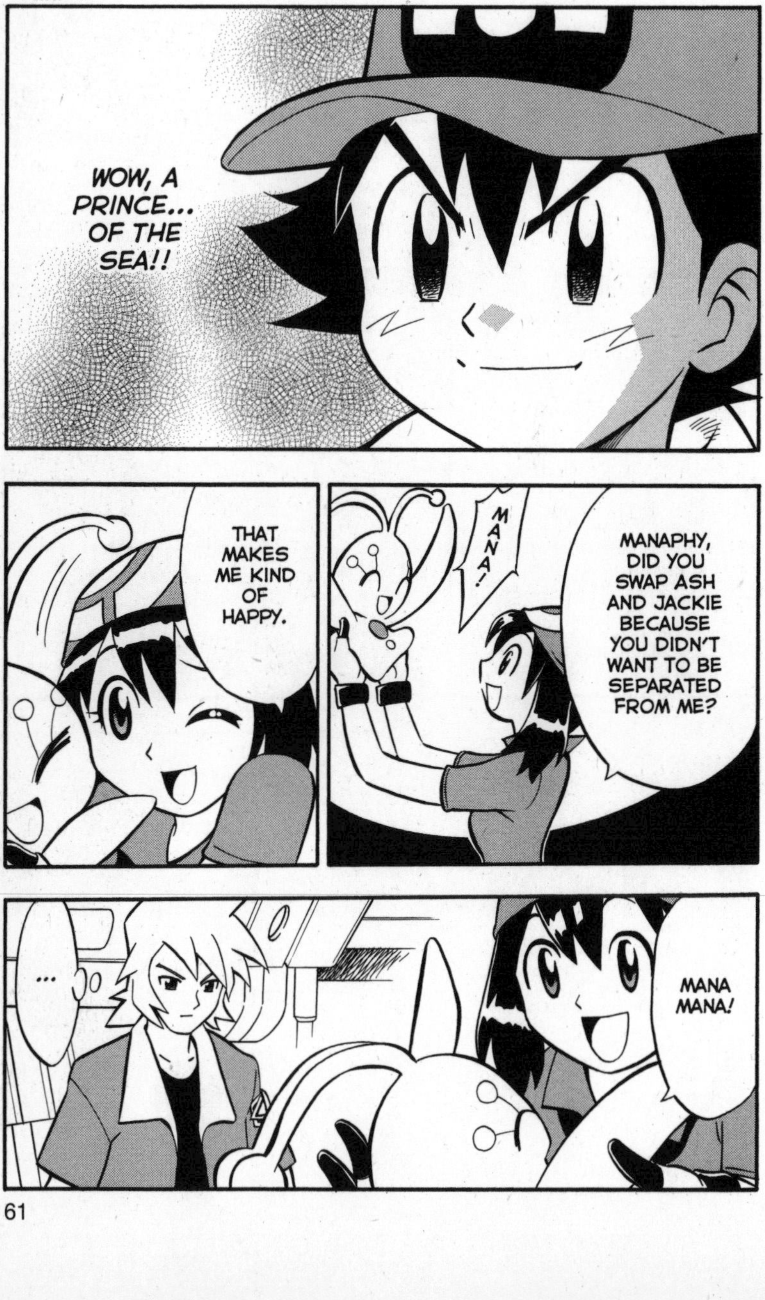

WOW, A PRINCE... OF THE SEA!!
MANAPHY, DID YOU SWAP ASH AND JACKIE BECAUSE YOU DIDN'T WANT TO BE SEPARATED FROM ME?
MANA!
THAT MAKES ME KIND OF HAPPY.
MANA MANA!
...

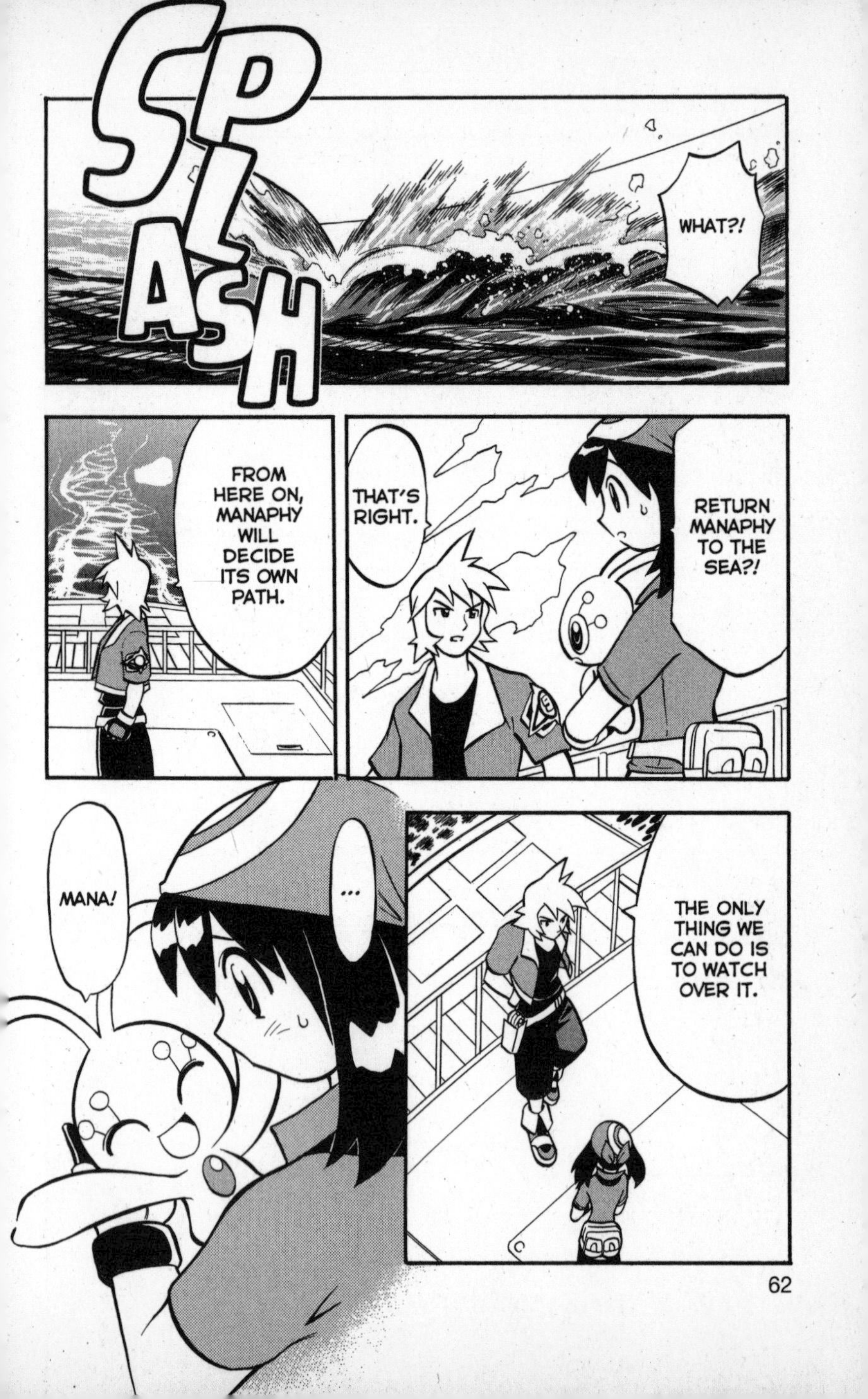
SPLASH
WHAT?!
RETURN MANAPHY TO THE SEA?!
THAT'S RIGHT.
FROM HERE ON, MANAPHY WILL DECIDE ITS OWN PATH.
THE ONLY THING WE CAN DO IS TO WATCH OVER IT.
...
MANA!

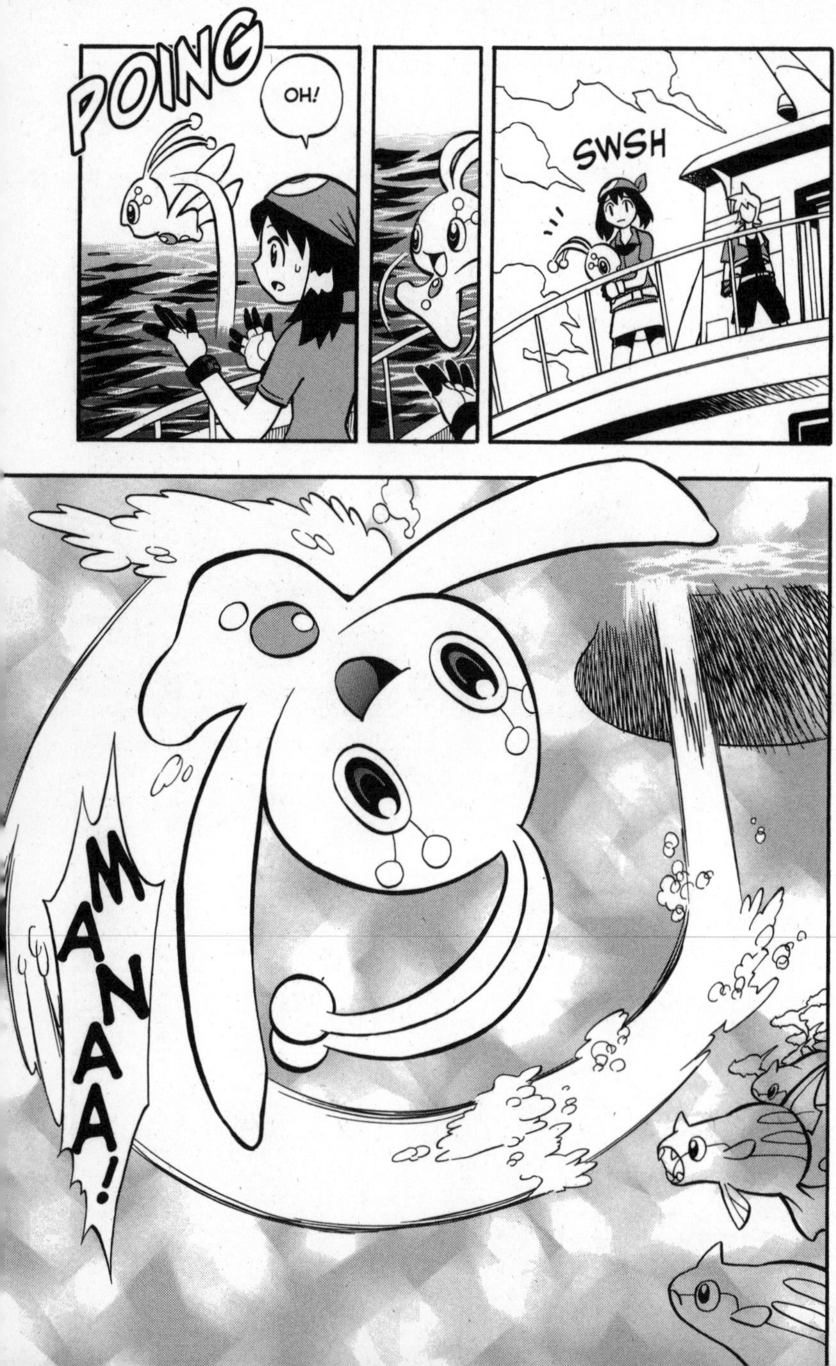
SWSH
POING
OH!
MANAA!

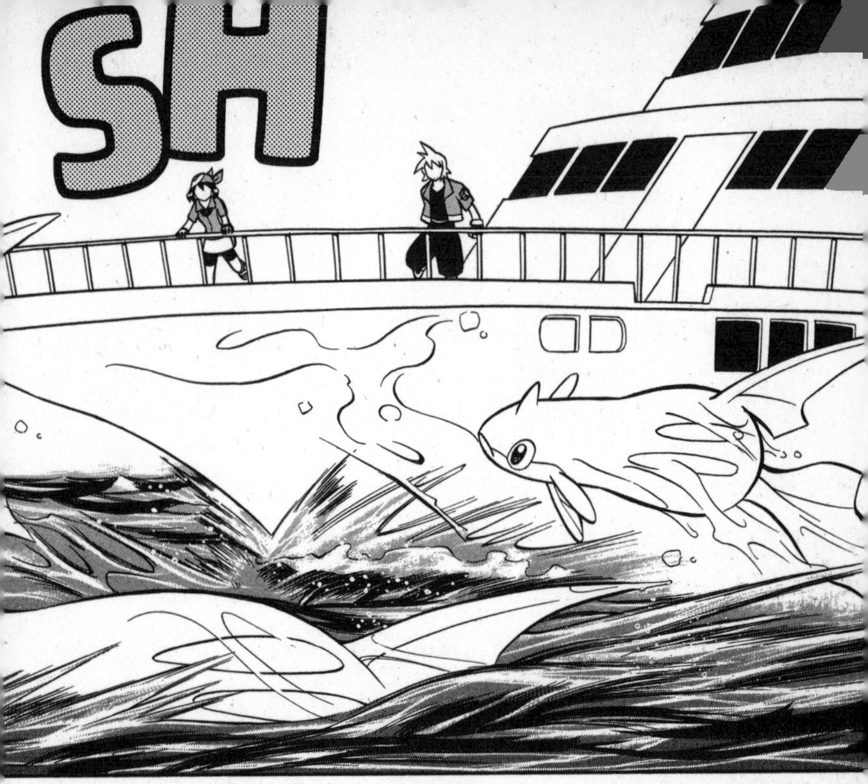
SH

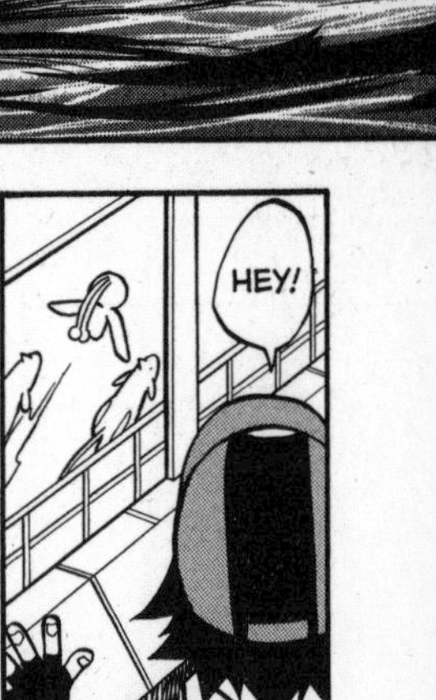
HEY!

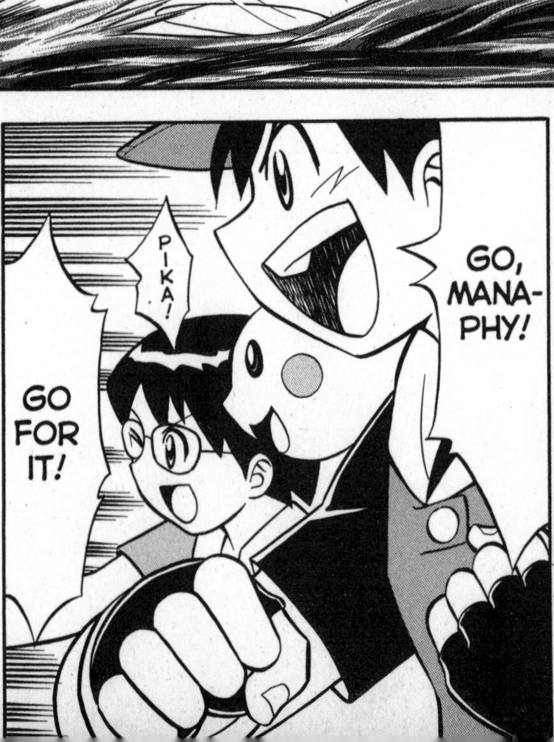
GO, MANA-PHY!
PIKA!
GO FOR IT!

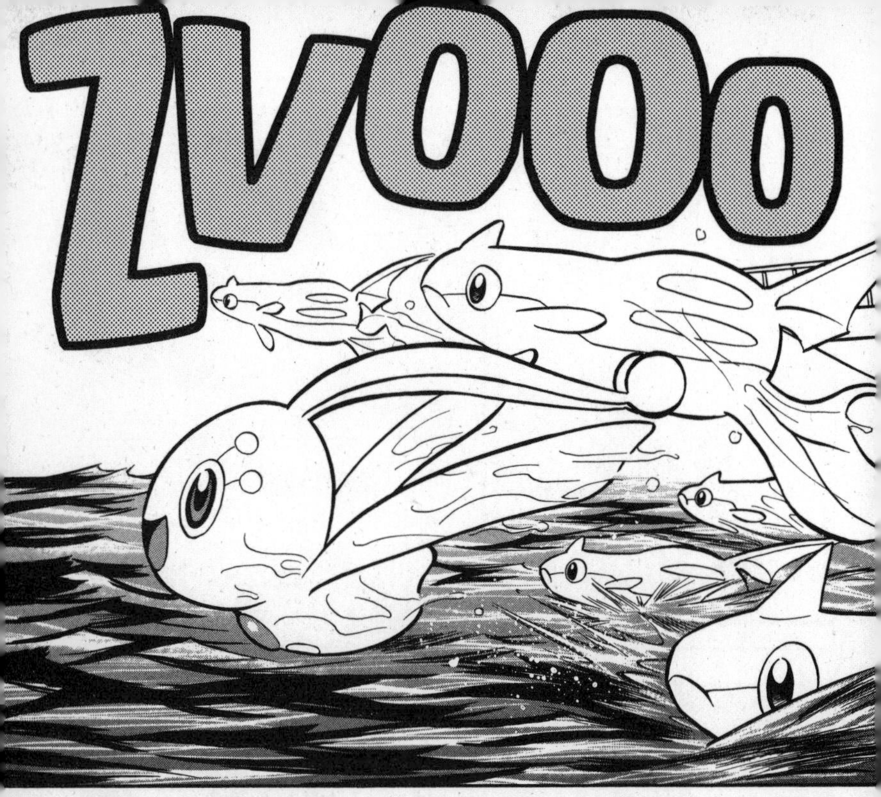
ZVOOO
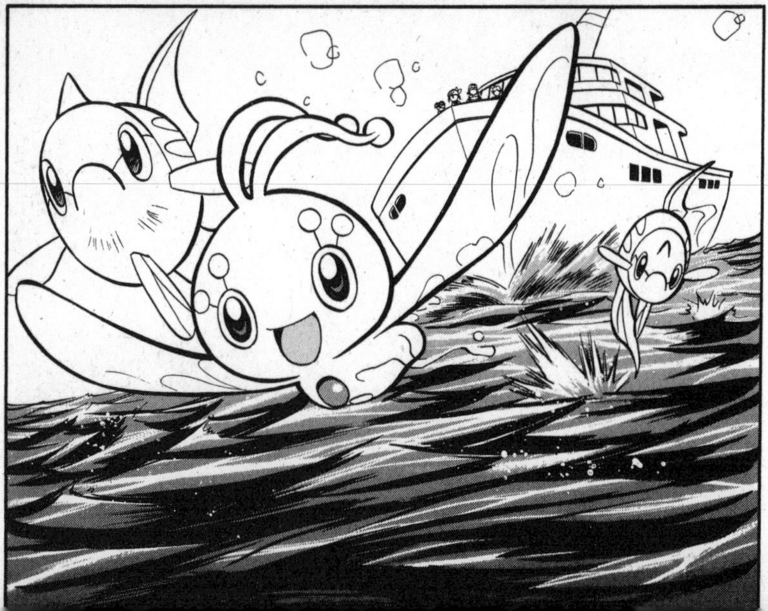

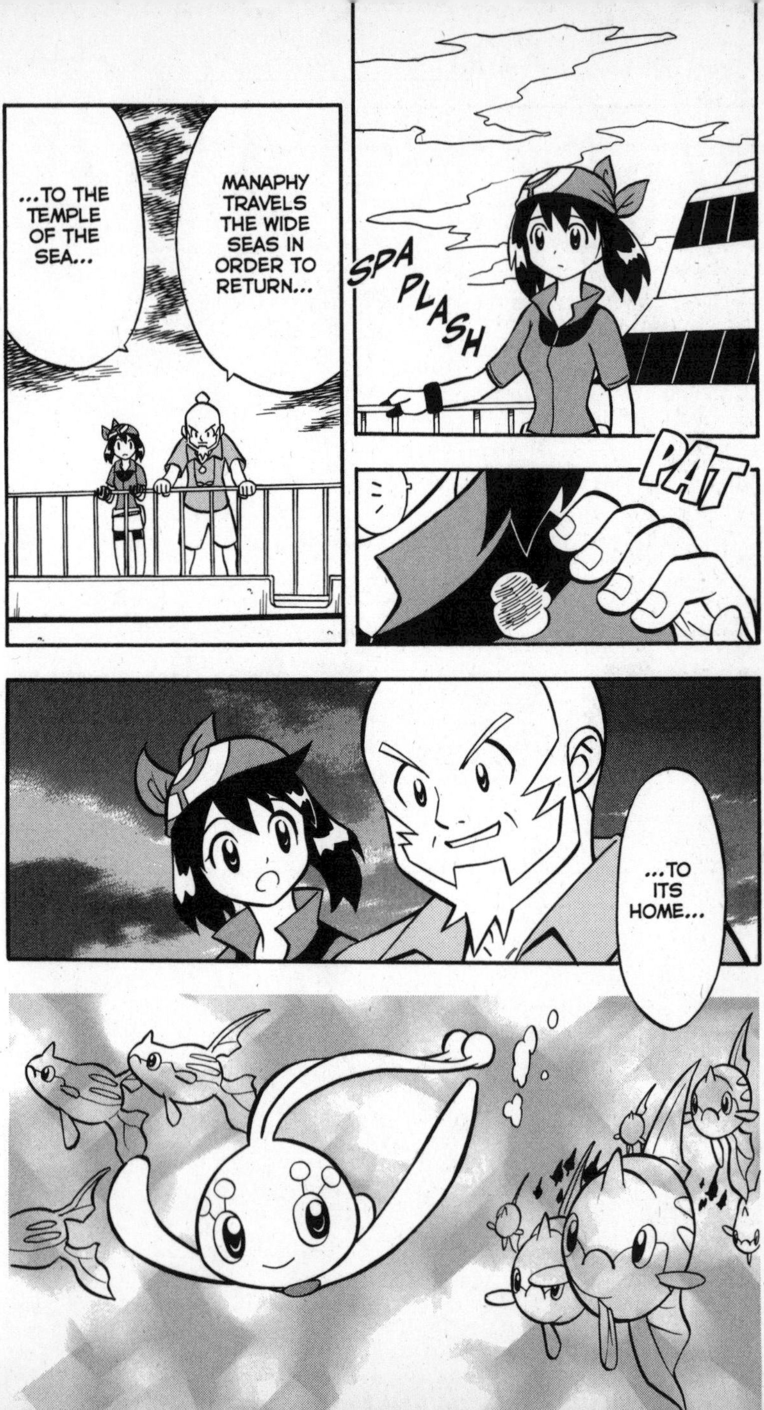
SPA
PLASH
PAT
MANAPHY TRAVELS THE WIDE SEAS IN ORDER TO RETURN...
...TO THE TEMPLE OF THE SEA...
...TO ITS HOME...

READ THIS WAY

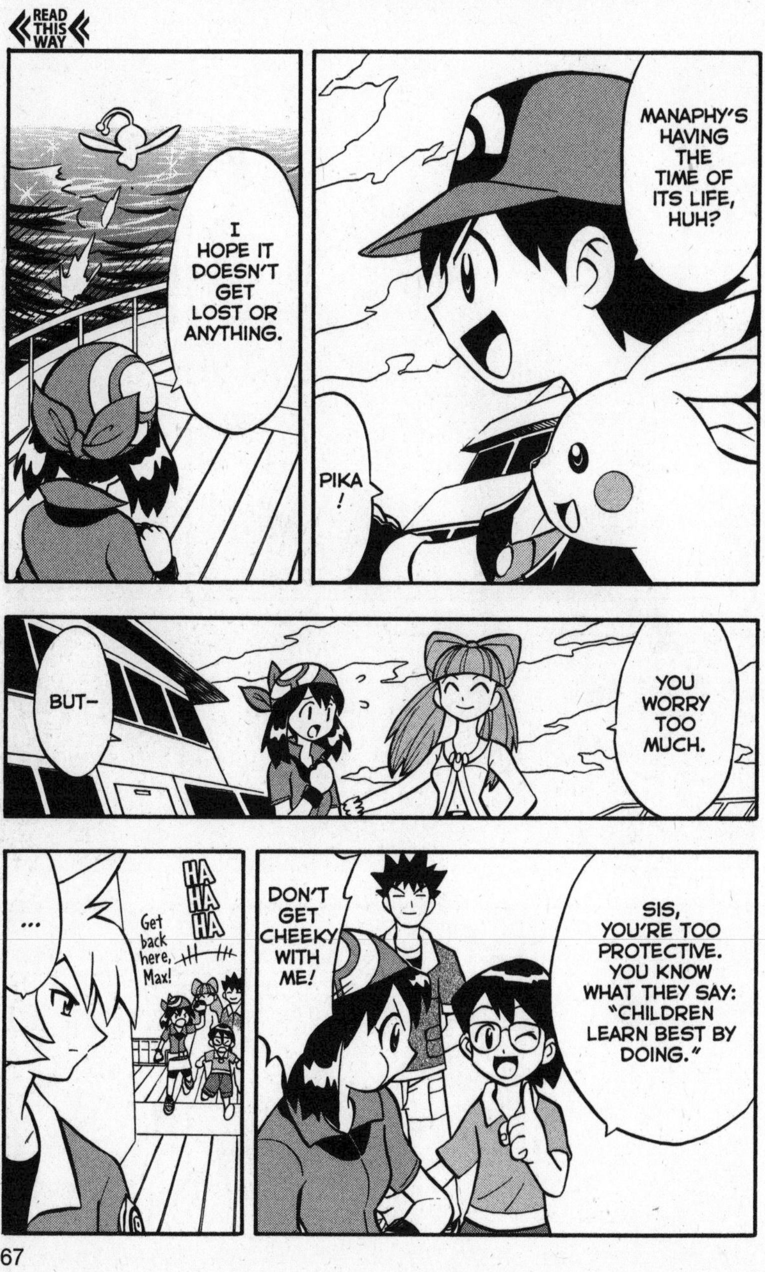

MANAPHY'S HAVING THE TIME OF ITS LIFE, HUH?
PIKA!
I HOPE IT DOESN'T GET LOST OR ANYTHING.
YOU WORRY TOO MUCH.
BUT–
SIS, YOU'RE TOO PROTECTIVE. YOU KNOW WHAT THEY SAY: "CHILDREN LEARN BEST BY DOING."
DON'T GET CHEEKY WITH ME!
HA HA HA
Get back here, Max!
...

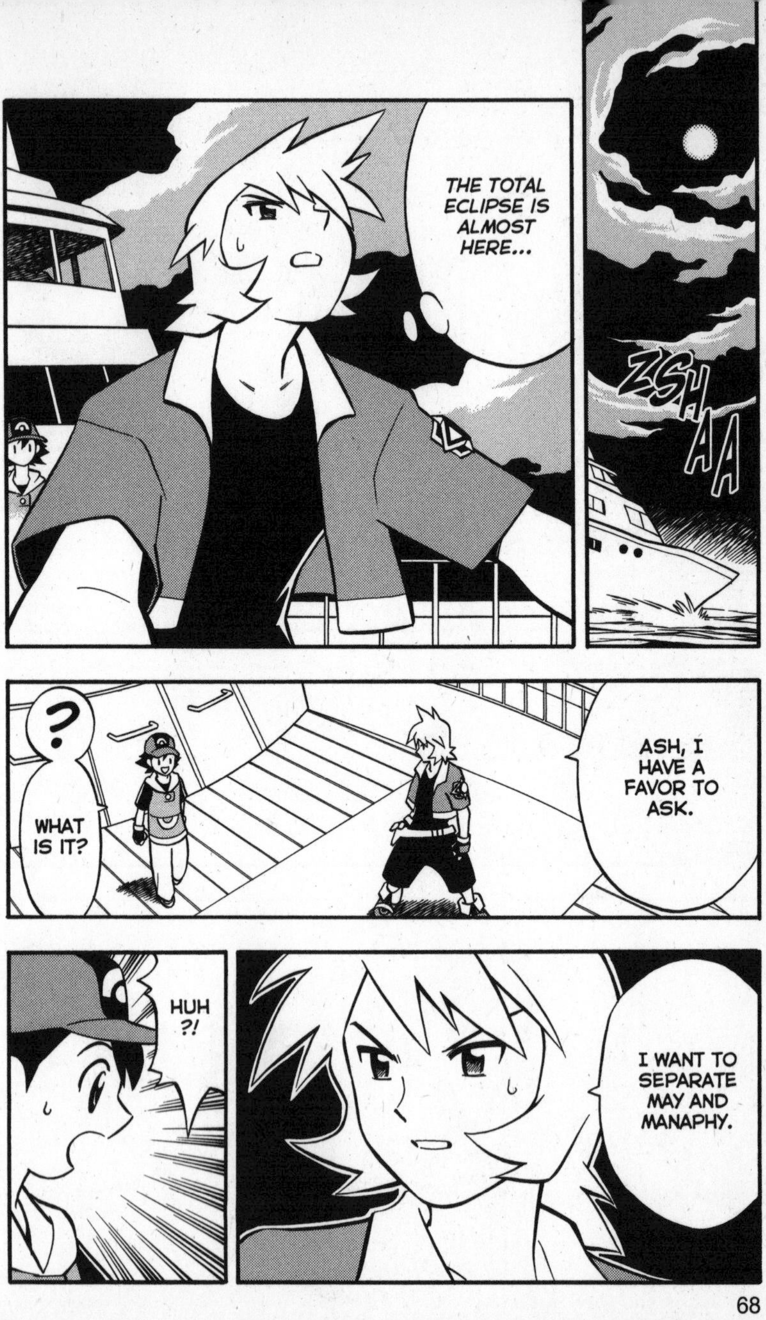
THE TOTAL ECLIPSE IS ALMOST HERE...
ZSHAA
ASH, I HAVE A FAVOR TO ASK.
WHAT IS IT?
HUH ?!
I WANT TO SEPARATE MAY AND MANAPHY.

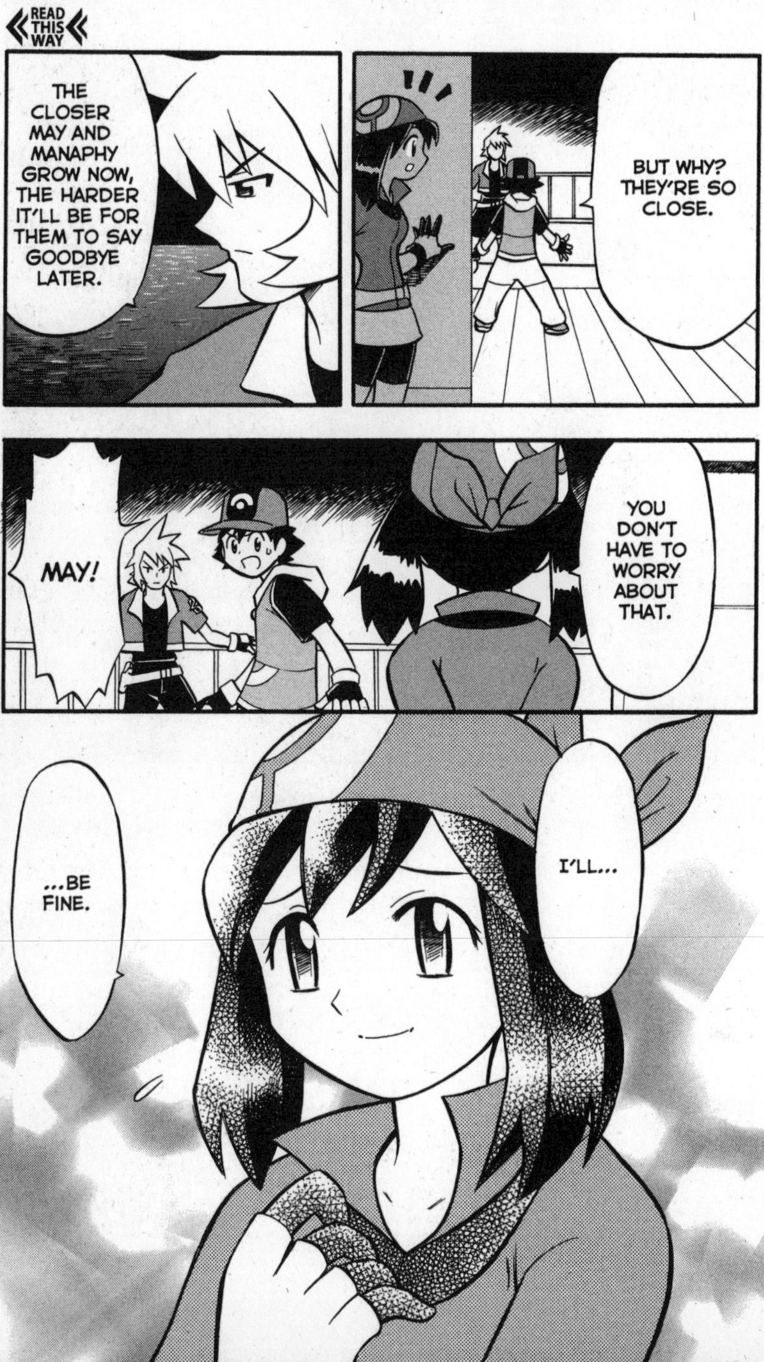
READ THIS WAY
BUT WHY? THEY'RE SO CLOSE.
THE CLOSER MAY AND MANAPHY GROW NOW, THE HARDER IT'LL BE FOR THEM TO SAY GOODBYE LATER.
YOU DON'T HAVE TO WORRY ABOUT THAT.
MAY!
I'LL...
...BE FINE.

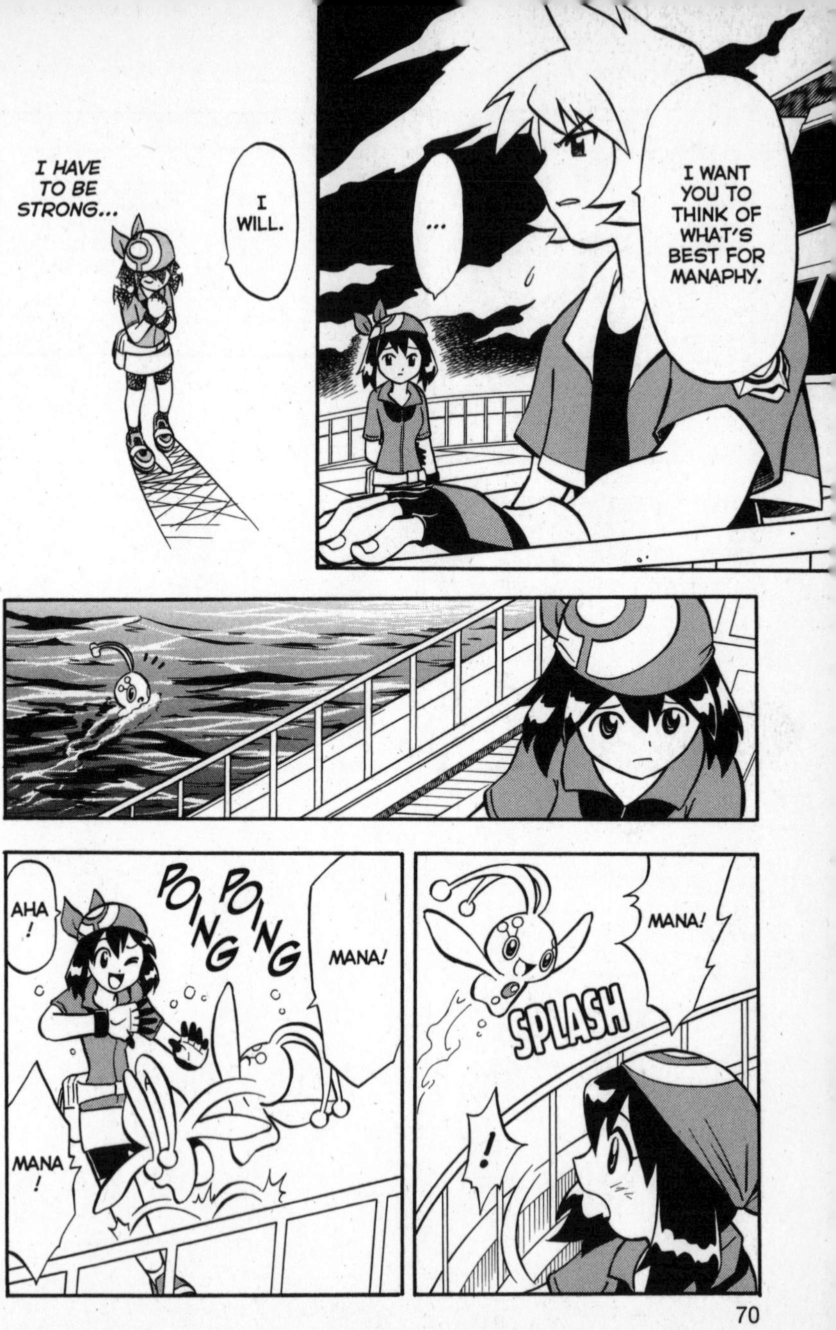
I WANT YOU TO THINK OF WHAT'S BEST FOR MANAPHY.
...
I WILL.
I HAVE TO BE STRONG...
MANA!
SPLASH
!
MANA!
POING POING
AHA!
MANA!

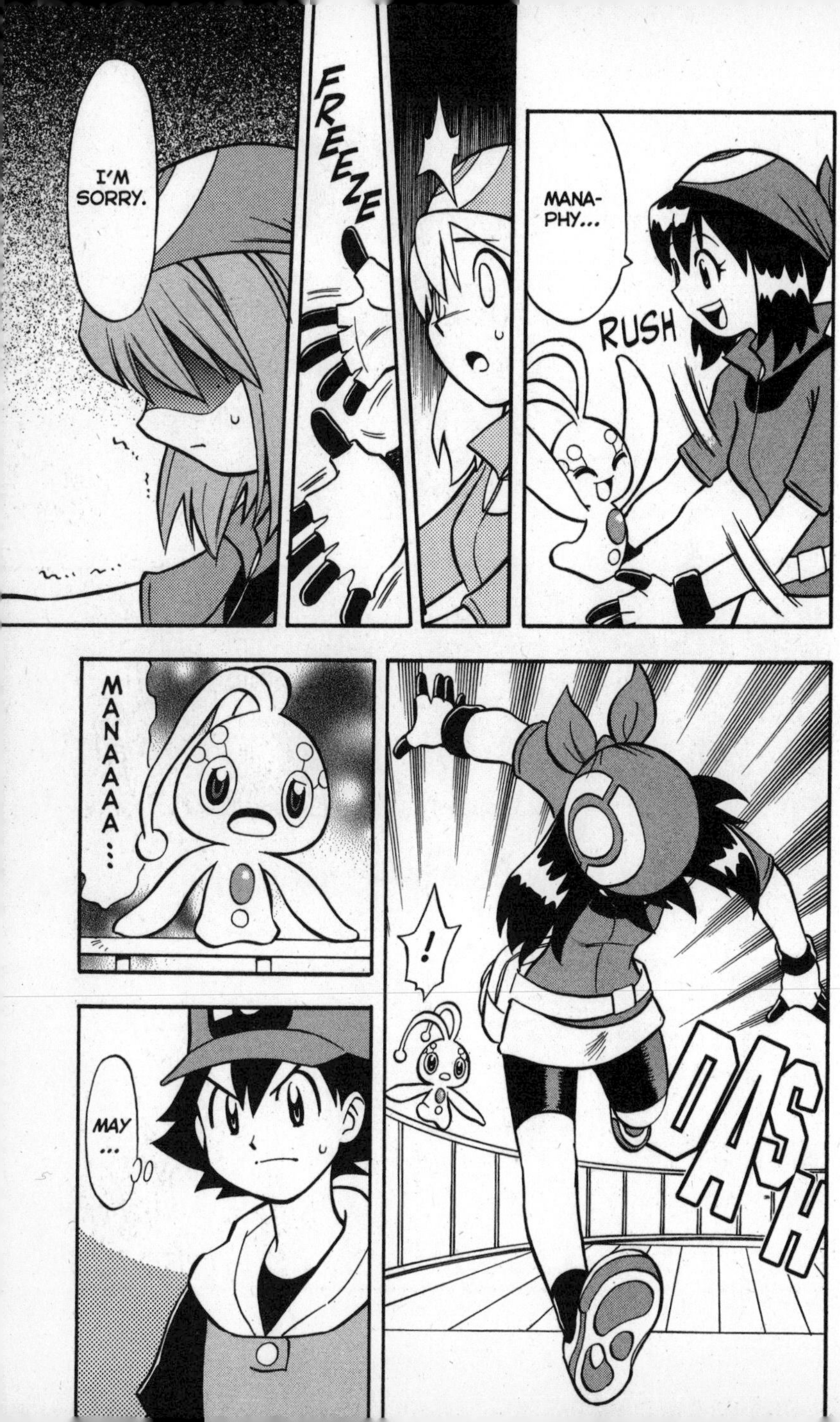
MANA-PHY...
RUSH
FREEZE
I'M SORRY.
!
DASH
MANAAAAA...
MAY ...

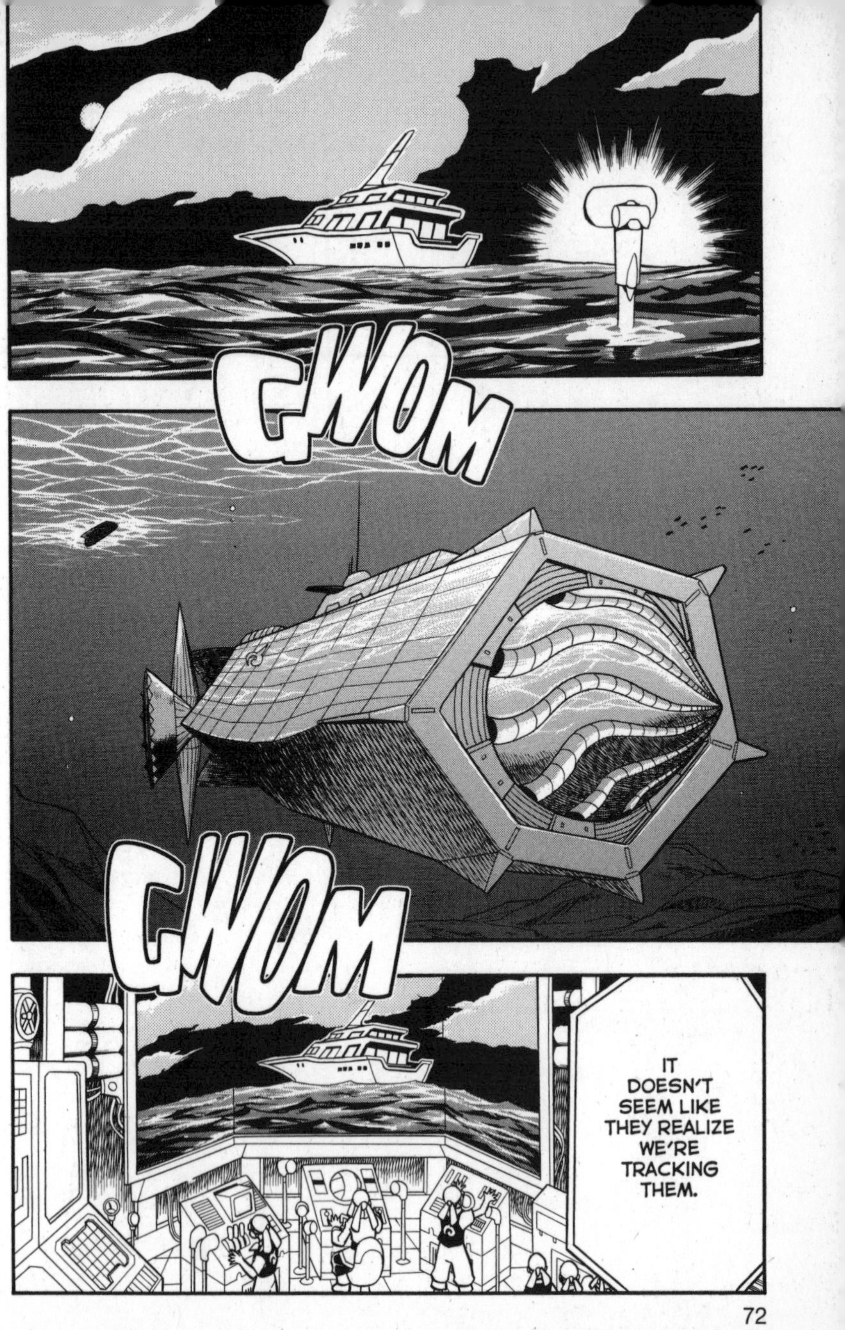
GWOM
GWOM
IT DOESN'T SEEM LIKE THEY REALIZE WE'RE TRACKING THEM.

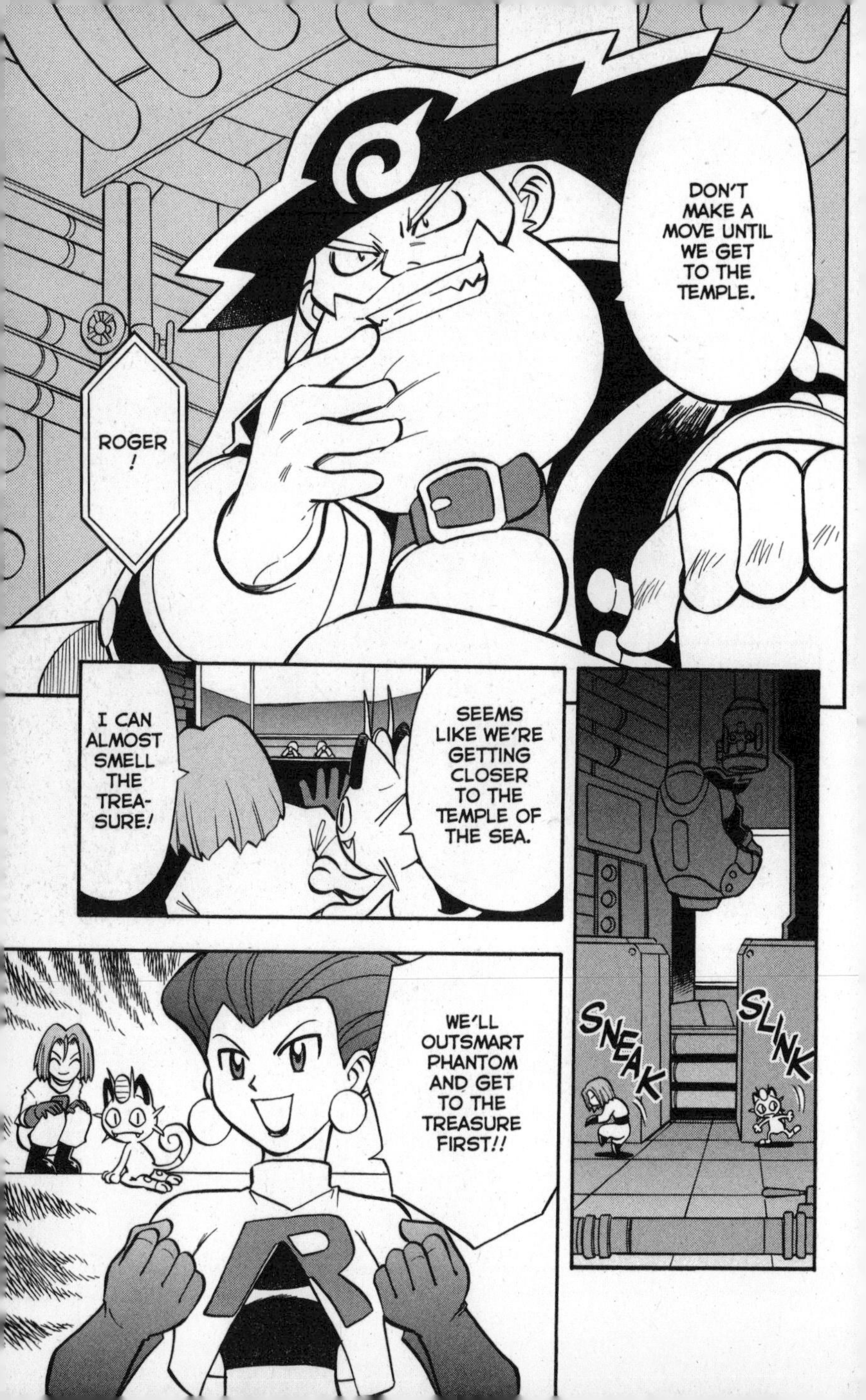
DON'T MAKE A MOVE UNTIL WE GET TO THE TEMPLE.
ROGER!
SLINK
SNEAK
SEEMS LIKE WE'RE GETTING CLOSER TO THE TEMPLE OF THE SEA.
I CAN ALMOST SMELL THE TREA-SURE!
WE'LL OUTSMART PHANTOM AND GET TO THE TREASURE FIRST!!

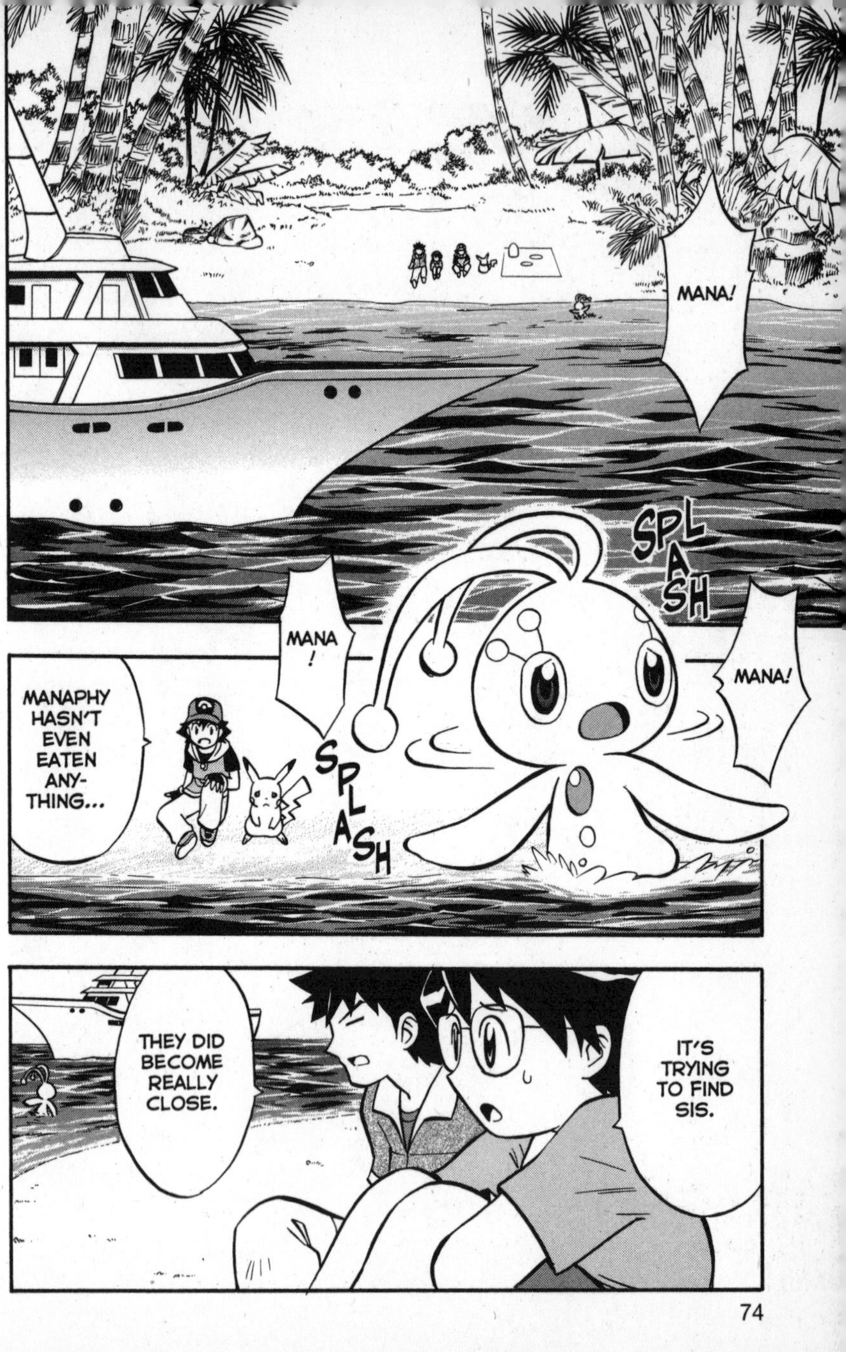
MANA!
SPLASH
MANA!
MANA!
SPLASH
MANAPHY HASN'T EVEN EATEN ANYTHING...
IT'S TRYING TO FIND SIS.
THEY DID BECOME REALLY CLOSE.

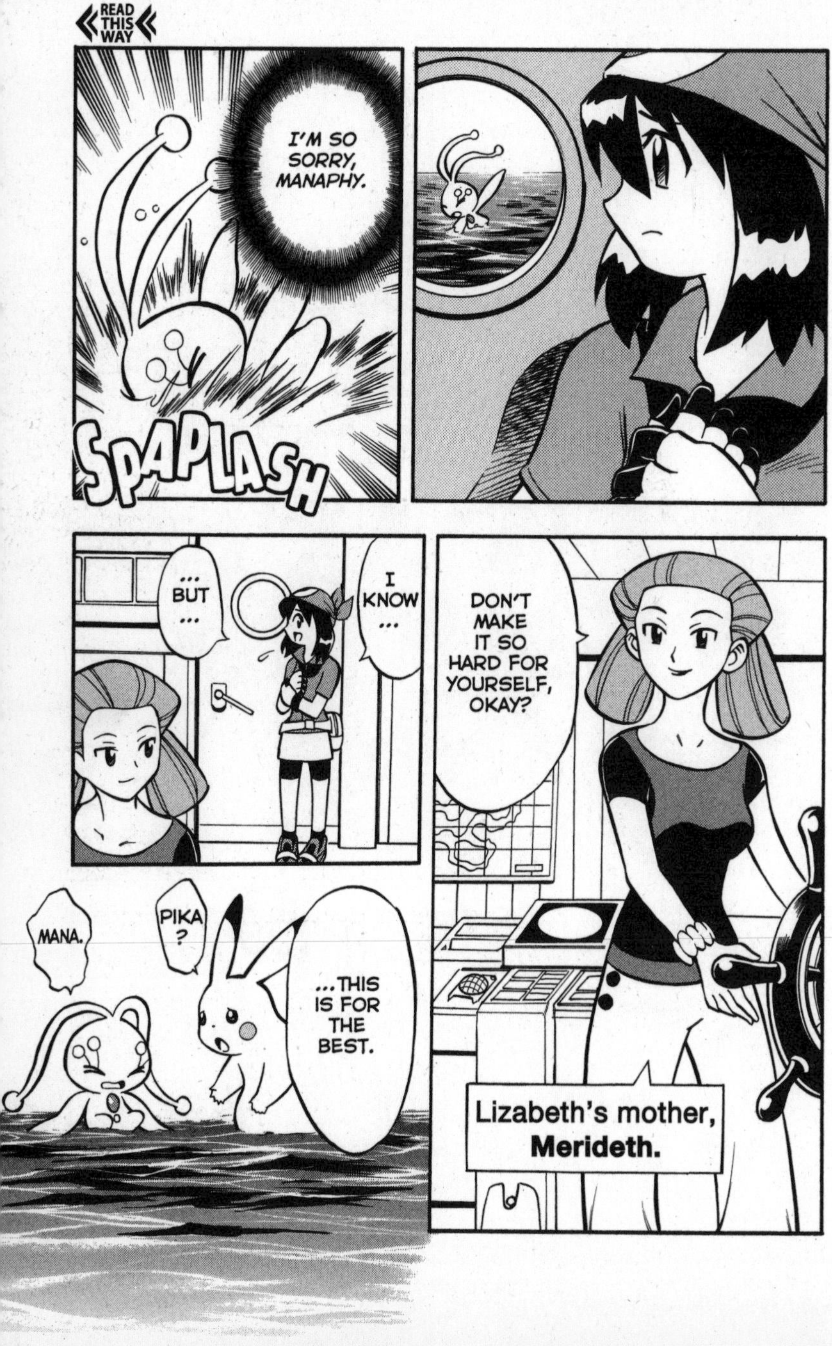
READ THIS WAY
I'M SO SORRY, MANAPHY.
SPAPLASH
DON'T MAKE IT SO HARD FOR YOURSELF, OKAY?
Lizabeth's mother, **Merideth.**
I KNOW...
...BUT...
...THIS IS FOR THE BEST.
PIKA?
MANA.

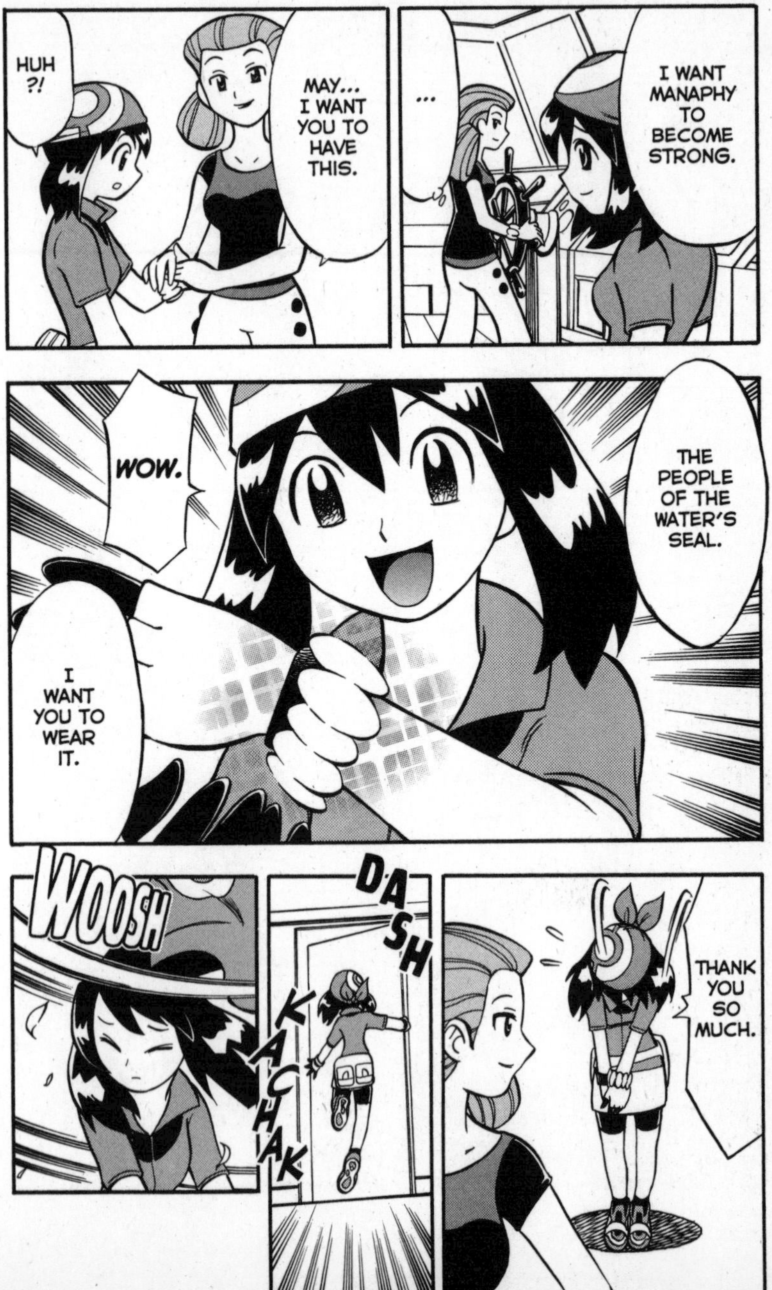
I WANT MANAPHY TO BECOME STRONG.
...
MAY... I WANT YOU TO HAVE THIS.
HUH ?!
THE PEOPLE OF THE WATER'S SEAL.
WOW.
I WANT YOU TO WEAR IT.
THANK YOU SO MUCH.
DASH
KACHAK
WOOSH

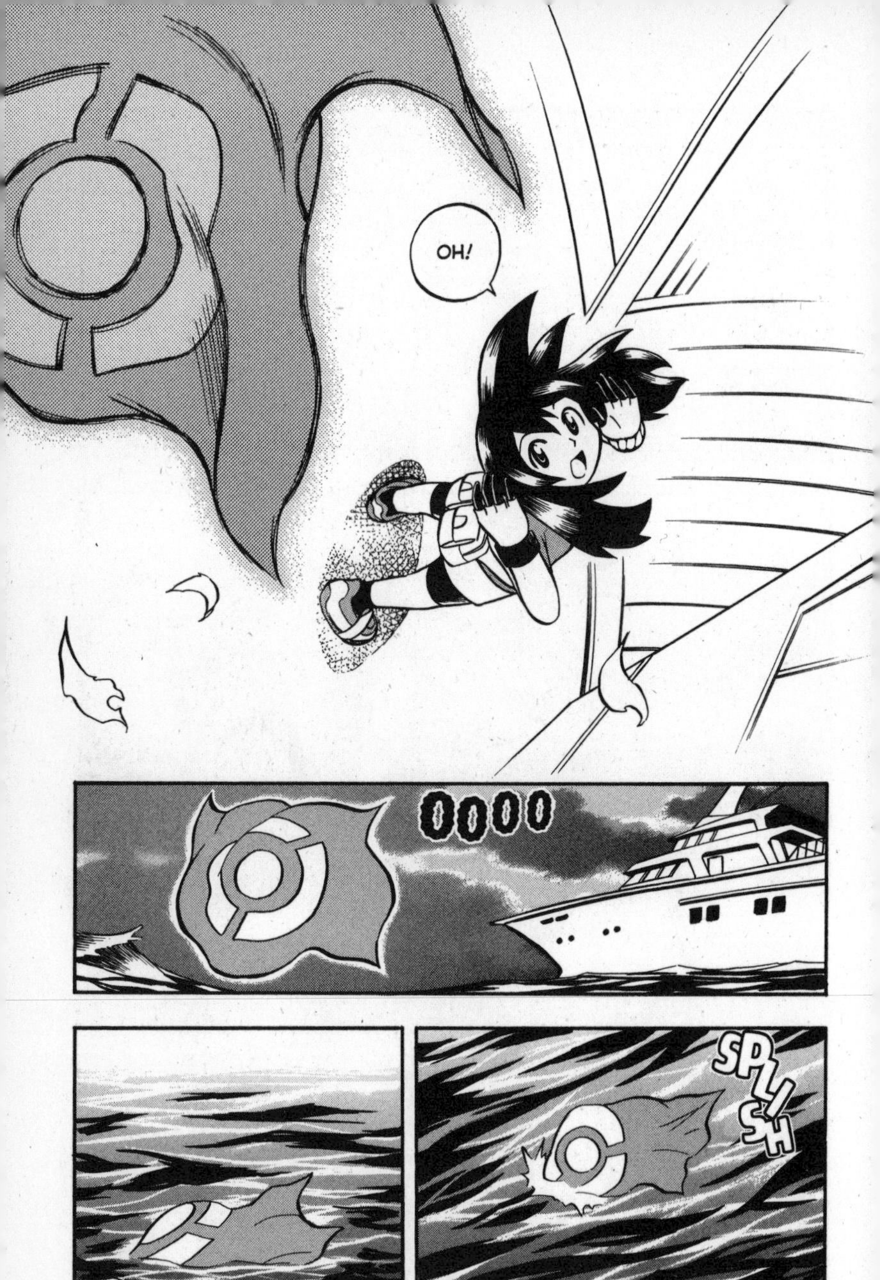
OH!
OOOO
SPLISH

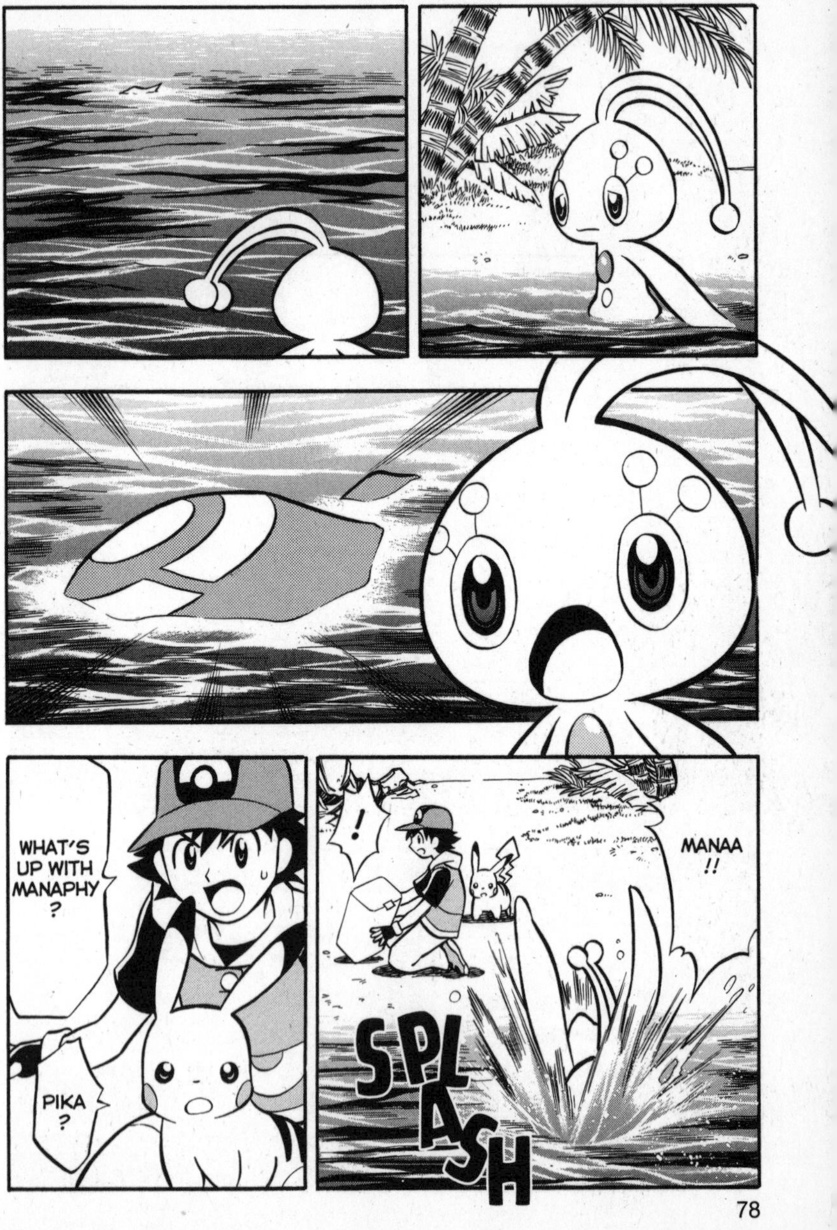
!
MANAA !!
SPLASH
WHAT'S UP WITH MANAPHY ?
PIKA ?

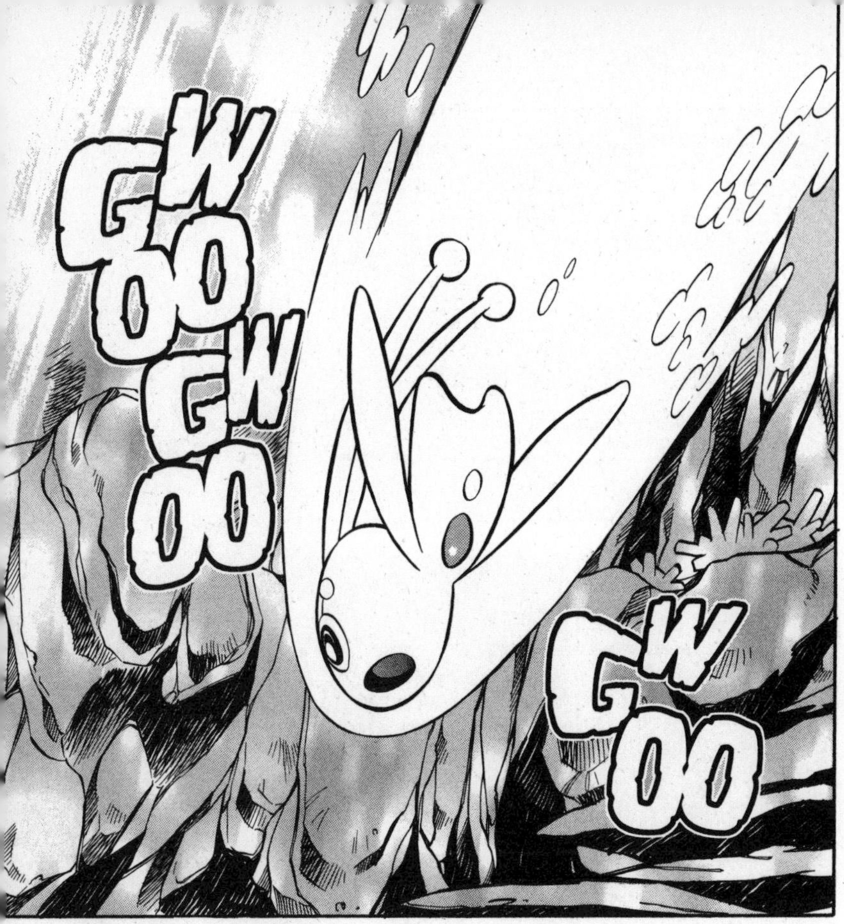
GWOO GWOO
GWOO

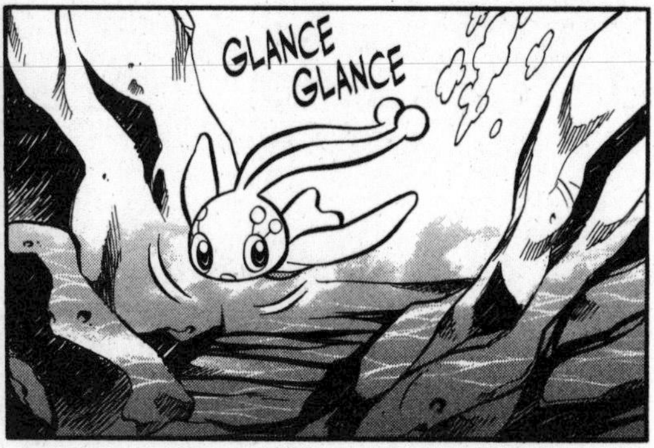
GLANCE GLANCE

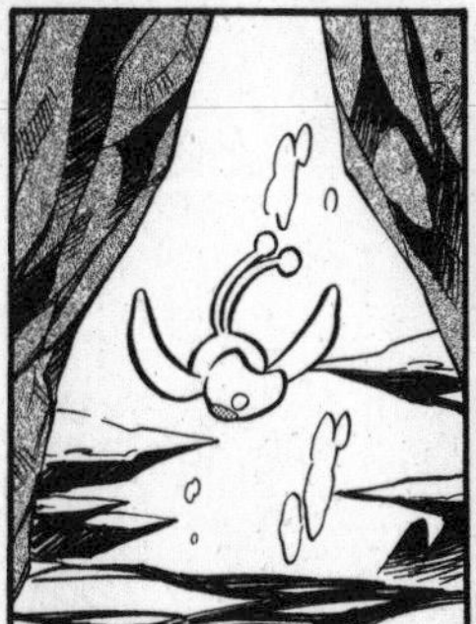

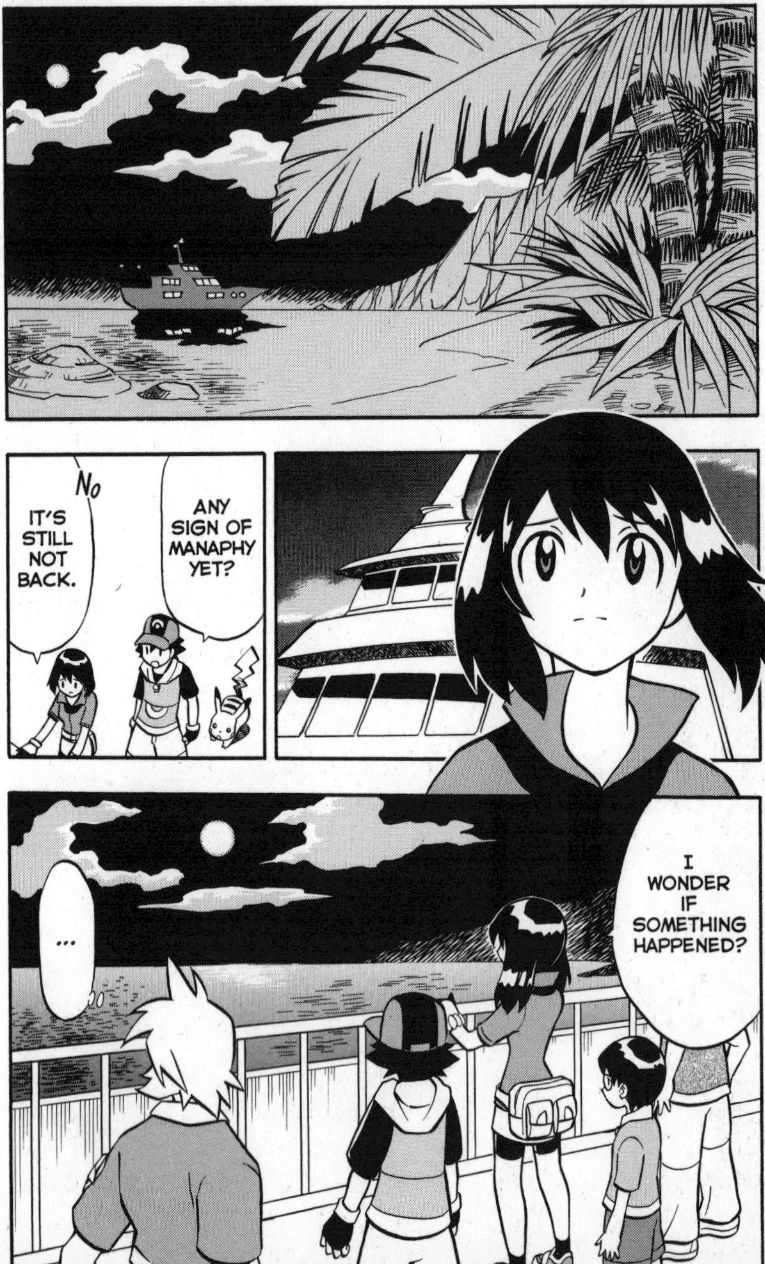
ANY SIGN OF MANAPHY YET?
No
IT'S STILL NOT BACK.
I WONDER IF SOMETHING HAPPENED?
...

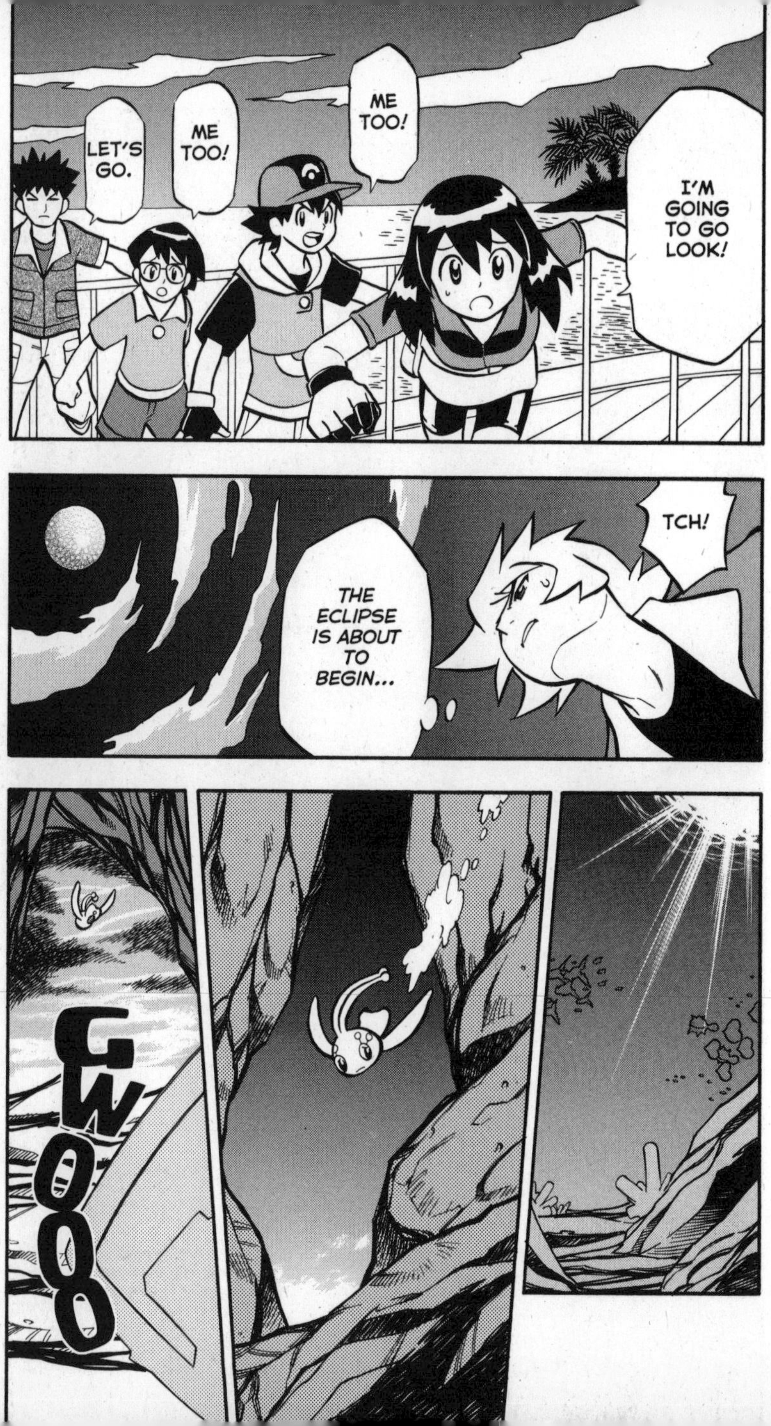
I'M GOING TO GO LOOK!
ME TOO!
ME TOO!
LET'S GO.
TCH!
THE ECLIPSE IS ABOUT TO BEGIN...
GWOOO

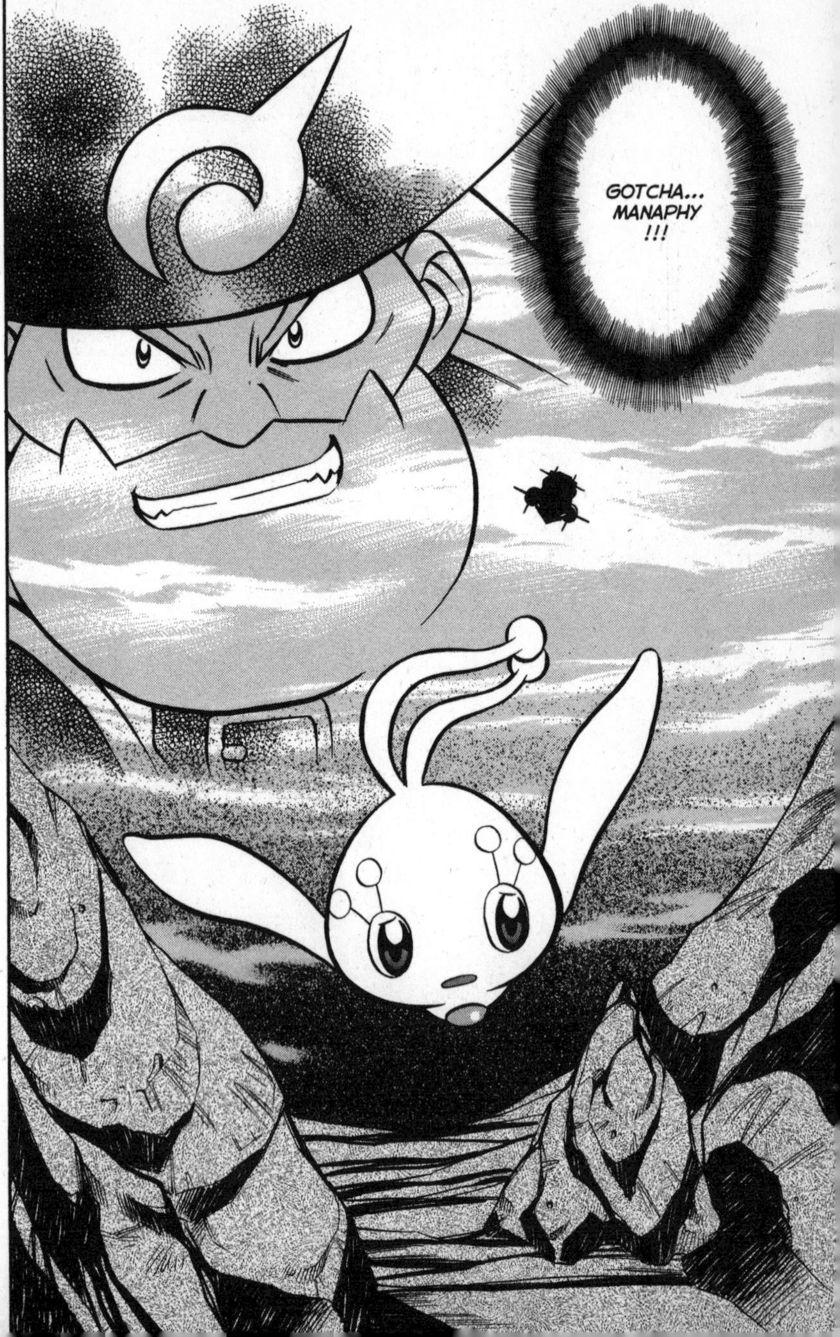
GOTCHA...
MANAPHY
!!!

Chapter 2: Bursting In!
Akusha, the Temple of the Sea

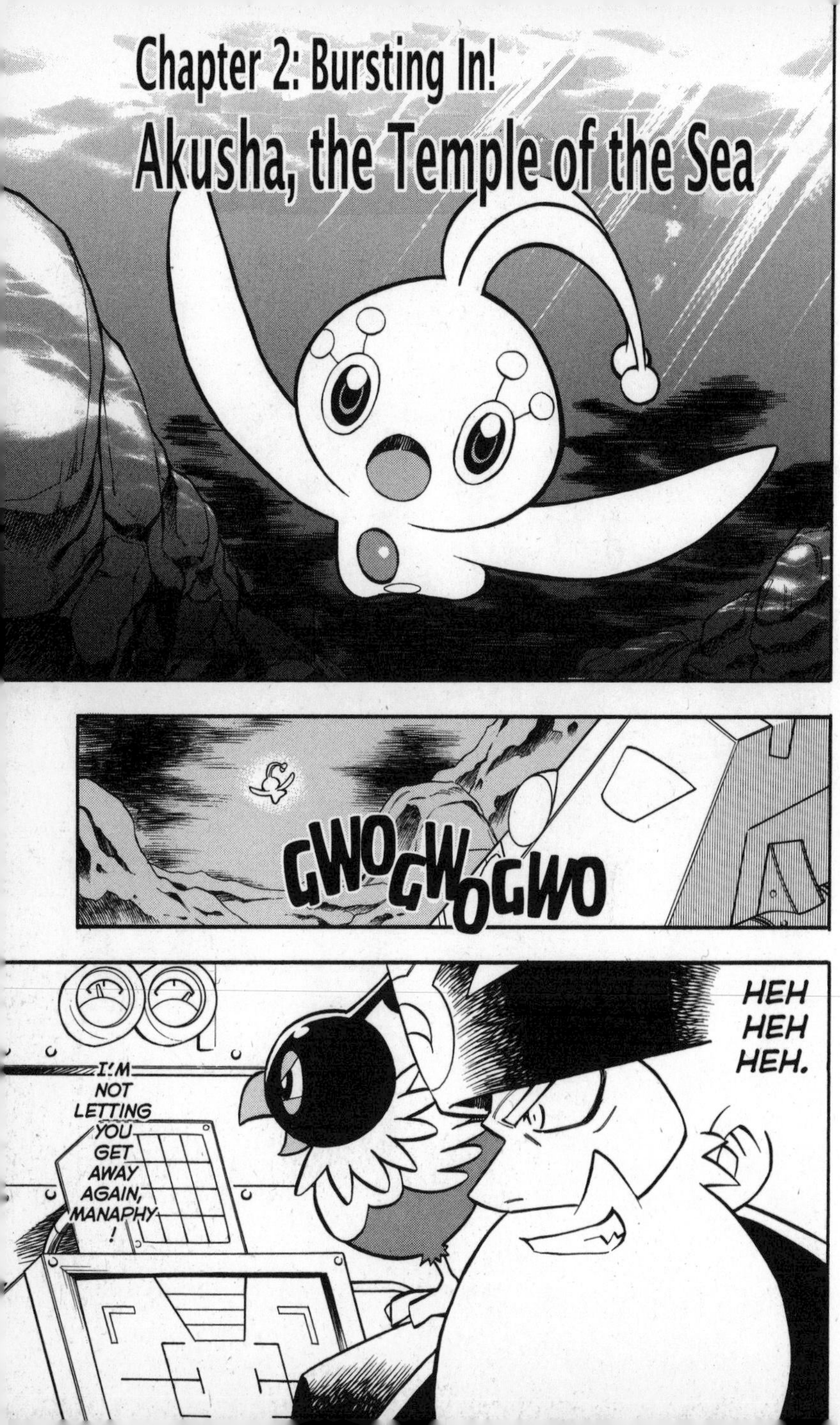
GWOGWOGWO
HEH HEH HEH.
I'M NOT LETTING YOU GET AWAY AGAIN, MANAPHY!

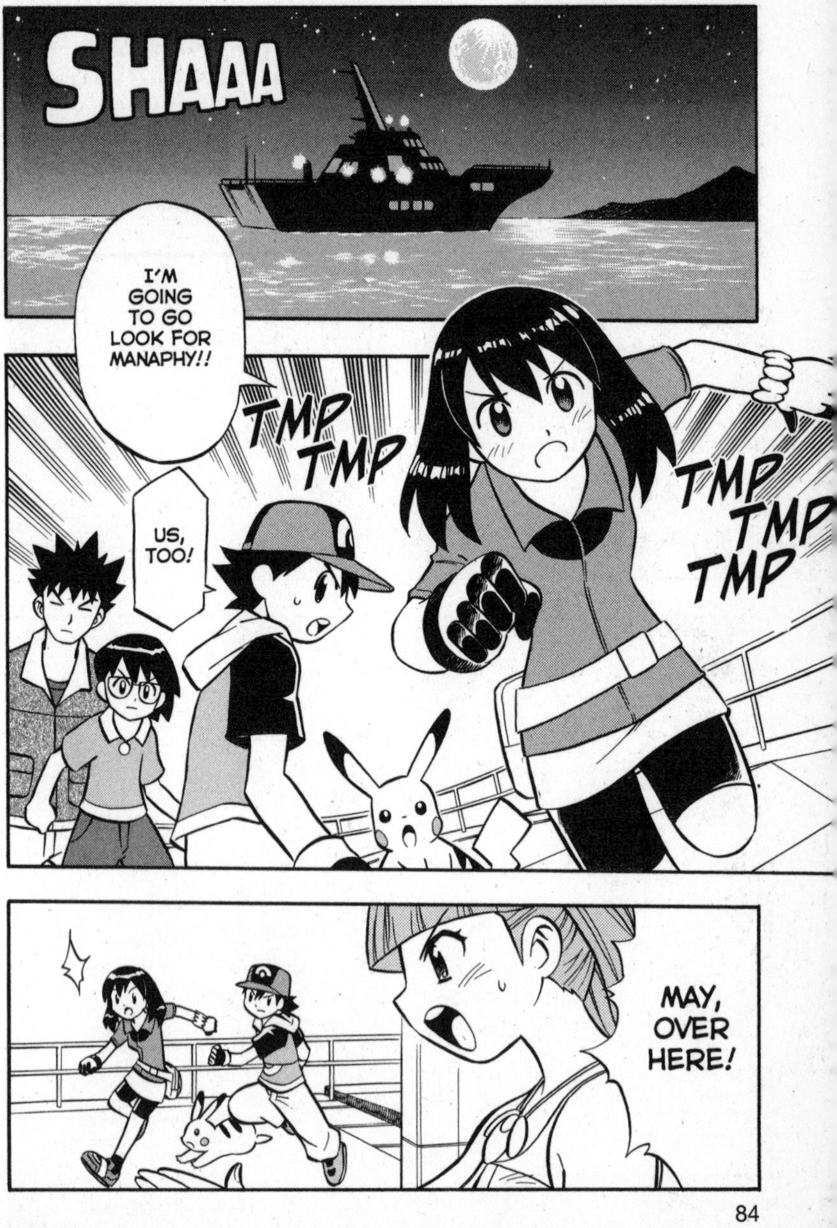
SHAAA
I'M GOING TO GO LOOK FOR MANAPHY!!
TMP TMP
US, TOO!
TMP TMP TMP
MAY, OVER HERE!

READ THIS WAY

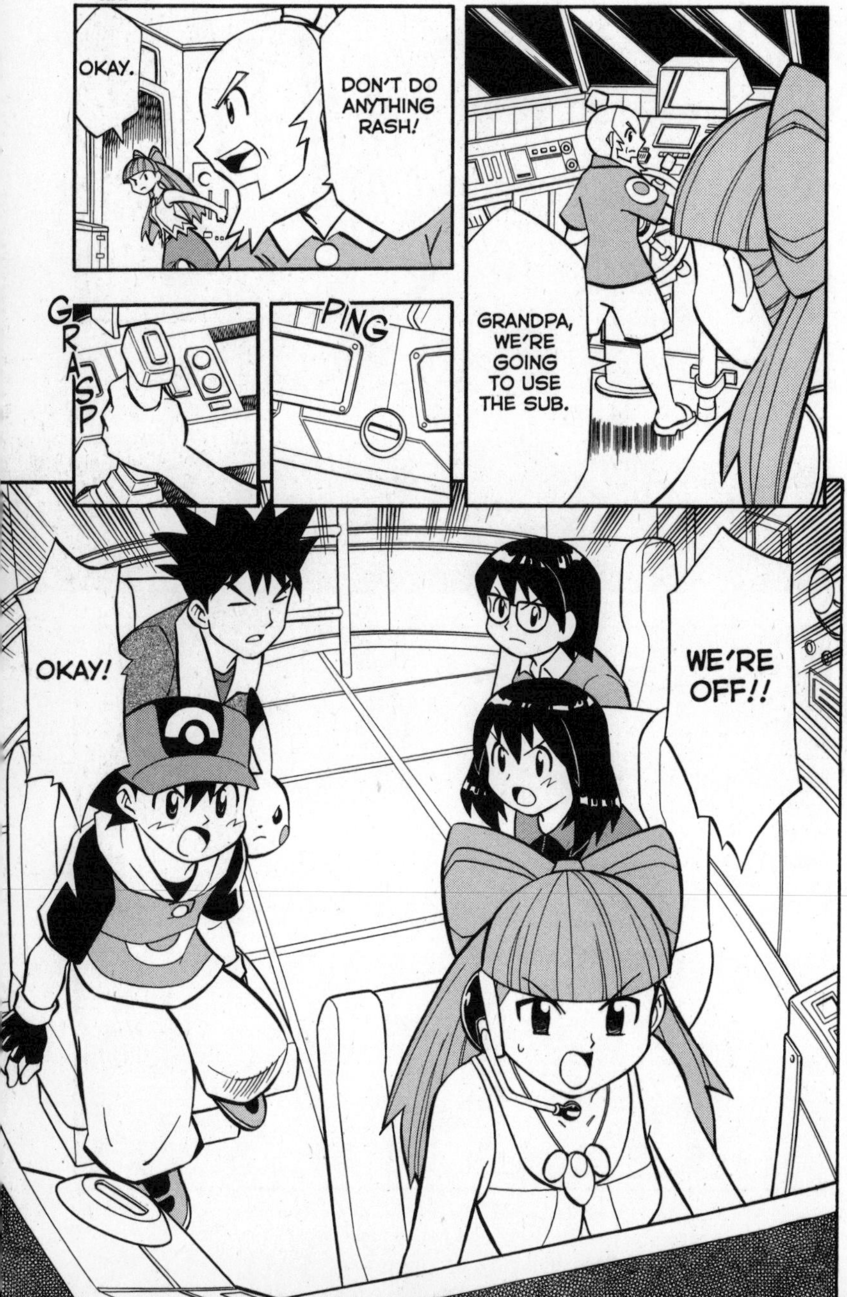
GRANDPA, WE'RE GOING TO USE THE SUB.
DON'T DO ANYTHING RASH!
OKAY.
PING
GRASP
WE'RE OFF!!
OKAY!

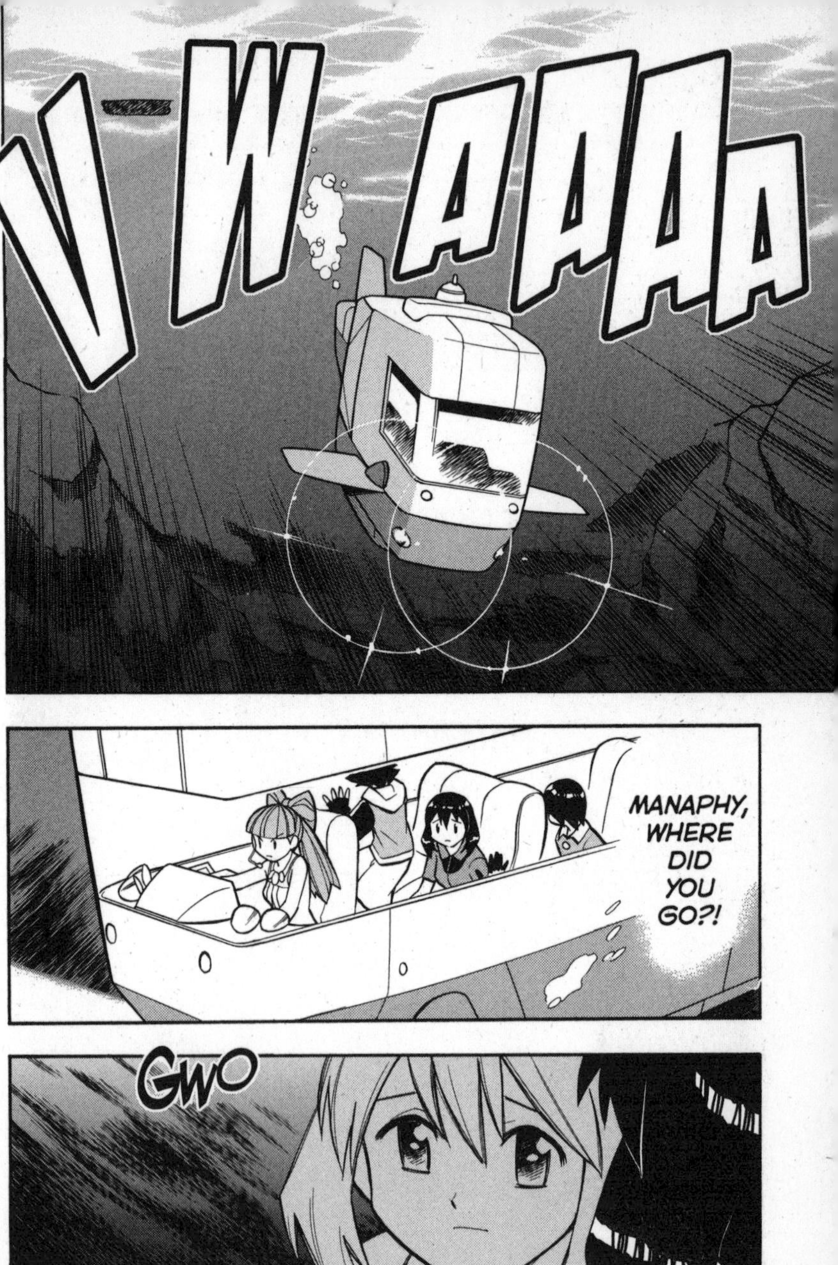
V-WAAAA
MANAPHY, WHERE DID YOU GO?!
GWO

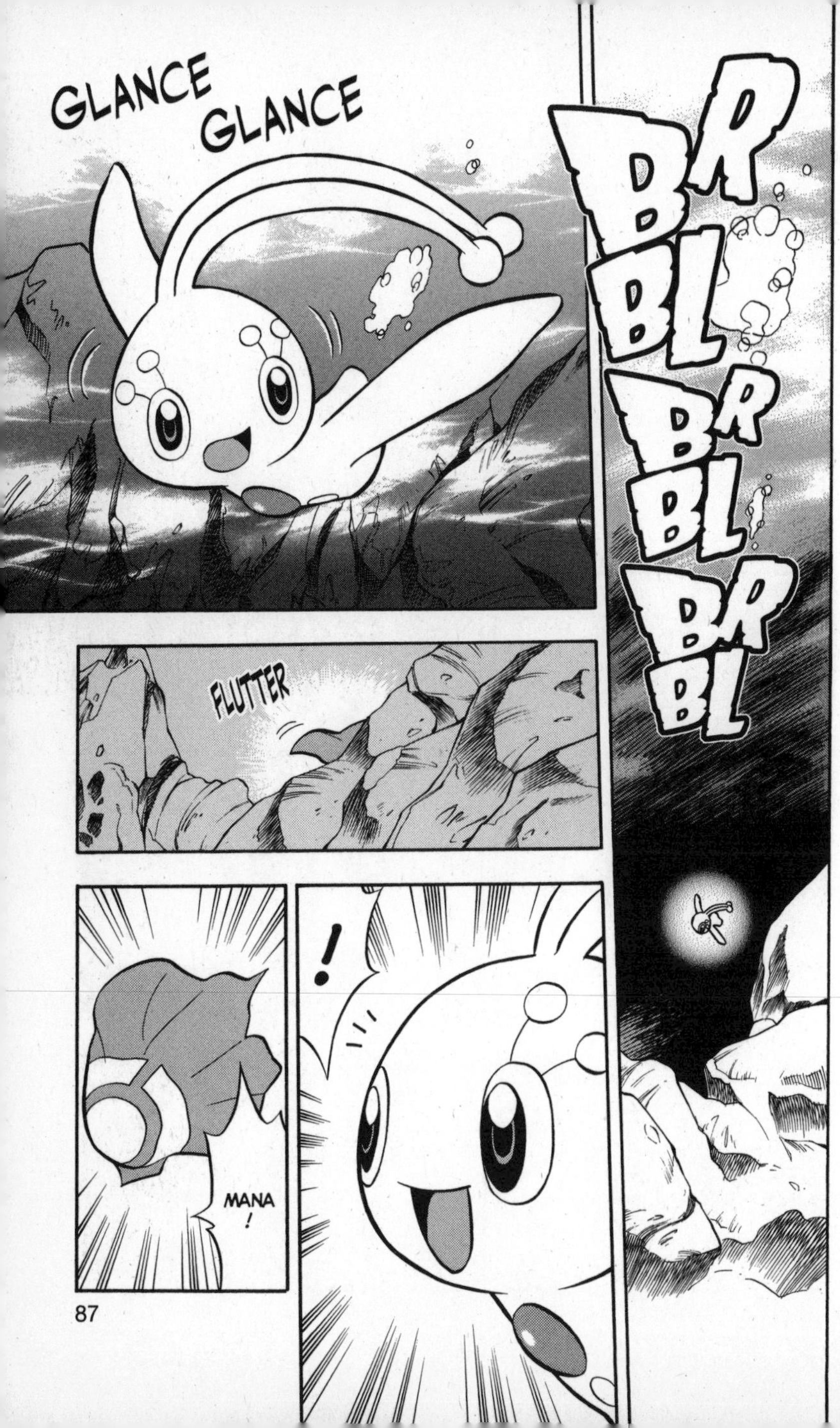
BRBLBRBLBRBL
GLANCE GLANCE
FLUTTER
!
MANA!

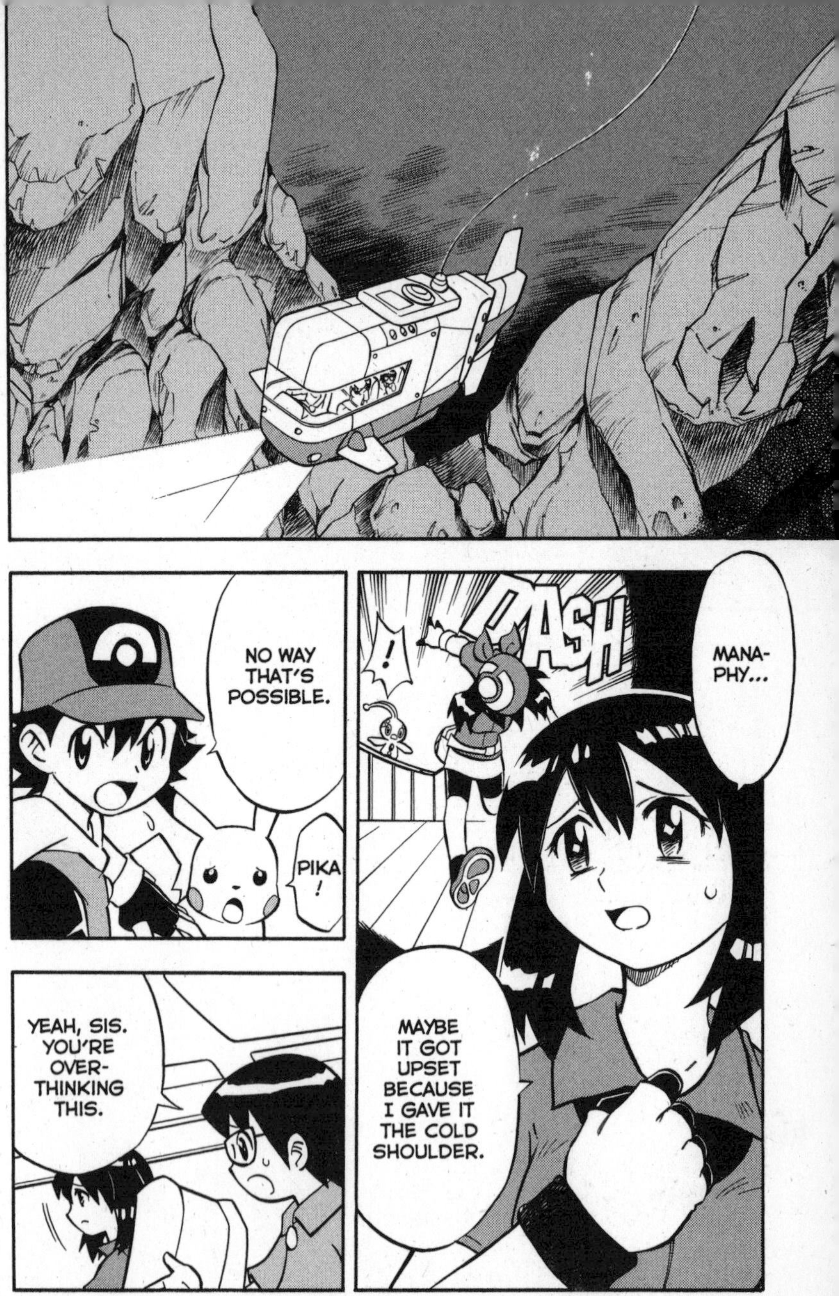
MANA-PHY...
DASH
!
MAYBE IT GOT UPSET BECAUSE I GAVE IT THE COLD SHOULDER.
NO WAY THAT'S POSSIBLE.
PIKA!
YEAH, SIS. YOU'RE OVER-THINKING THIS.

READ THIS WAY

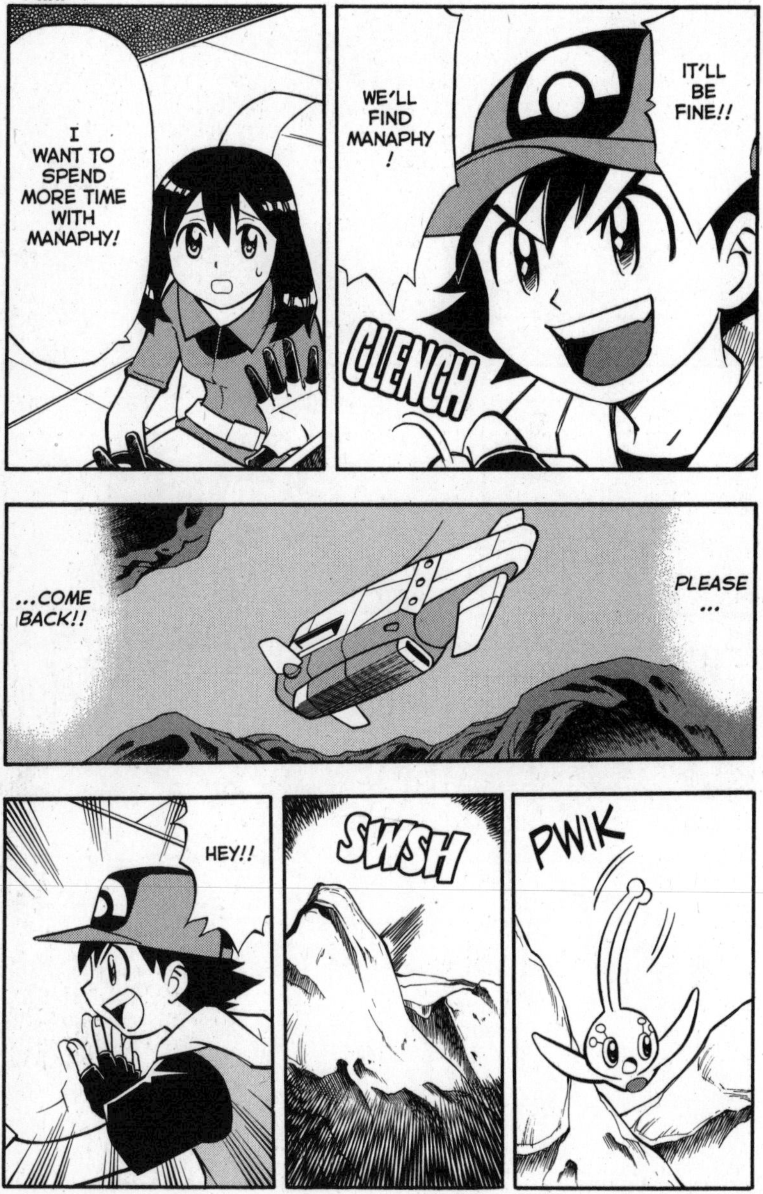

IT'LL BE FINE!!
WE'LL FIND MANAPHY!
CLENCH
I WANT TO SPEND MORE TIME WITH MANAPHY!
PLEASE...
...COME BACK!!
PWIK
SWSH
HEY!!

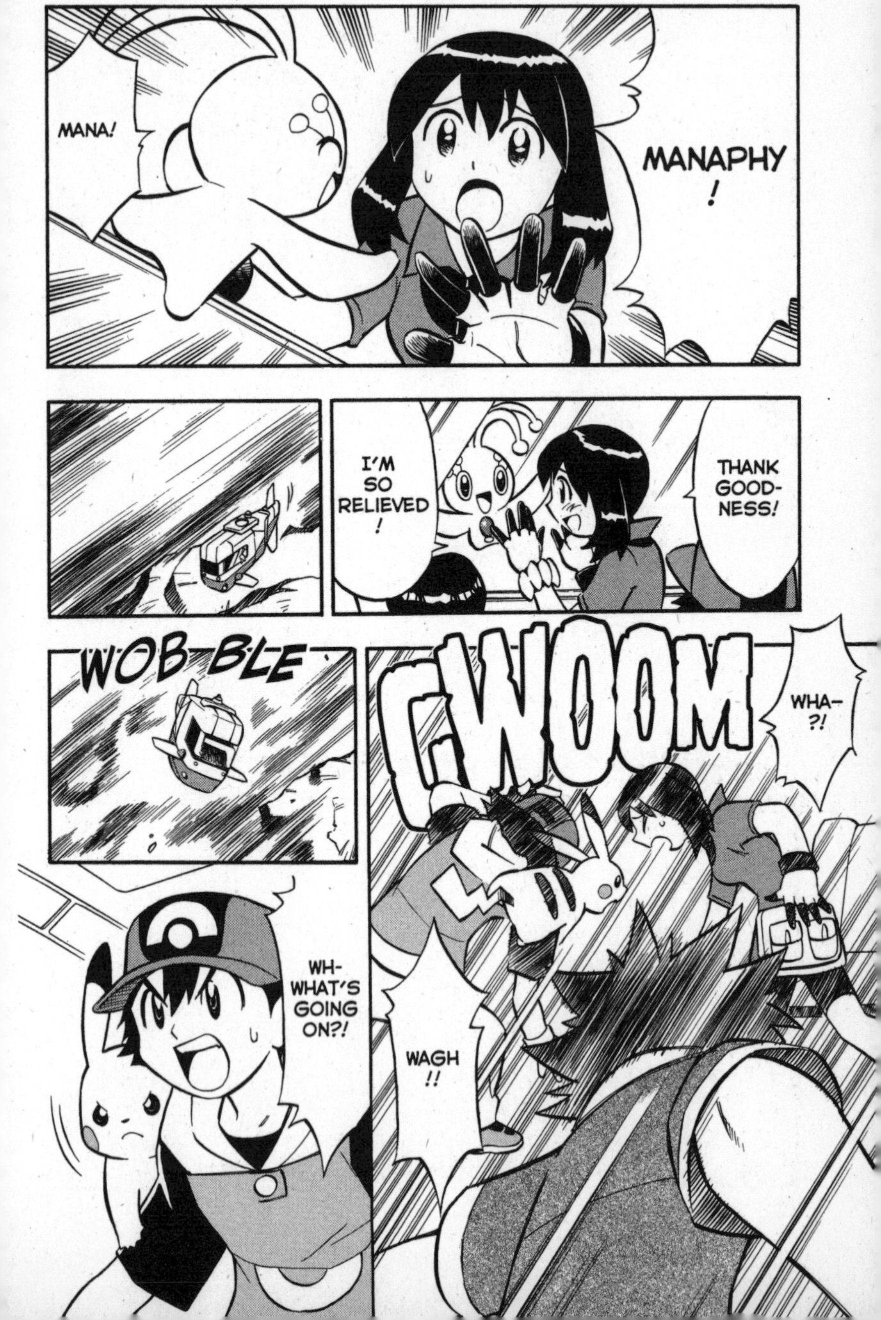
MANAPHY!
MANA!
THANK GOODNESS!
I'M SO RELIEVED!
GWOOM
WHA-?!
WAGH!!
WOB-BLE
WH-WHAT'S GOING ON?!

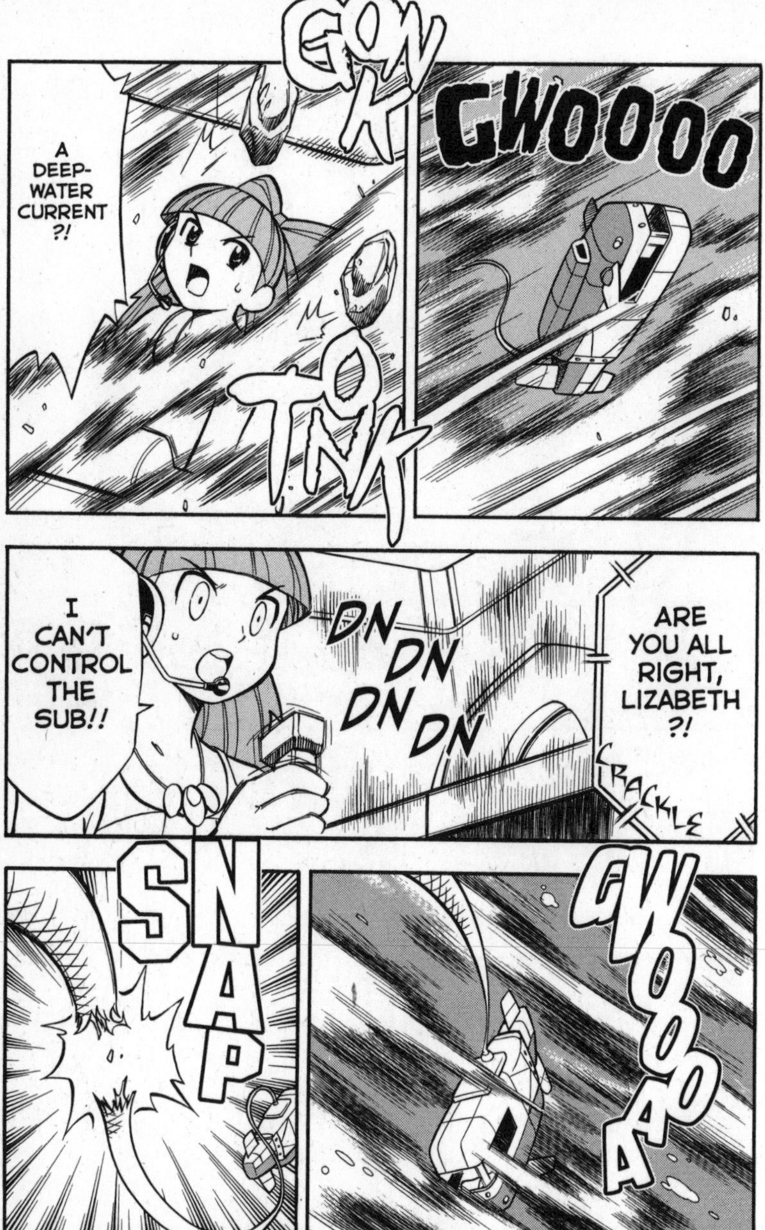
GWOOOOO
GONK
A DEEP-WATER CURRENT?!
TNK
ARE YOU ALL RIGHT, LIZABETH?!
CRACKLE
DN DN DN DN DN DN
I CAN'T CONTROL THE SUB!!
GWOOOOAA
SNAP

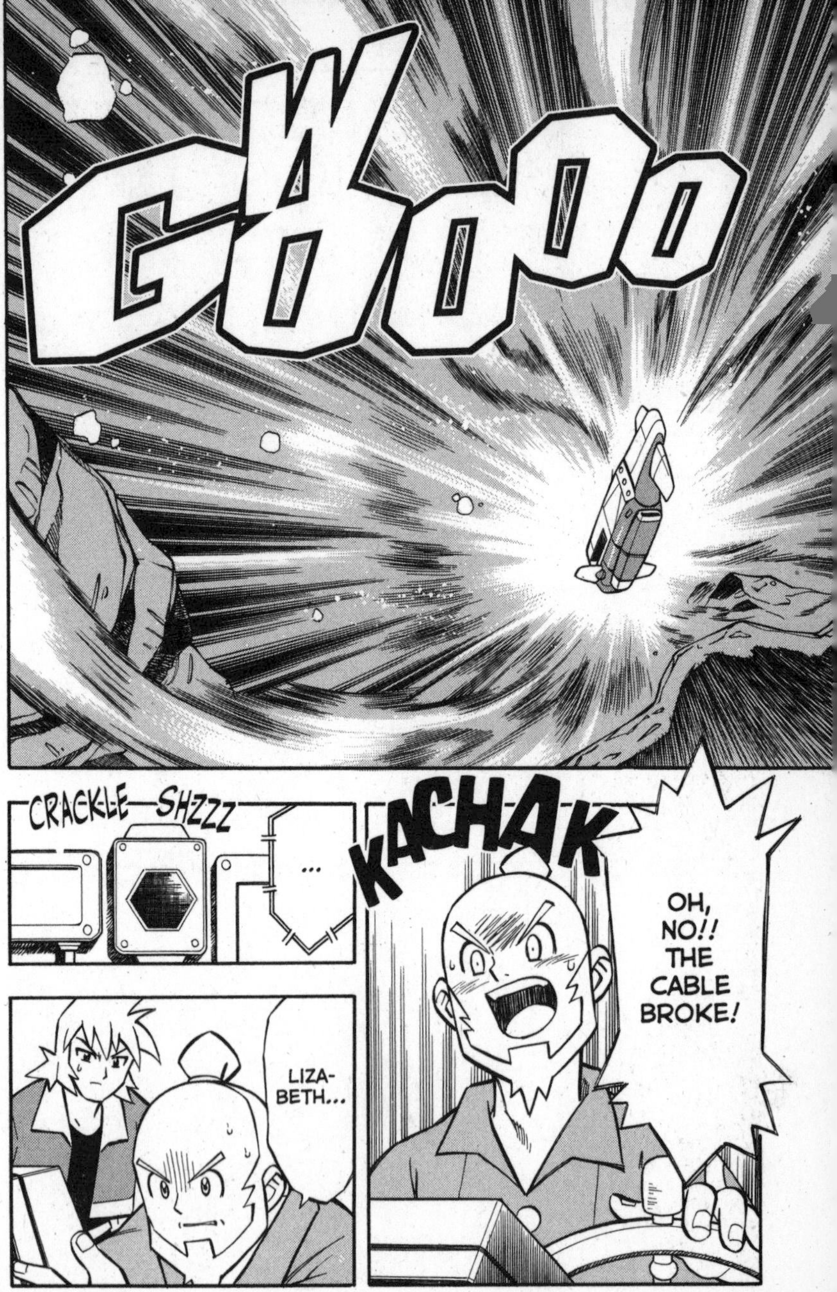
GWOOOO
KACHAK
OH, NO!! THE CABLE BROKE!
CRACKLE SHZZZ
...
LIZA-BETH...

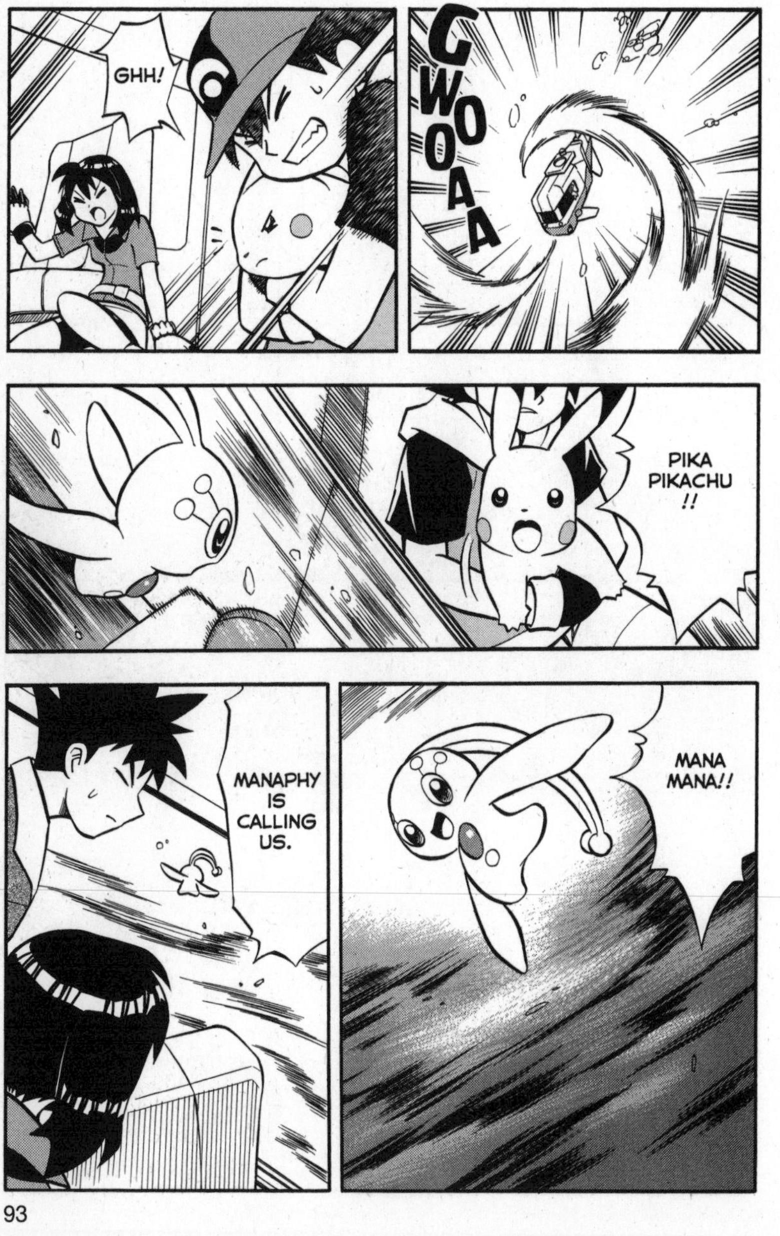
GWOOAA
GHH!
PIKA PIKACHU!!
MANA MANA!!
MANAPHY IS CALLING US.

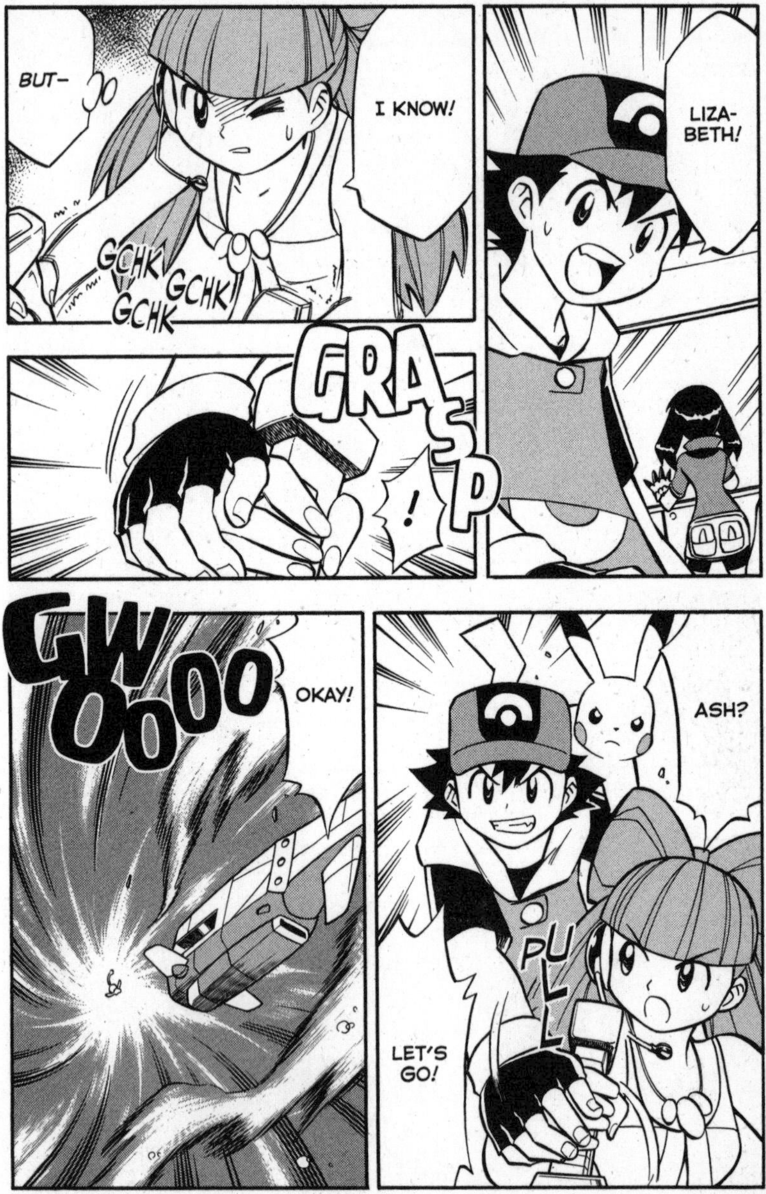
LIZA-BETH!
I KNOW!
BUT—
GCHK GCHK GCHK
GRASP
!
ASH?
PULL
LET'S GO!
GWOOOOO
OKAY!

READ THIS WAY

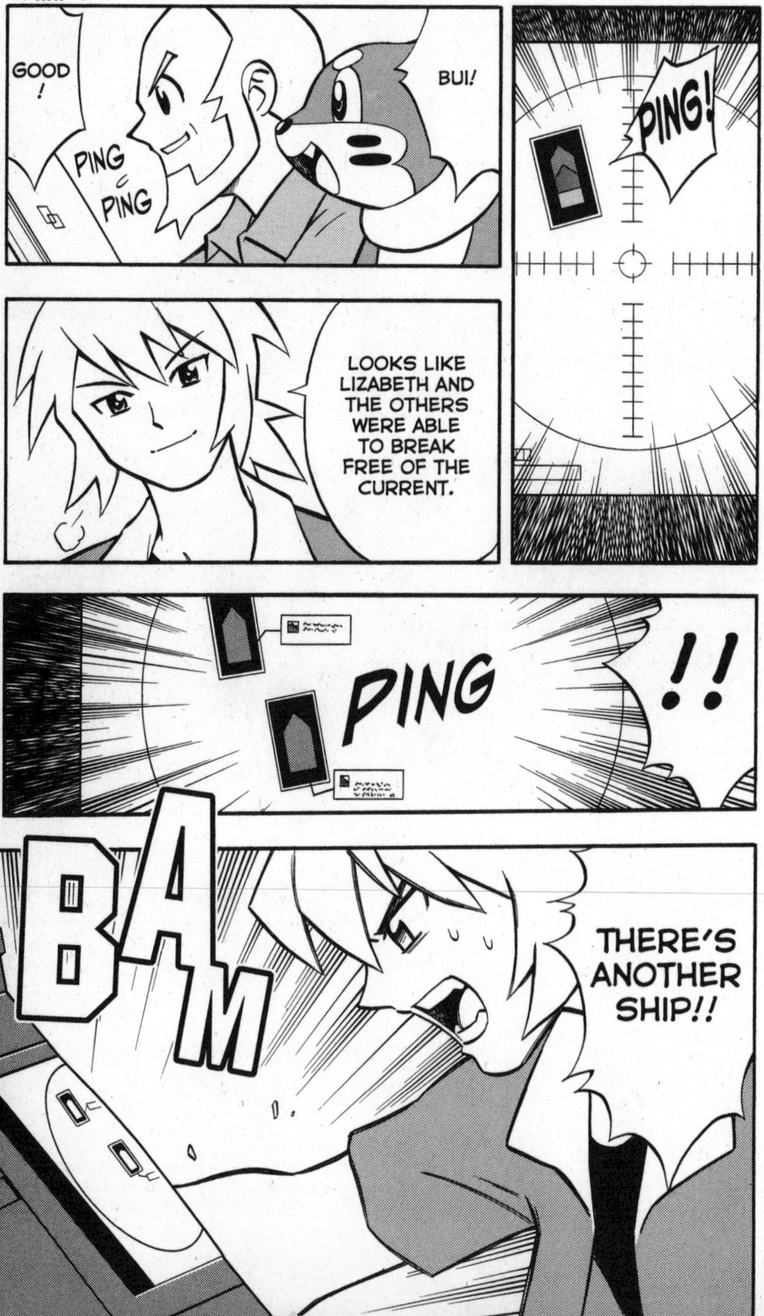

PING!
BUI!
GOOD!
PING PING
LOOKS LIKE LIZABETH AND THE OTHERS WERE ABLE TO BREAK FREE OF THE CURRENT.
PING
!!
THERE'S ANOTHER SHIP!!
BAM

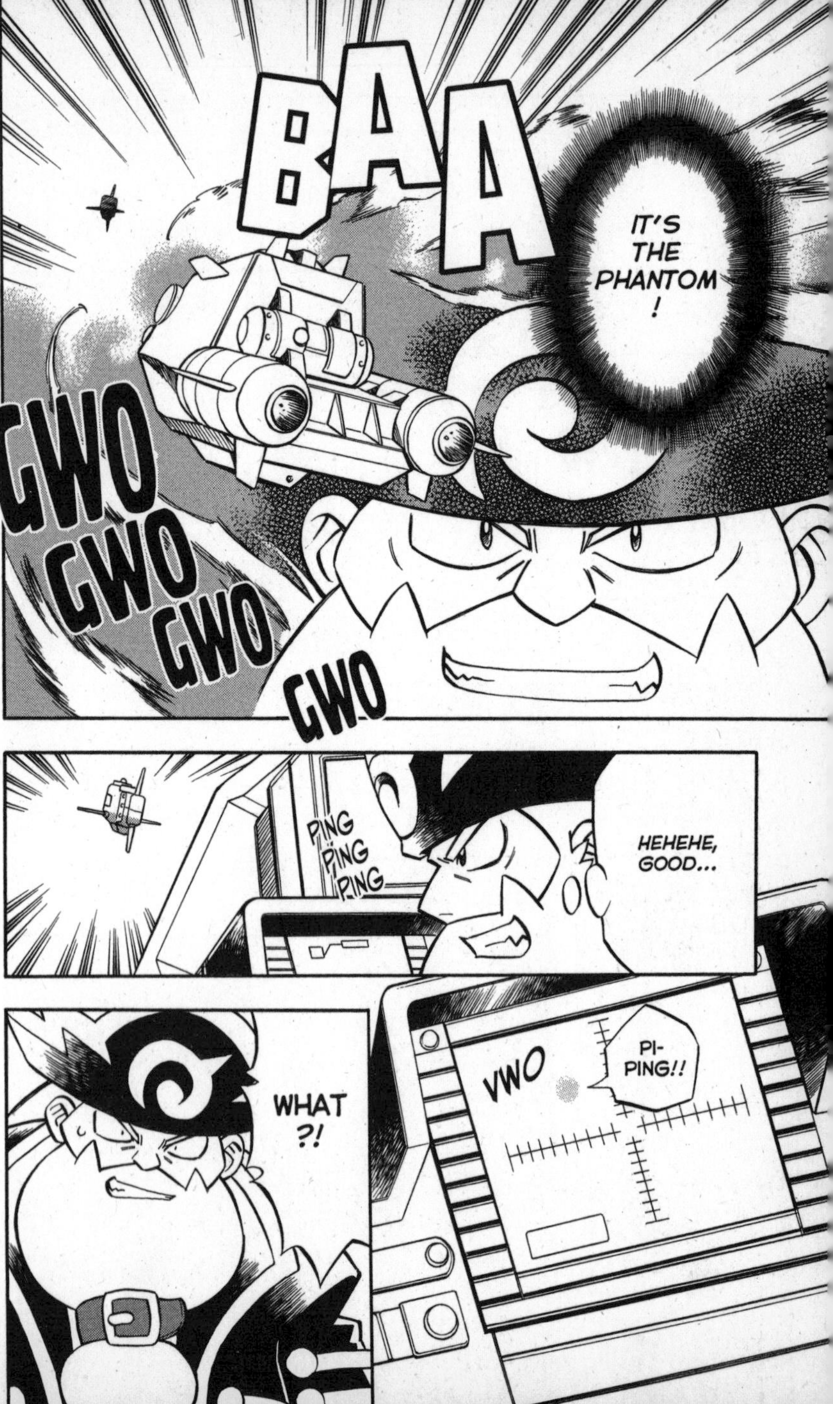
BAAO
IT'S THE PHANTOM!
GWO GWO GWO
GWO
HEHEHE, GOOD...
PING PING PING
PI-PING!!
VWO
WHAT?!

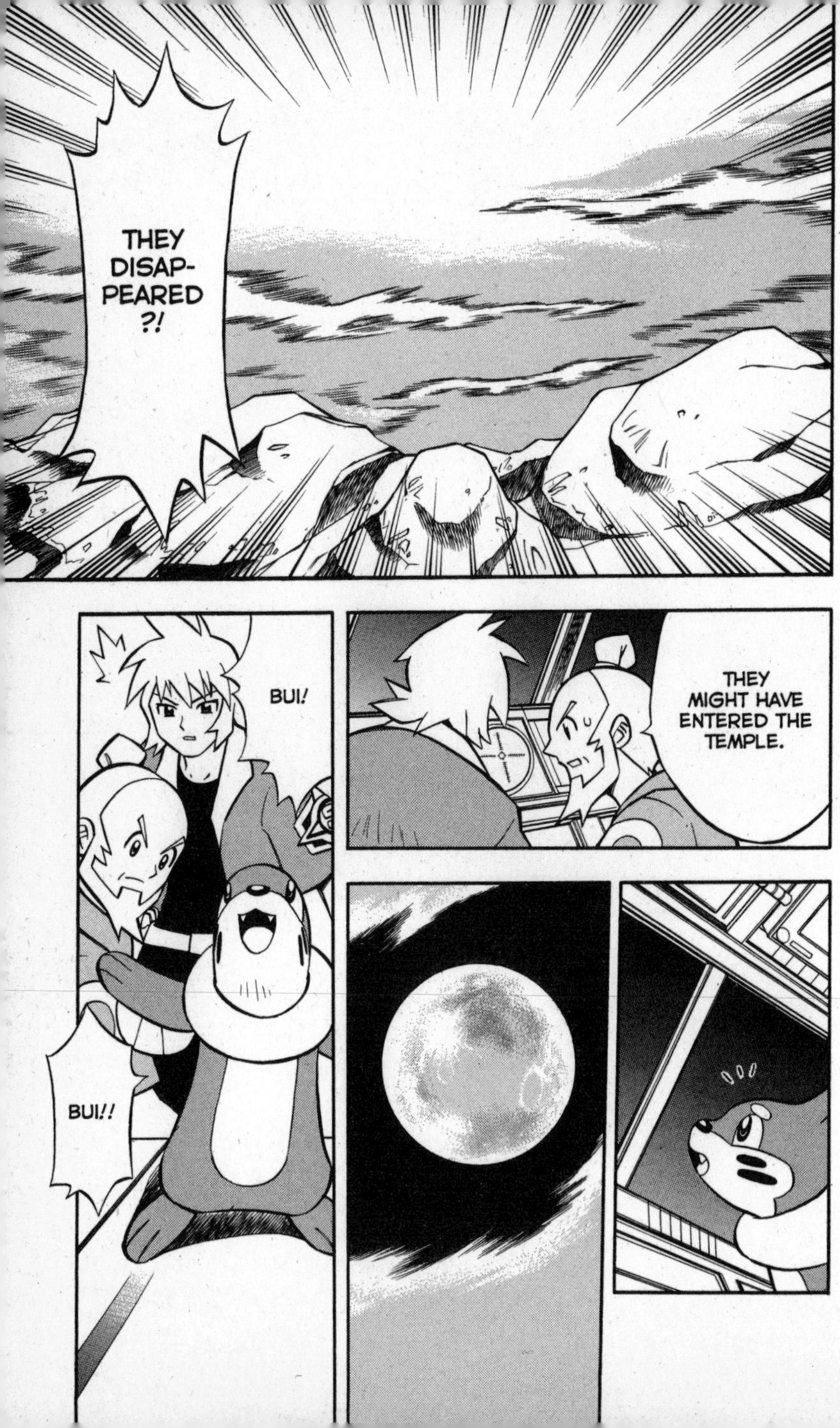
THEY DISAP-PEARED ?!
THEY MIGHT HAVE ENTERED THE TEMPLE.
BUI!
BUI!!

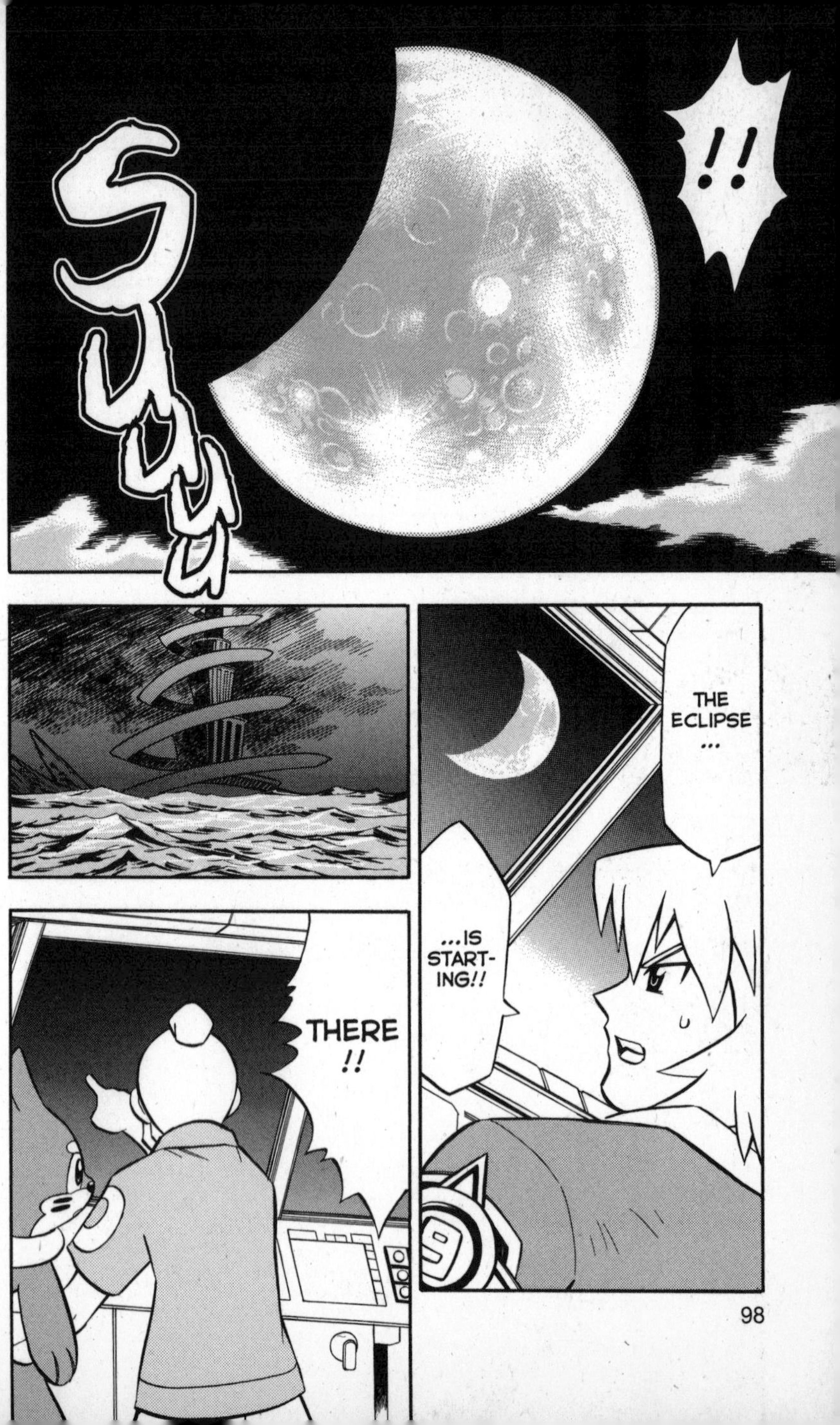

!!
SUUUU
THE ECLIPSE ...
...IS START-ING!!
THERE !!

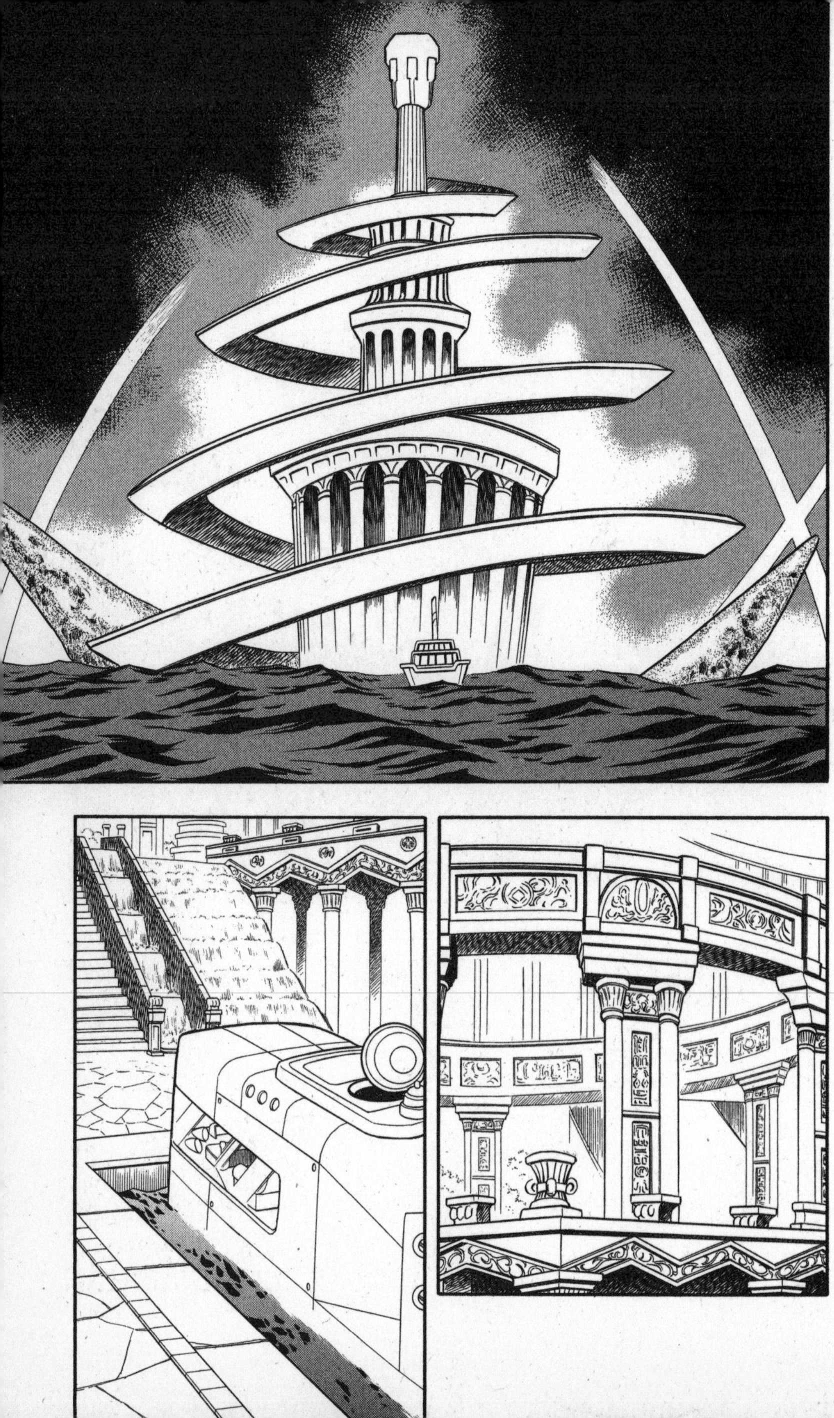

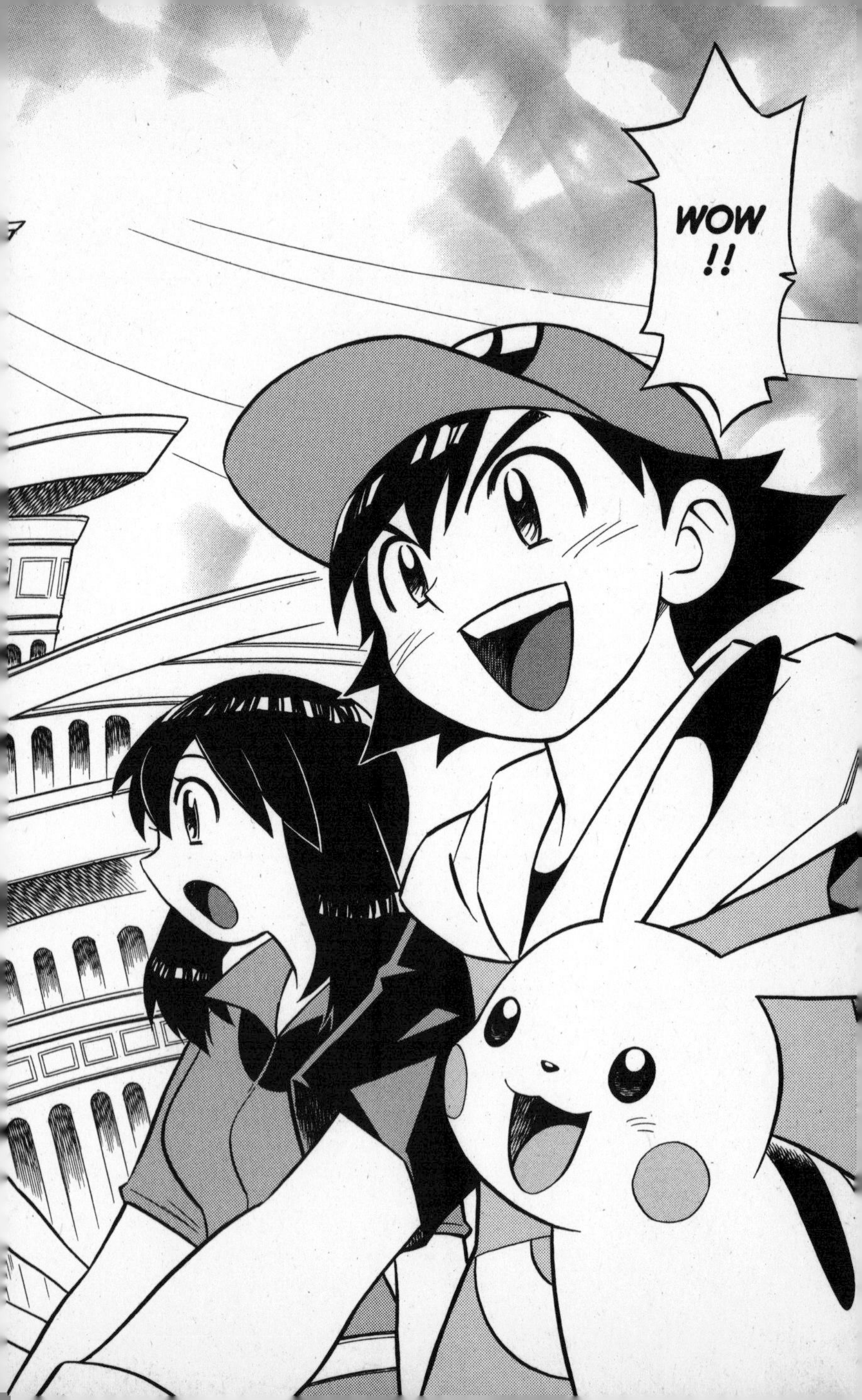
WOW !!

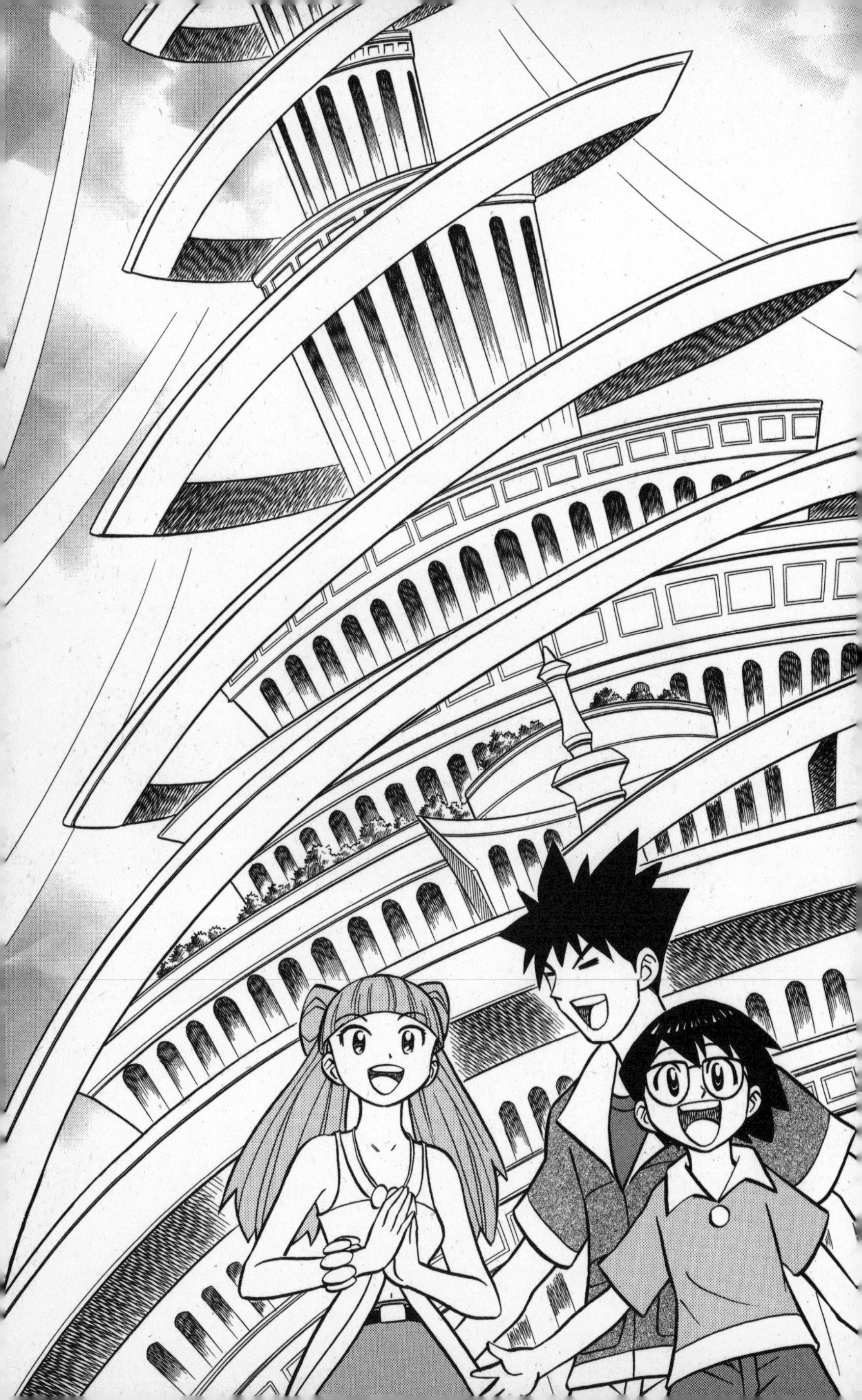

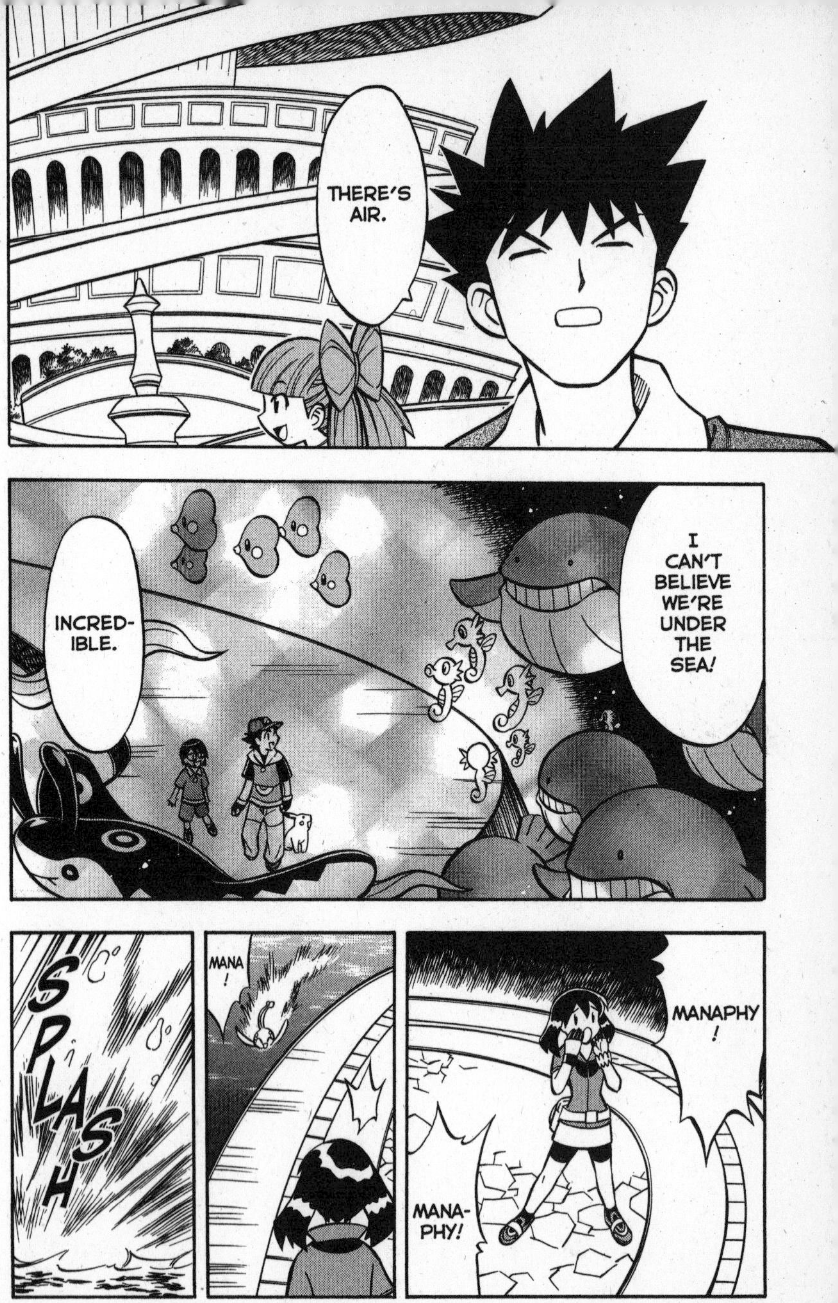
THERE'S AIR.
I CAN'T BELIEVE WE'RE UNDER THE SEA!
INCRED-IBLE.
MANAPHY!
MANA-PHY!
MANA!
SPLASH

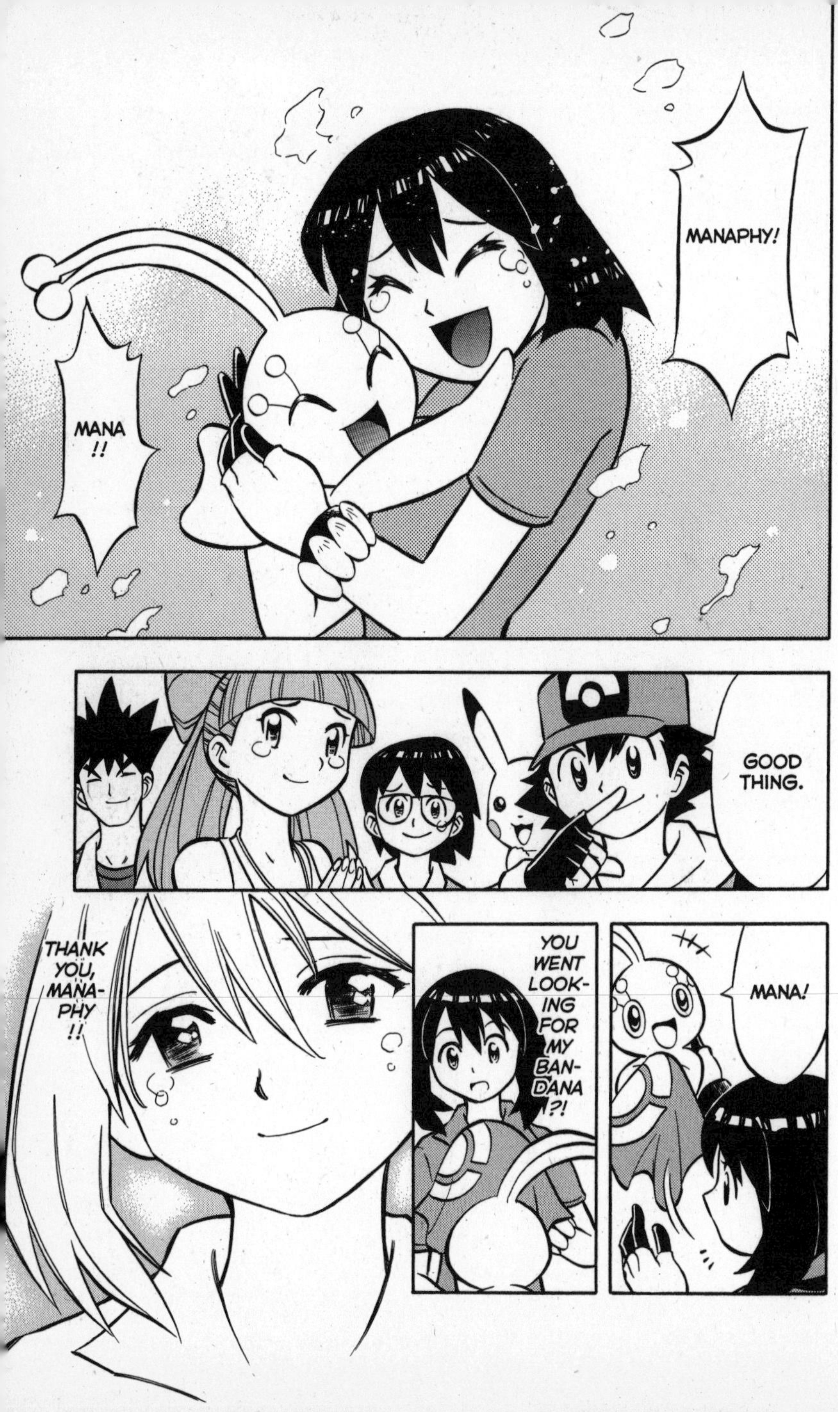
MANAPHY!
MANA !!
GOOD THING.
MANA!
YOU WENT LOOKING FOR MY BANDANA ?!
THANK YOU, MANAPHY !!

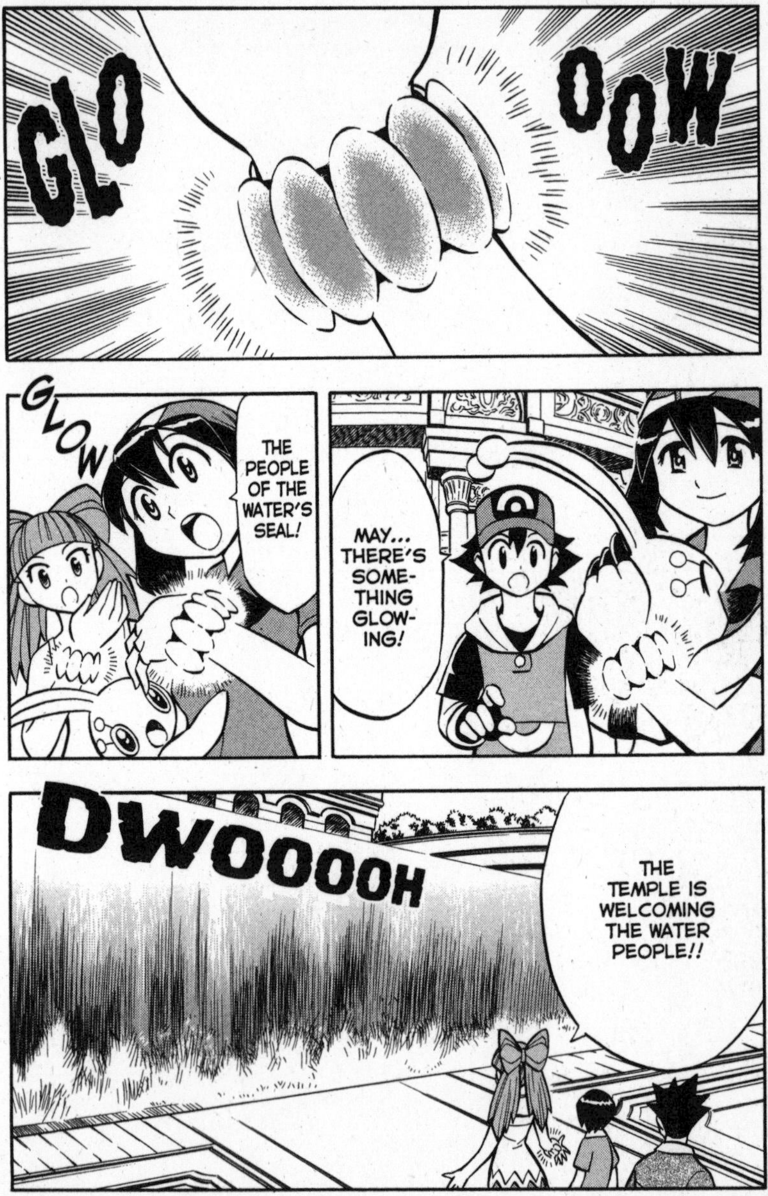

GLO
OOW
MAY... THERE'S SOME-THING GLOW-ING!
GLOW
THE PEOPLE OF THE WATER'S SEAL!
DWOOOOOH
THE TEMPLE IS WELCOMING THE WATER PEOPLE!!

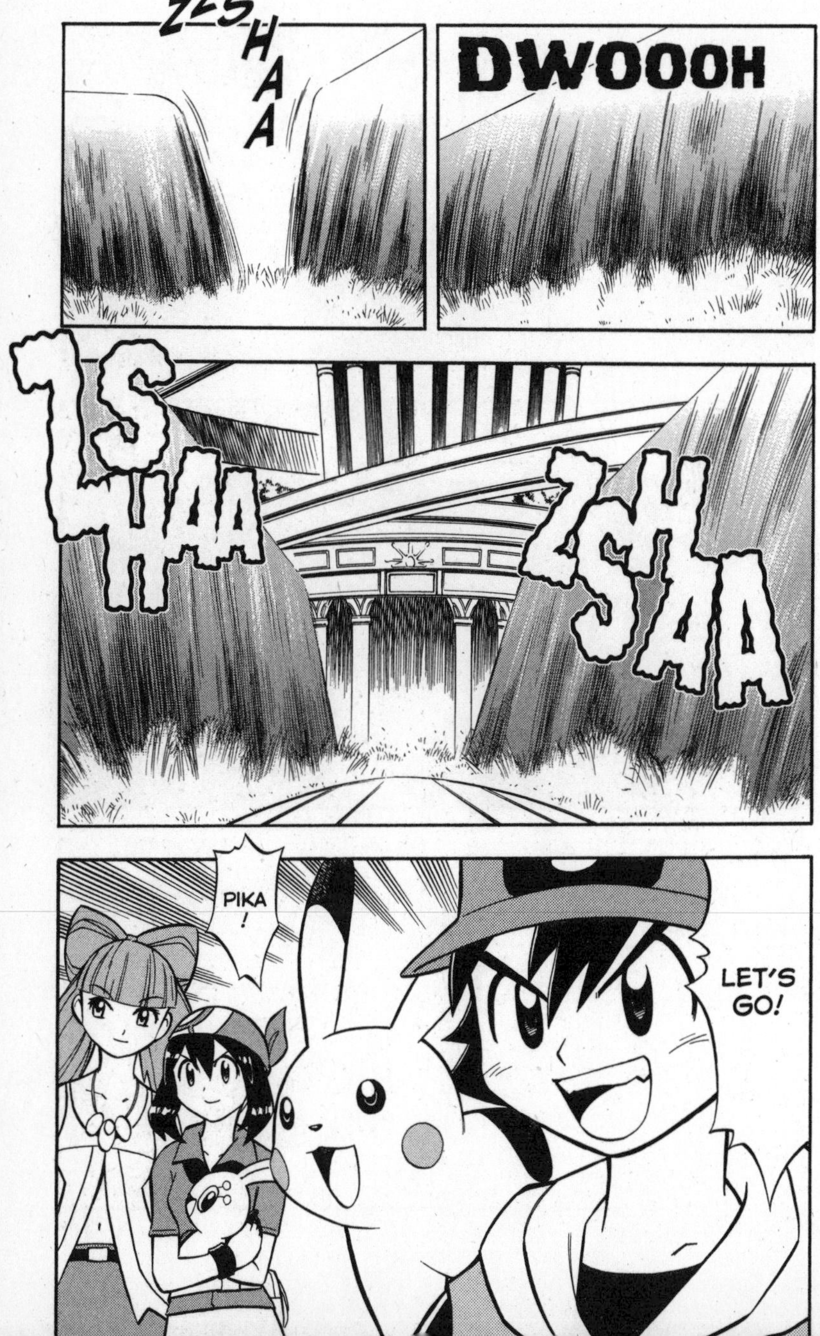
DWOOOH
ZZSHAAA
ZSHAA
ZSHAA
LET'S GO!
PIKA!

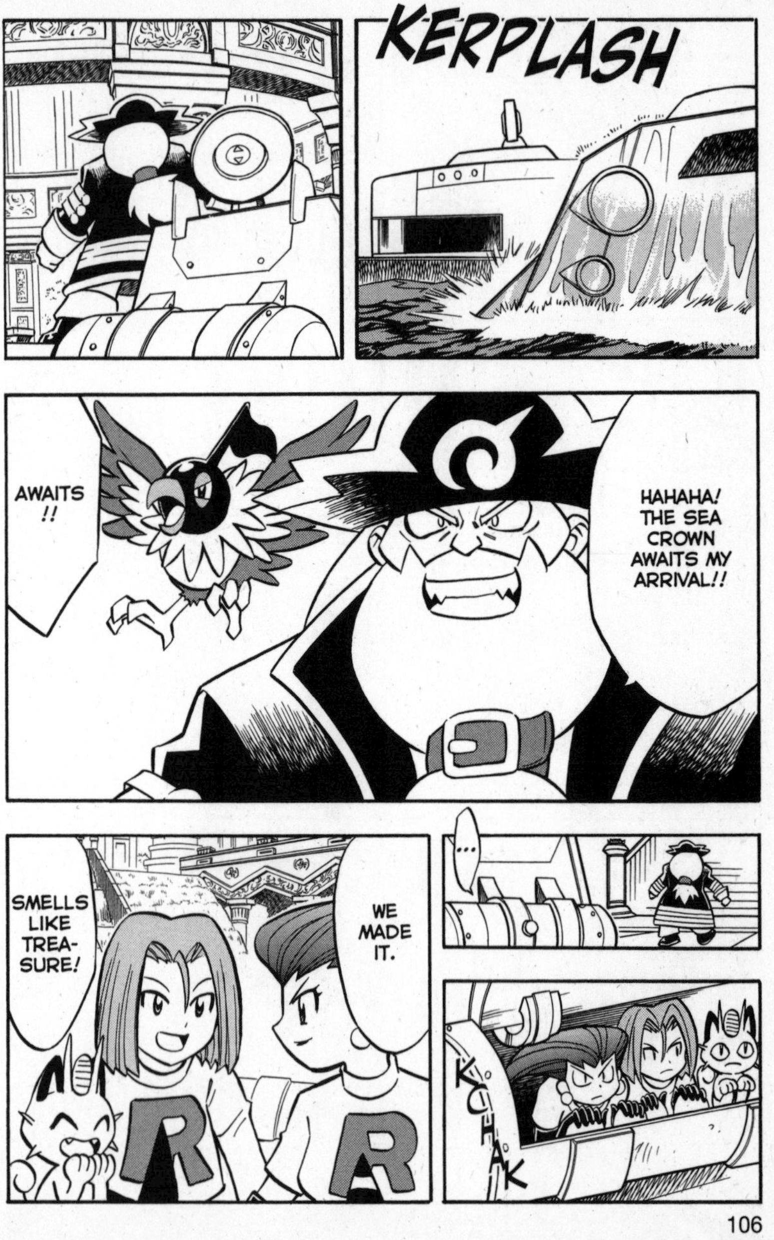
KERPLASH
HAHAHA! THE SEA CROWN AWAITS MY ARRIVAL!!
AWAITS !!
...
KCHAK
WE MADE IT.
SMELLS LIKE TREASURE!

READ THIS WAY

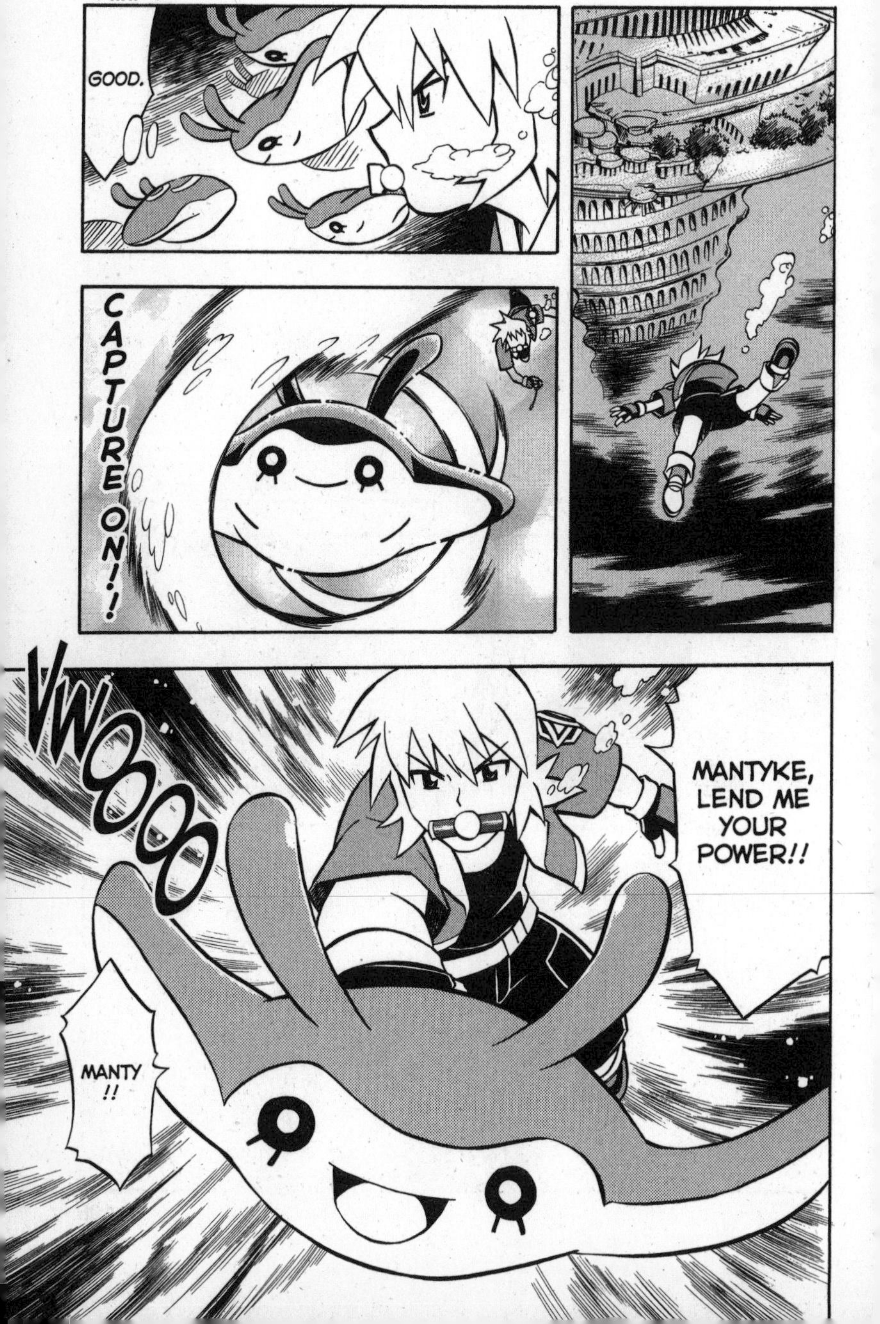
GOOD.
CAPTURE ON!!
MANTYKE, LEND ME YOUR POWER!!
VWOOOO
MANTY !!

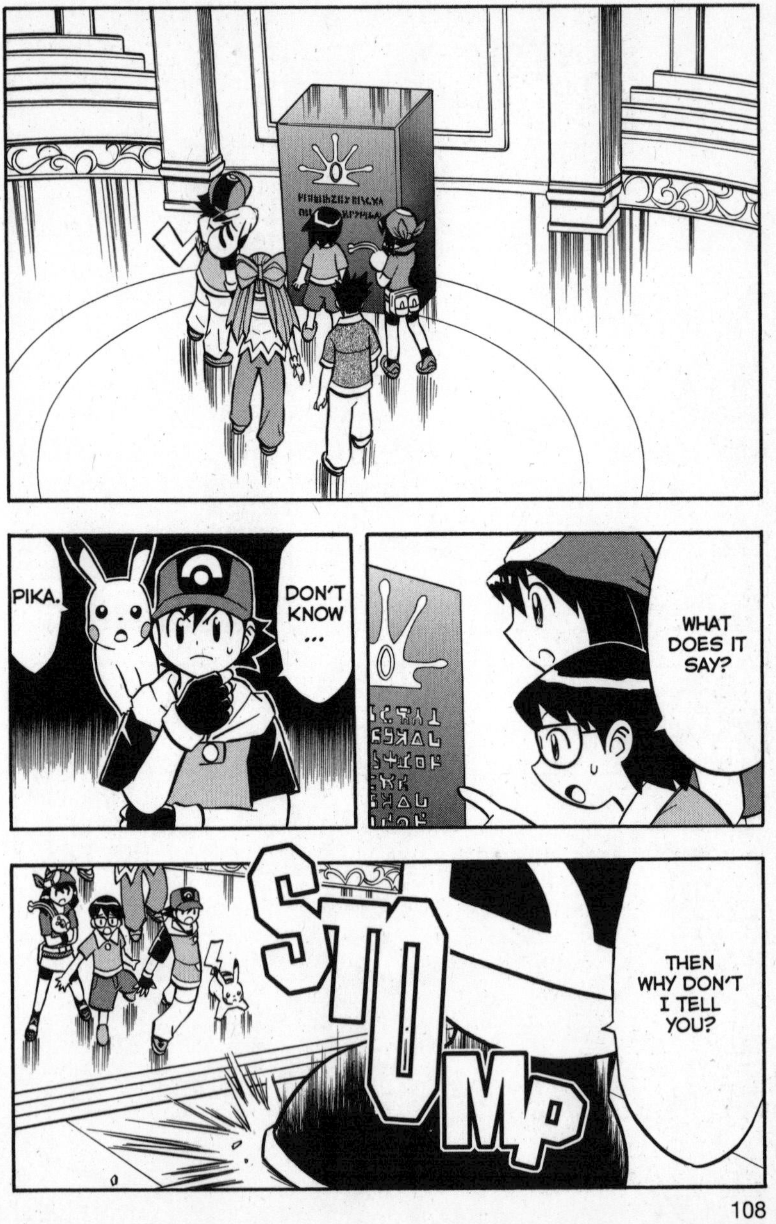
WHAT DOES IT SAY?
DON'T KNOW ...
PIKA.
THEN WHY DON'T I TELL YOU?
STOMP

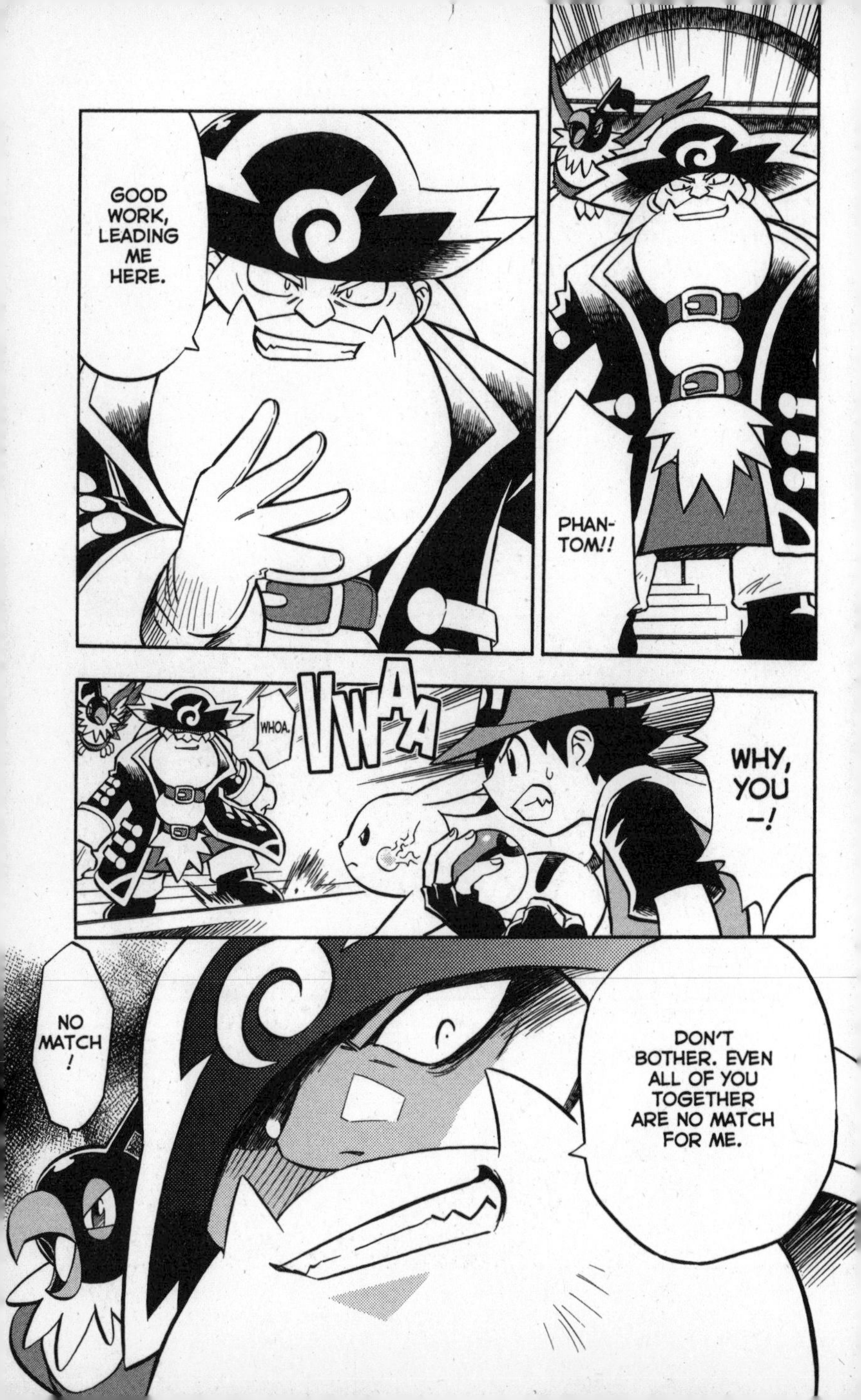
PHAN-TOM!!
GOOD WORK, LEADING ME HERE.
WHY, YOU—!
VWAA
WHOA.
DON'T BOTHER. EVEN ALL OF YOU TOGETHER ARE NO MATCH FOR ME.
NO MATCH!

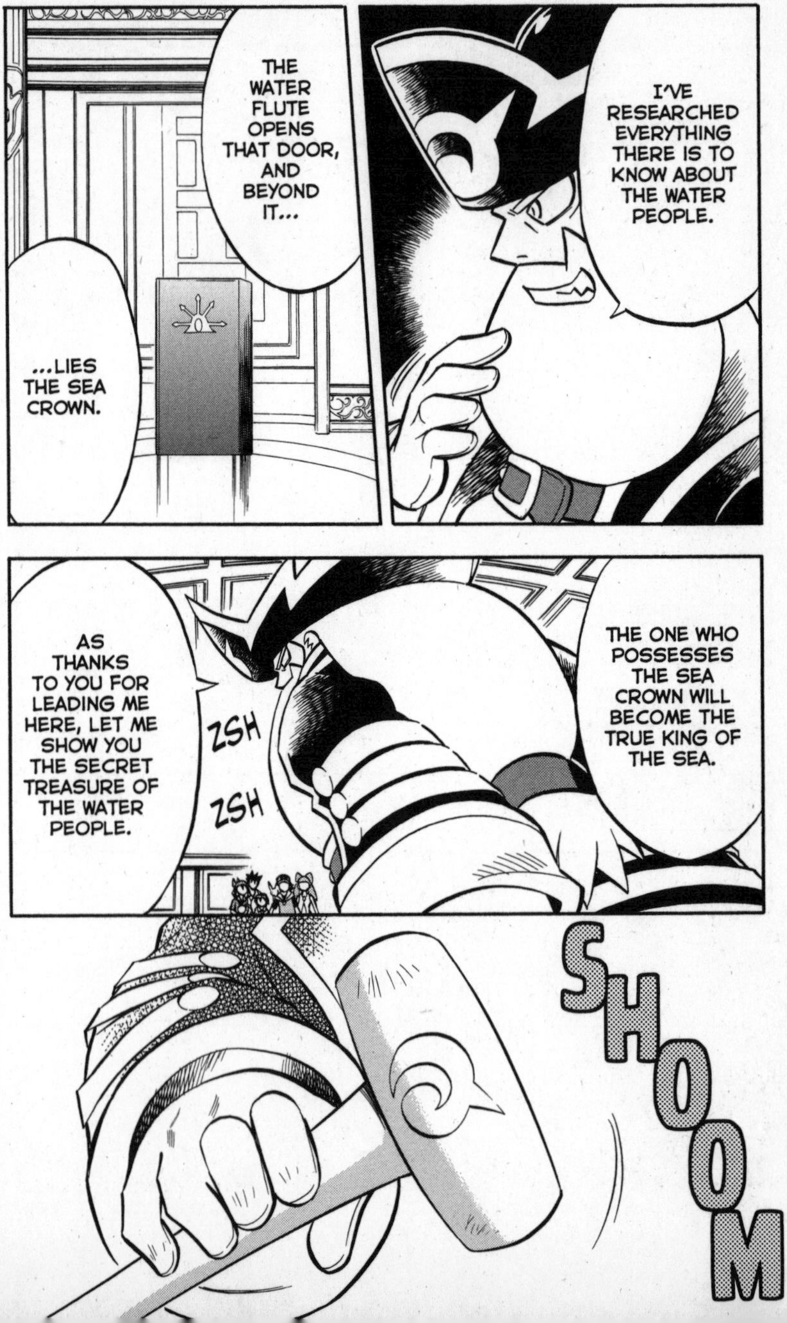
I'VE RESEARCHED EVERYTHING THERE IS TO KNOW ABOUT THE WATER PEOPLE.
THE WATER FLUTE OPENS THAT DOOR, AND BEYOND IT...
...LIES THE SEA CROWN.
THE ONE WHO POSSESSES THE SEA CROWN WILL BECOME THE TRUE KING OF THE SEA.
AS THANKS TO YOU FOR LEADING ME HERE, LET ME SHOW YOU THE SECRET TREASURE OF THE WATER PEOPLE.
ZSH
ZSH
SHOOOM

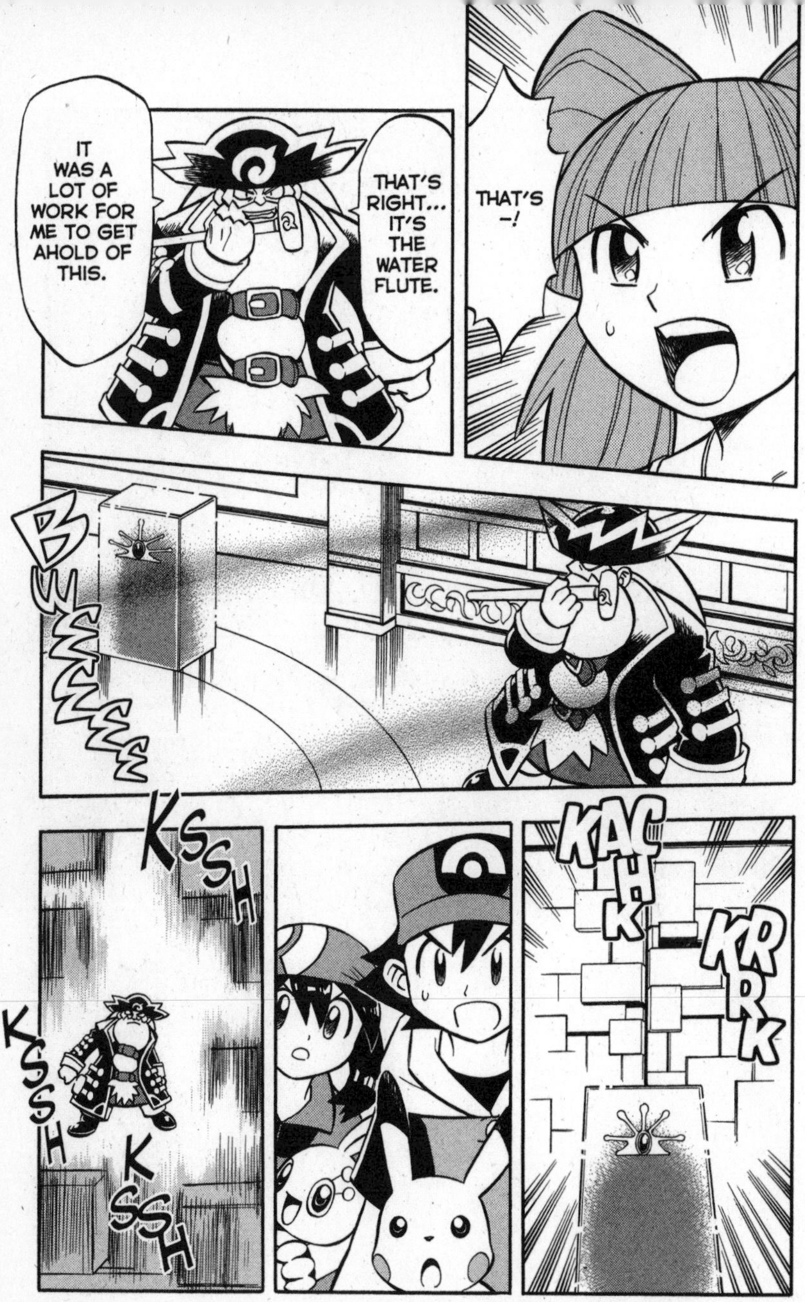
THAT'S —!
THAT'S RIGHT... IT'S THE WATER FLUTE.
IT WAS A LOT OF WORK FOR ME TO GET AHOLD OF THIS.
BWEEEEEE
KACHK
KRRRK
KSSH
KSSSH
KSSH

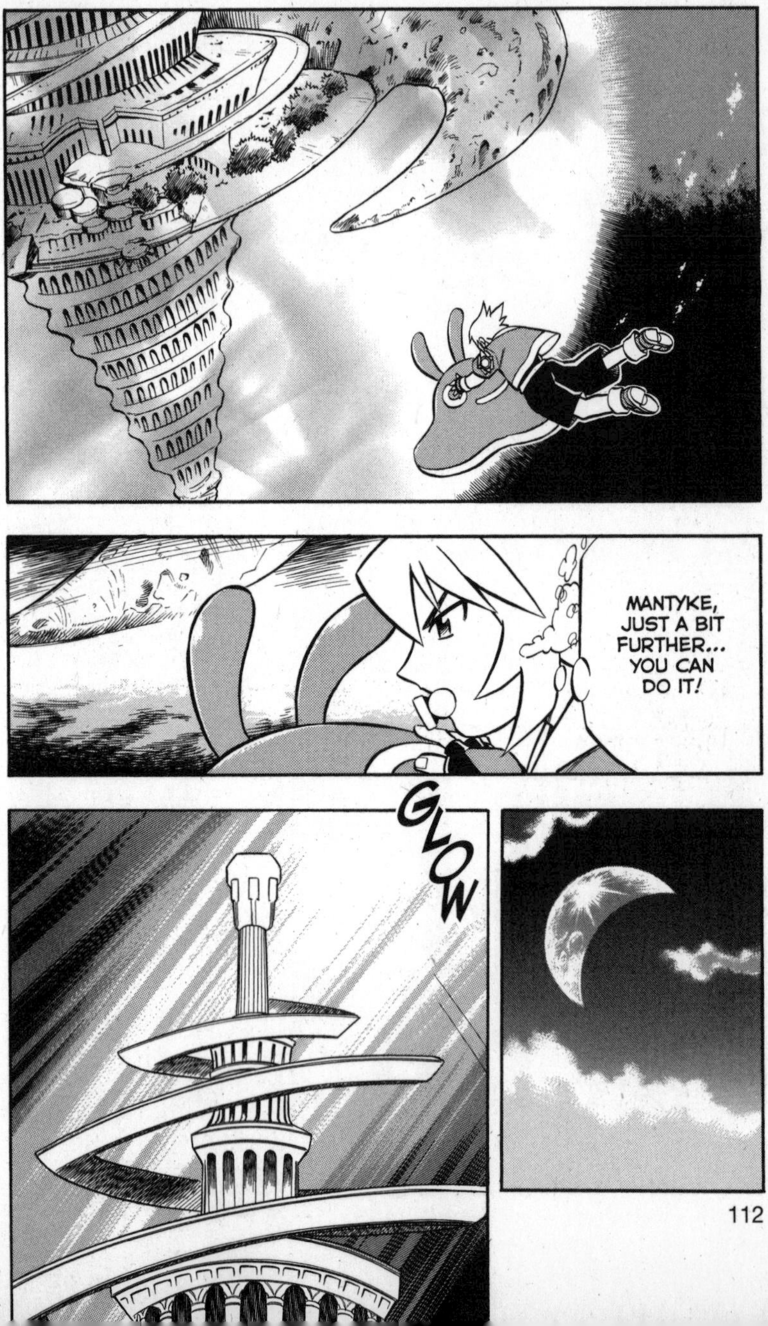
MANTYKE, JUST A BIT FURTHER... YOU CAN DO IT!
GLOW

READ THIS WAY

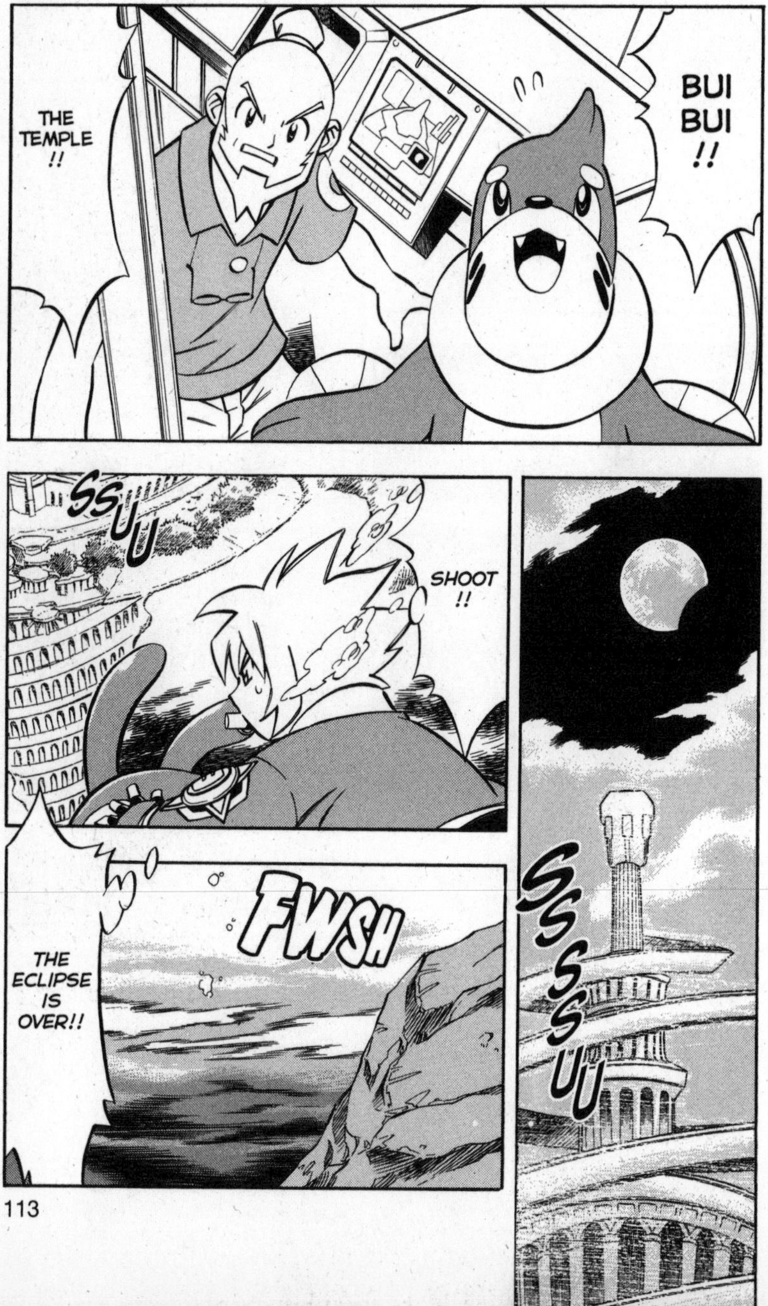
BUI BUI!!
THE TEMPLE!!
SSSSUU
SSUU
SHOOT!!
FWSH
THE ECLIPSE IS OVER!!

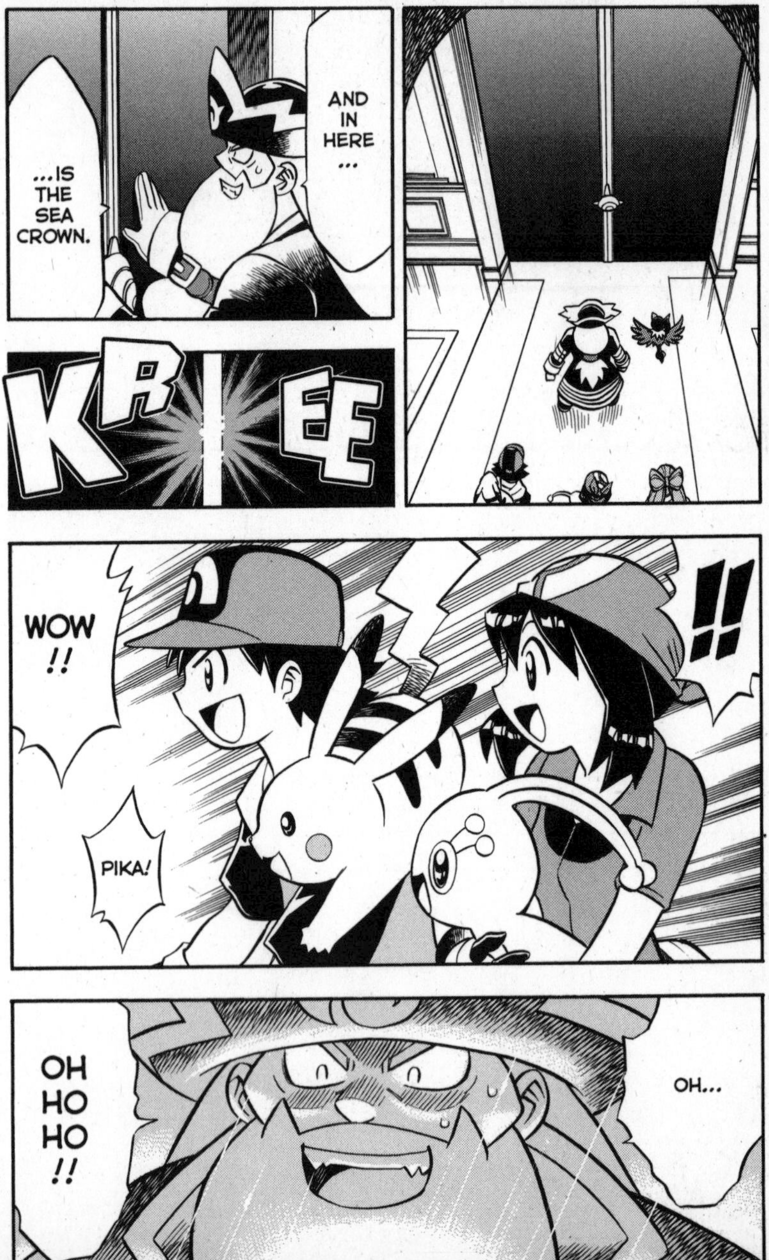

AND IN HERE ...
...IS THE SEA CROWN.
KR EE
!!
WOW !!
PIKA!
OH...
OH HO HO !!

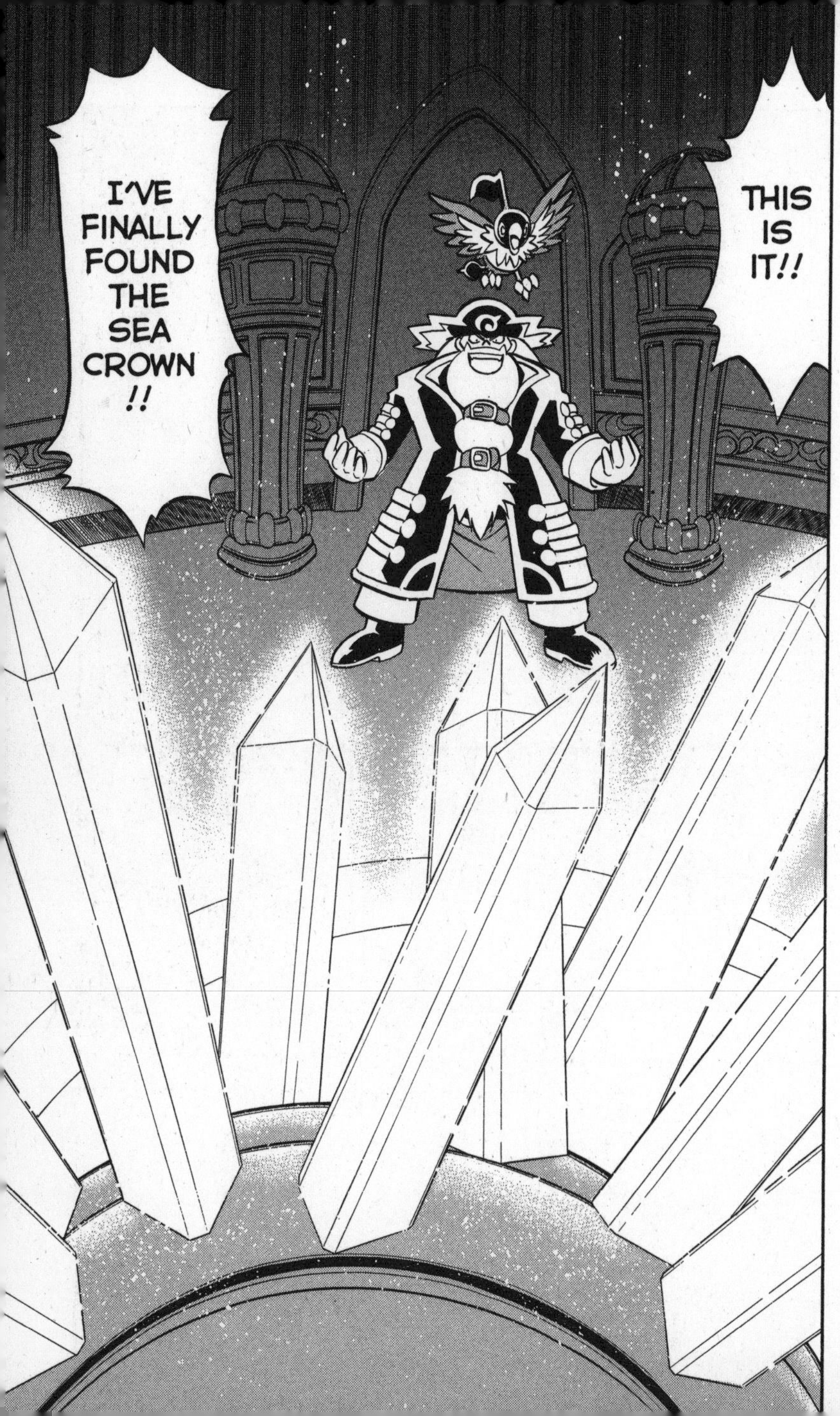
THIS IS IT!!
I'VE FINALLY FOUND THE SEA CROWN!!

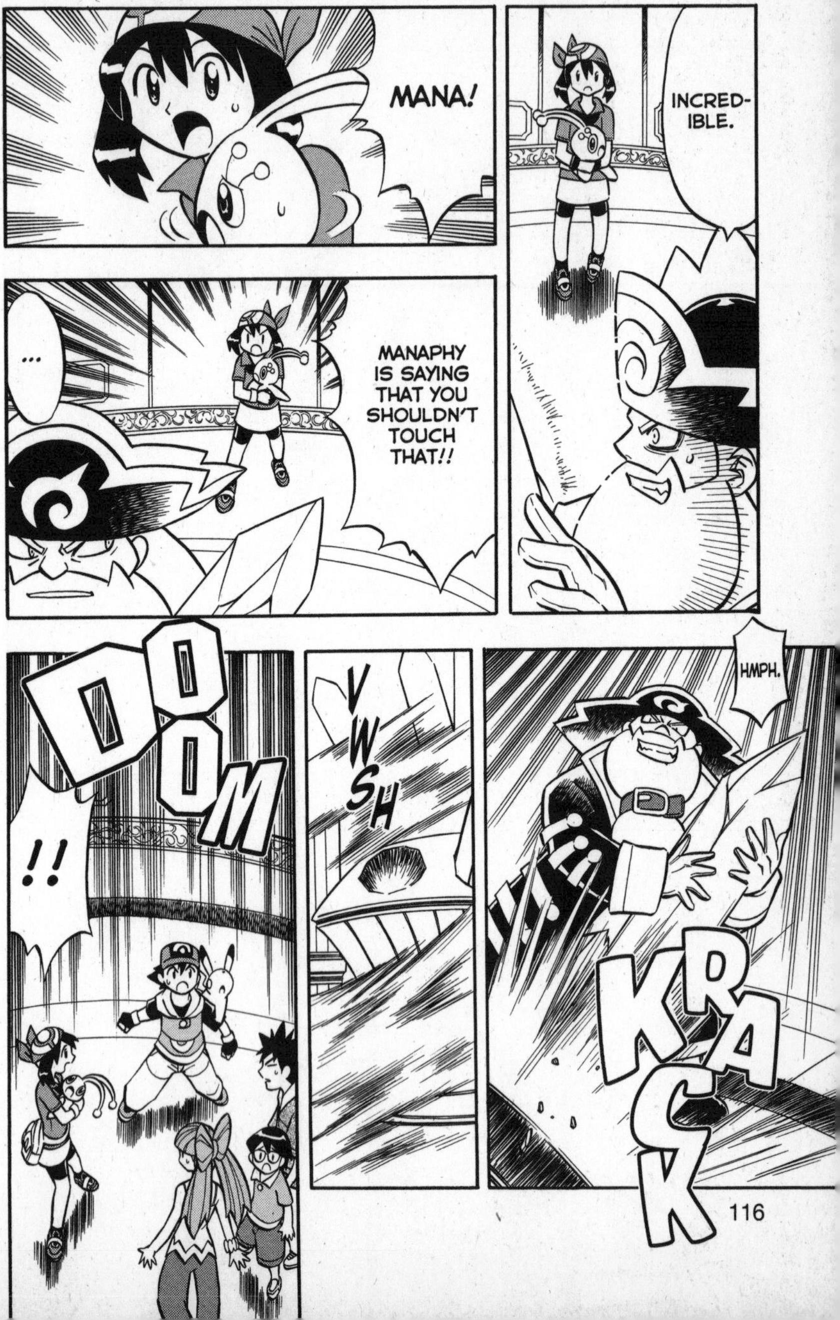
INCRED-IBLE.
MANA!
MANAPHY IS SAYING THAT YOU SHOULDN'T TOUCH THAT!!
...
HMPH.
KRACK
VWSH
DOOM
!!

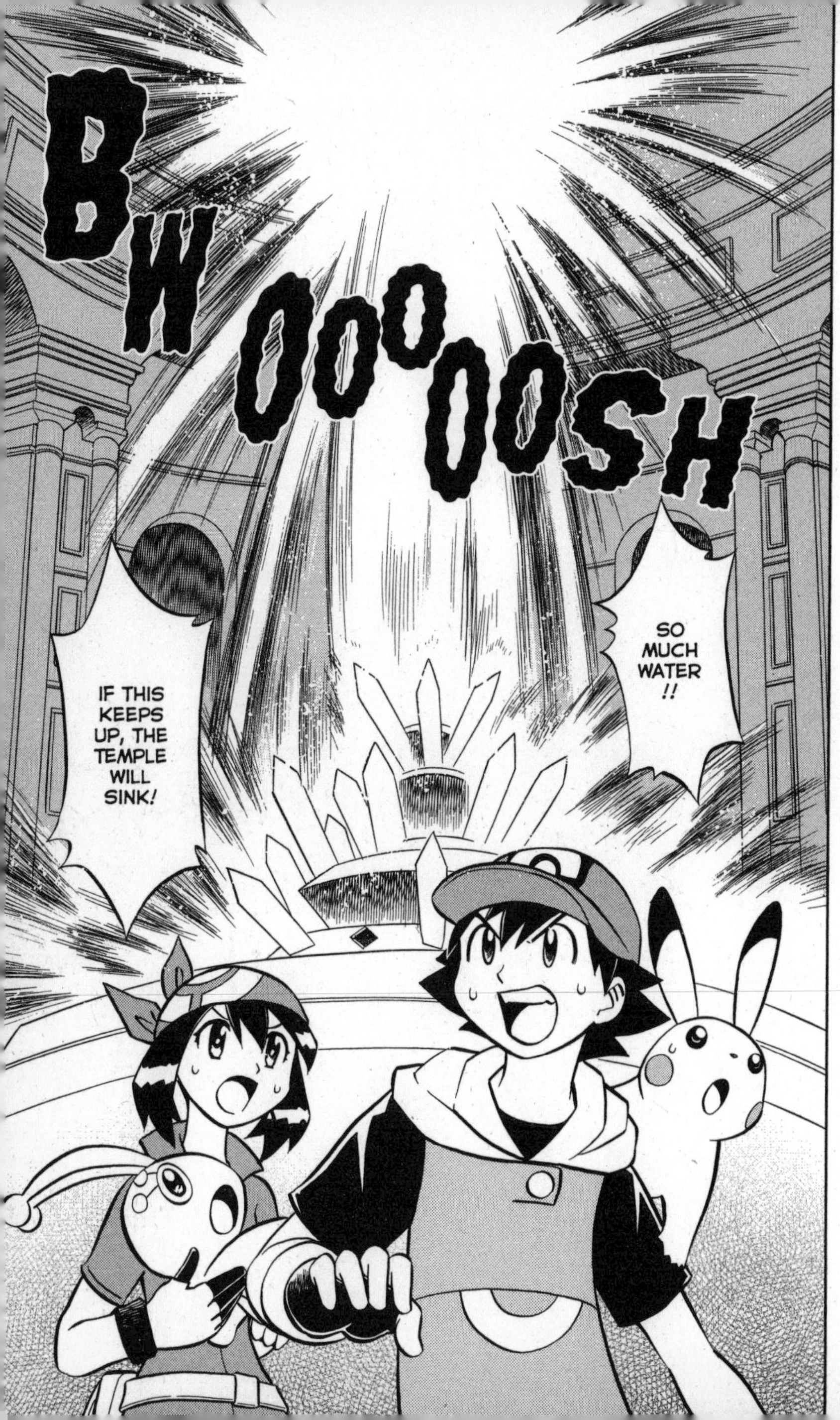
BWOOOOOSH
SO MUCH WATER!!
IF THIS KEEPS UP, THE TEMPLE WILL SINK!

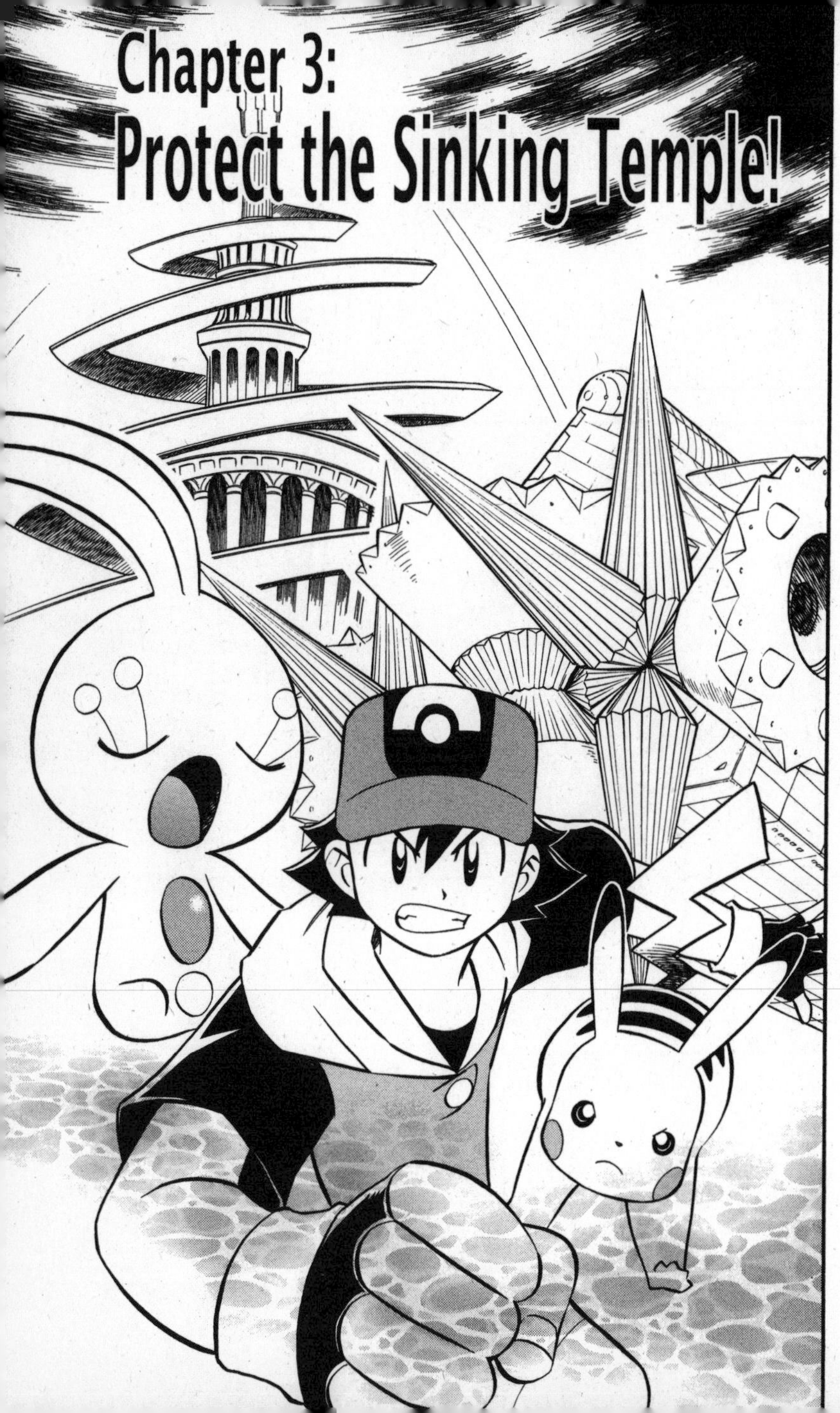
Chapter 3:
Protect the Sinking Temple!

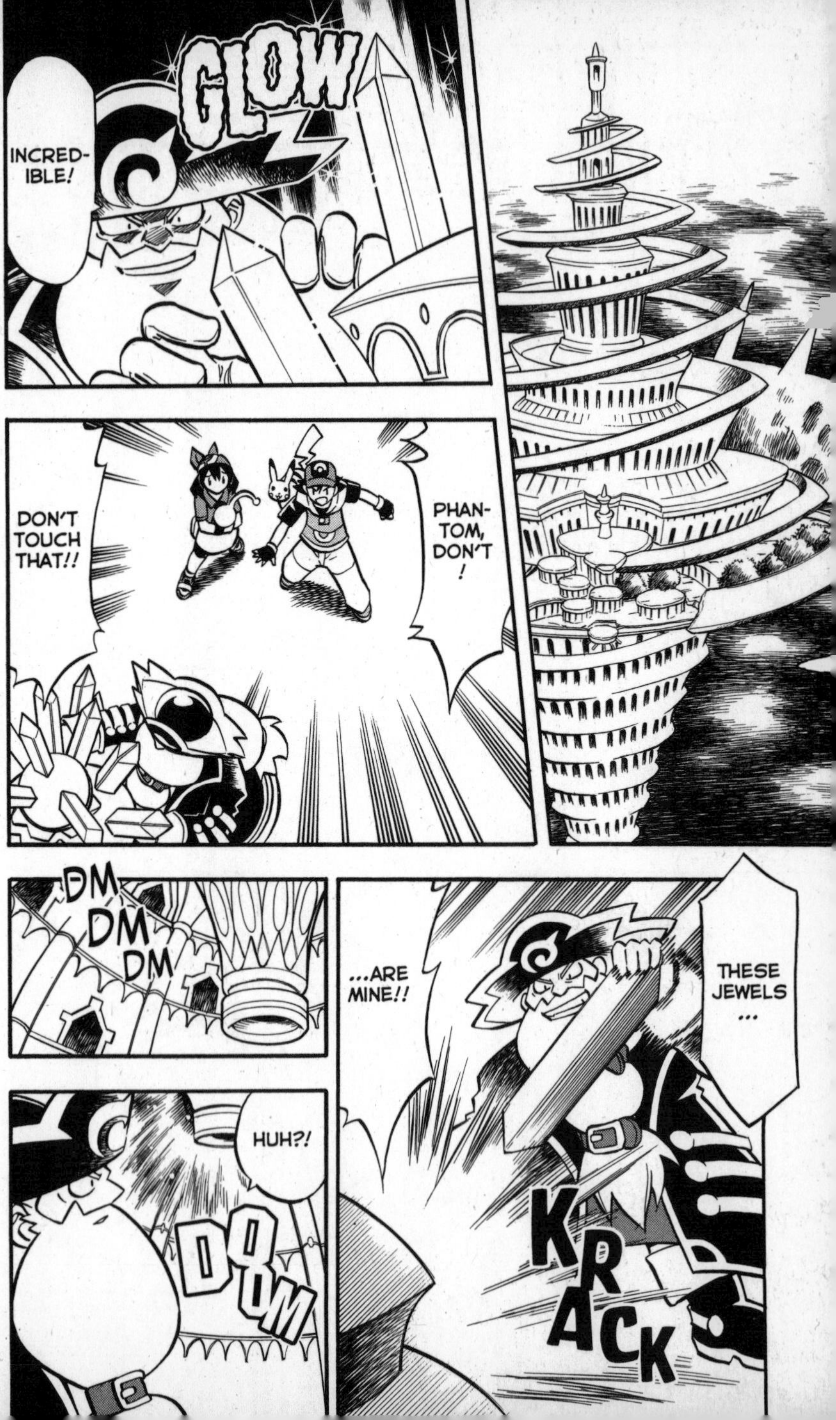
GLOW
INCREDIBLE!
PHANTOM, DON'T!
DON'T TOUCH THAT!!
THESE JEWELS...
...ARE MINE!!
KRACK
DM DM DM
HUH?!
DOOM

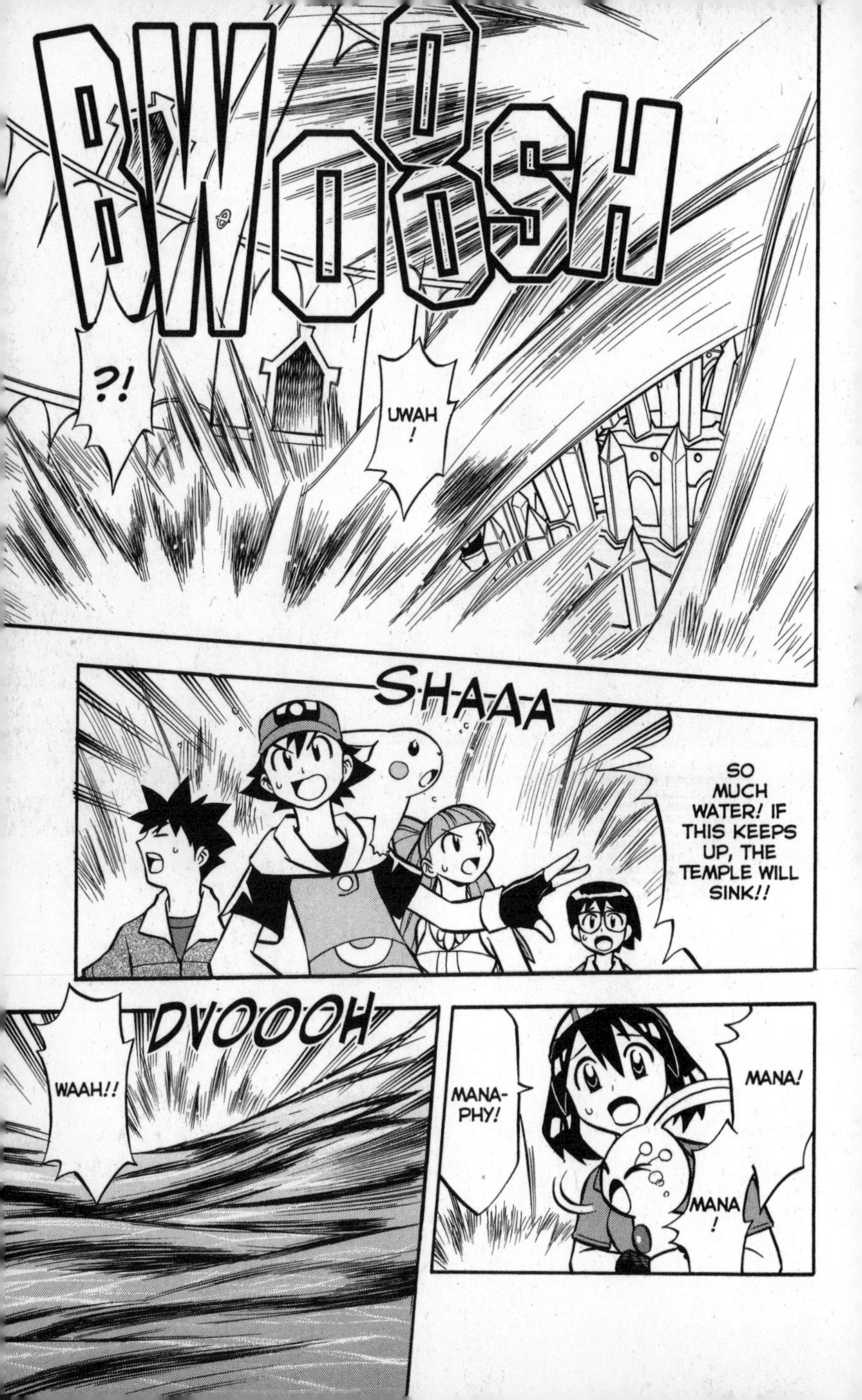
BWOOOSH
UWAH!
?!
SHAAA
SO MUCH WATER! IF THIS KEEPS UP, THE TEMPLE WILL SINK!!
MANA!
MANA-PHY!
MANA!
DVOOOH
WAAH!!

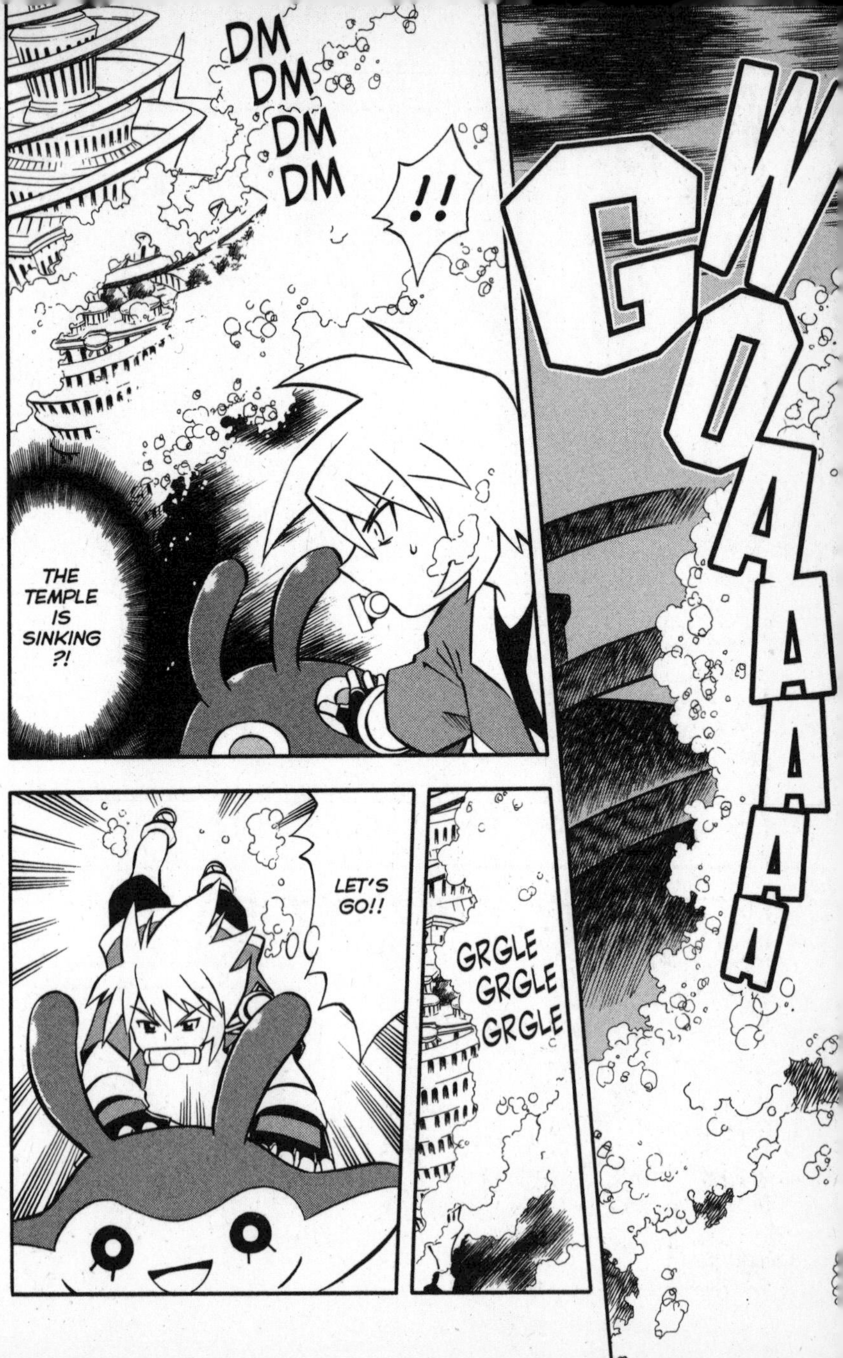
GWOAAAAAA
DM DM DM DM
!!
THE TEMPLE IS SINKING ?!
GRGLE GRGLE GRGLE
LET'S GO!!

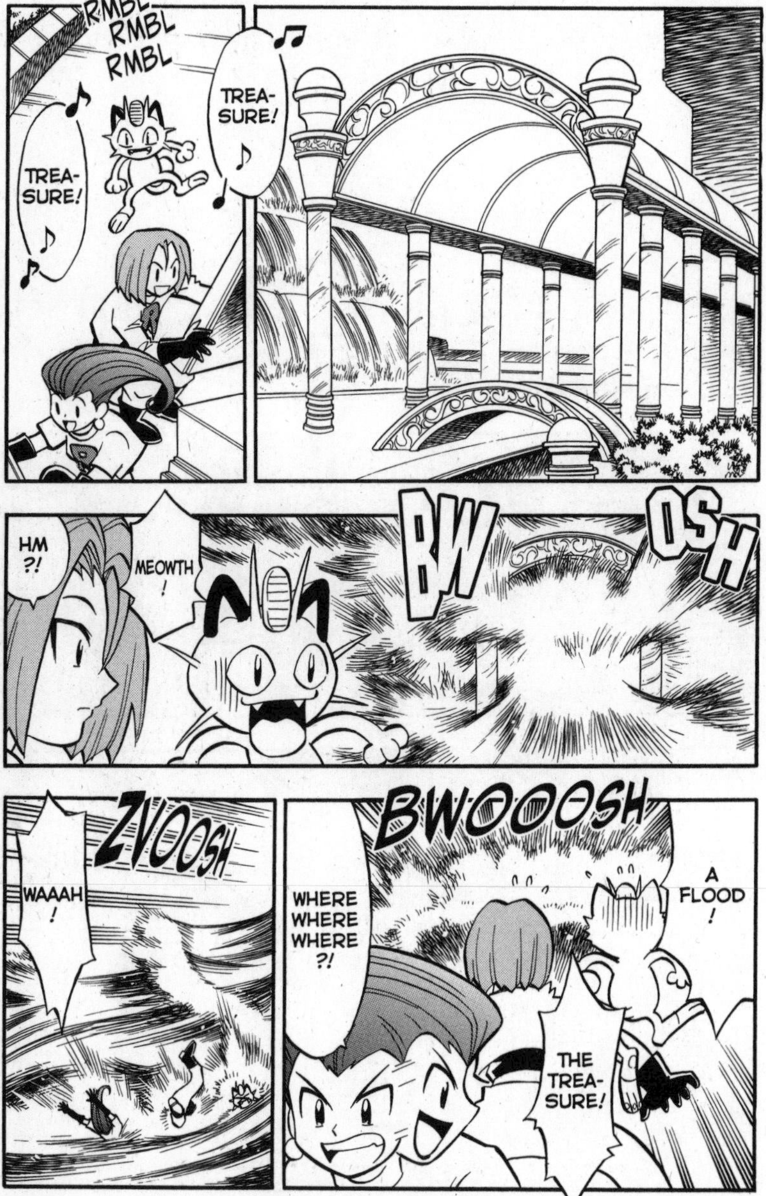
RMBL RMBL RMBL
TREA-SURE!
TREA-SURE!
HM?!
MEOWTH!
BWOSH
ZVOOSH
WAAAH!
BWOOOSH
WHERE WHERE WHERE?!
A FLOOD!
THE TREA-SURE!

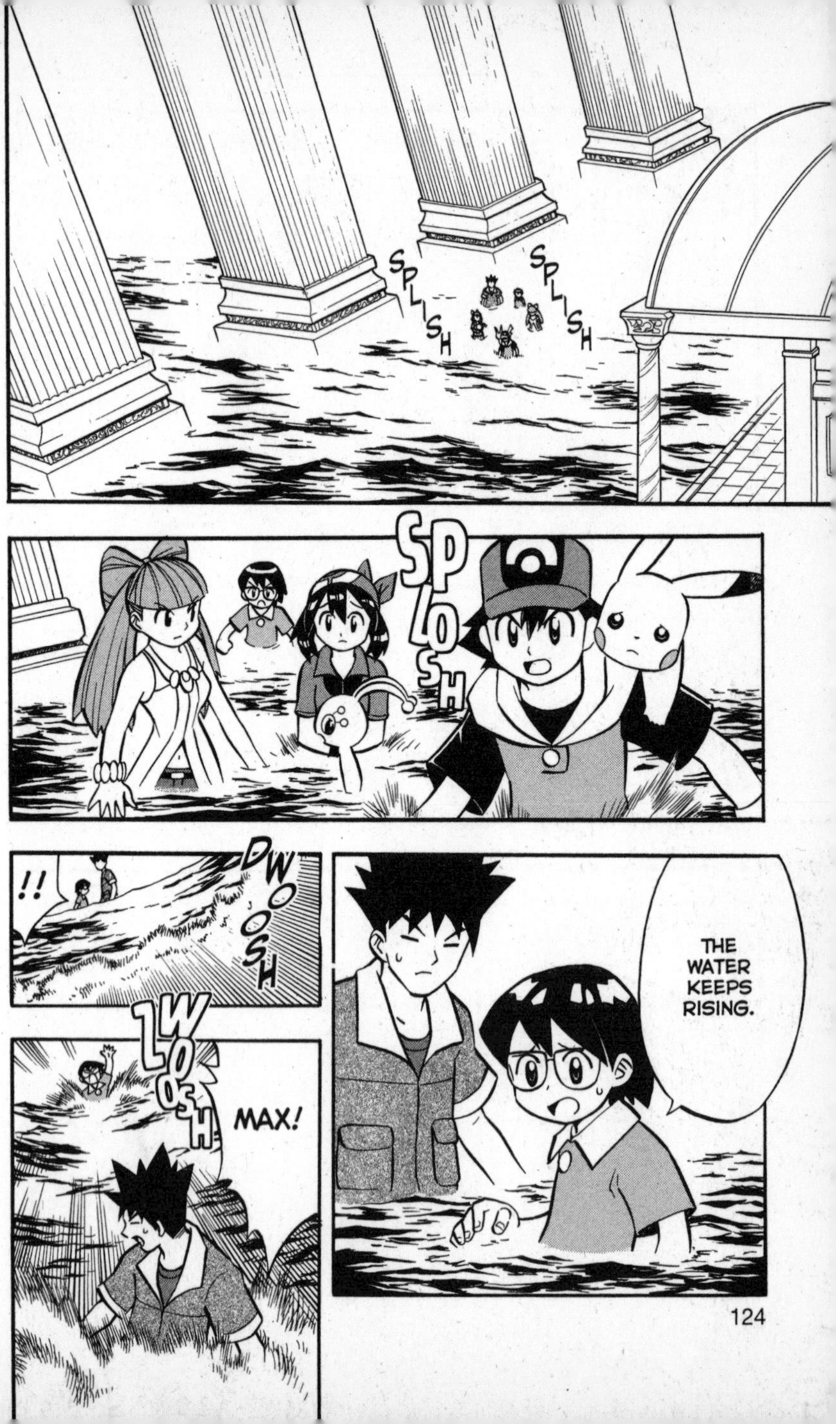
SPLISH
SPLISH
SPLOSH
THE WATER KEEPS RISING.
!!
DWOOSH
ZWOOSH
MAX!

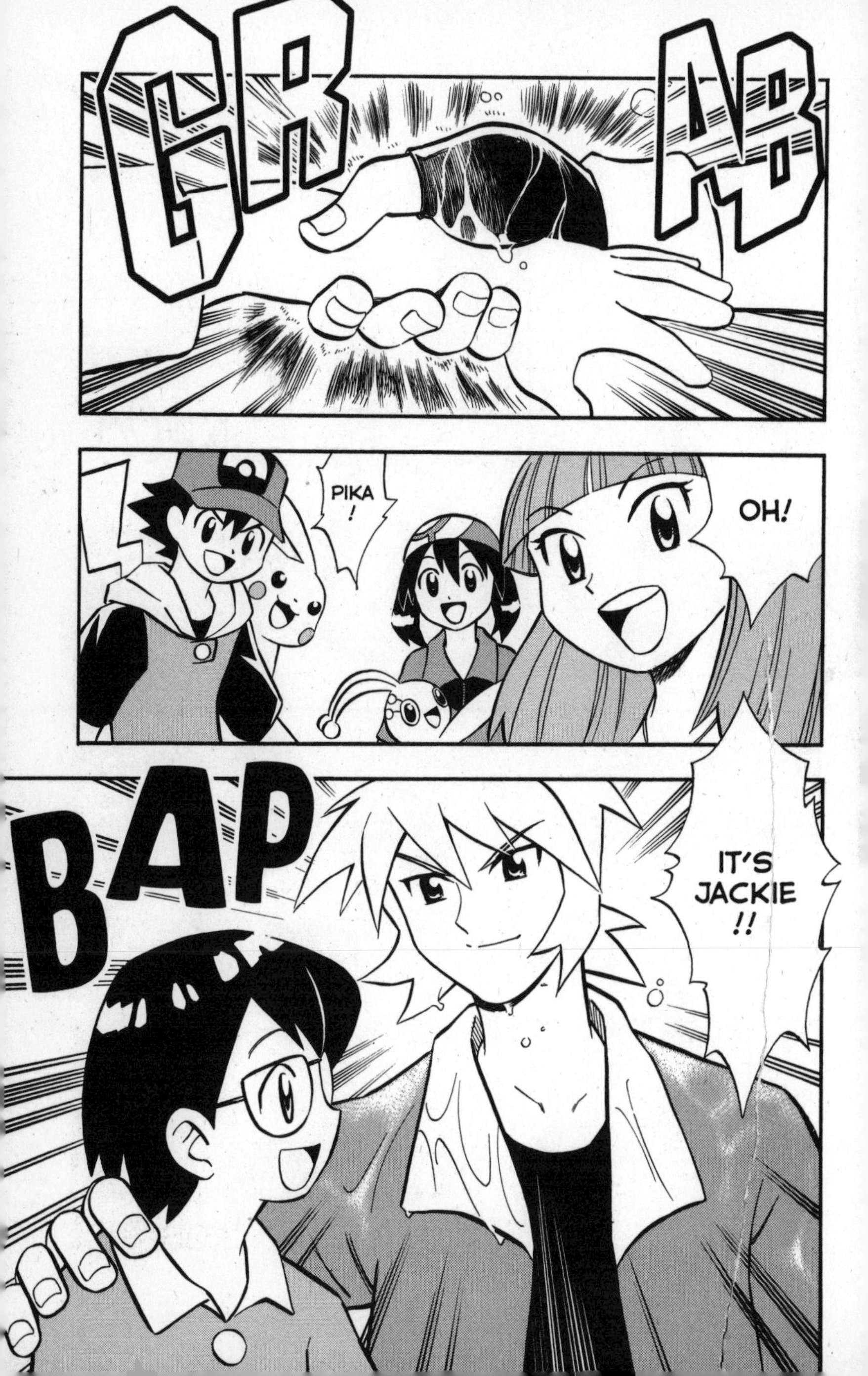
GRAB
OH!
PIKA !
BAP
IT'S JACKIE !!

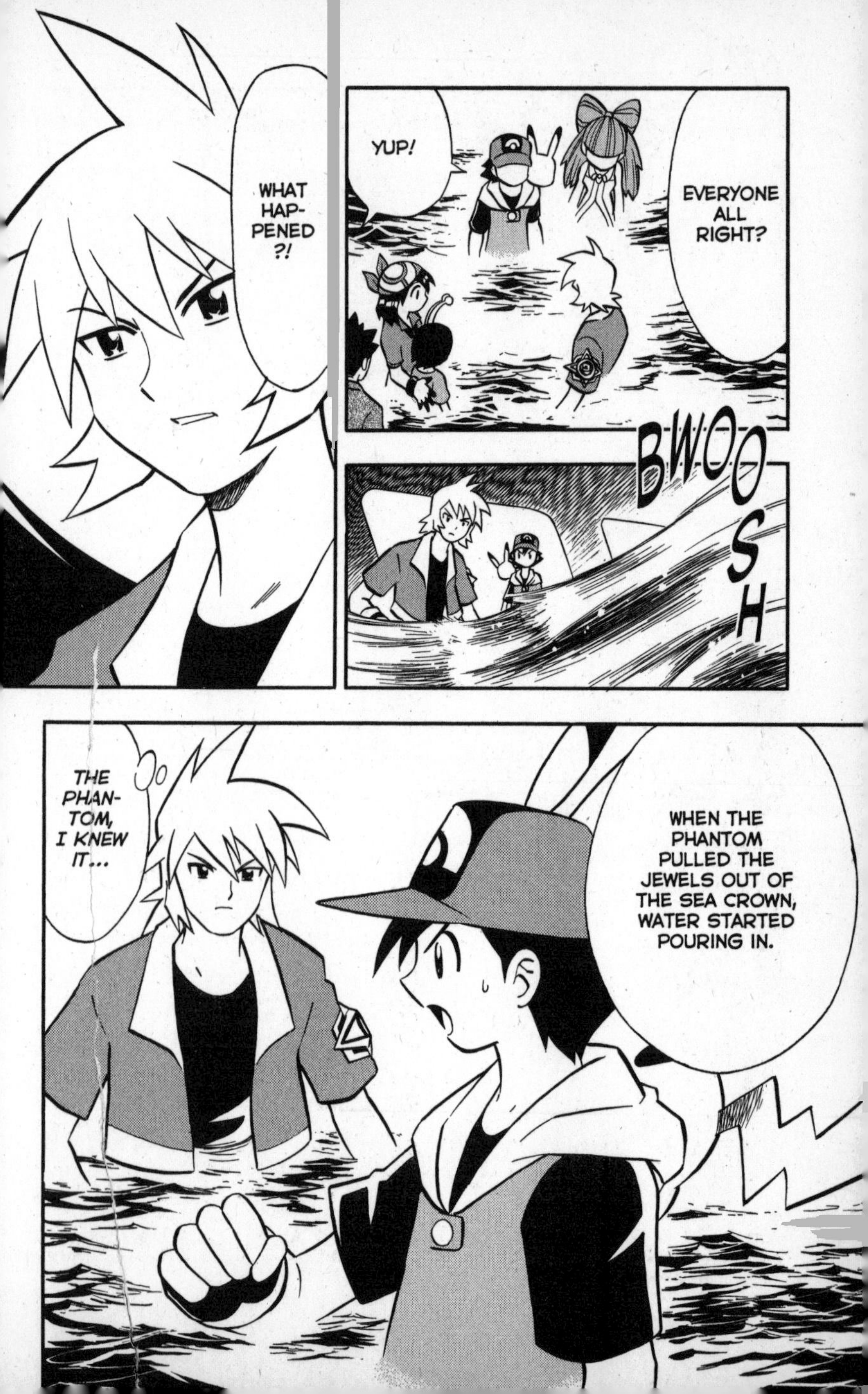
EVERYONE ALL RIGHT?
YUP!
BWOOSH
WHAT HAP-PENED ?!
WHEN THE PHANTOM PULLED THE JEWELS OUT OF THE SEA CROWN, WATER STARTED POURING IN.
THE PHAN-TOM, I KNEW IT...

READ THIS WAY

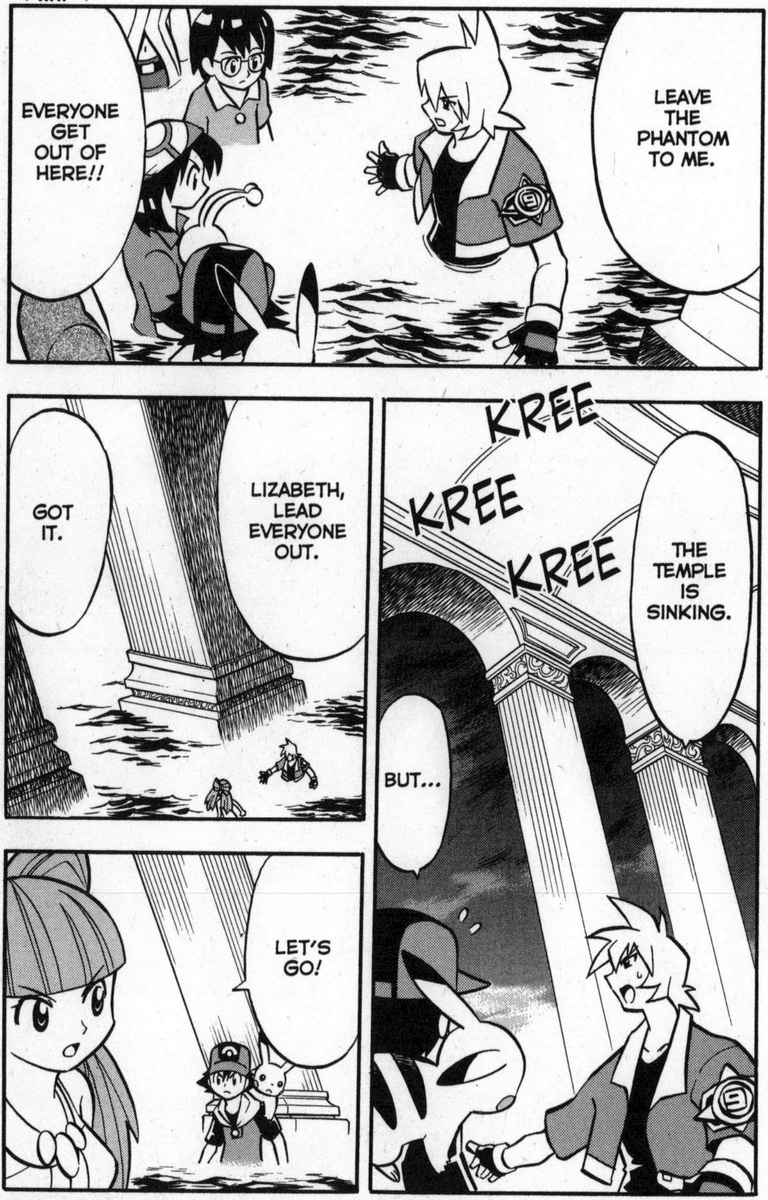
LEAVE THE PHANTOM TO ME.
EVERYONE GET OUT OF HERE!!
KREE
KREE
KREE
THE TEMPLE IS SINKING.
BUT...
LIZABETH, LEAD EVERYONE OUT.
GOT IT.
LET'S GO!

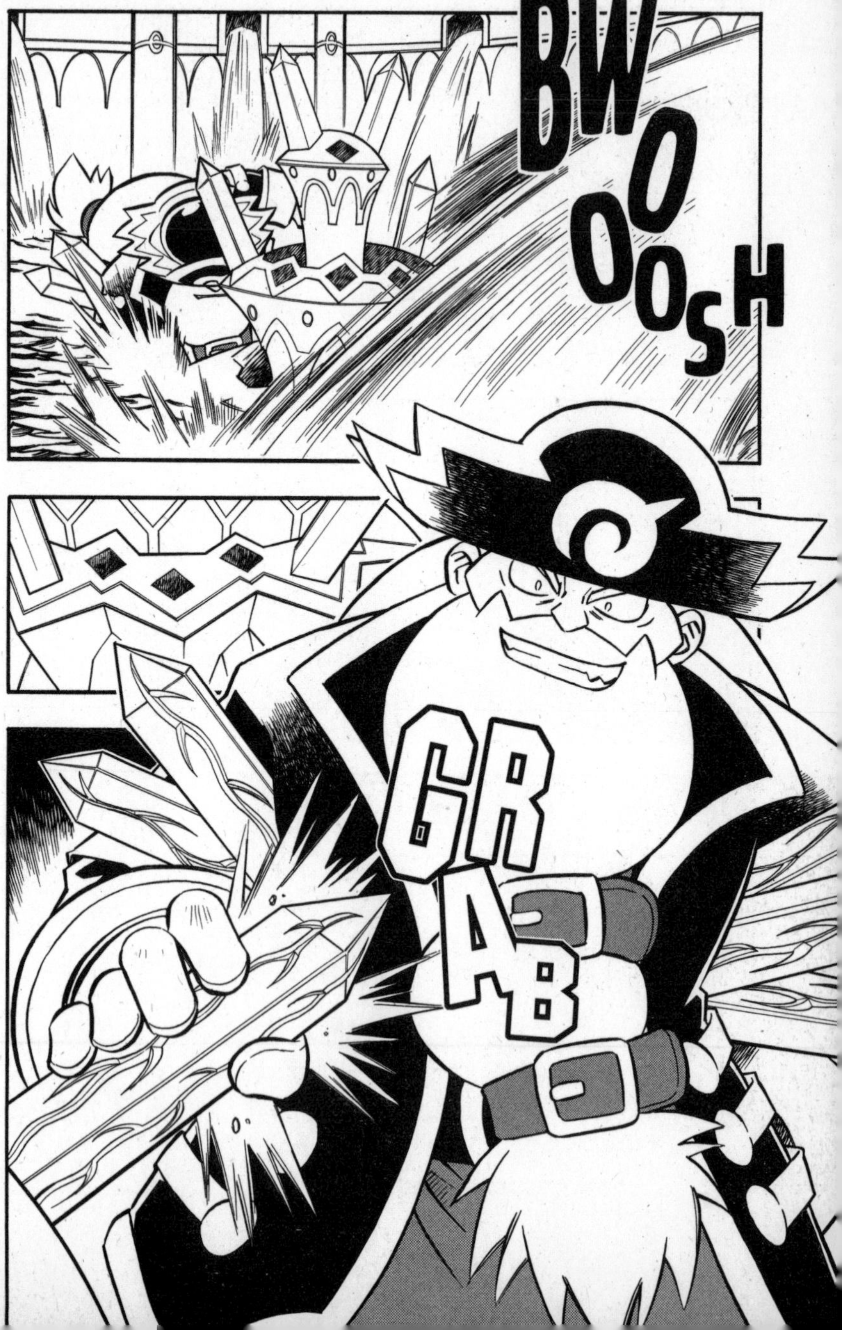
BWOOOOSH
GRAB

READ THIS WAY

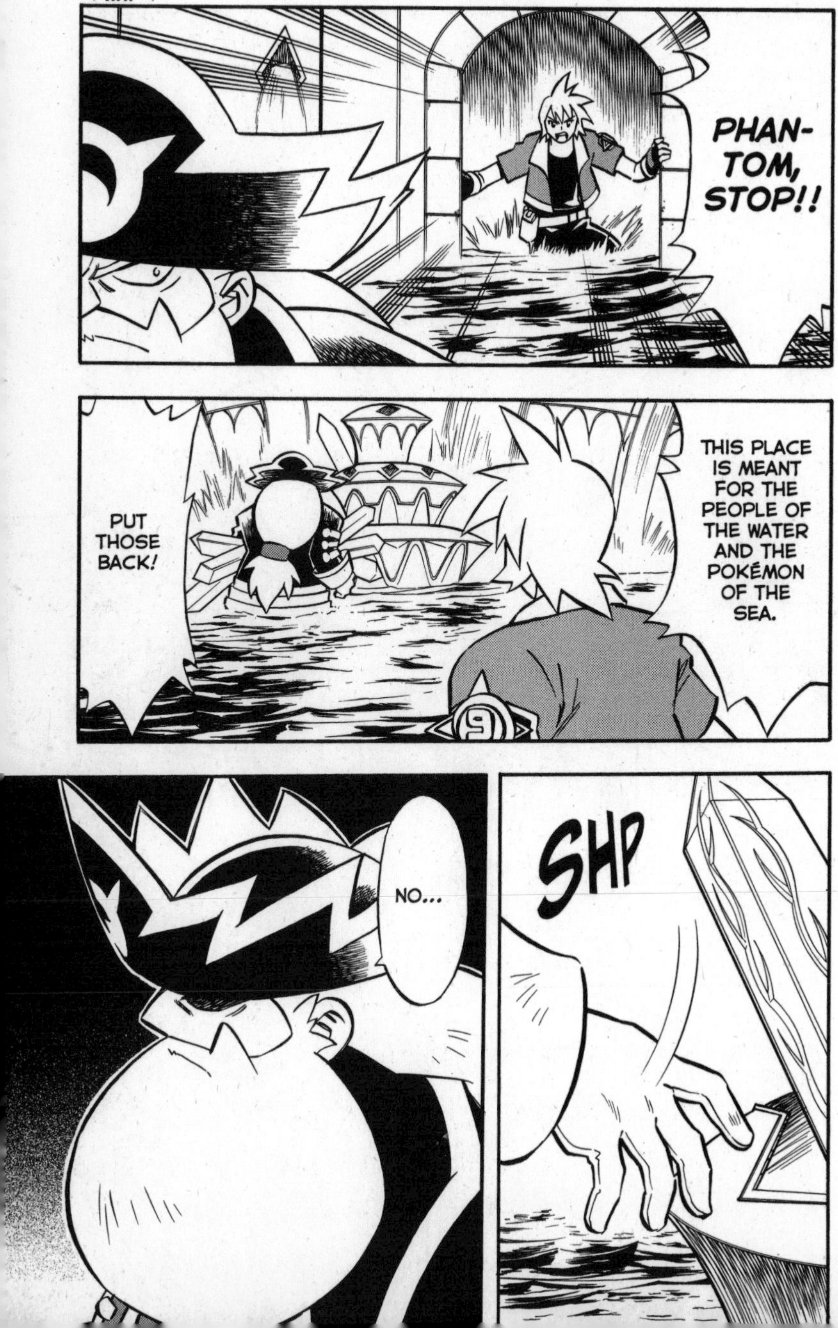
PHAN-TOM, STOP!!
THIS PLACE IS MEANT FOR THE PEOPLE OF THE WATER AND THE POKÉMON OF THE SEA.
PUT THOSE BACK!
SHP
NO...

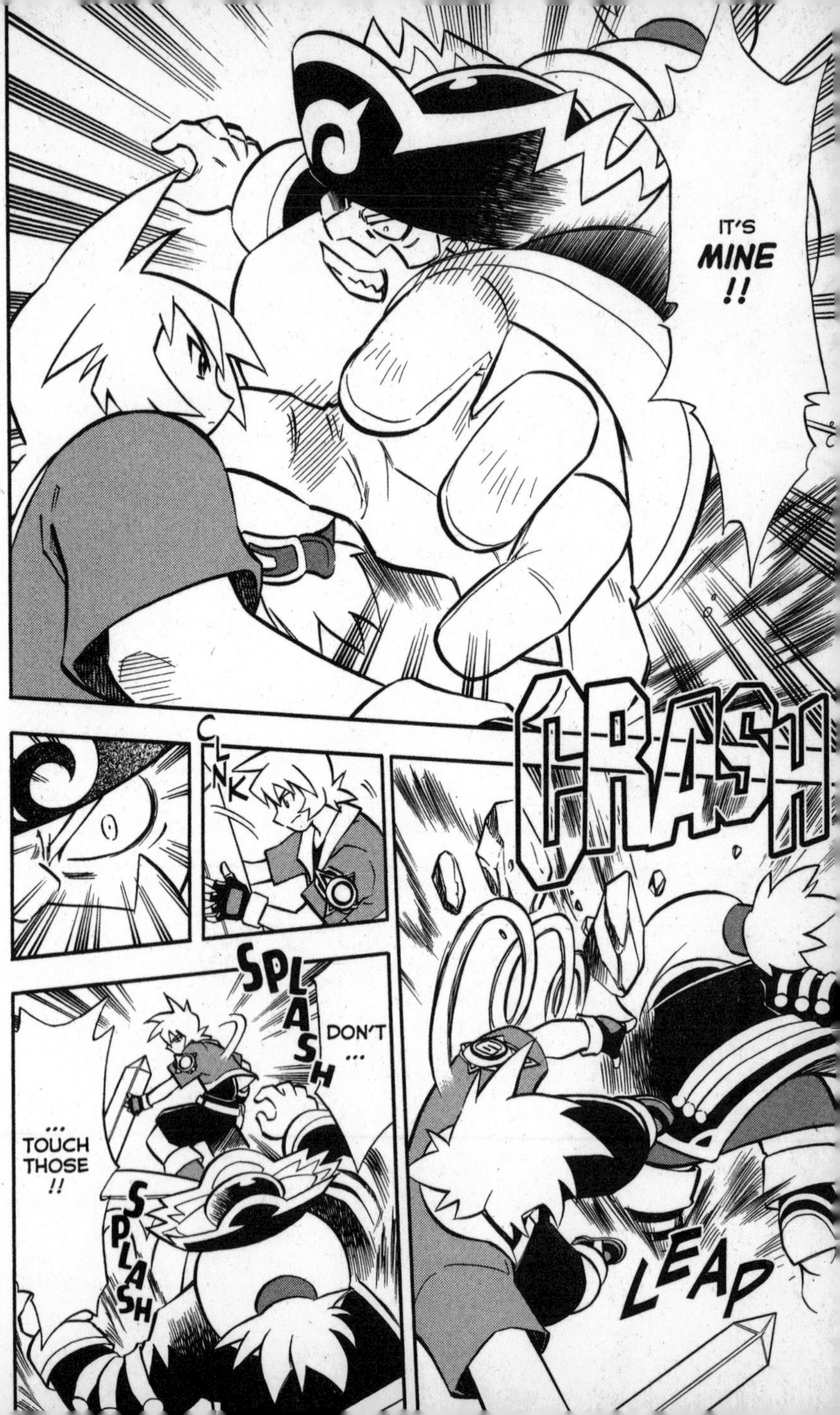
IT'S MINE !!
CRASH
LEAP
CLNK
SPLASH
DON'T ...
... TOUCH THOSE !!
SPLASH

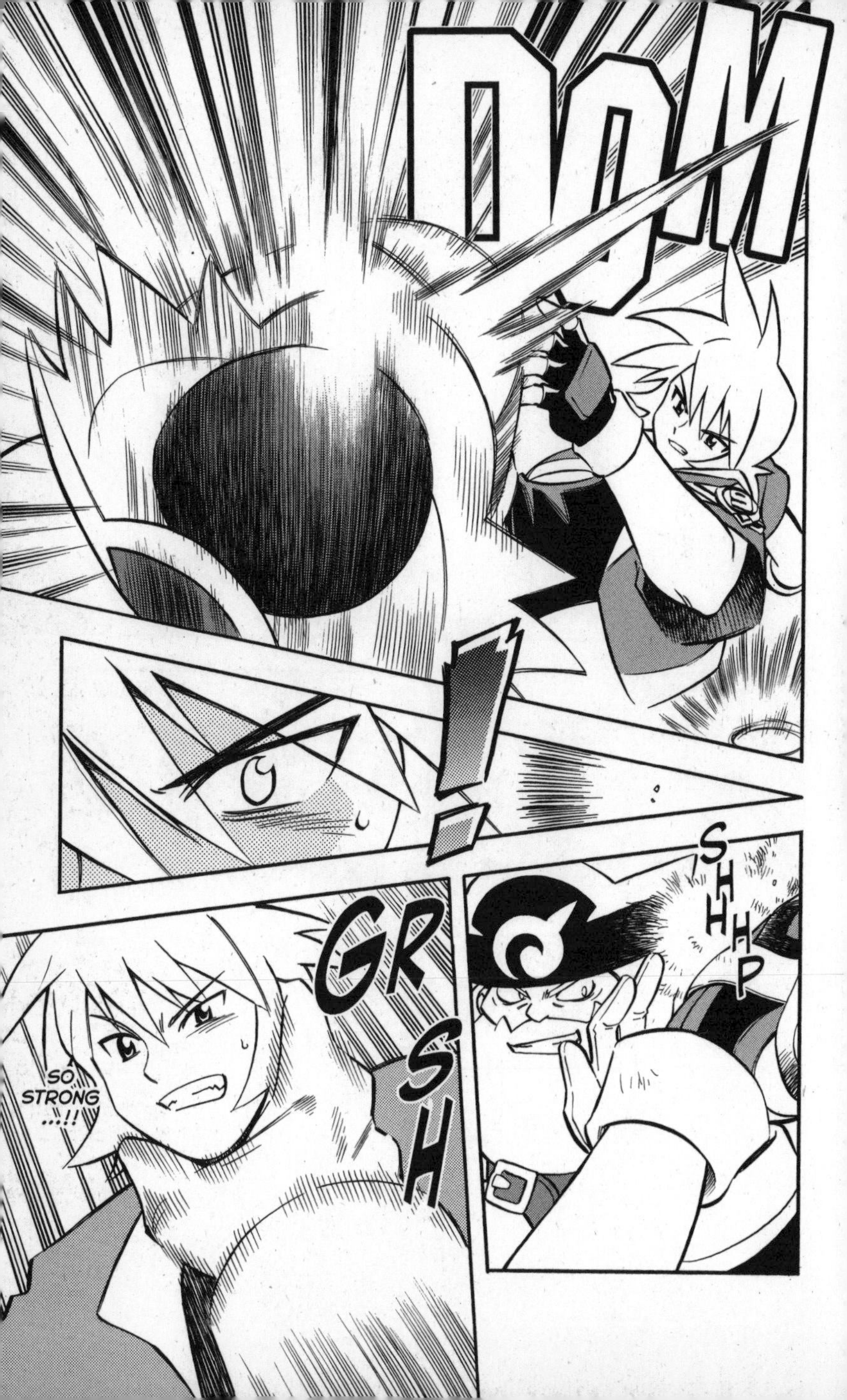
DOM
!
SHHHP
GRSH
SO STRONG ...!!

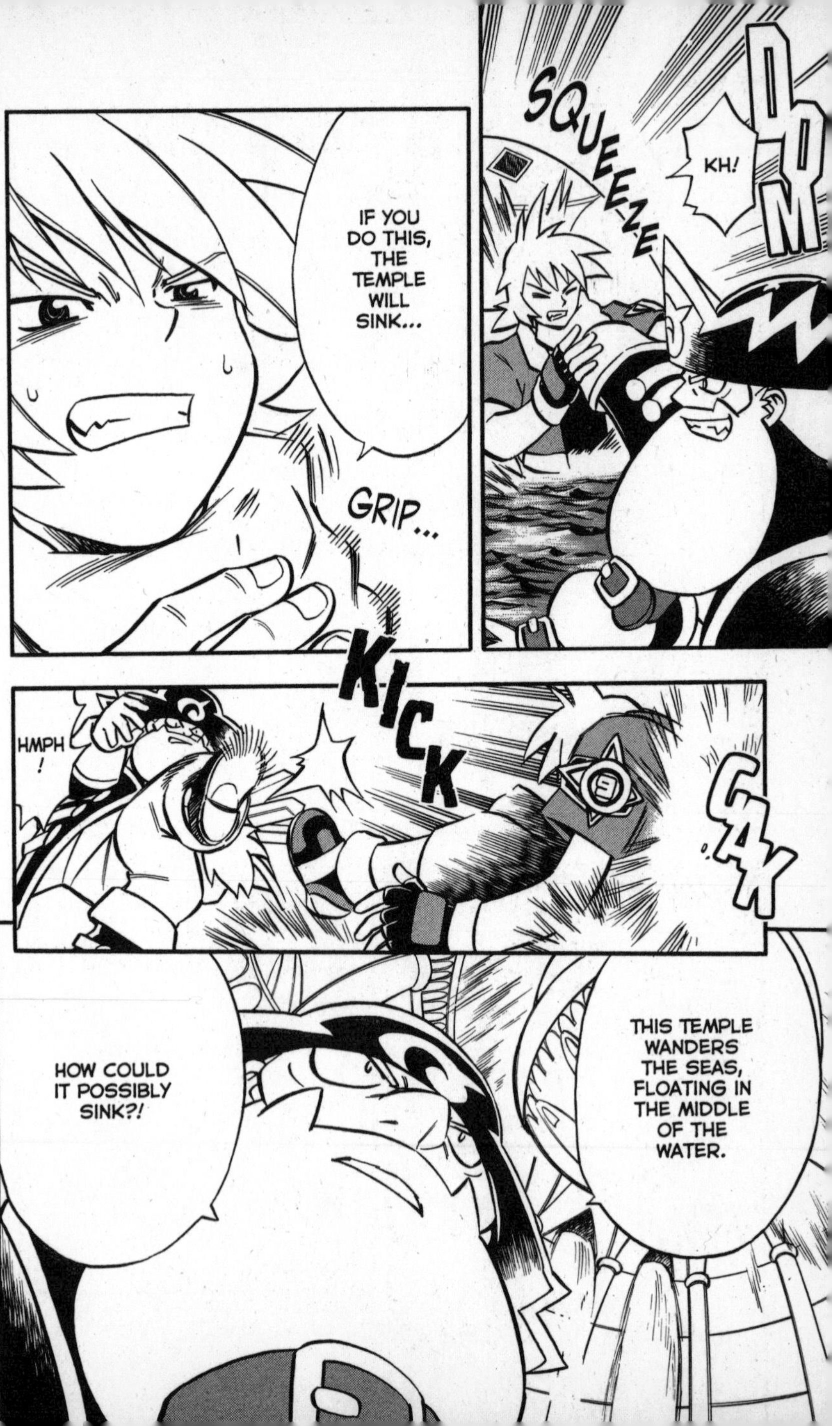
DOOM
KH!
SQUEEZE
IF YOU DO THIS, THE TEMPLE WILL SINK...
GRIP...
GAK
KICK
HMPH!
THIS TEMPLE WANDERS THE SEAS, FLOATING IN THE MIDDLE OF THE WATER.
HOW COULD IT POSSIBLY SINK?!

READ THIS WAY

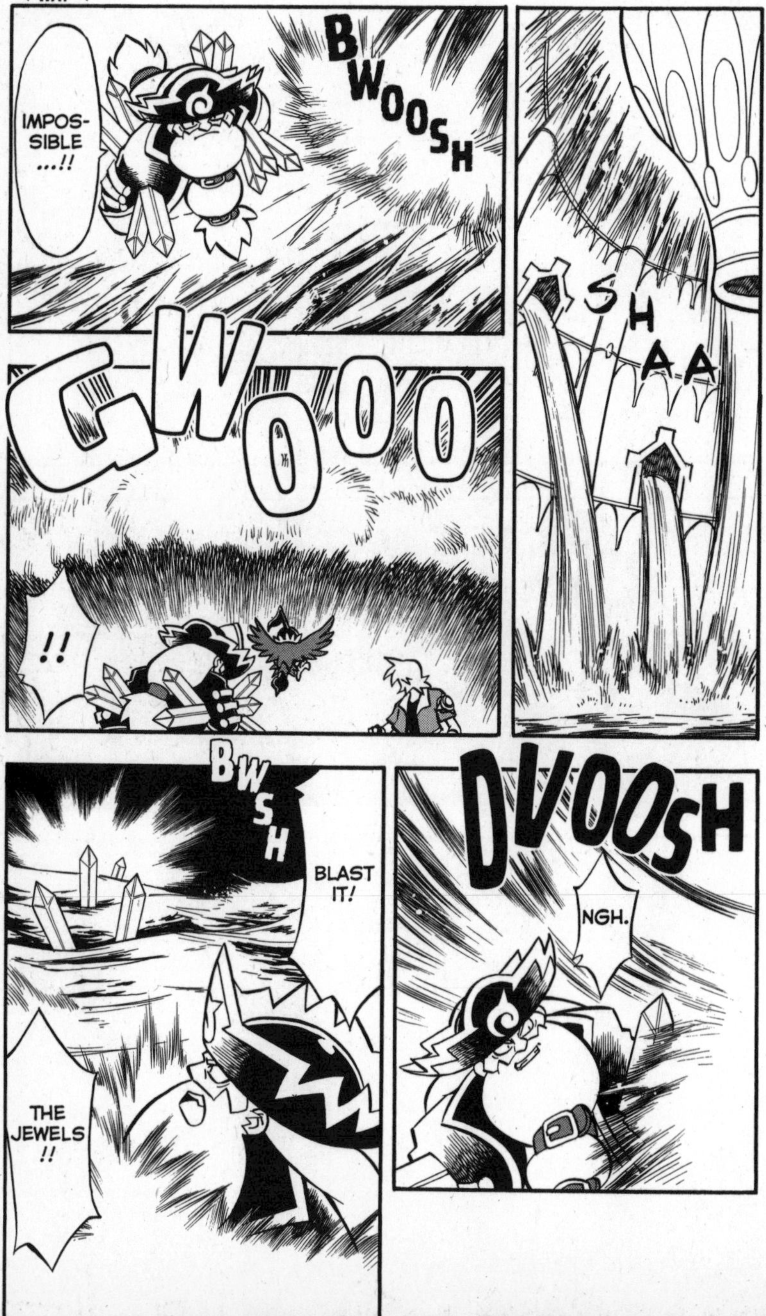
SHAA
BWOOSH
IMPOSSIBLE ...!!
GWOOO
!!
DVOOSH
NGH.
BWSH
BLAST IT!
THE JEWELS!!

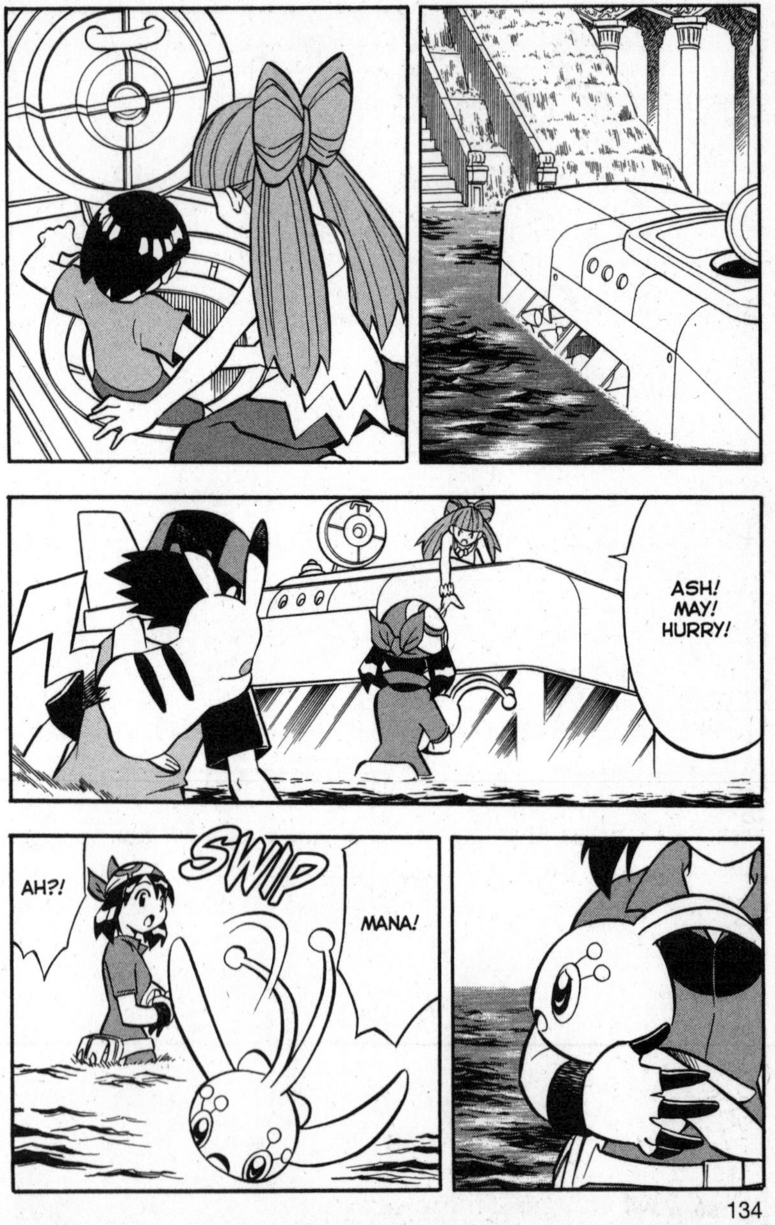
ASH! MAY! HURRY!
MANA!
SWIP
AH?!

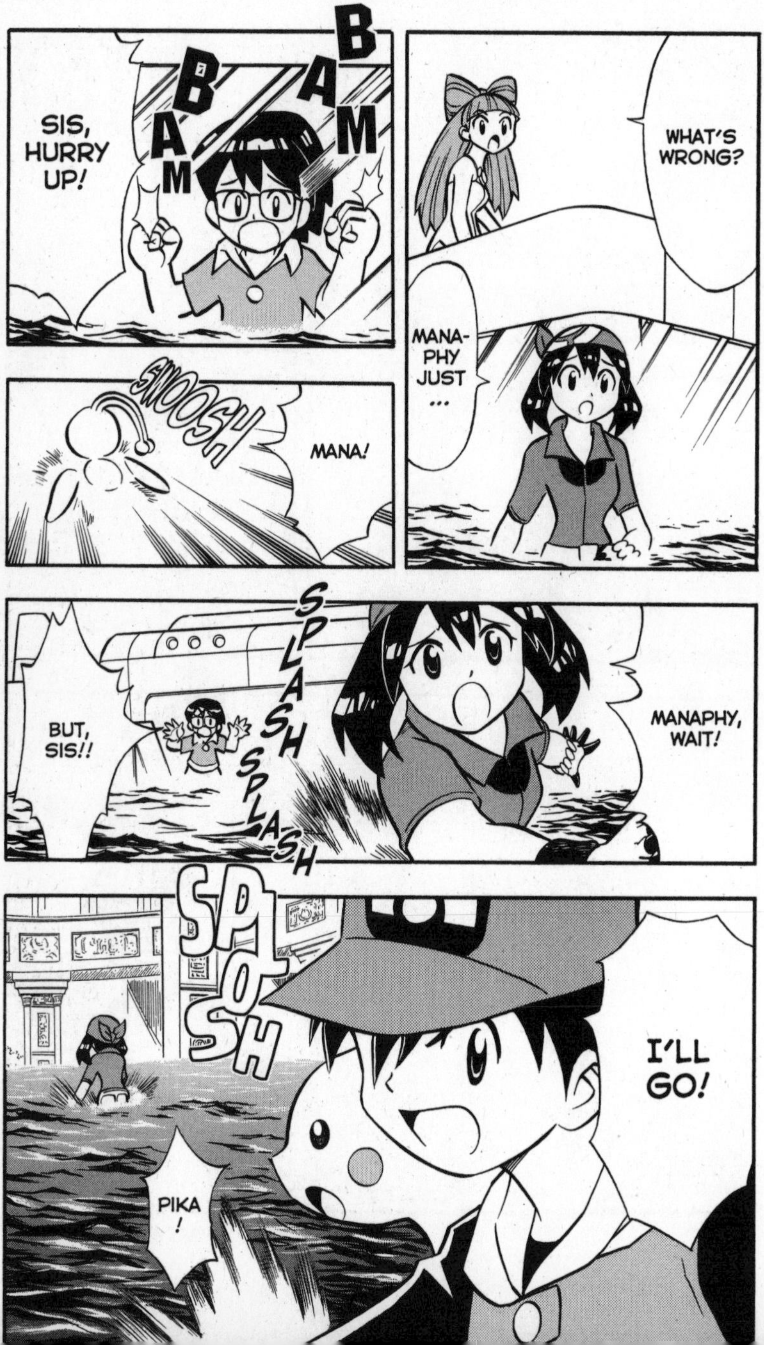
WHAT'S WRONG?
MANAPHY JUST...
BAM
BAM
SIS, HURRY UP!
SWOOSH
MANA!
MANAPHY, WAIT!
SPLASH
SPLASH
BUT, SIS!!
I'LL GO!
SPLOOSH
PIKA!

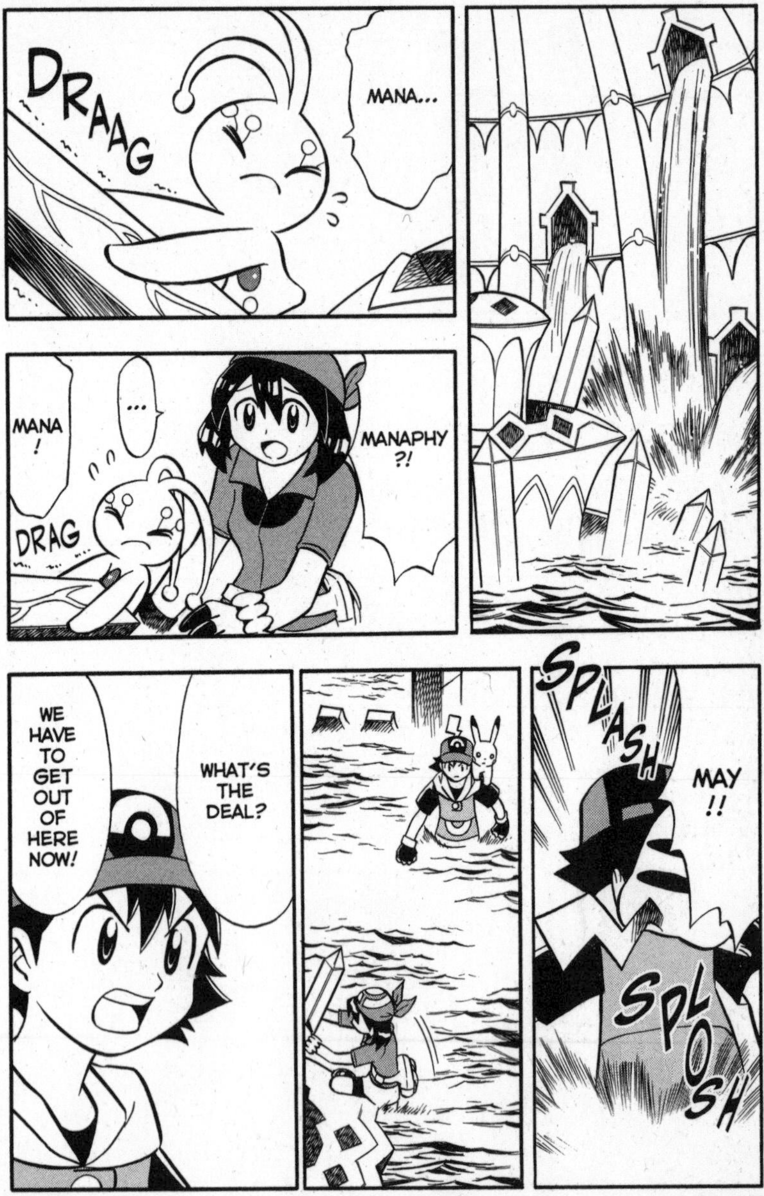
MANA...
DRAAG
MANAPHY ?!
...
MANA !
DRAG
SPLASH
MAY !!
SPLOSH
WHAT'S THE DEAL?
WE HAVE TO GET OUT OF HERE NOW!

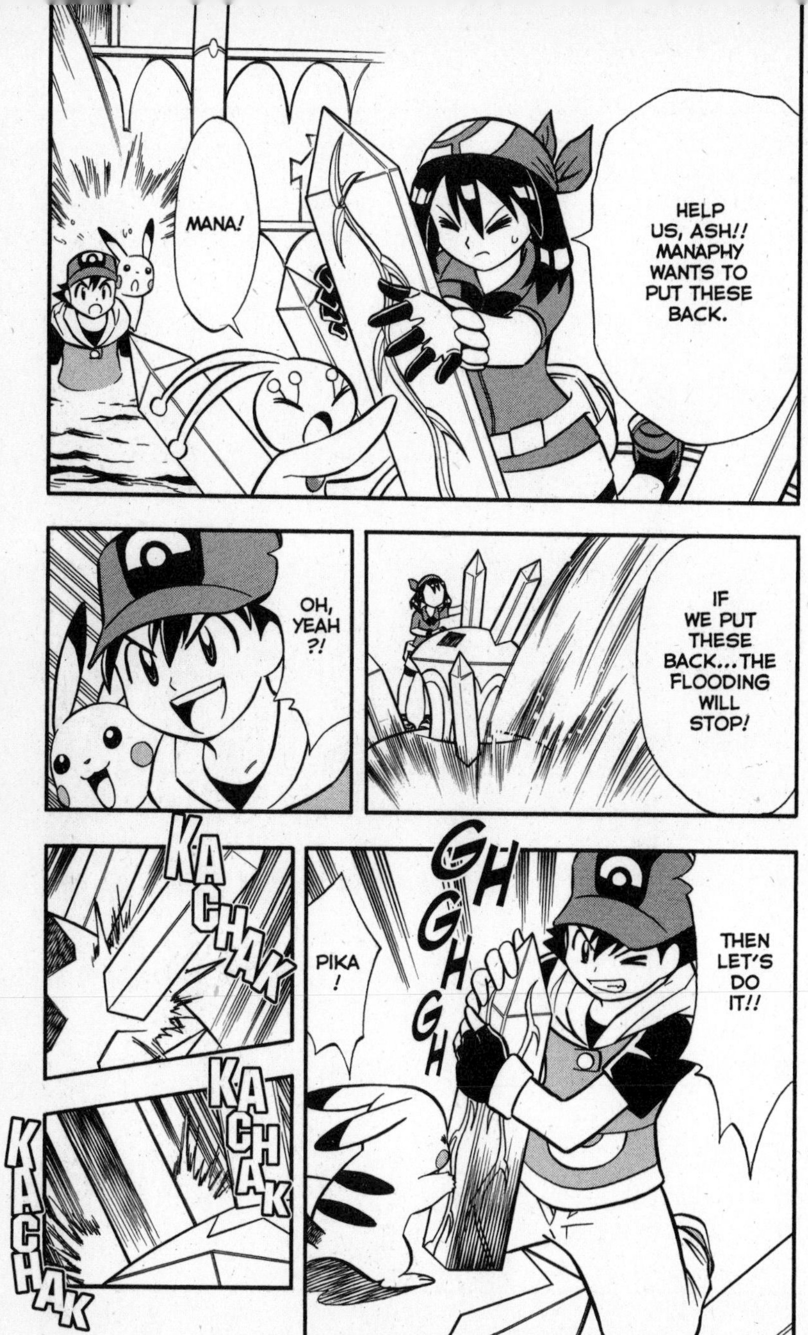
HELP US, ASH!! MANAPHY WANTS TO PUT THESE BACK.
MANA!
IF WE PUT THESE BACK...THE FLOODING WILL STOP!
OH, YEAH ?!
THEN LET'S DO IT!!
GHGHGHGH
PIKA !
KACHAK
KACHAK
KACHAK

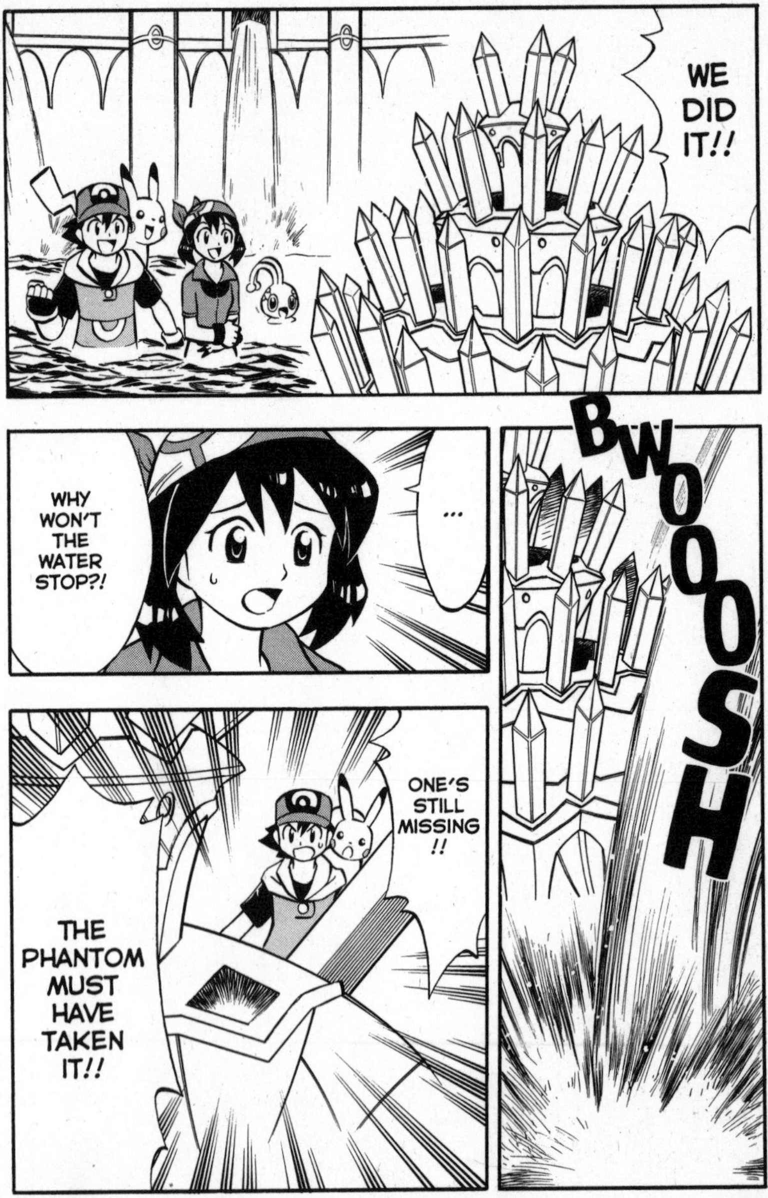
WE DID IT!!
BWOOOOSH
...
WHY WON'T THE WATER STOP?!
ONE'S STILL MISSING!!
THE PHANTOM MUST HAVE TAKEN IT!!

READ THIS WAY

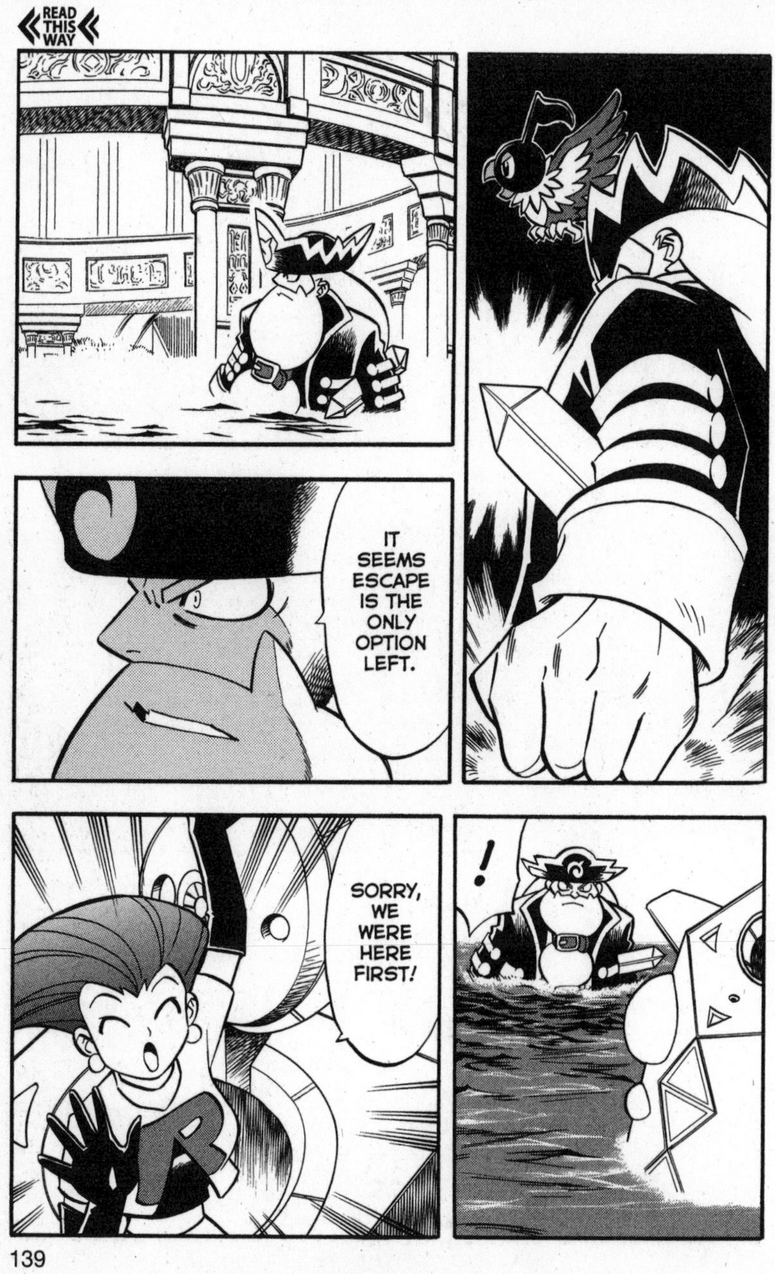
IT SEEMS ESCAPE IS THE ONLY OPTION LEFT.
!
SORRY, WE WERE HERE FIRST!

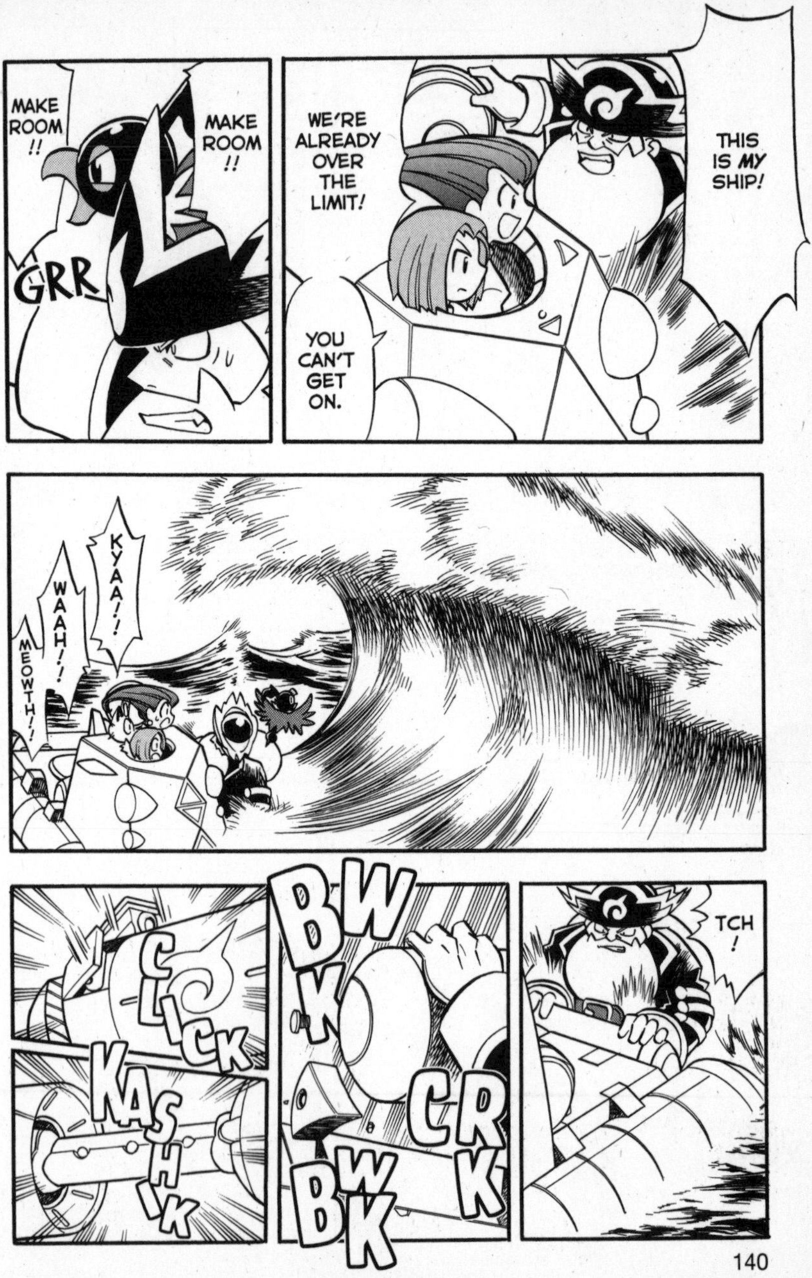
THIS IS MY SHIP!
WE'RE ALREADY OVER THE LIMIT!
YOU CAN'T GET ON.
MAKE ROOM!!
MAKE ROOM!!
GRR
KYAA!!
WAAAH!!
MEOWTH!!
TCH!
BWK
CRK
BWK
CLICK
KASHIK

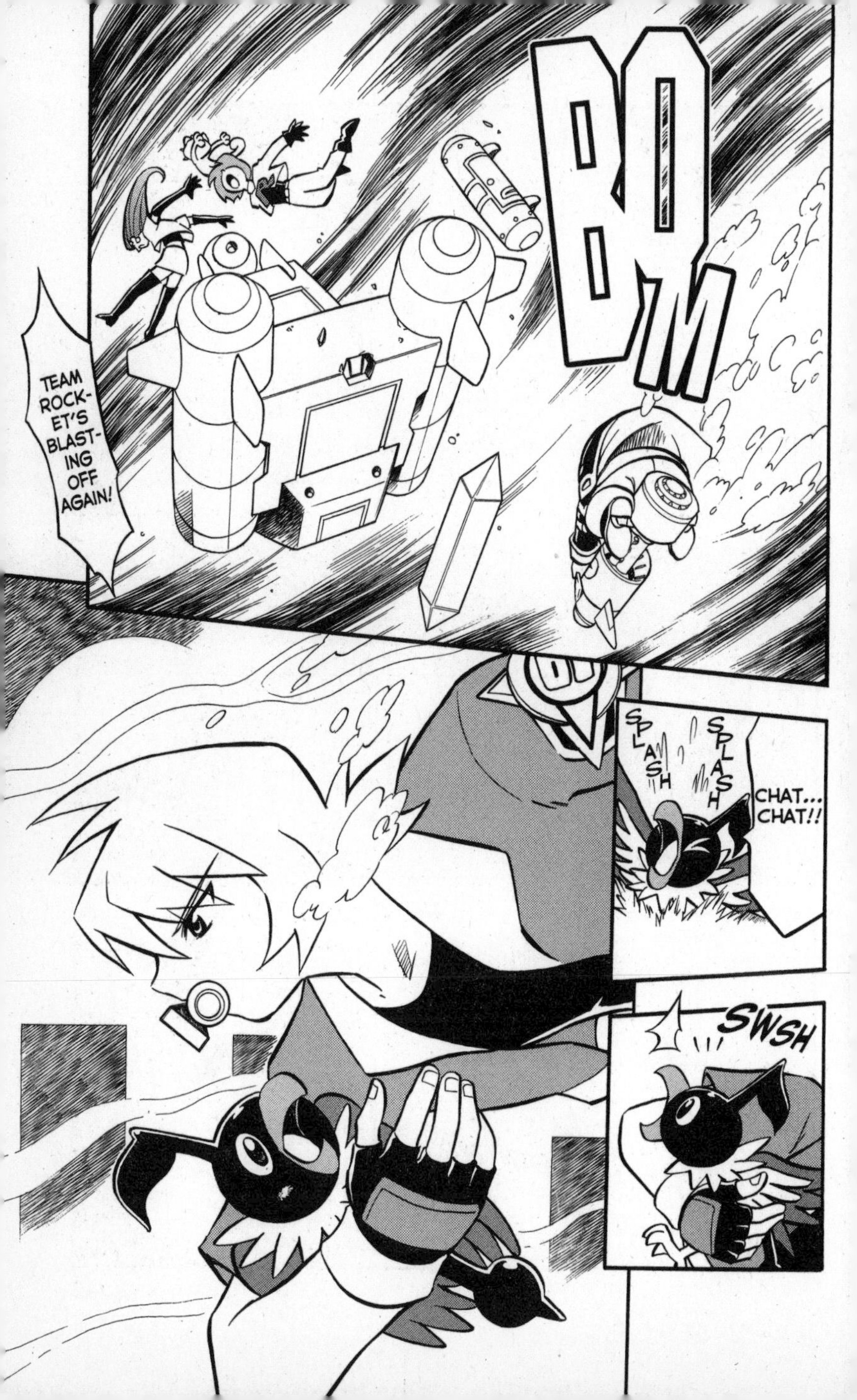
BOOM
TEAM ROCKET'S BLASTING OFF AGAIN!
SPLASH SPLASH
CHAT... CHAT!!
SWSH

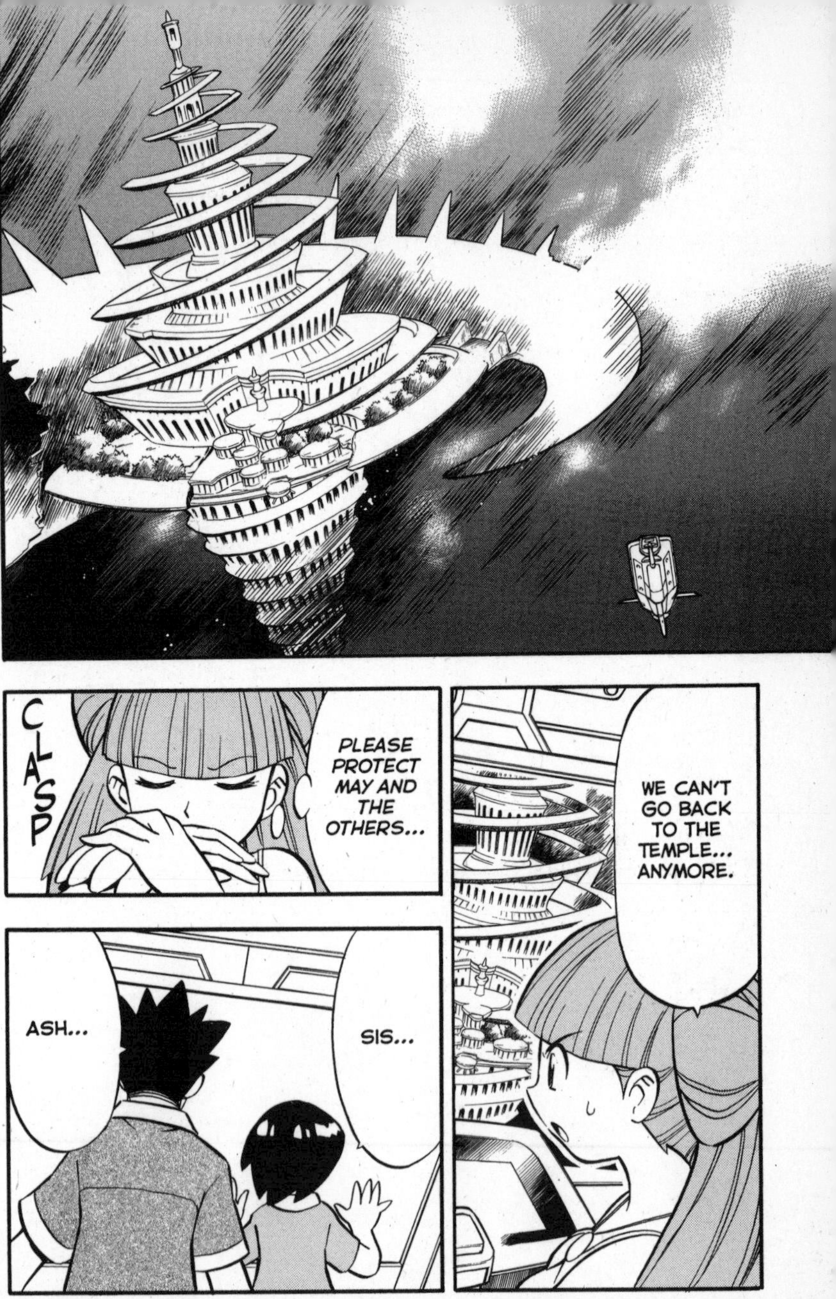
WE CAN'T GO BACK TO THE TEMPLE... ANYMORE.
CLASP
PLEASE PROTECT MAY AND THE OTHERS...
SIS...
ASH...

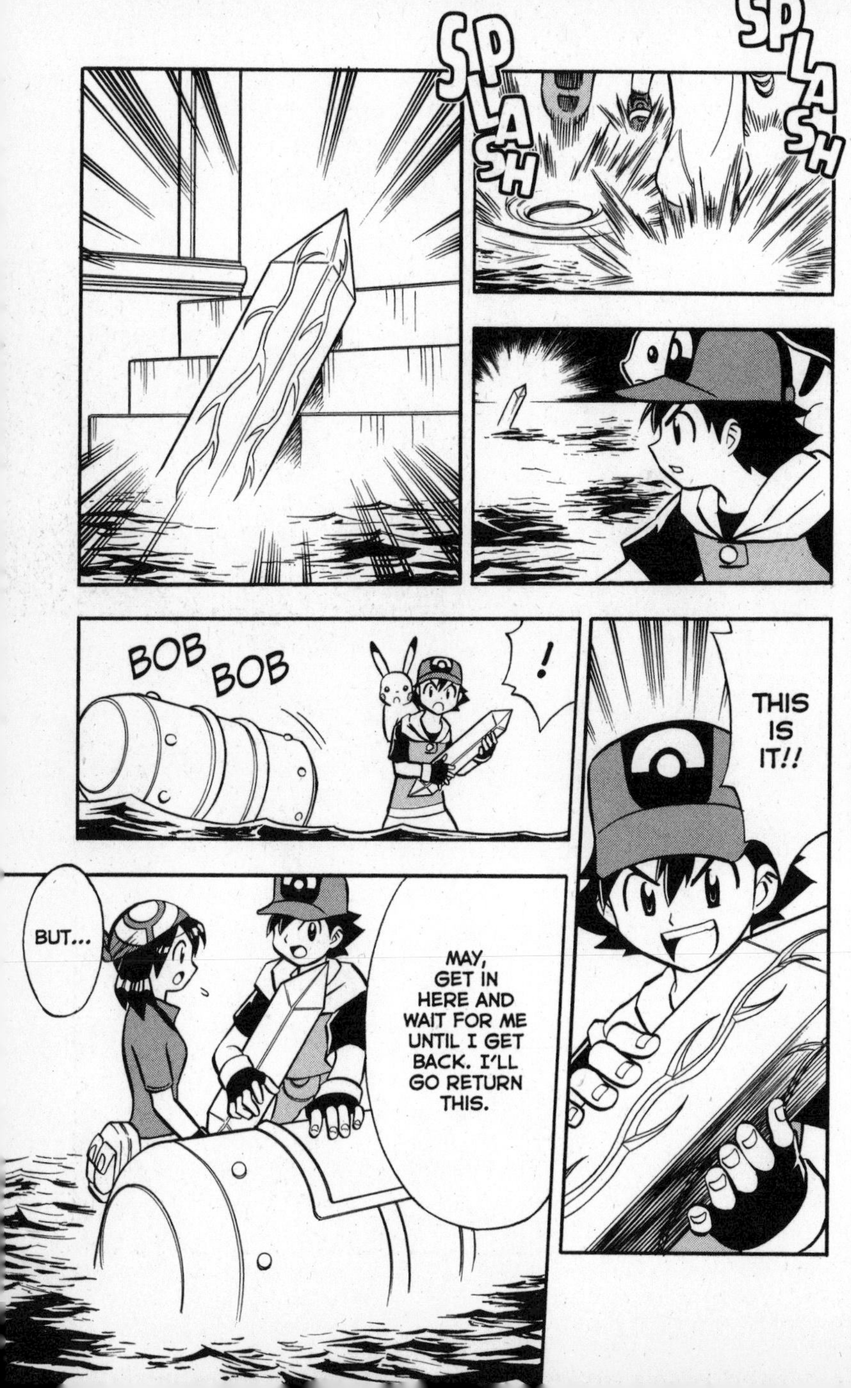
SPLASH
SPLASH
!
BOB BOB
THIS IS IT!!
MAY, GET IN HERE AND WAIT FOR ME UNTIL I GET BACK. I'LL GO RETURN THIS.
BUT...

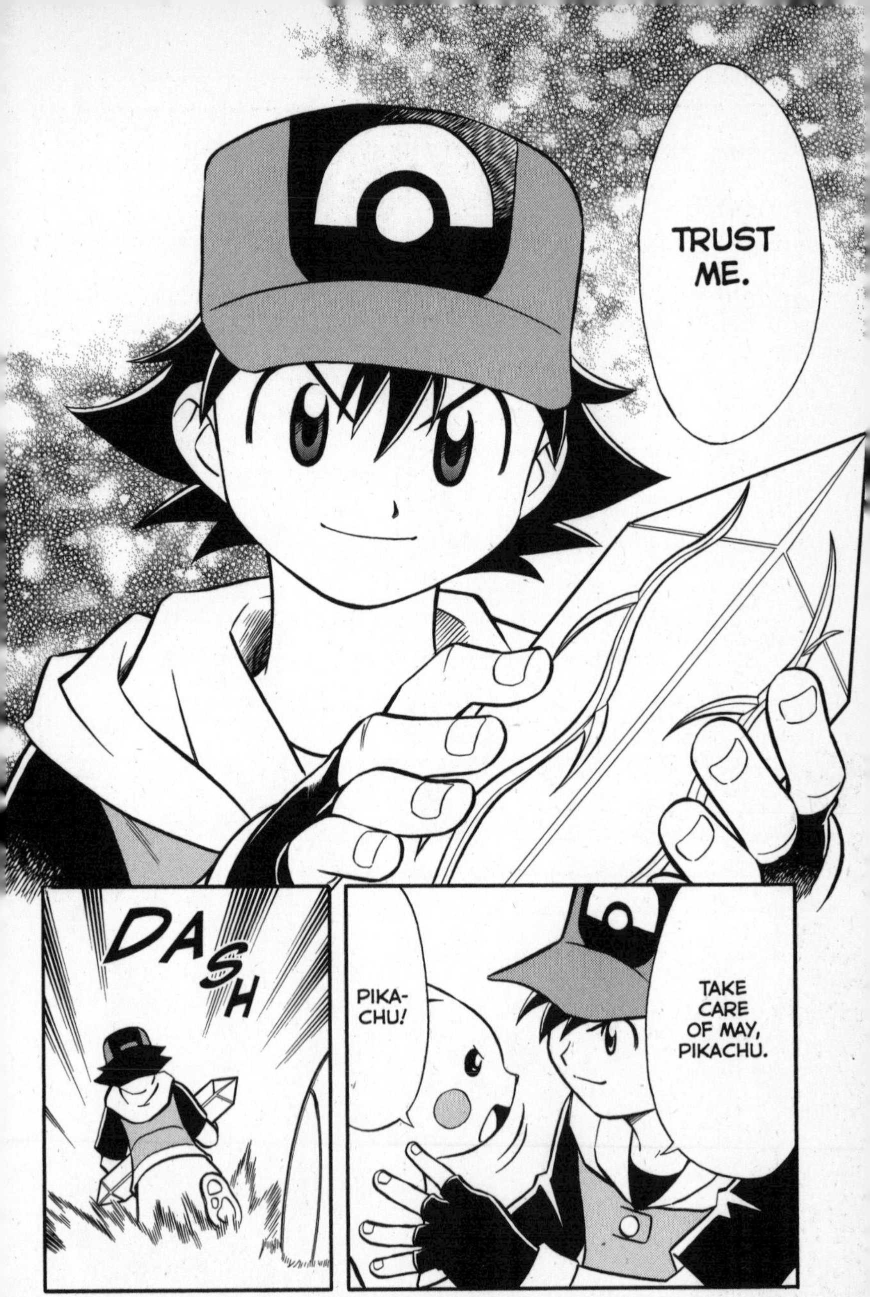
TRUST ME.
TAKE CARE OF MAY, PIKACHU.
PIKA-CHU!
DASH

READ THIS WAY

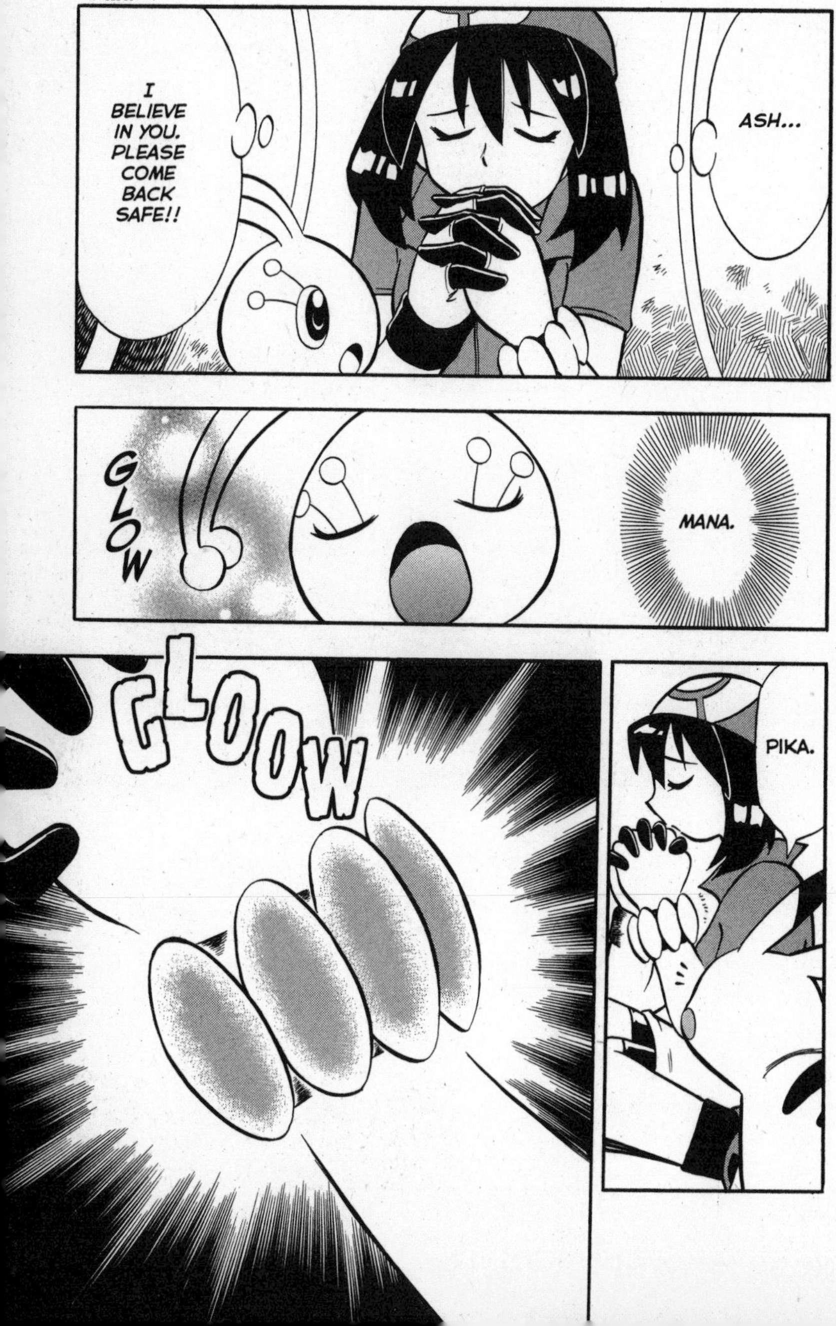
ASH...
I BELIEVE IN YOU. PLEASE COME BACK SAFE!!
MANA.
GLOW
PIKA.
GLOOW

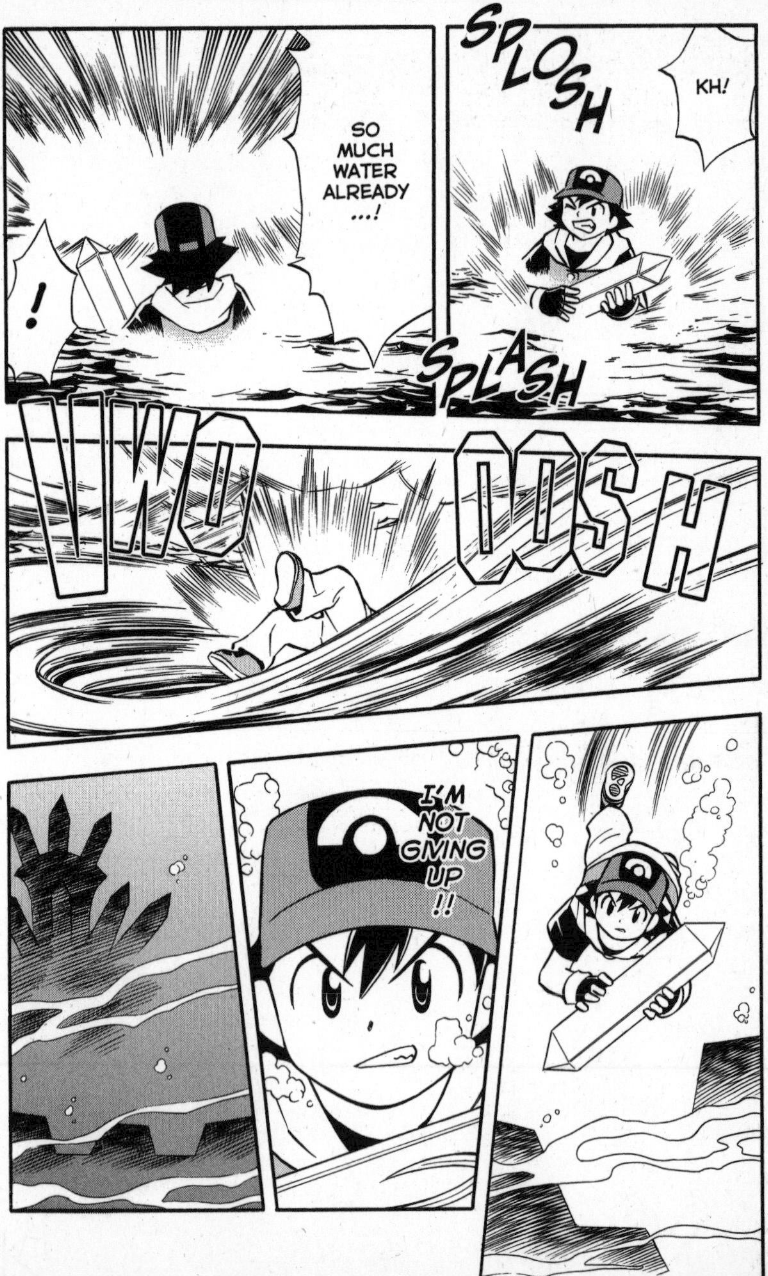
SPLOSH
KH!
SPLASH
SO MUCH WATER ALREADY ...!
!
VWOOOSH
I'M NOT GIVING UP !!

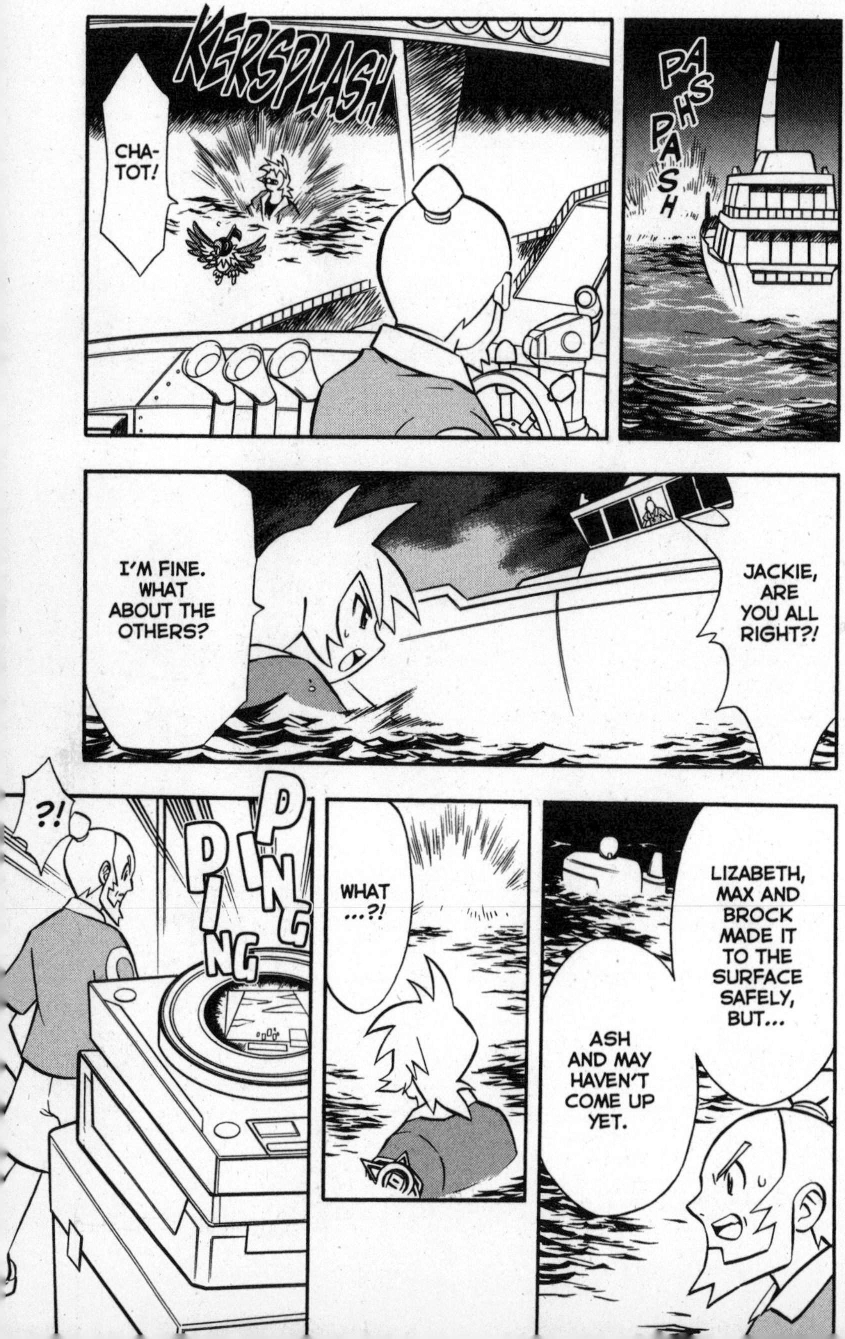
PASH
PASH
KERSPLASH
CHATOT!
JACKIE, ARE YOU ALL RIGHT?!
I'M FINE. WHAT ABOUT THE OTHERS?
LIZABETH, MAX AND BROCK MADE IT TO THE SURFACE SAFELY, BUT...
ASH AND MAY HAVEN'T COME UP YET.
WHAT ...?!
?!
PING
PING

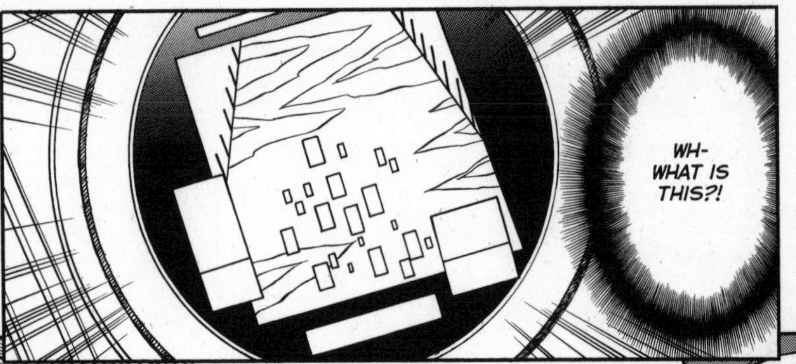
WH-
WHAT IS
THIS?!
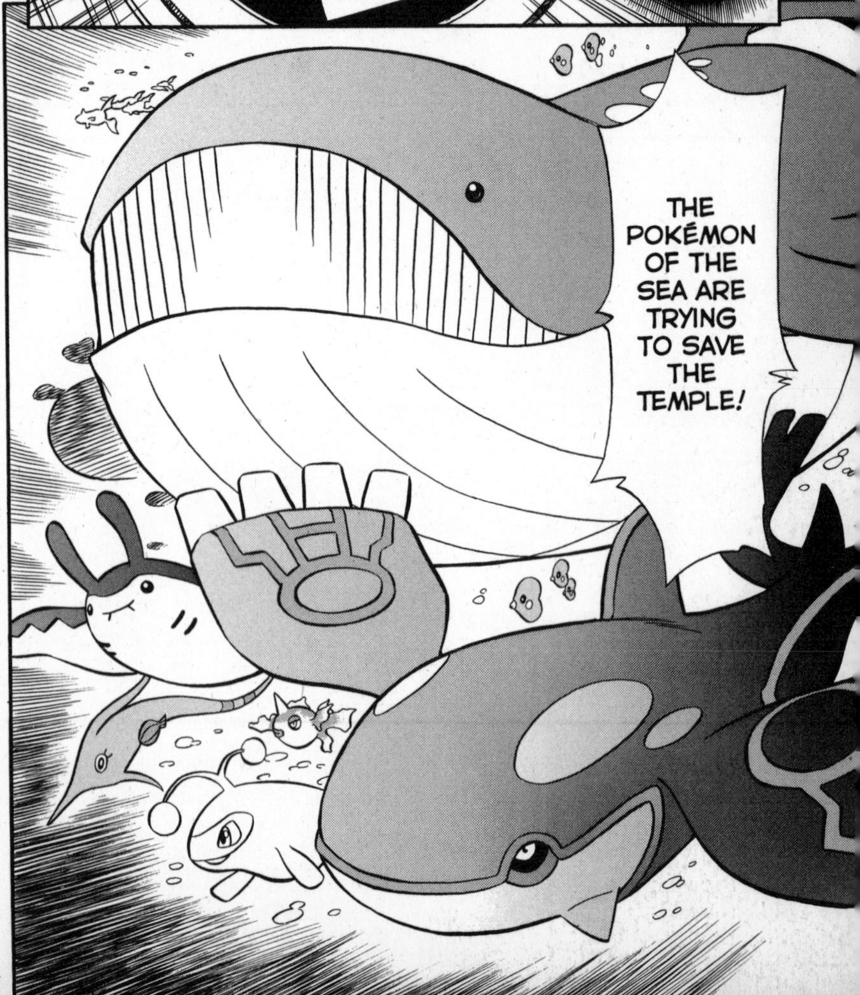
THE
POKÉMON
OF THE
SEA ARE
TRYING
TO SAVE
THE
TEMPLE!

READ THIS WAY

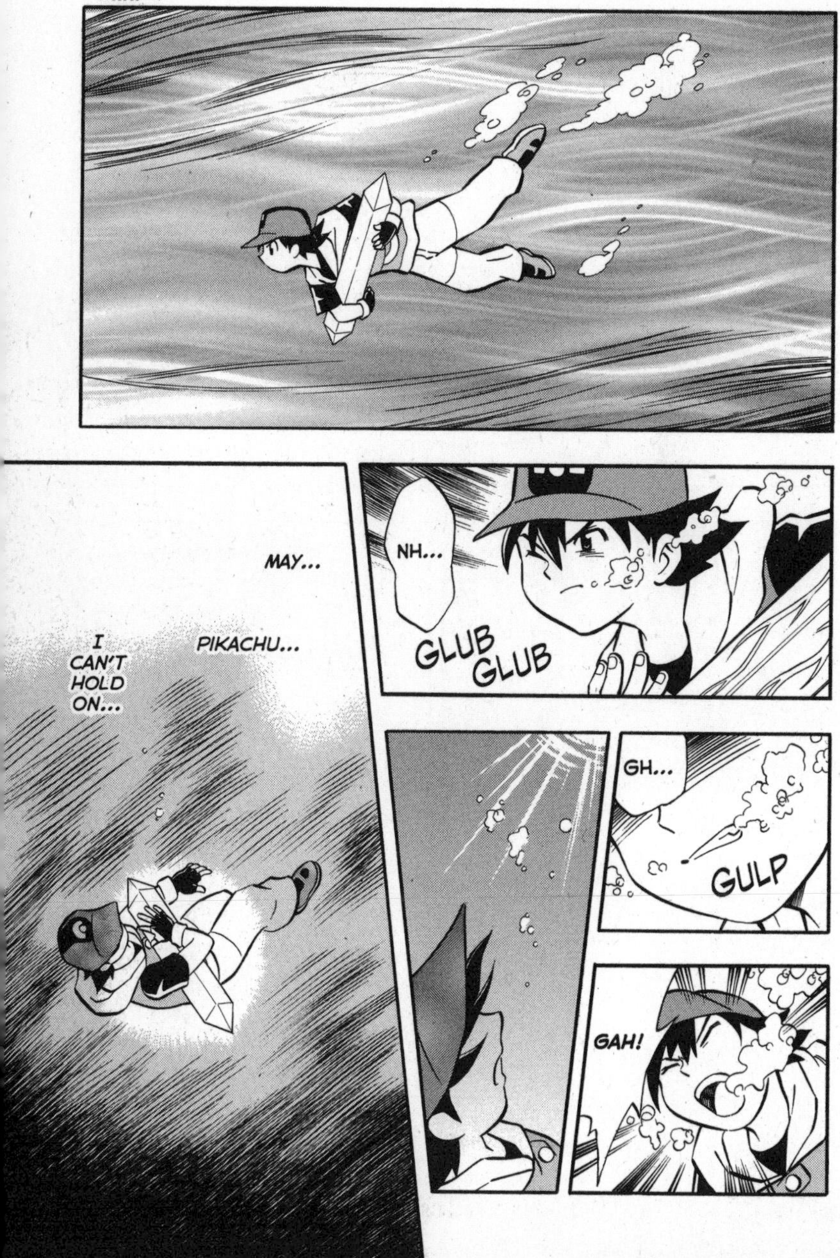
NH...
GLUB GLUB
GH...
GULP
GAH!
MAY...
PIKACHU...
I CAN'T HOLD ON...

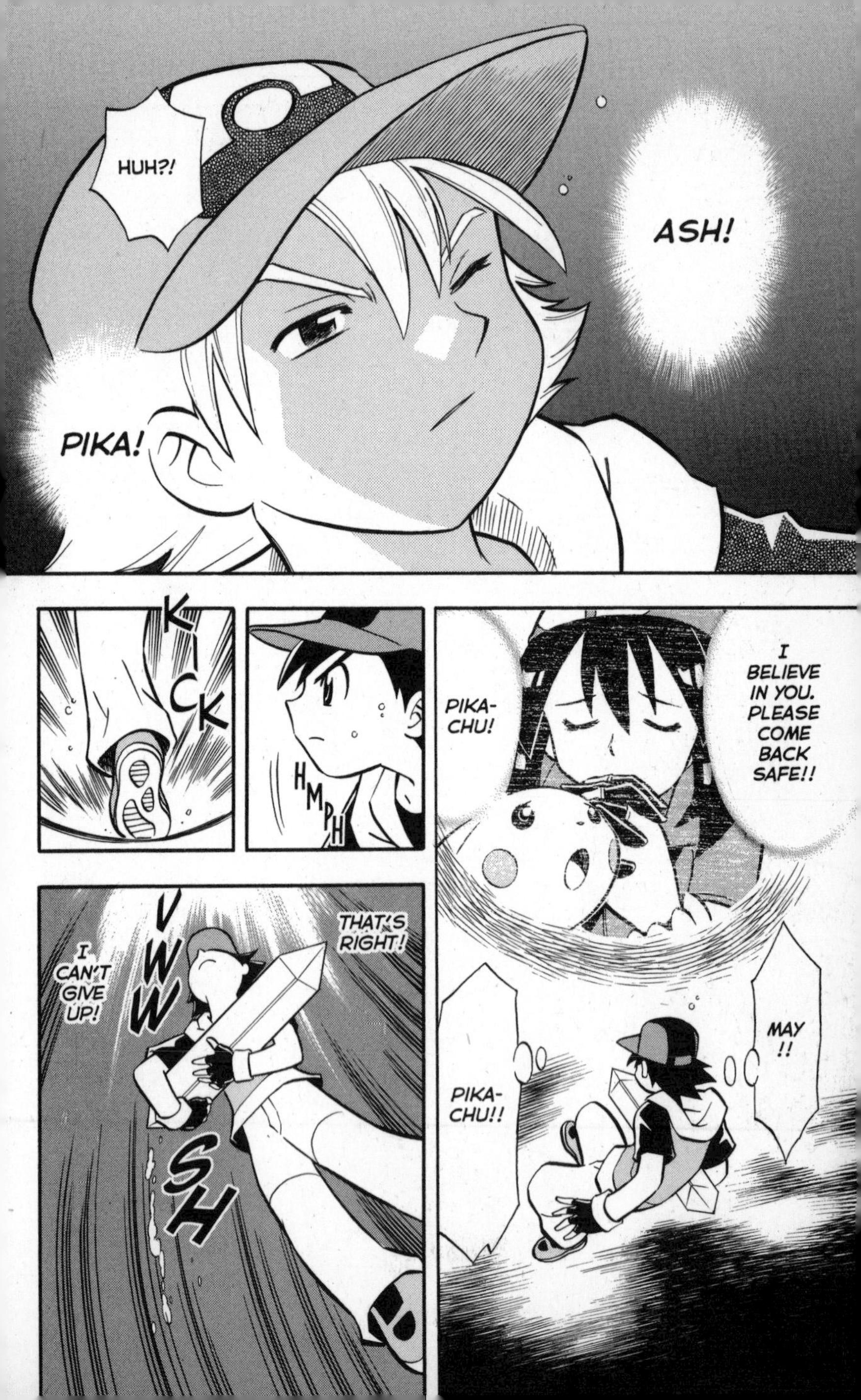

ASH!
HUH?!
PIKA!
I BELIEVE IN YOU. PLEASE COME BACK SAFE!!
PIKA-CHU!
MAY!!
PIKA-CHU!!
HMPH
KICK
THAT'S RIGHT!
I CAN'T GIVE UP!
WHOOSH

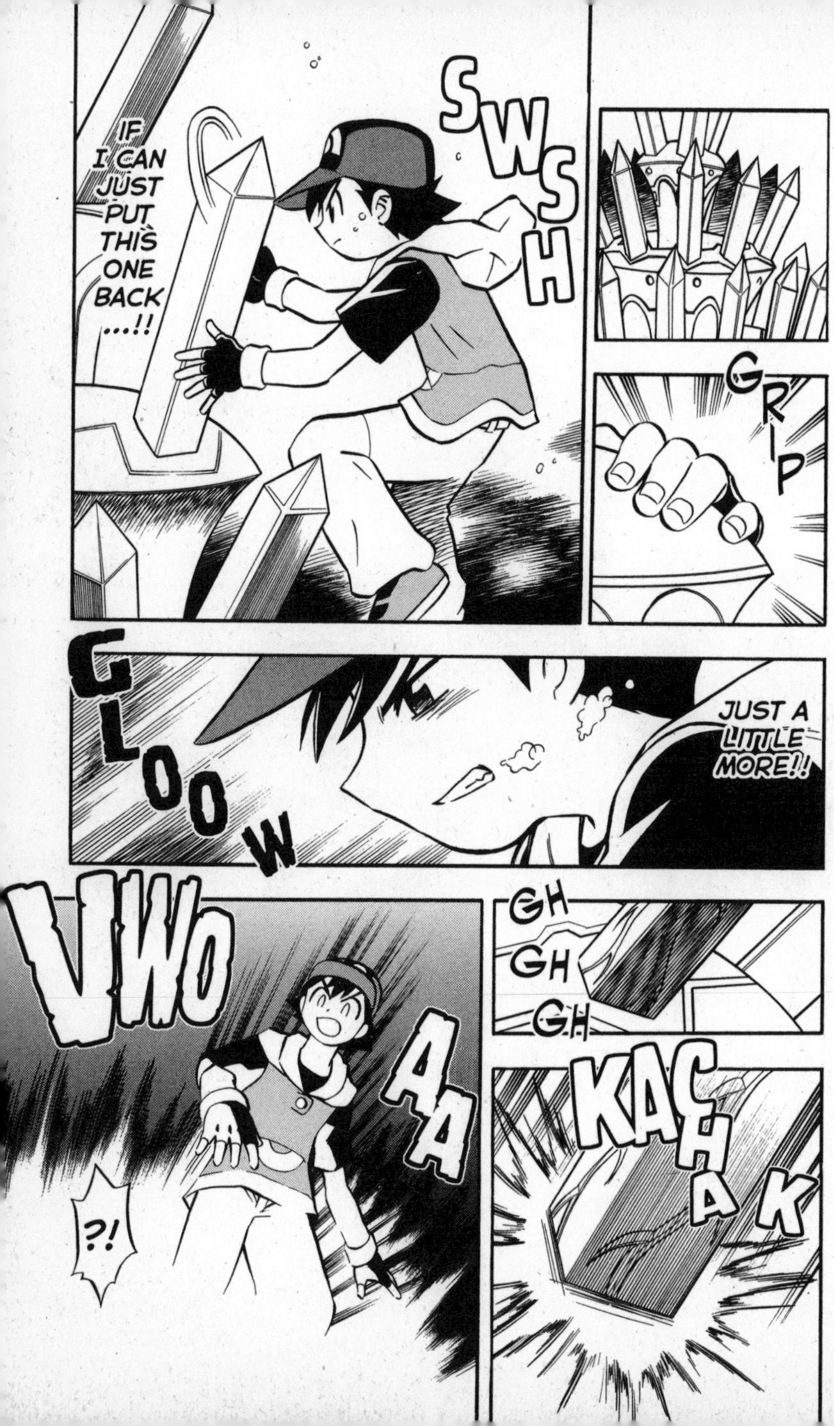
GRIP
SWSH
IF I CAN JUST PUT THIS ONE BACK...!!
JUST A LITTLE MORE!!
GLOOOW
GH GH GH
KACHAK
VWOAA
?!

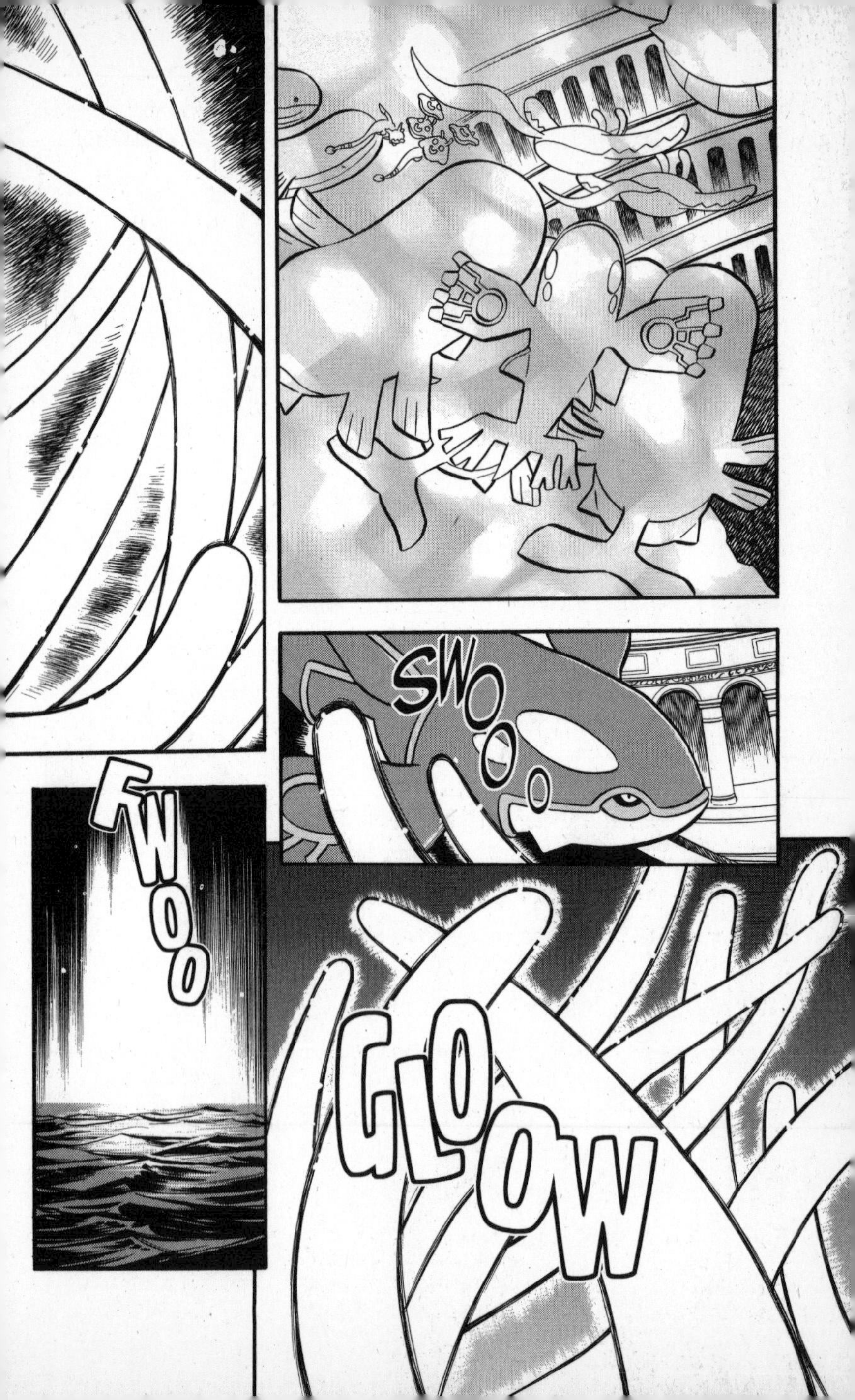
SWOOO
GLOOW
FWOO

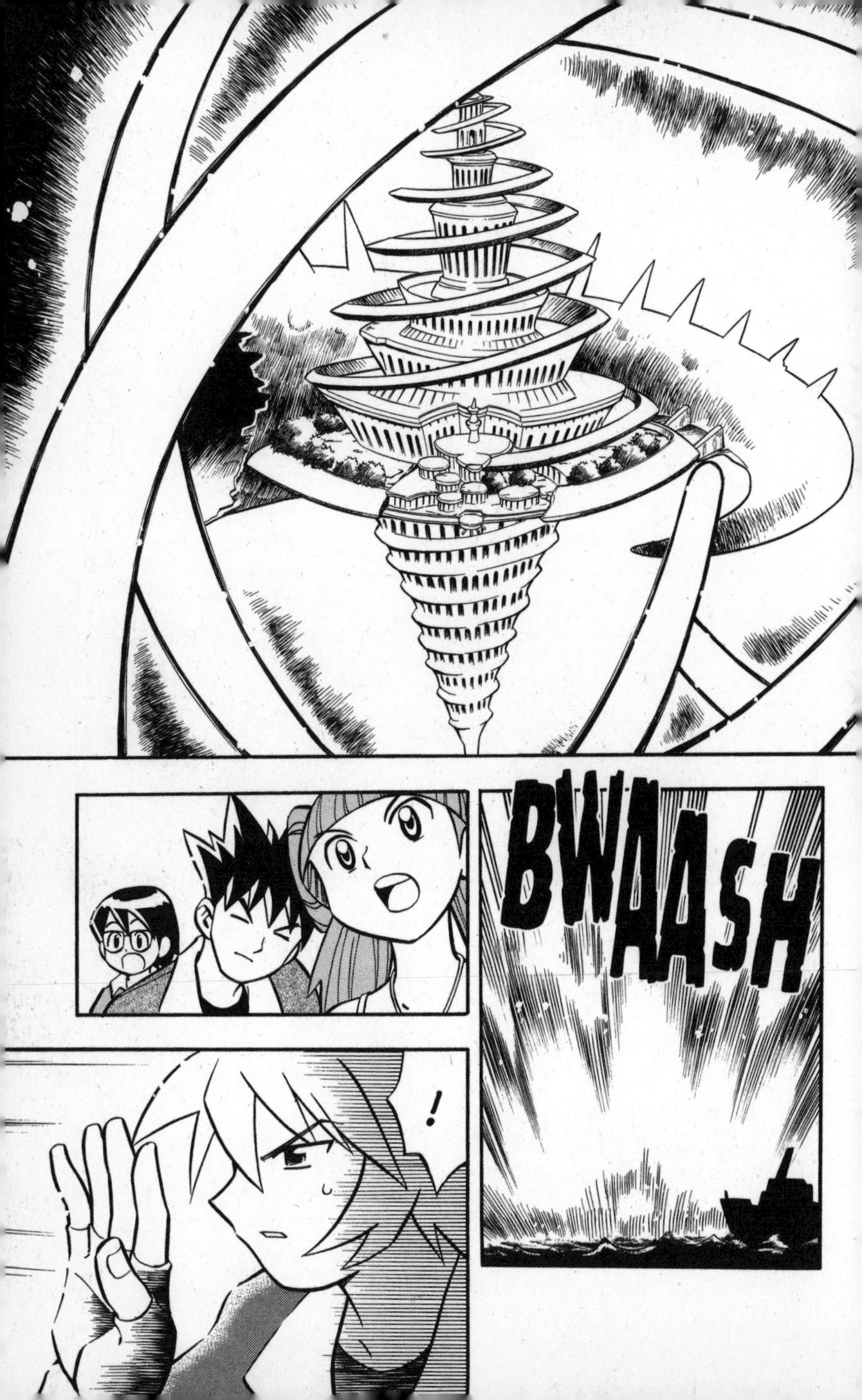
BWAASH
!

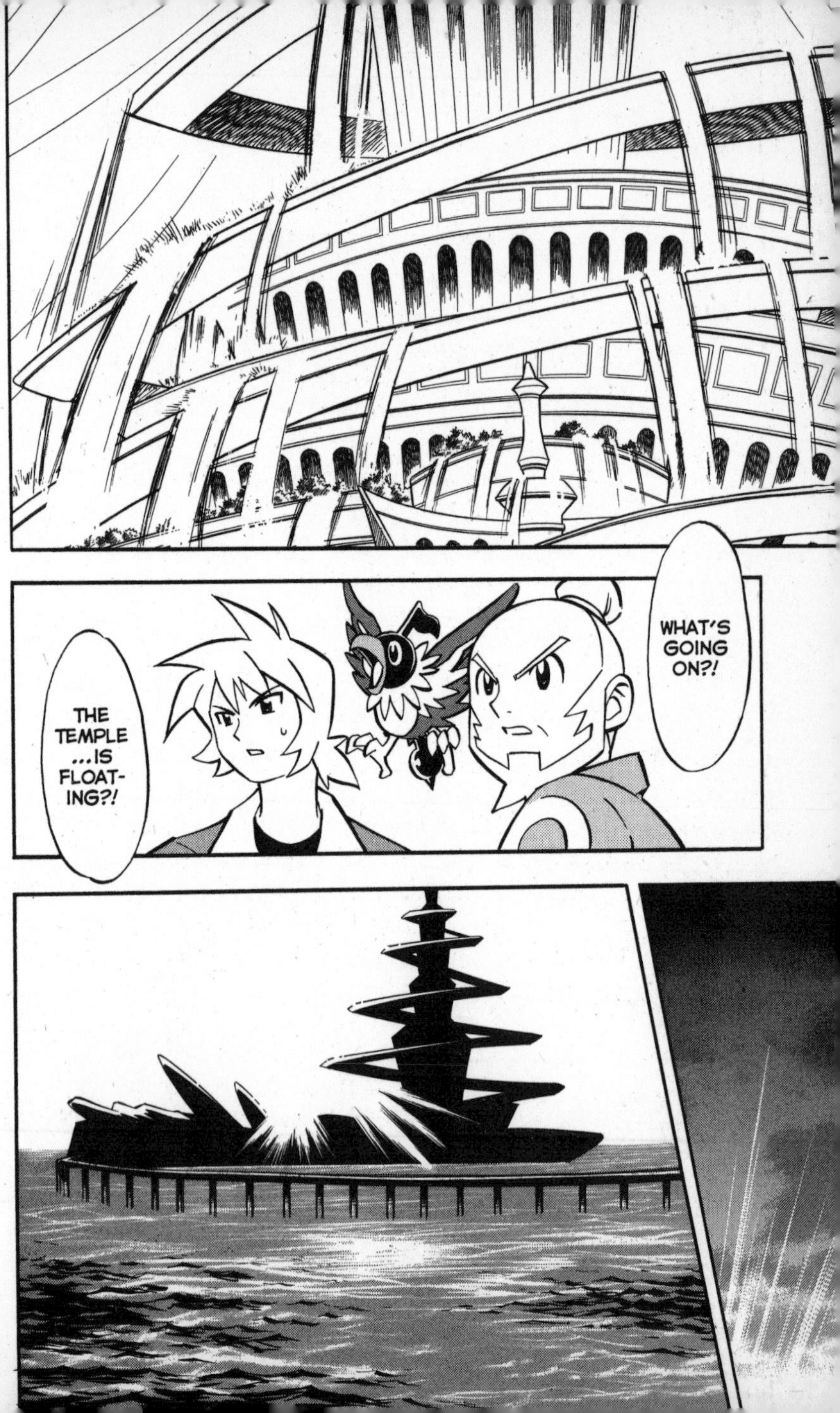
WHAT'S GOING ON?!
THE TEMPLE ...IS FLOAT-ING?!

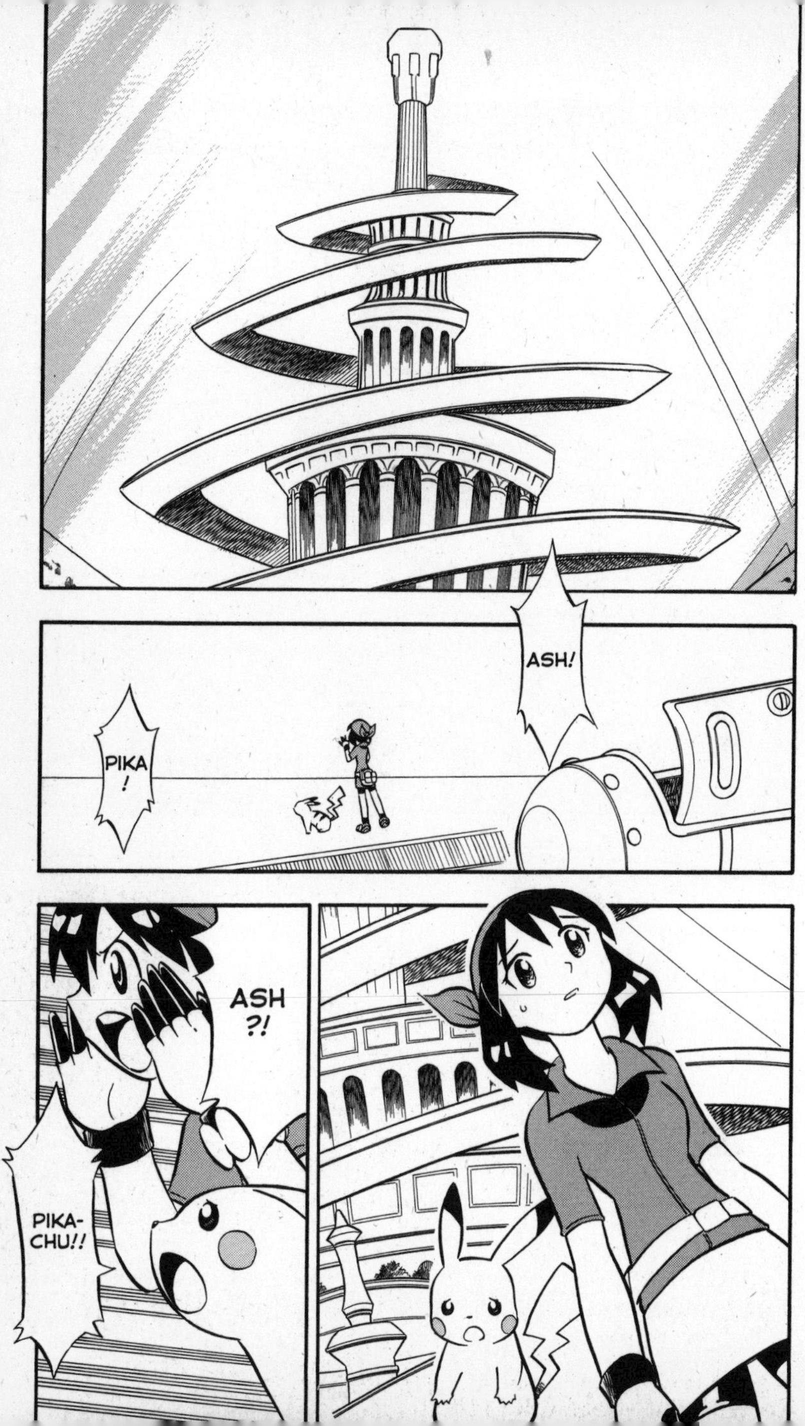
ASH!
PIKA!
ASH?!
PIKA-CHU!!

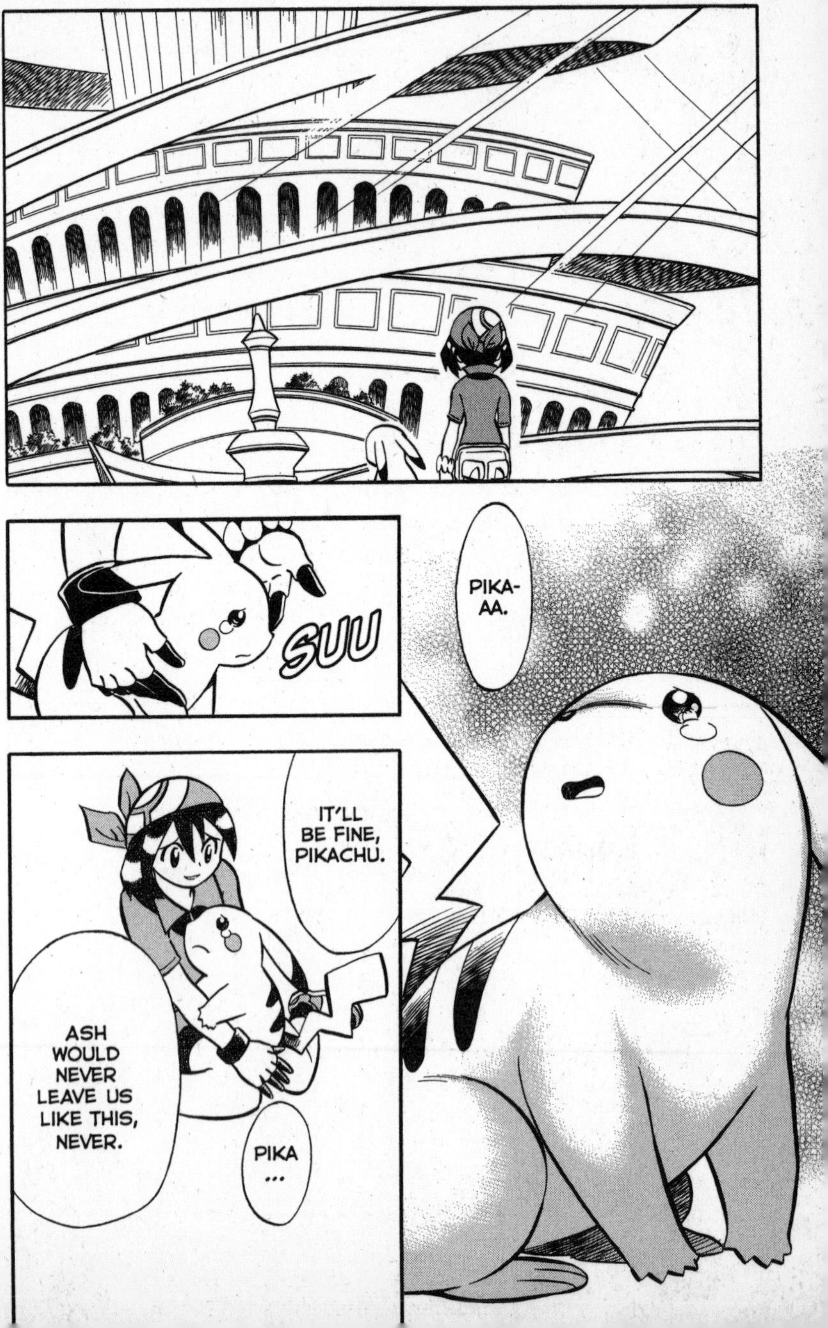
PIKA-AA.
SUU
IT'LL BE FINE, PIKACHU.
ASH WOULD NEVER LEAVE US LIKE THIS, NEVER.
PIKA...

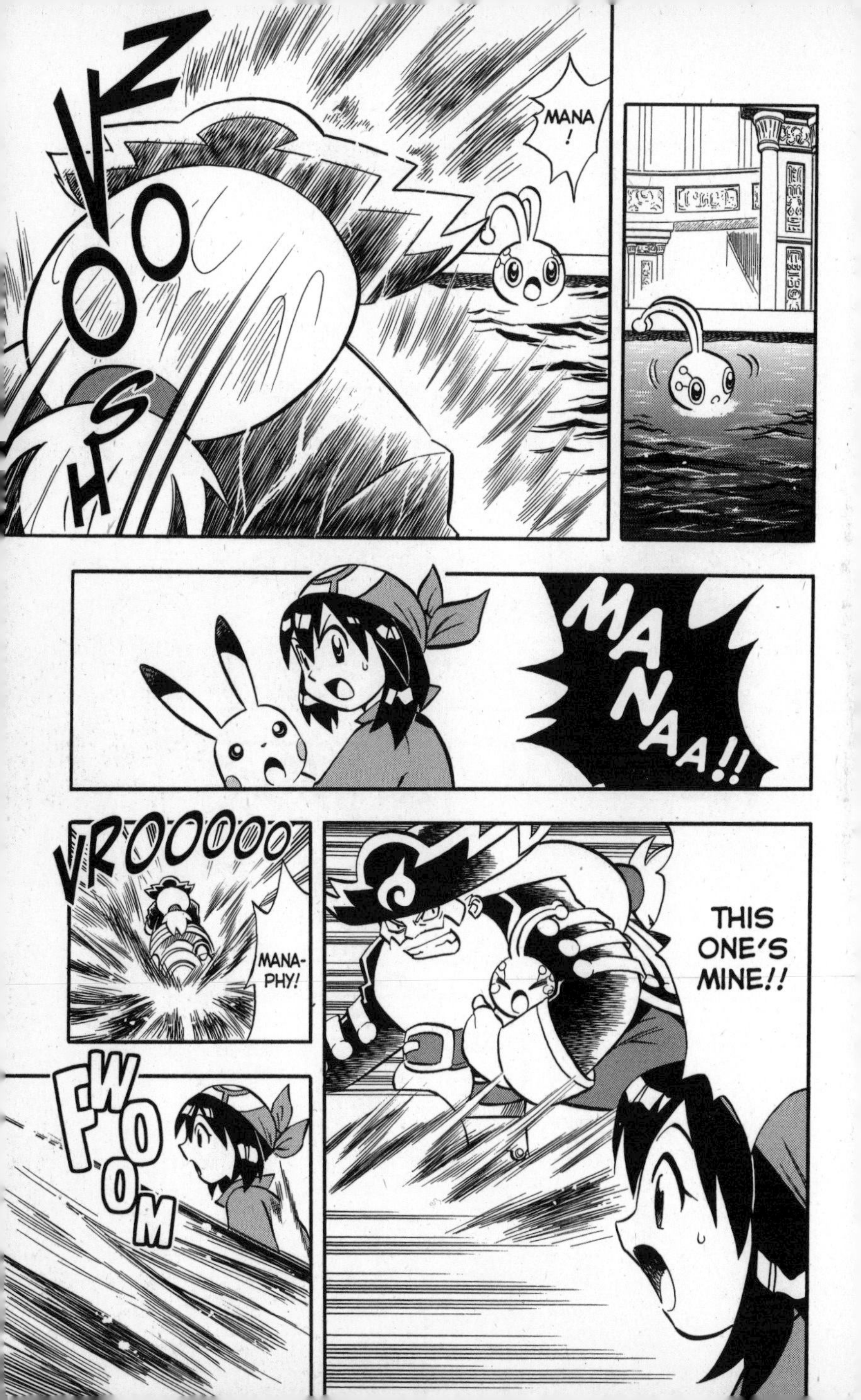
MANA!
MANAAA!!
THIS ONE'S MINE!!
VROOOOO
MANA-PHY!
FWOOM

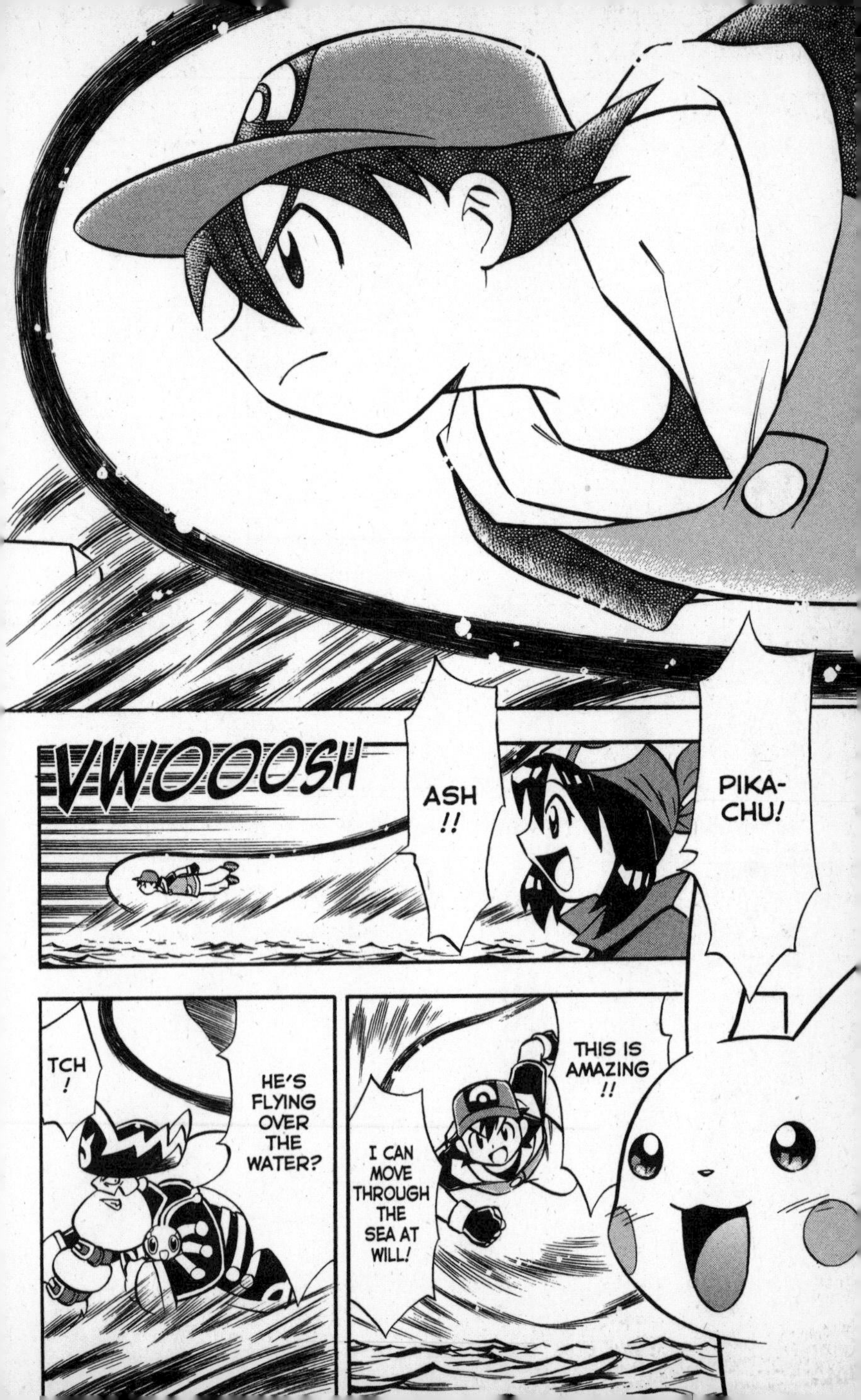
PIKA-CHU!
ASH!!
VWOOOSH
THIS IS AMAZING!!
I CAN MOVE THROUGH THE SEA AT WILL!
HE'S FLYING OVER THE WATER?
TCH!

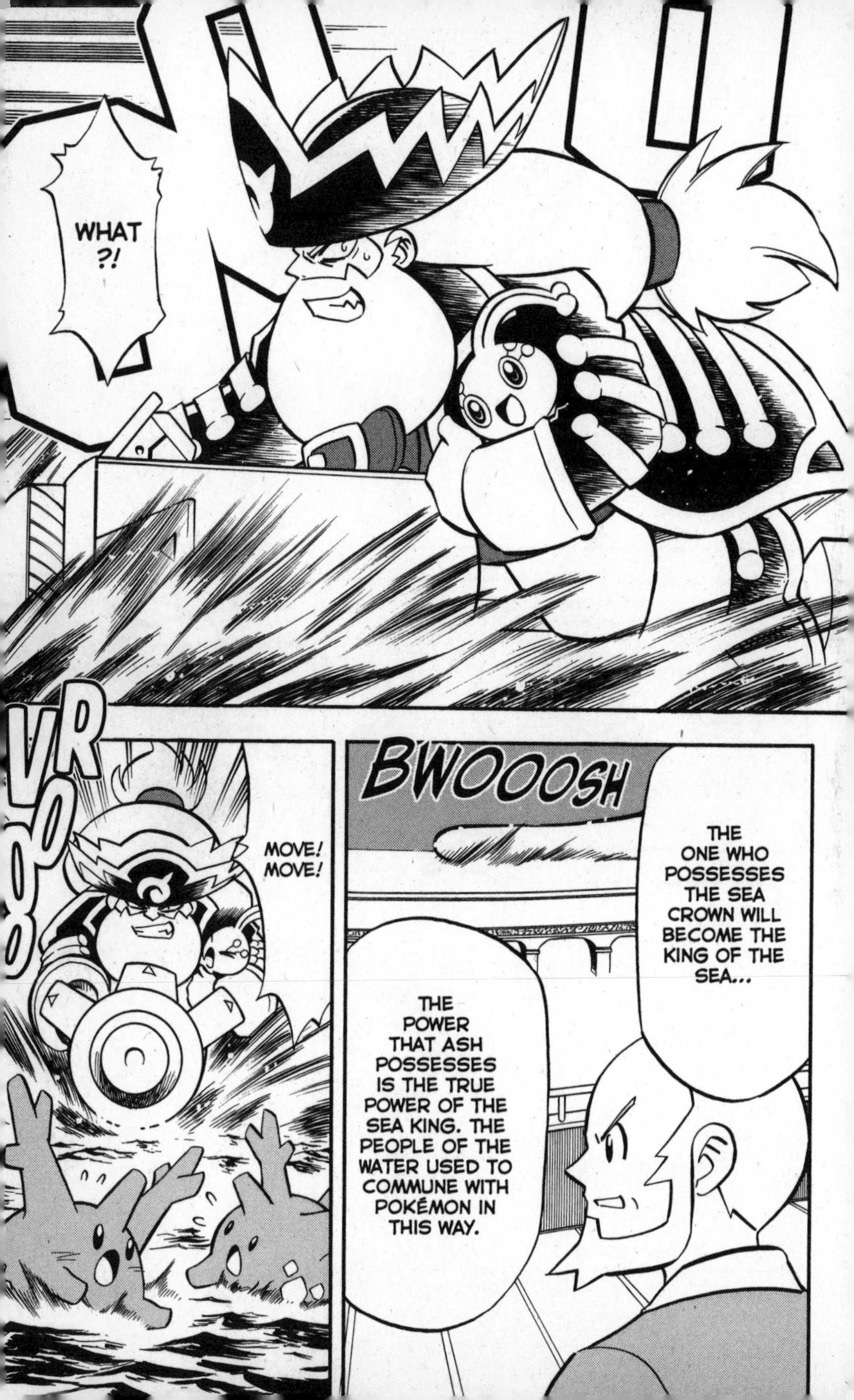
WHAT ?!
BWOOOSH
THE ONE WHO POSSESSES THE SEA CROWN WILL BECOME THE KING OF THE SEA...
THE POWER THAT ASH POSSESSES IS THE TRUE POWER OF THE SEA KING. THE PEOPLE OF THE WATER USED TO COMMUNE WITH POKÉMON IN THIS WAY.
VROOOO
MOVE! MOVE!

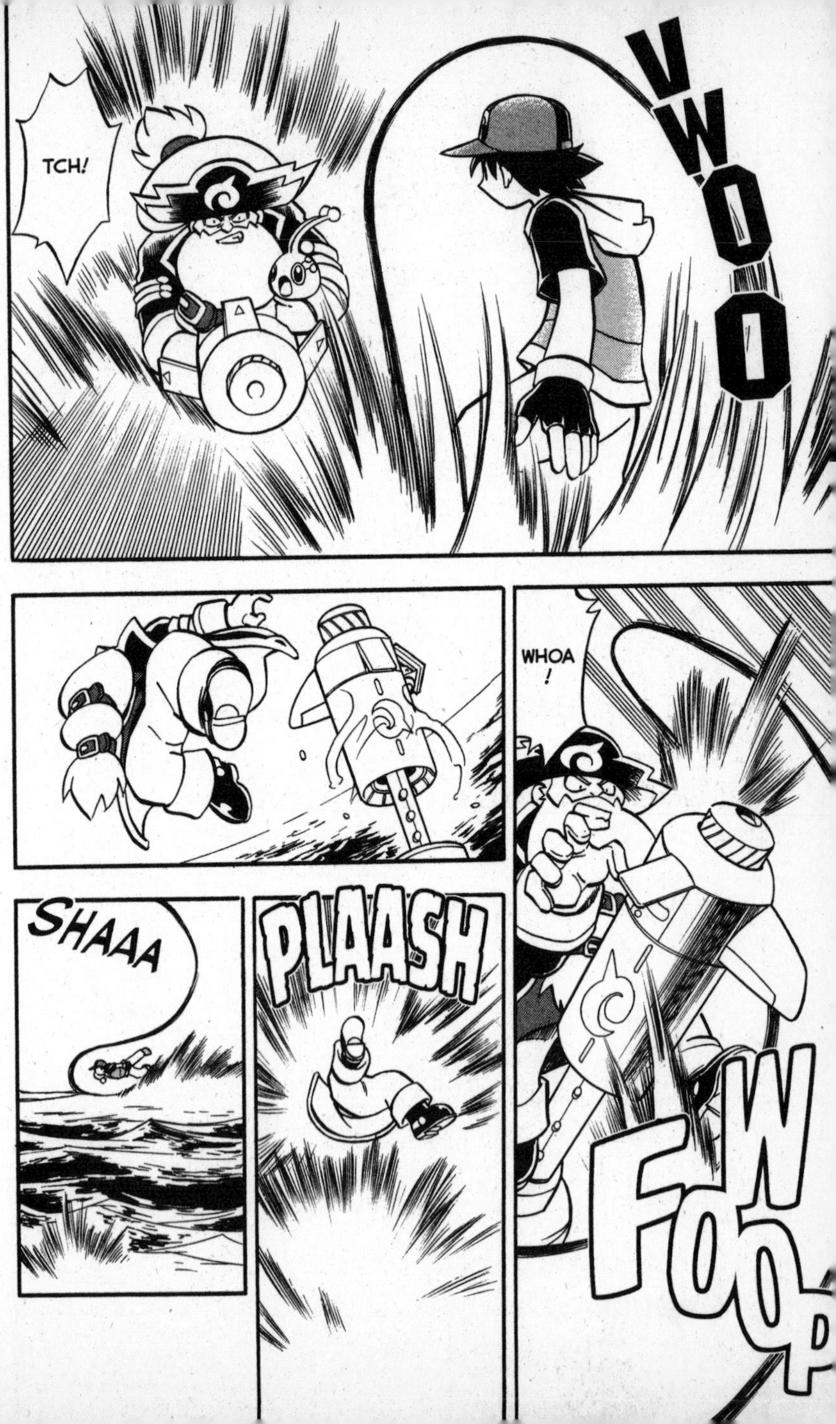
VWOOO
TCH!
WHOA!
FWOOOP
PLAASH
SHAAA

READ THIS WAY

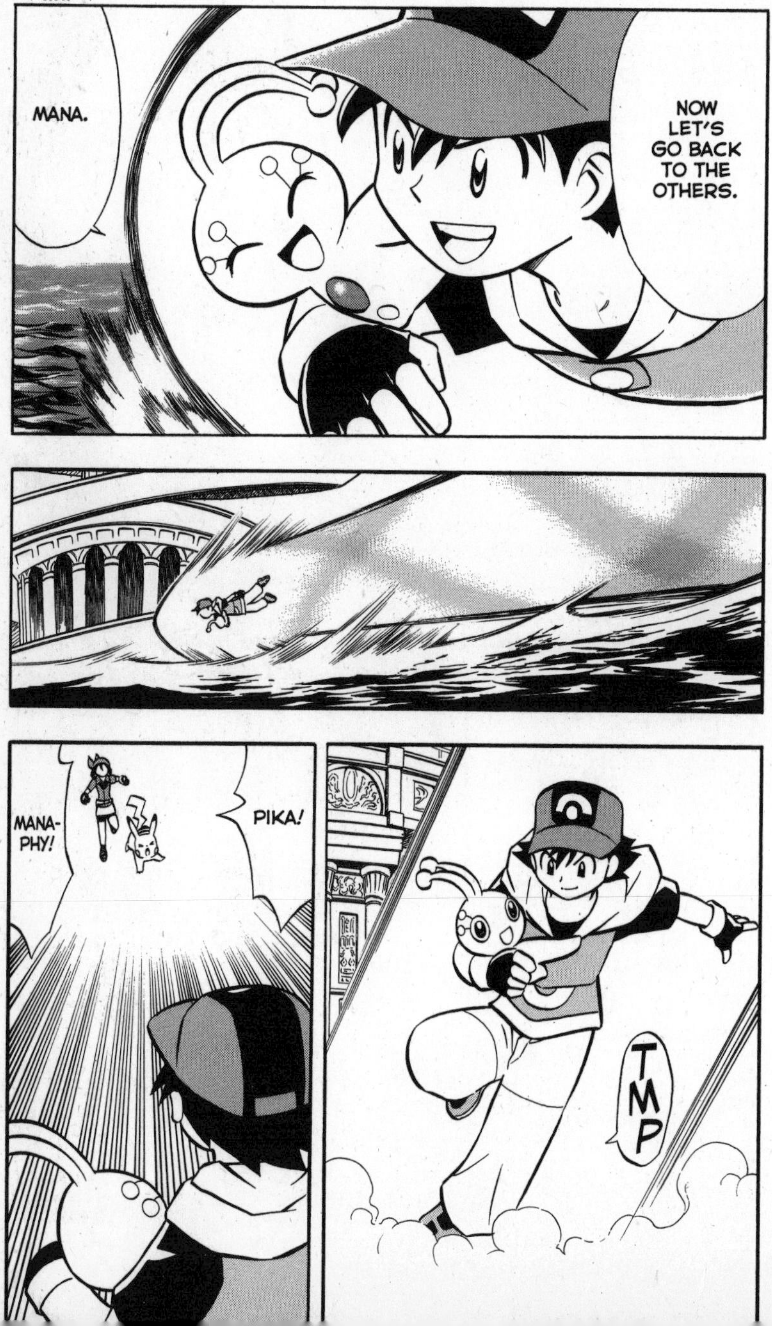
NOW LET'S GO BACK TO THE OTHERS.
MANA.
TMP
PIKA!
MANA-PHY!

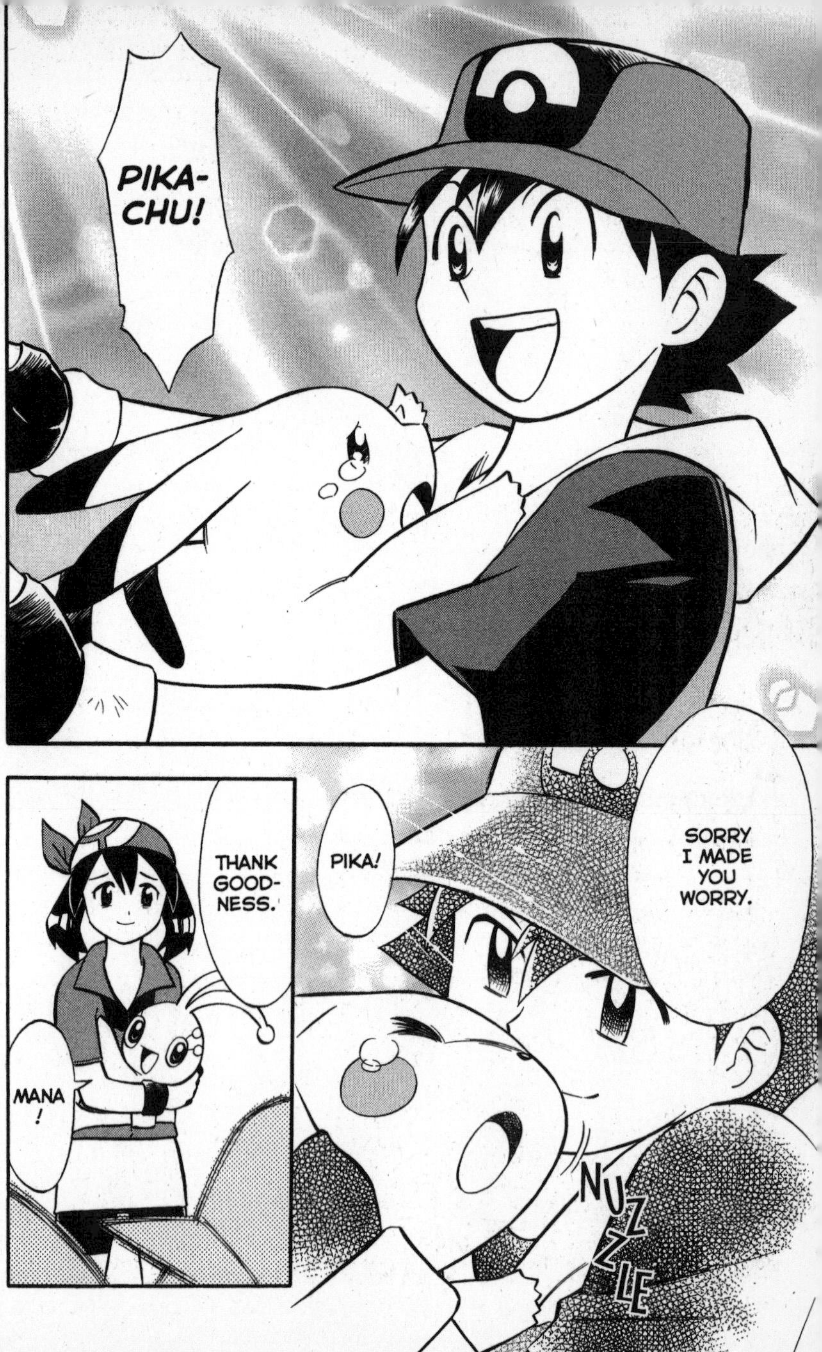
PIKA-CHU!
SORRY I MADE YOU WORRY.
PIKA!
NUZZLE
THANK GOOD-NESS.
MANA!

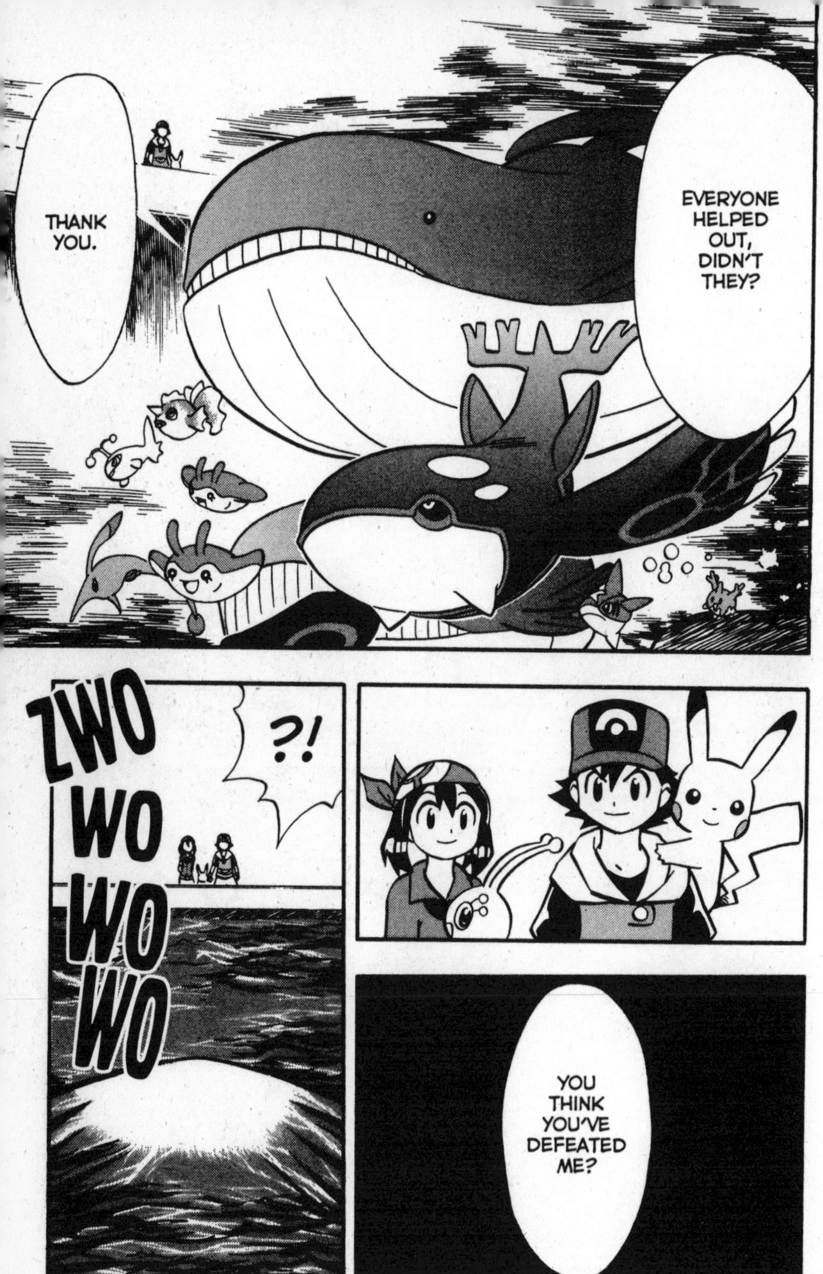
EVERYONE HELPED OUT, DIDN'T THEY?
THANK YOU.
YOU THINK YOU'VE DEFEATED ME?
?!
ZWO WO WO WO WO

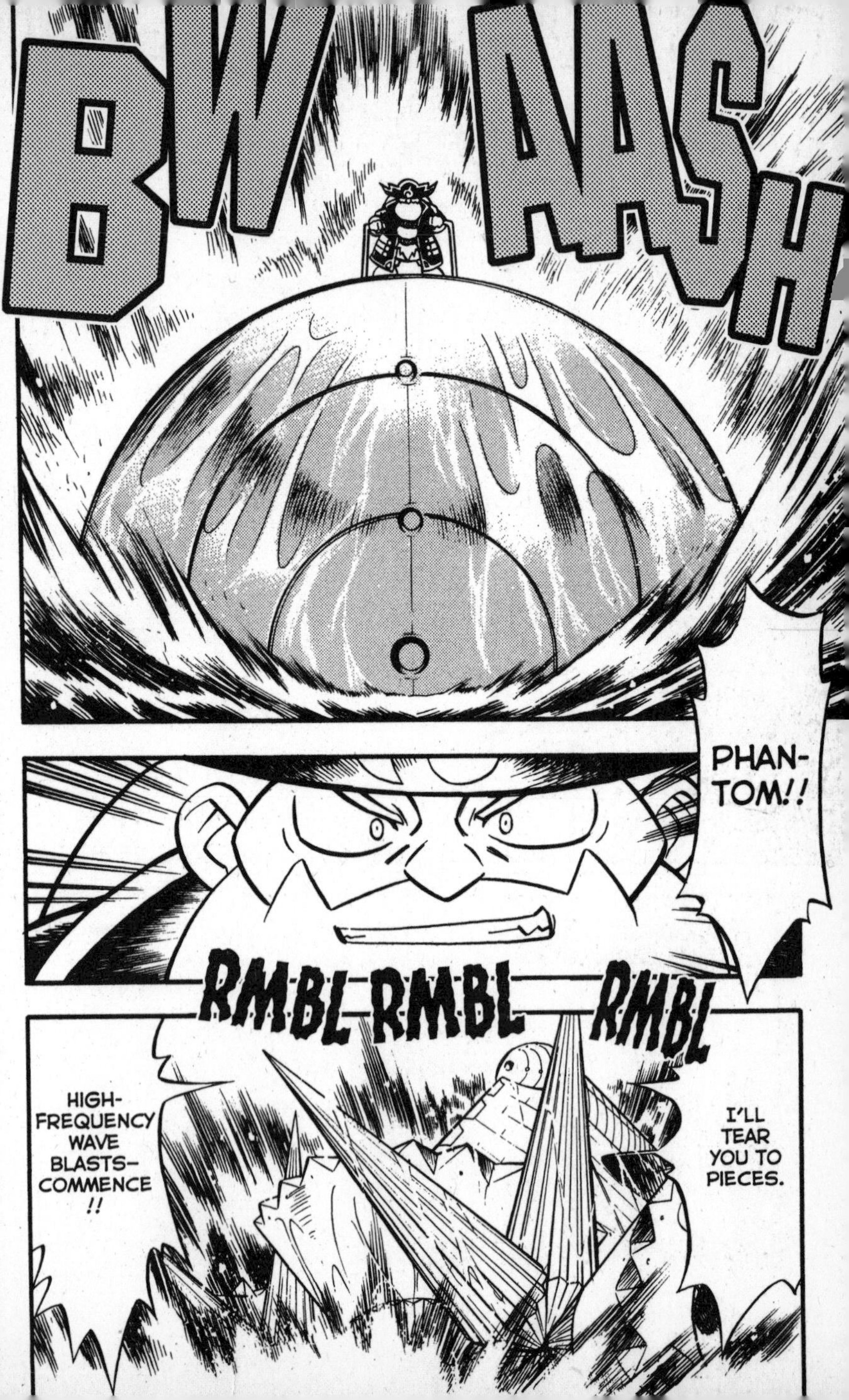
BWAASH
PHAN-TOM!!
RMBL RMBL RMBL
I'LL TEAR YOU TO PIECES.
HIGH-FREQUENCY WAVE BLASTS—COMMENCE!!

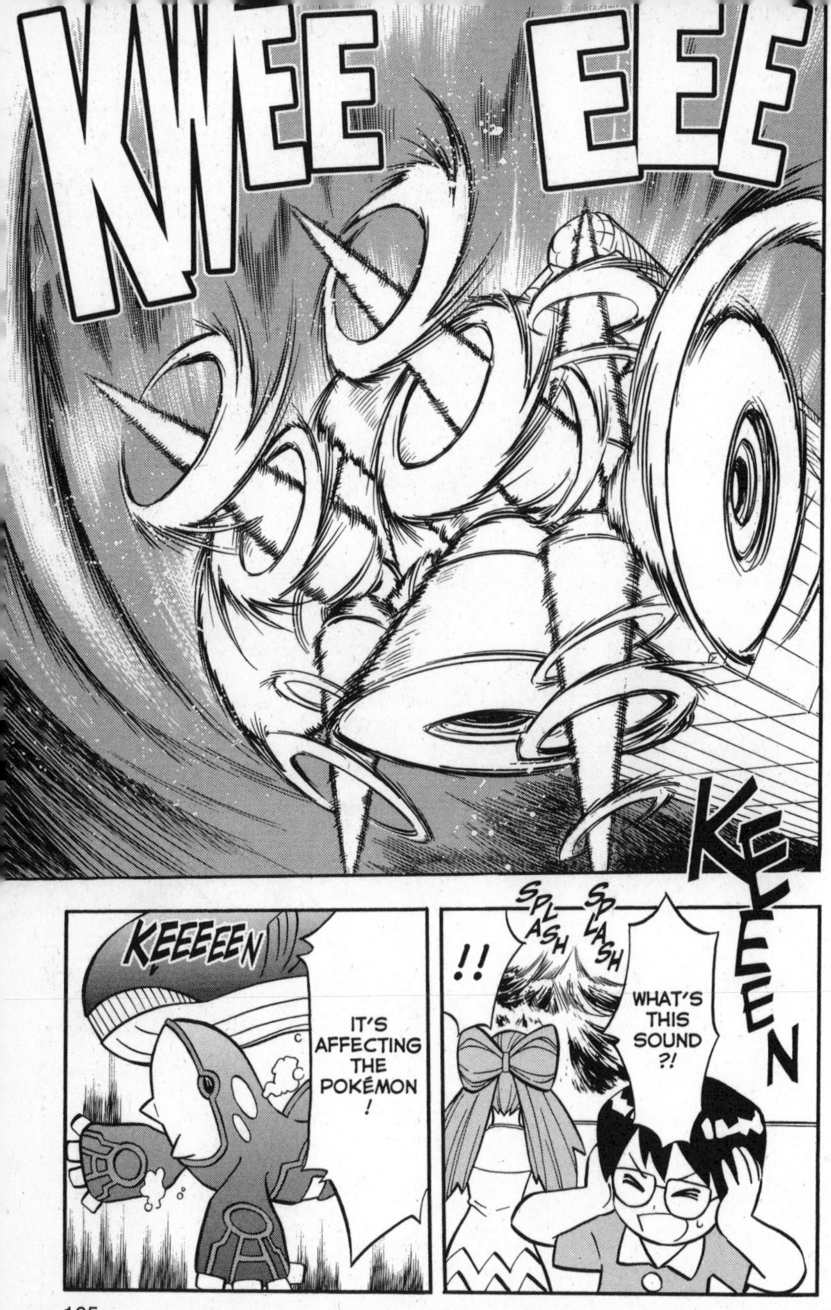
KWEE EEE
KEEEEN
SPLASH SPLASH
!!
WHAT'S THIS SOUND?!
KEEEEEN
IT'S AFFECTING THE POKÉMON!

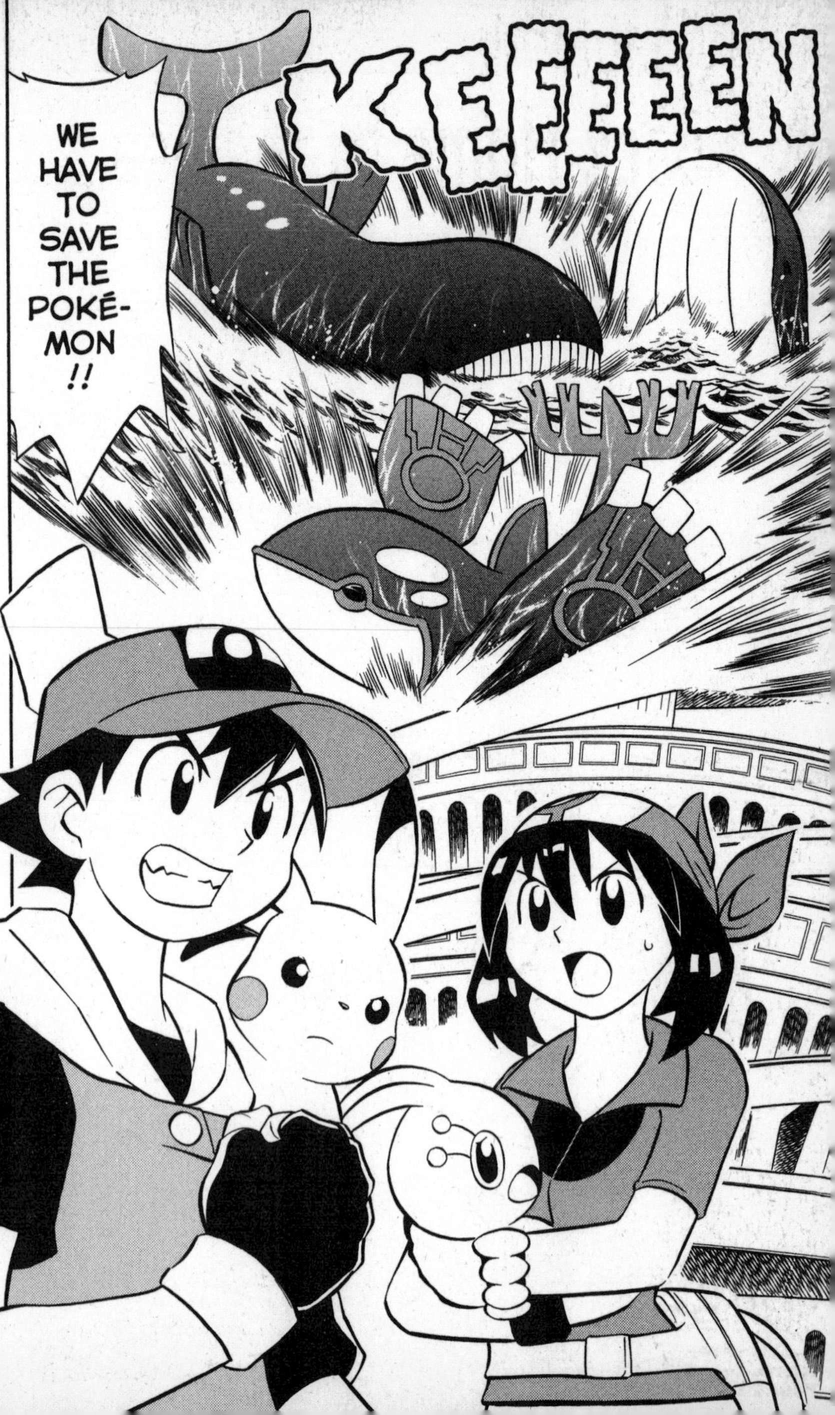
KEEEEEN
WE HAVE TO SAVE THE POKÉ-MON!!

Chapter 4:
Back Home to the Sea

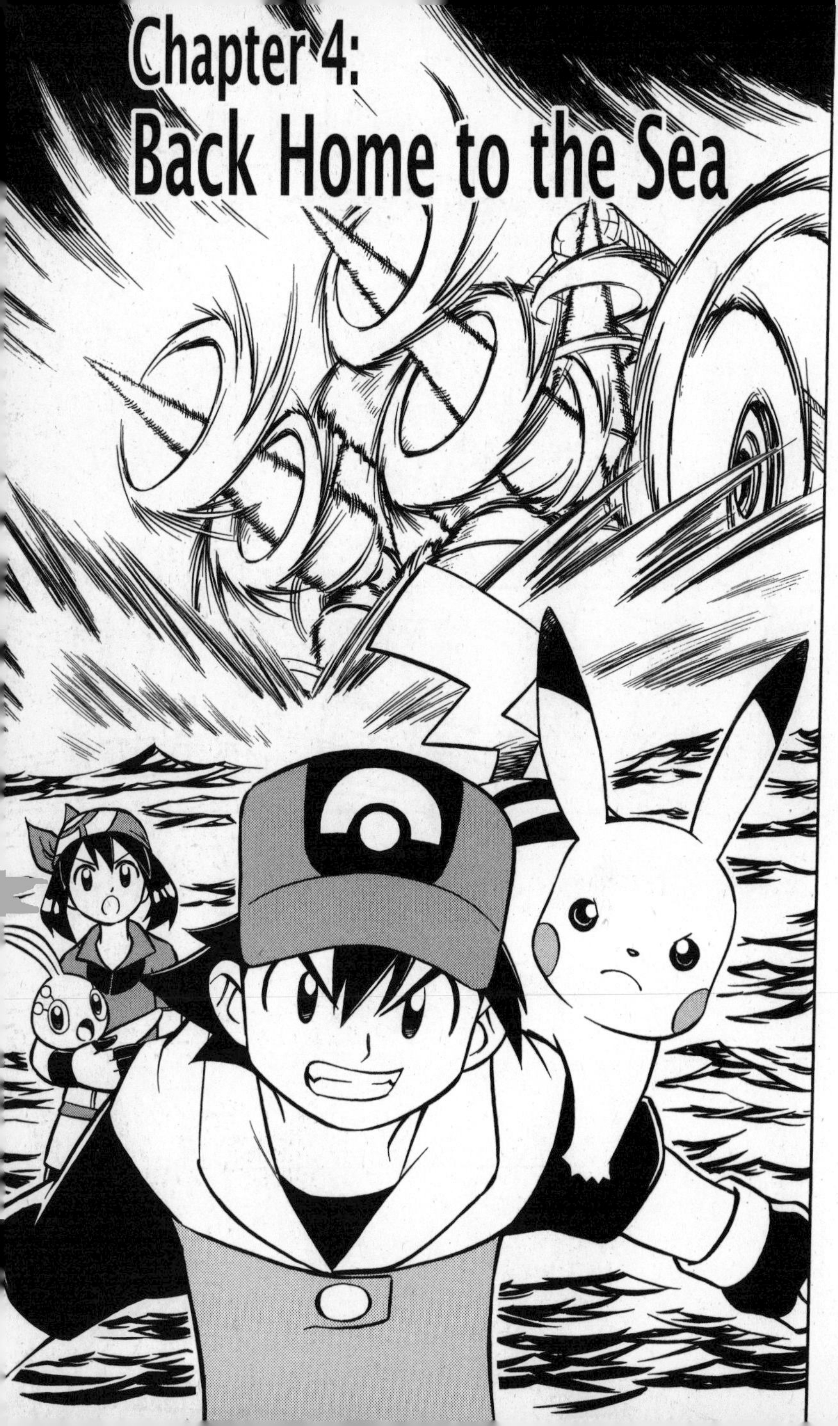

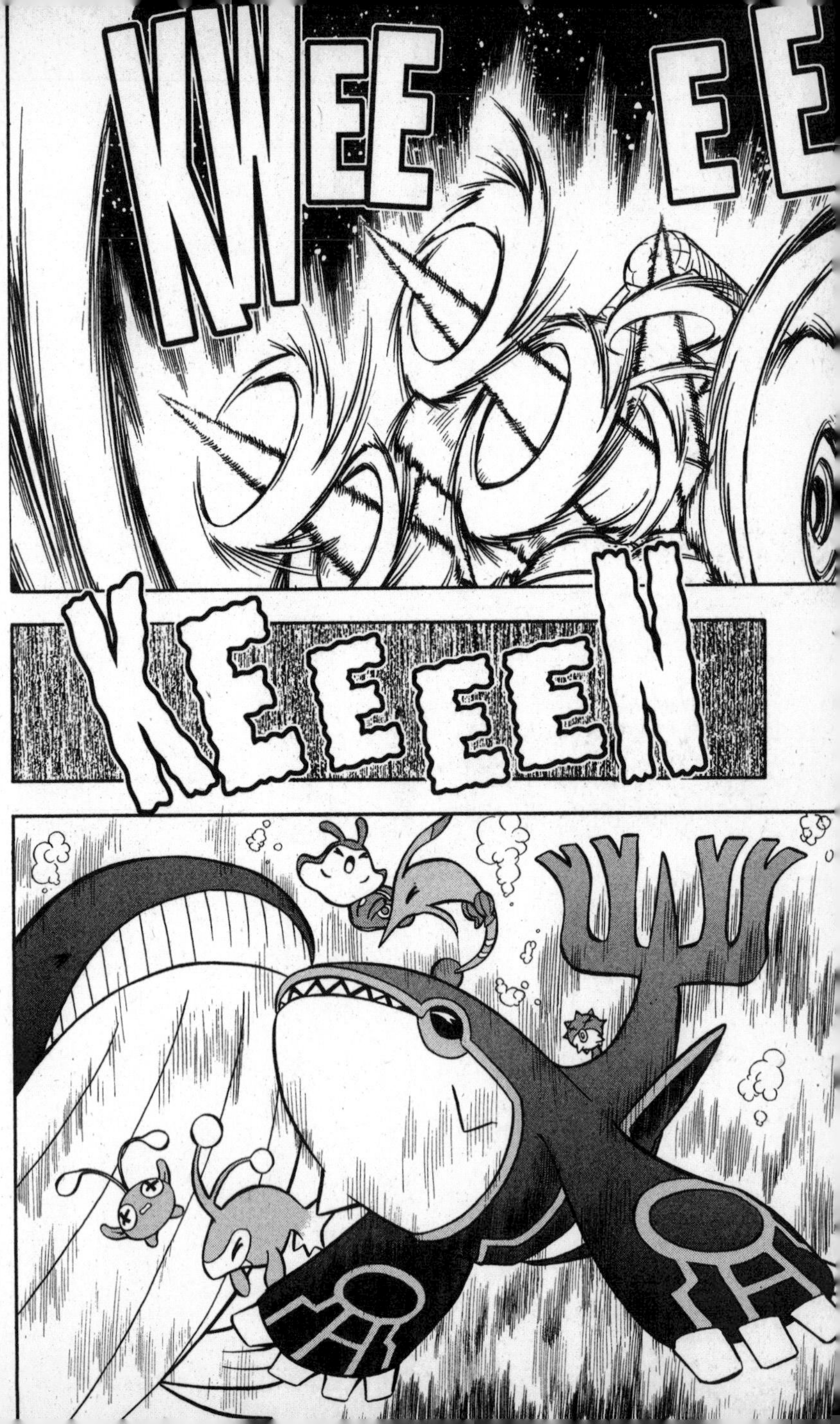
KWEE EE
KEEEN

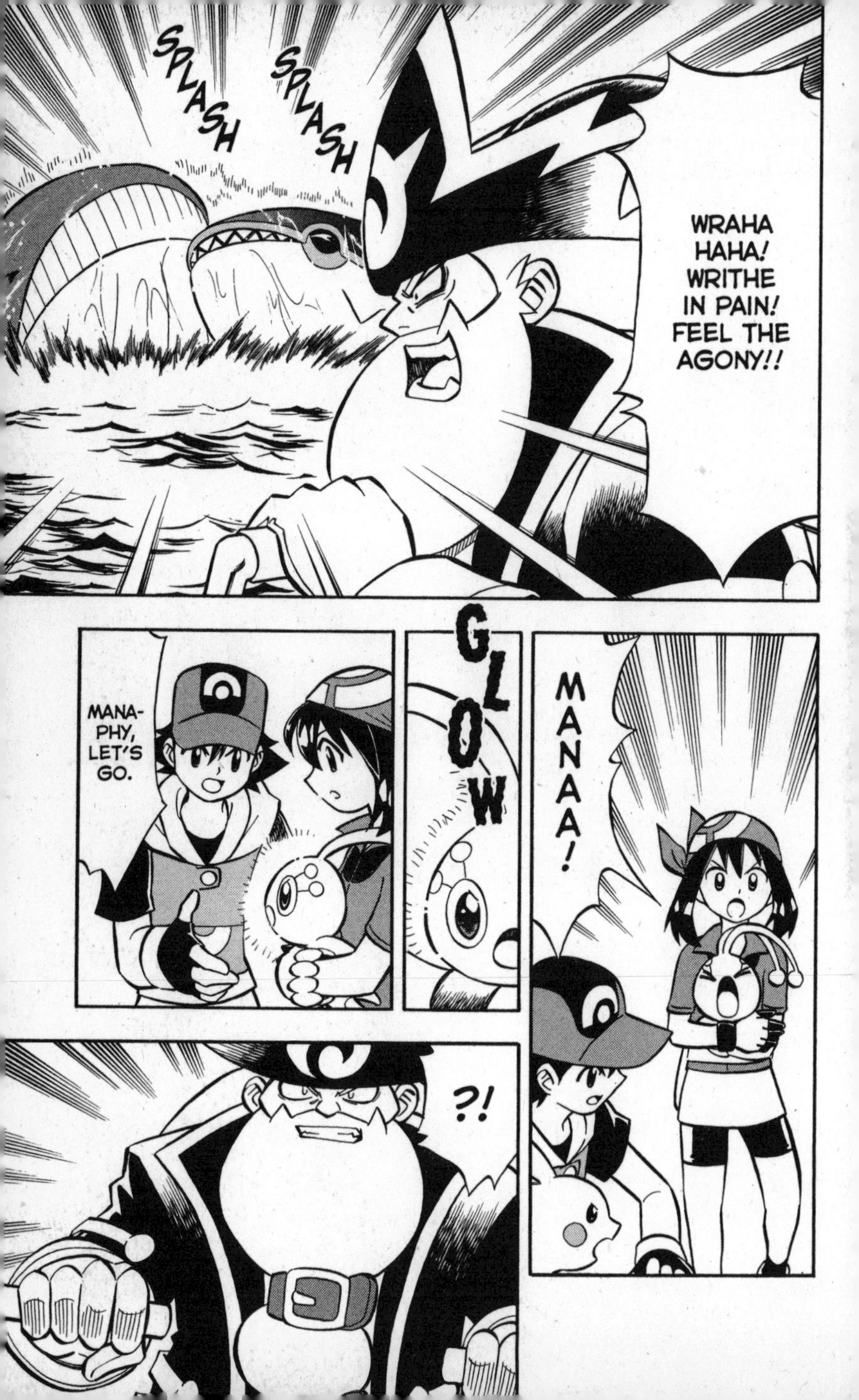
SPLASH
SPLASH
WRAHA HAHA! WRITHE IN PAIN! FEEL THE AGONY!!
MANAAA!
GLOW
MANA-PHY, LET'S GO.
?!

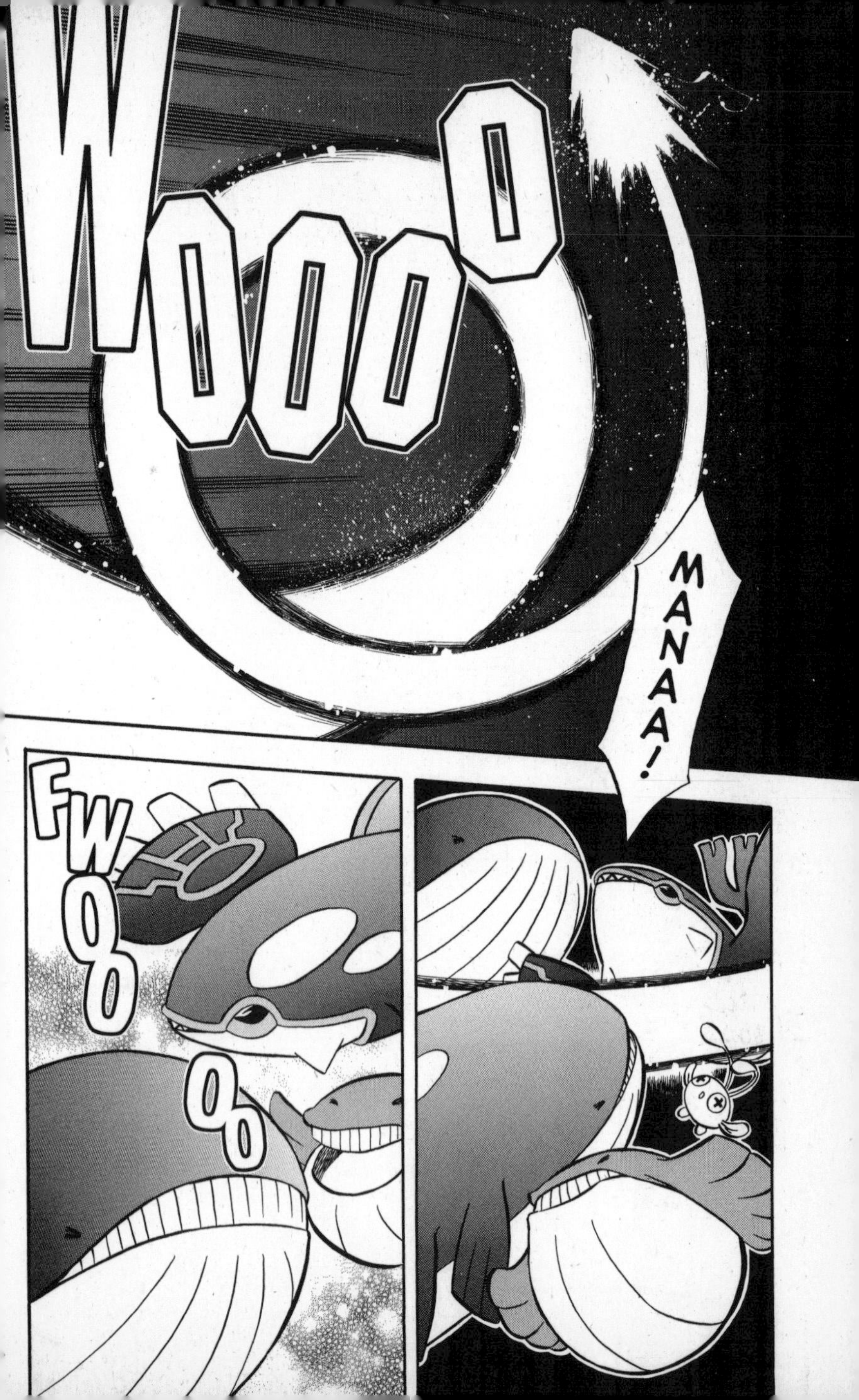
WOOOO
MANAAA!
FWOOOO

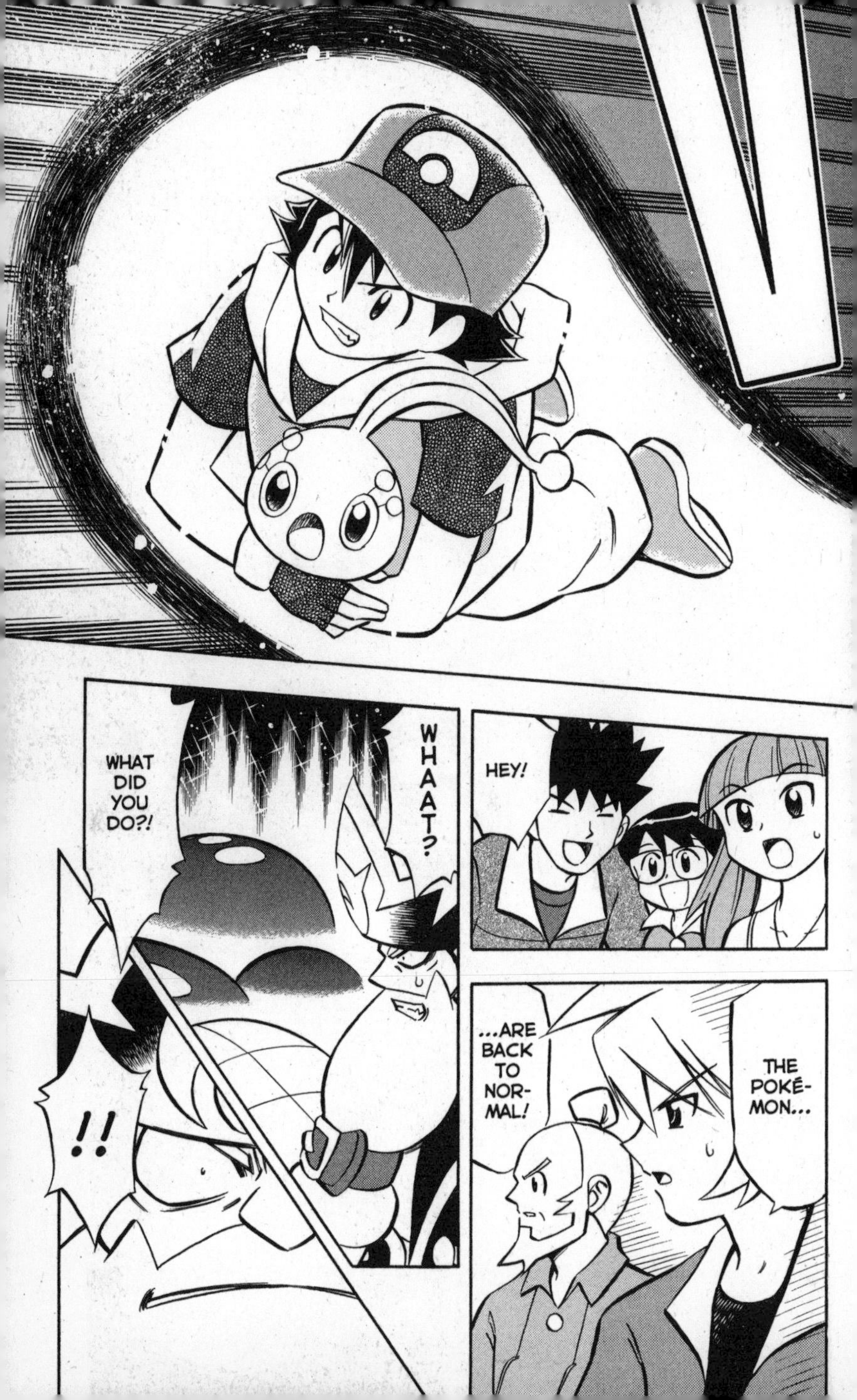
HEY!
THE POKÉMON...
...ARE BACK TO NORMAL!
WHAAAT?
WHAT DID YOU DO?!
!!

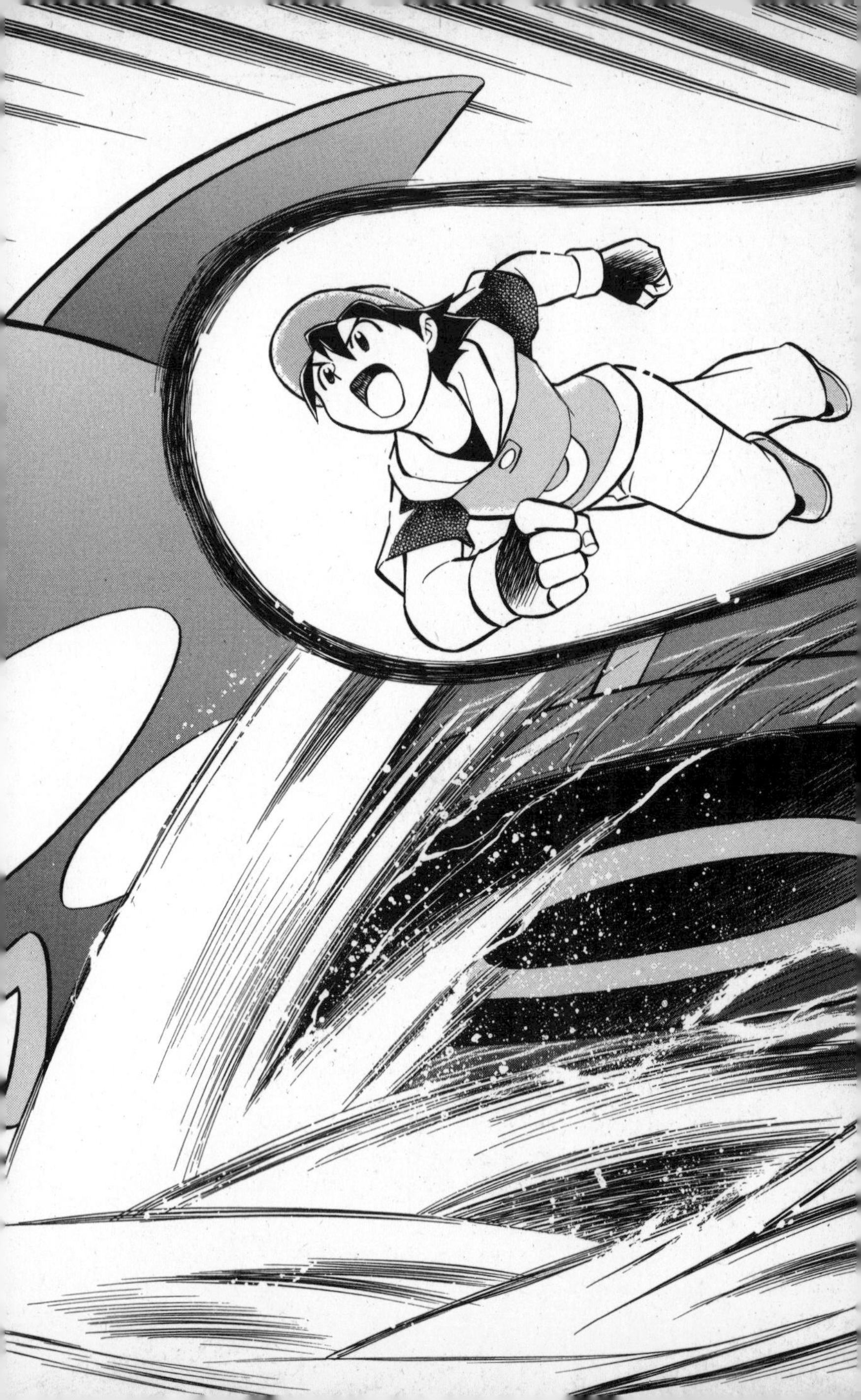

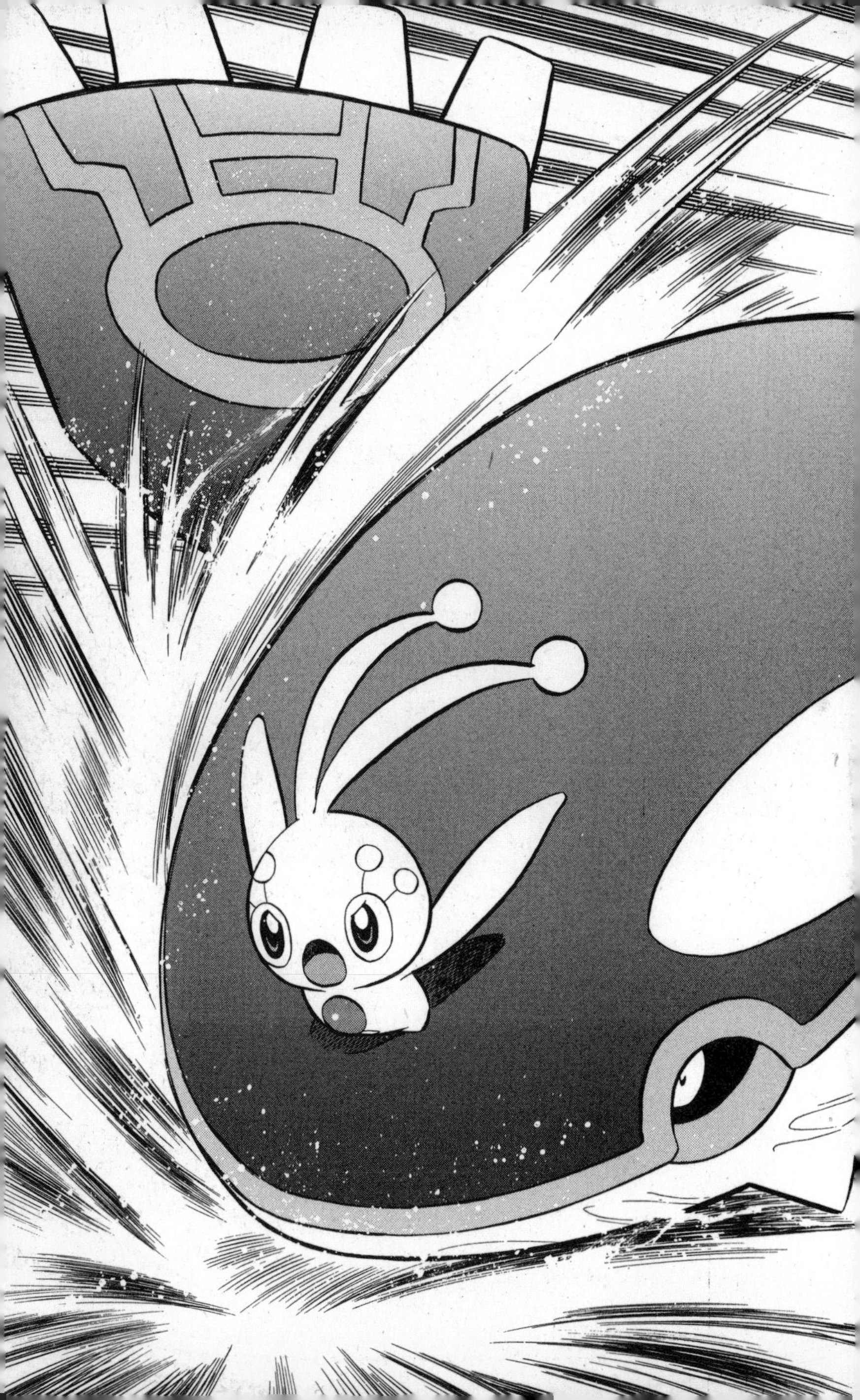

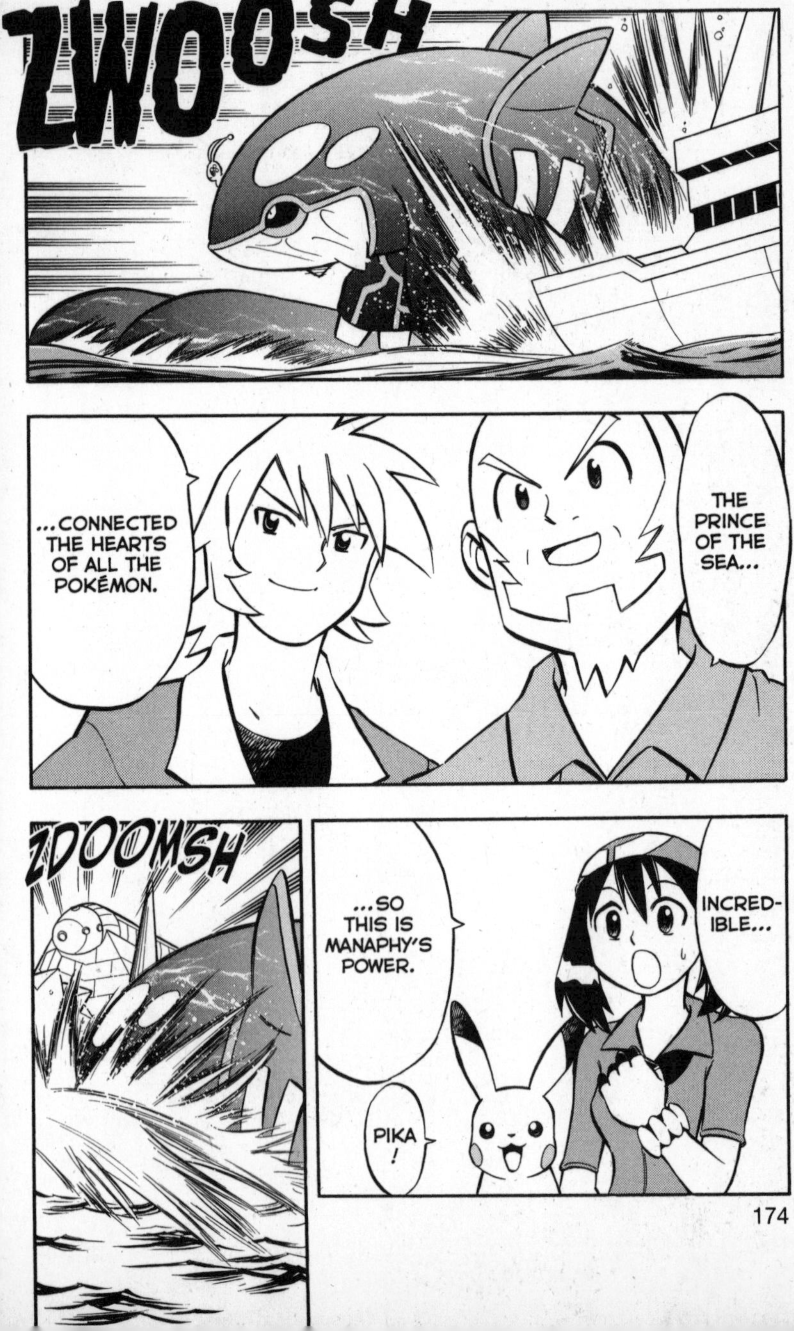
ZWOOSH
THE PRINCE OF THE SEA...
...CONNECTED THE HEARTS OF ALL THE POKÉMON.
INCRED-IBLE...
...SO THIS IS MANAPHY'S POWER.
PIKA !
ZDOOMSH

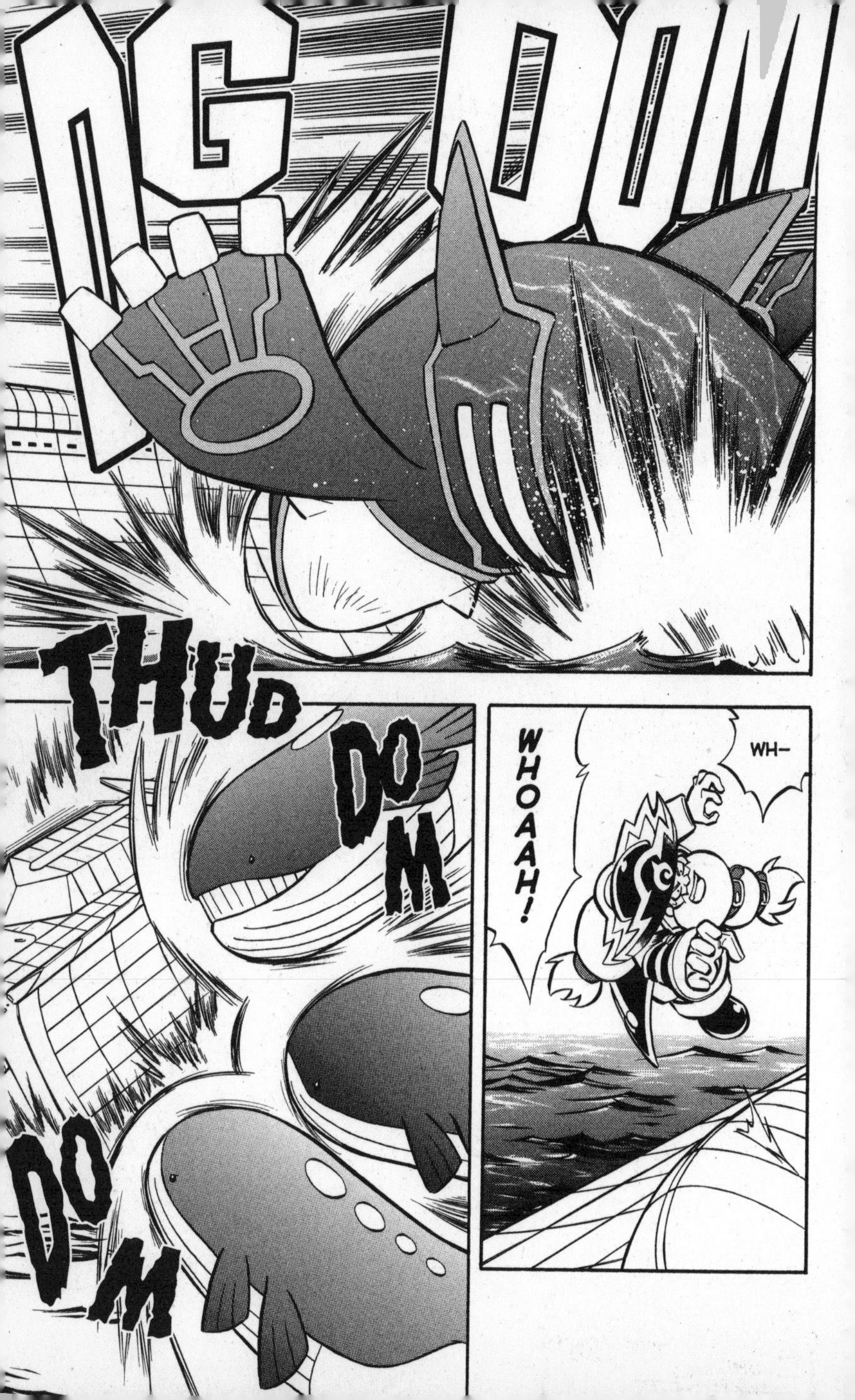
WH-
WHOAAH!
THUD
DOOM
DOOM

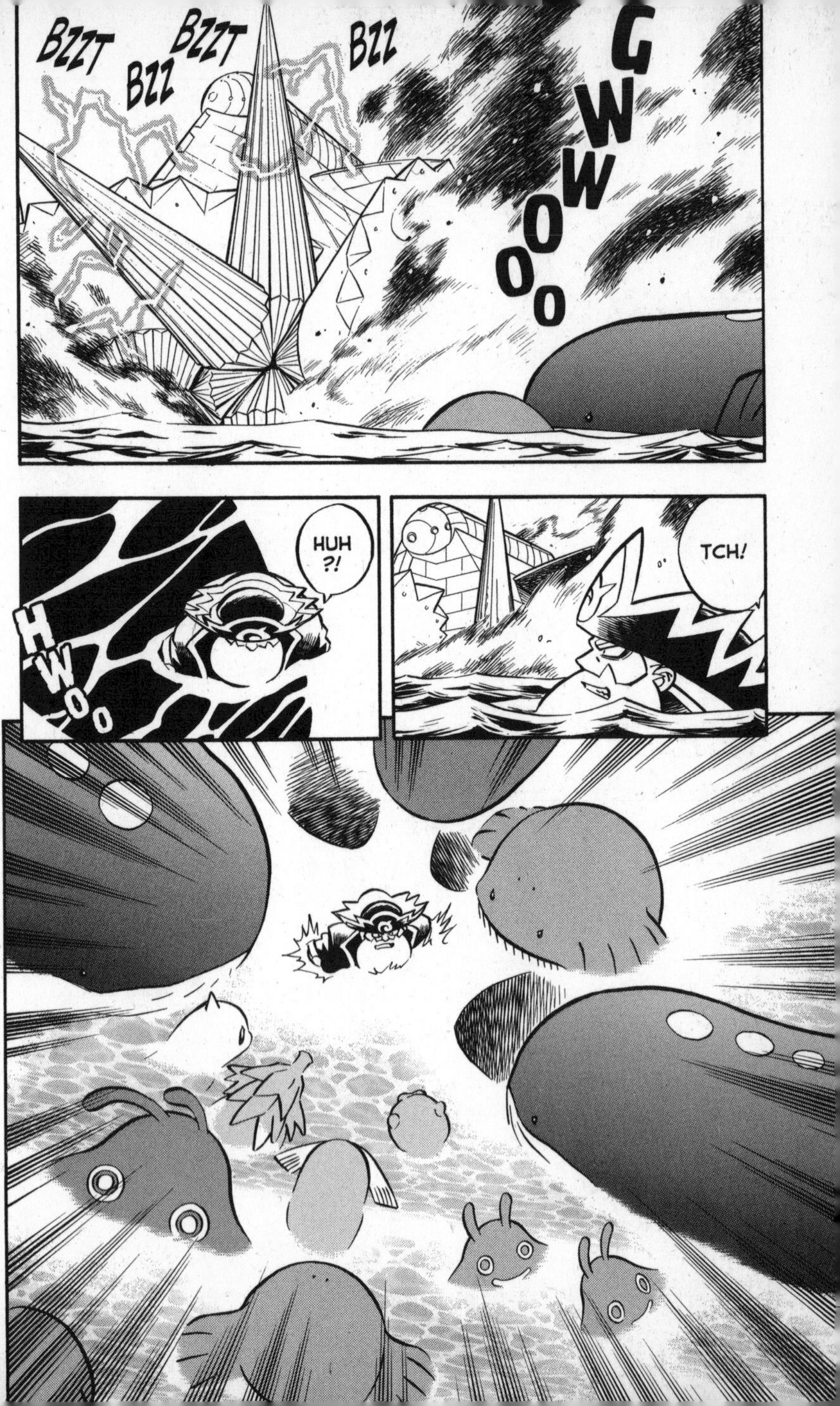
GWWOOOO
BZZ
BZZT
BZZ
BZZT
TCH!
HUH ?!
HWOO

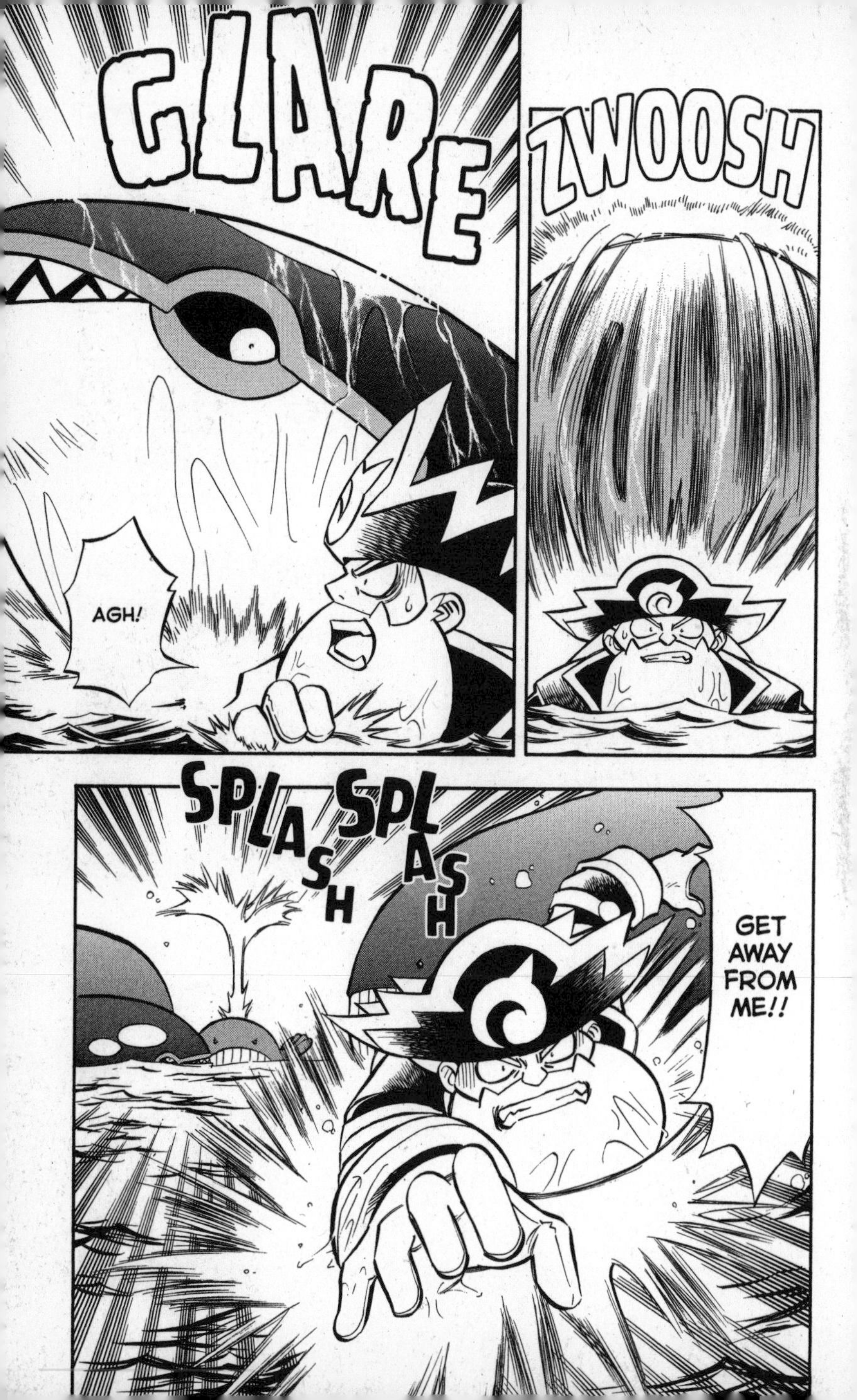
ZWOOSH
GLARE
AGH!
SPLASH
SPLASH
GET AWAY FROM ME!!

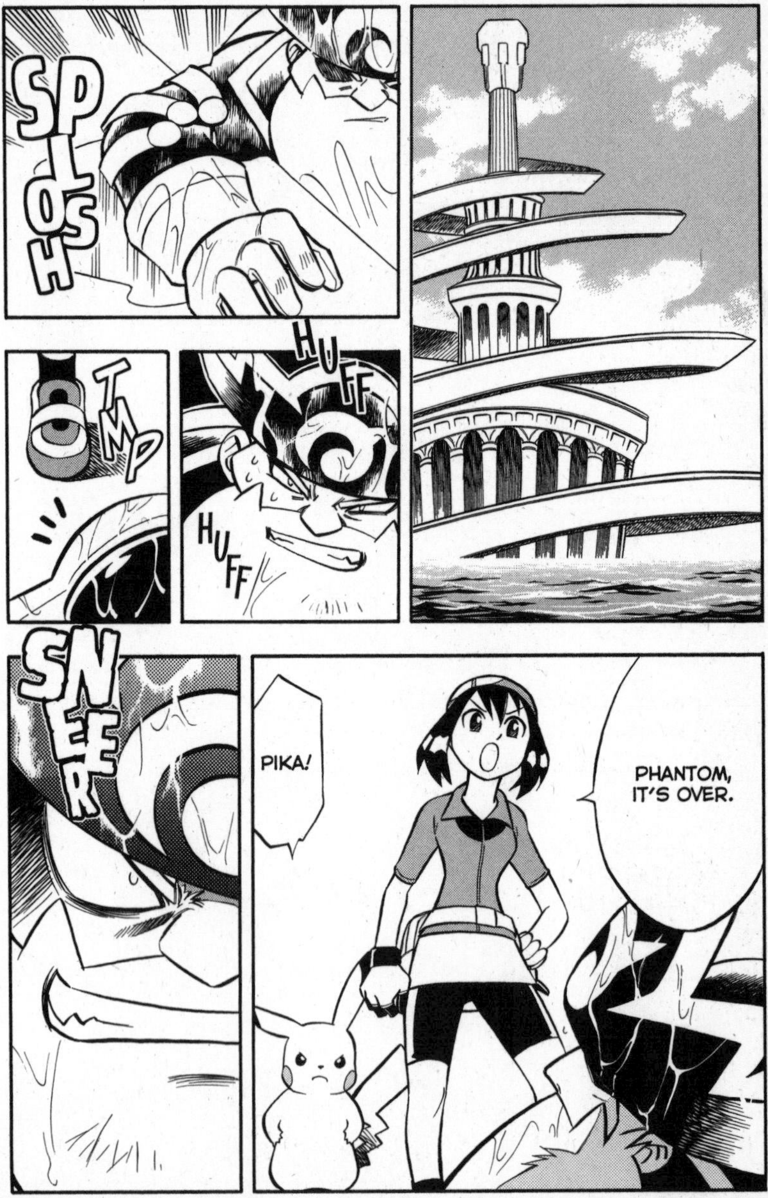
SPLOSH
HUFF
HUFF
TMP
PHANTOM, IT'S OVER.
PIKA!
SNEER

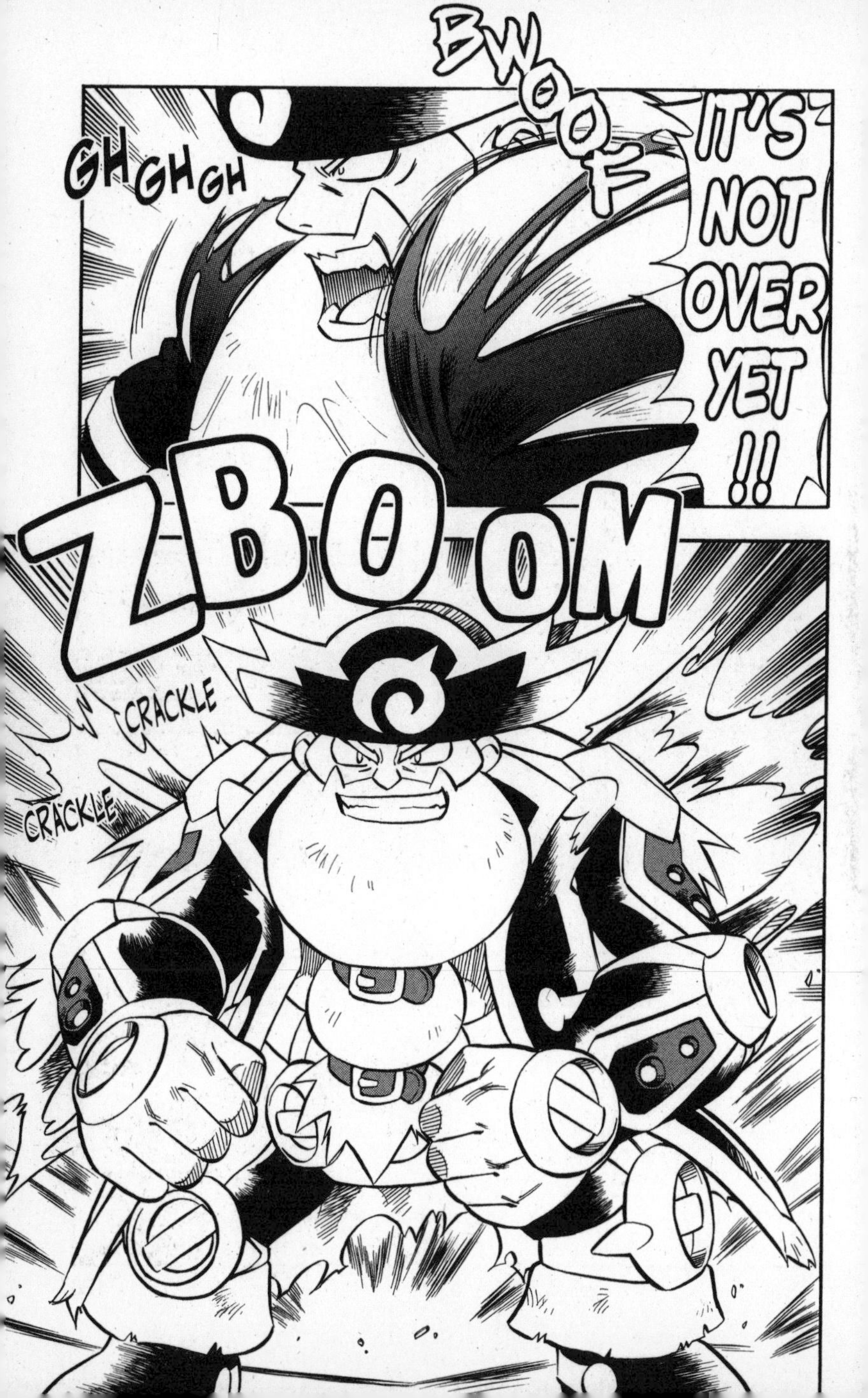
BWOOOF
IT'S NOT OVER YET!!
GH GH GH
ZBOOM
CRACKLE
CRACKLE

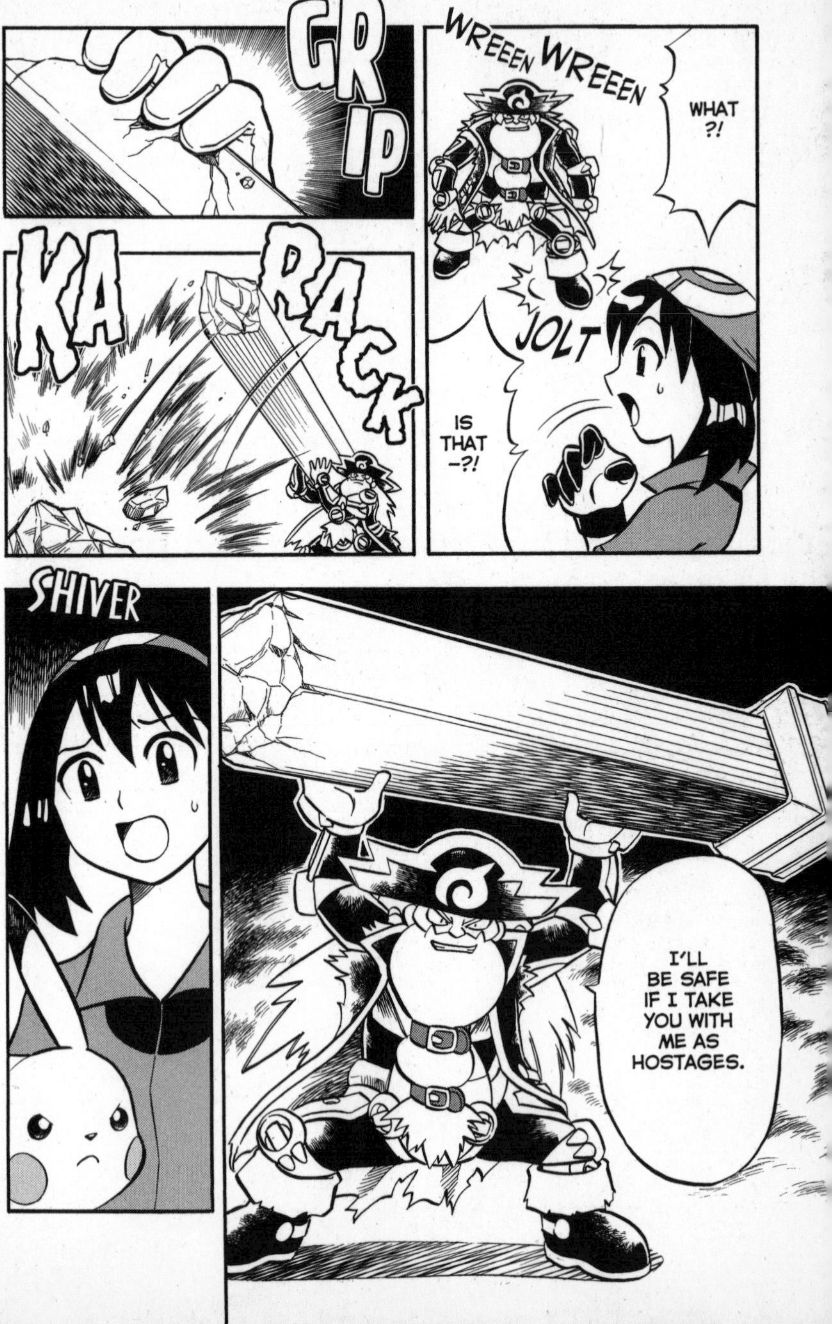
WREEEN WREEEN
WHAT?!
JOLT
IS THAT—?!
GRIP
KARACK
I'LL BE SAFE IF I TAKE YOU WITH ME AS HOSTAGES.
SHIVER

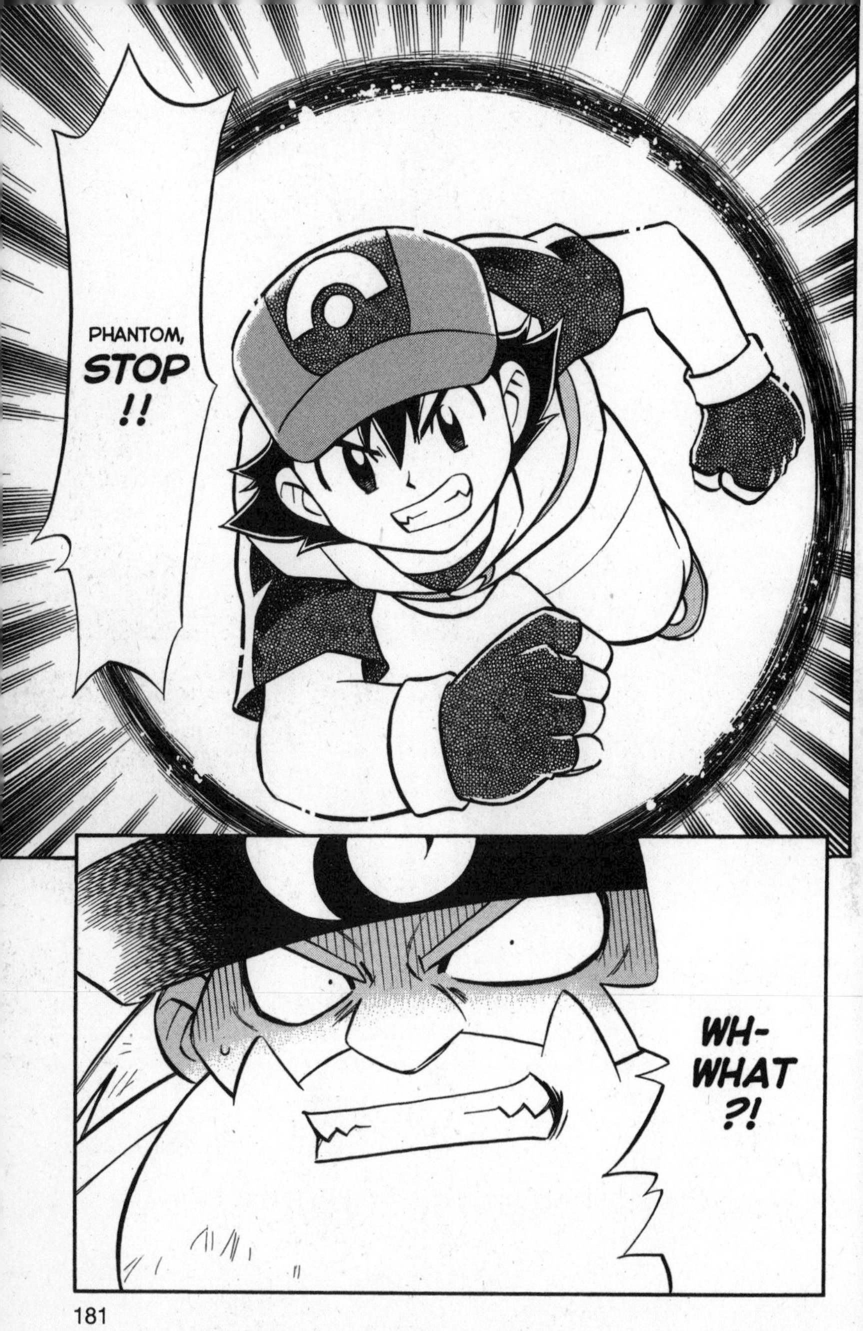
PHANTOM, STOP !!
WH- WHAT ?!

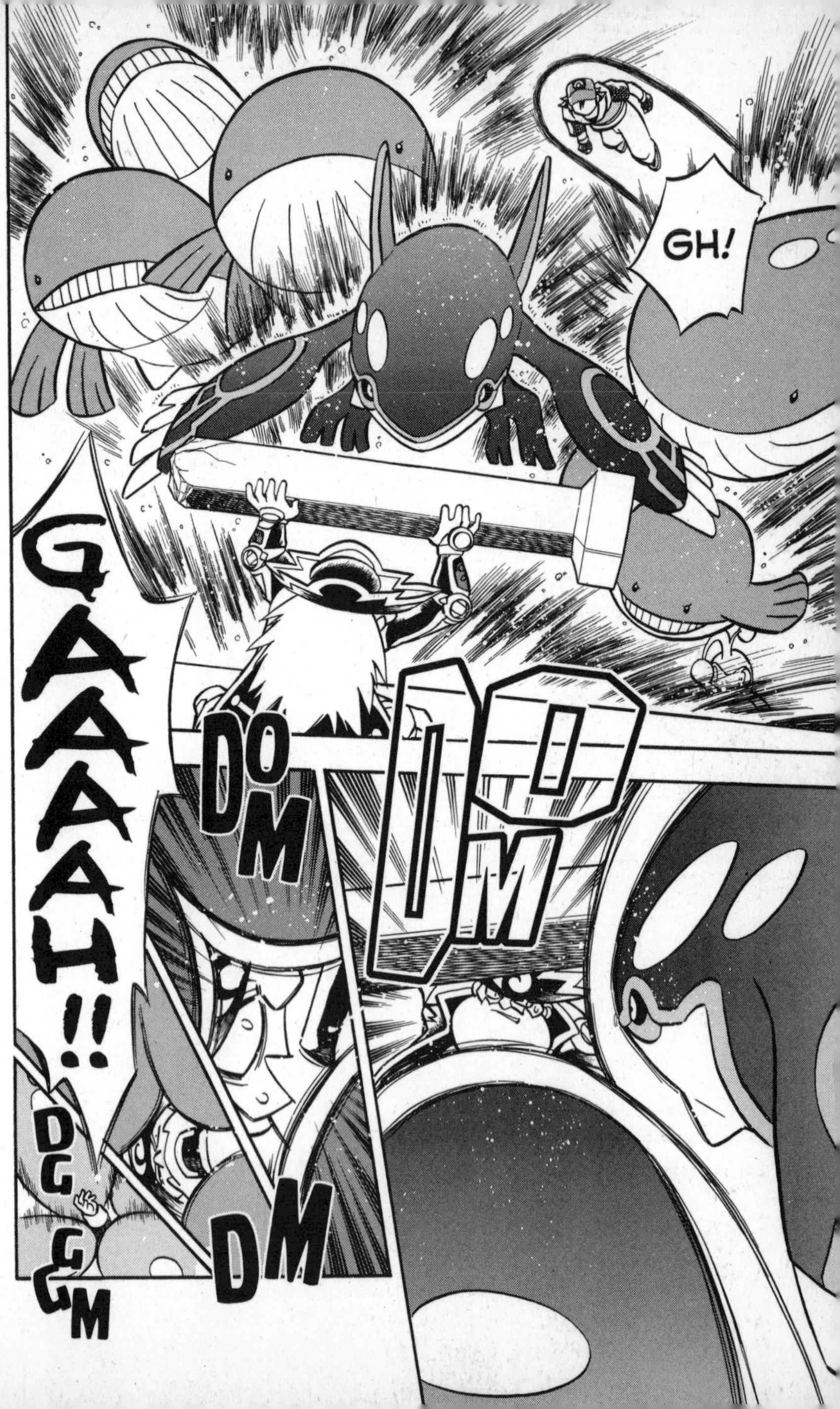
GH!
DOM
DOM
GAAAAH!!
DM
DGGGM

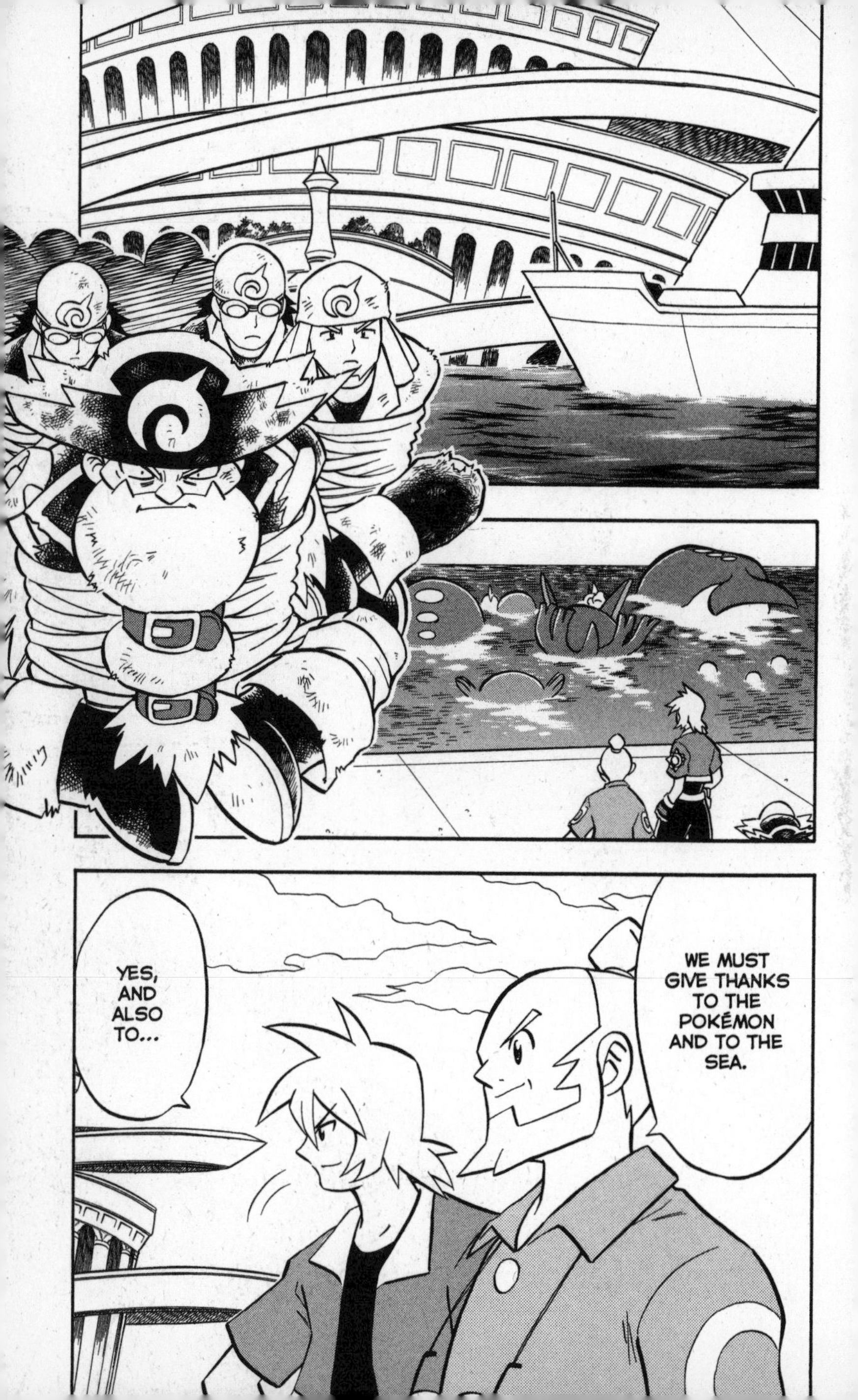
WE MUST GIVE THANKS TO THE POKÉMON AND TO THE SEA.
YES, AND ALSO TO...

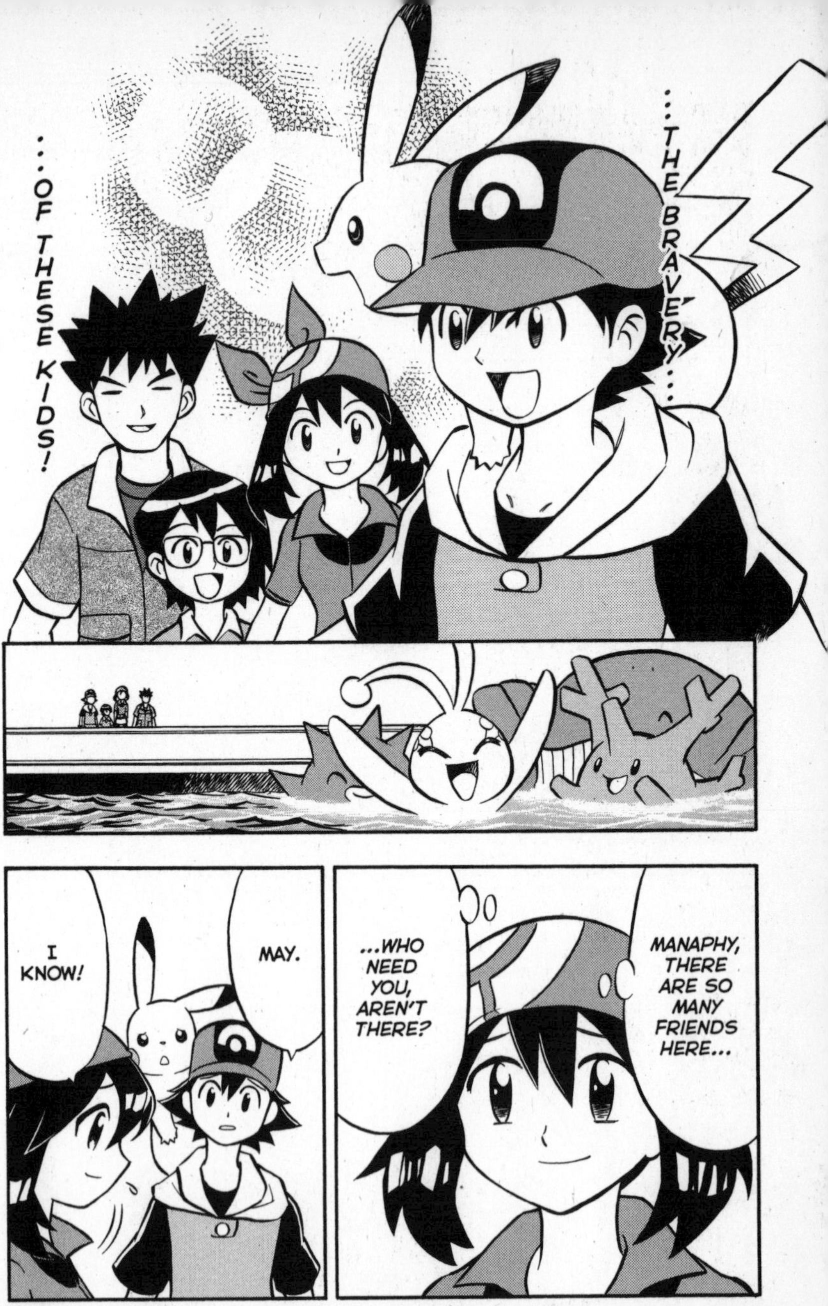
...THE BRAVERY...
...OF THESE KIDS!
MANAPHY, THERE ARE SO MANY FRIENDS HERE...
...WHO NEED YOU, AREN'T THERE?
MAY.
I KNOW!

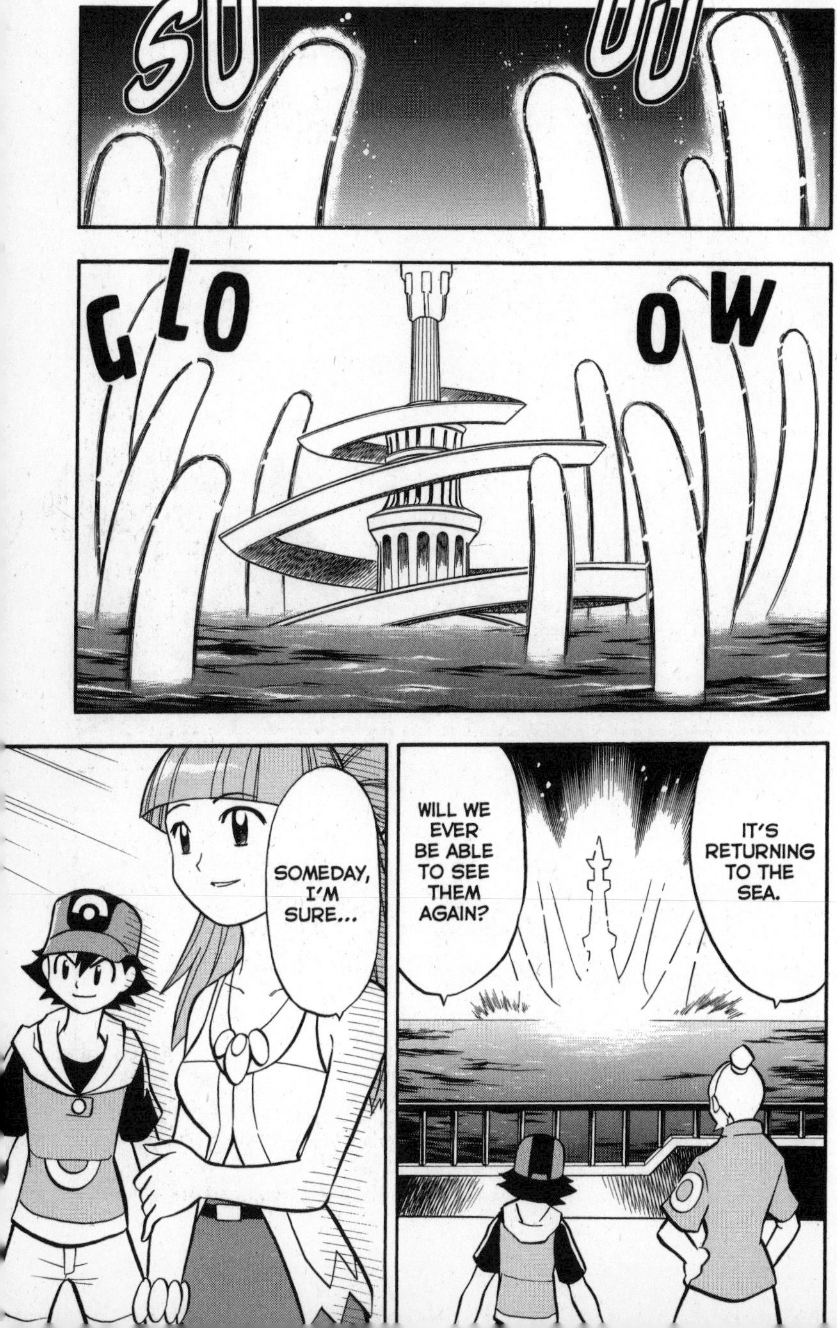
SU UU
GLO OW
IT'S RETURNING TO THE SEA.
WILL WE EVER BE ABLE TO SEE THEM AGAIN?
SOMEDAY, I'M SURE...

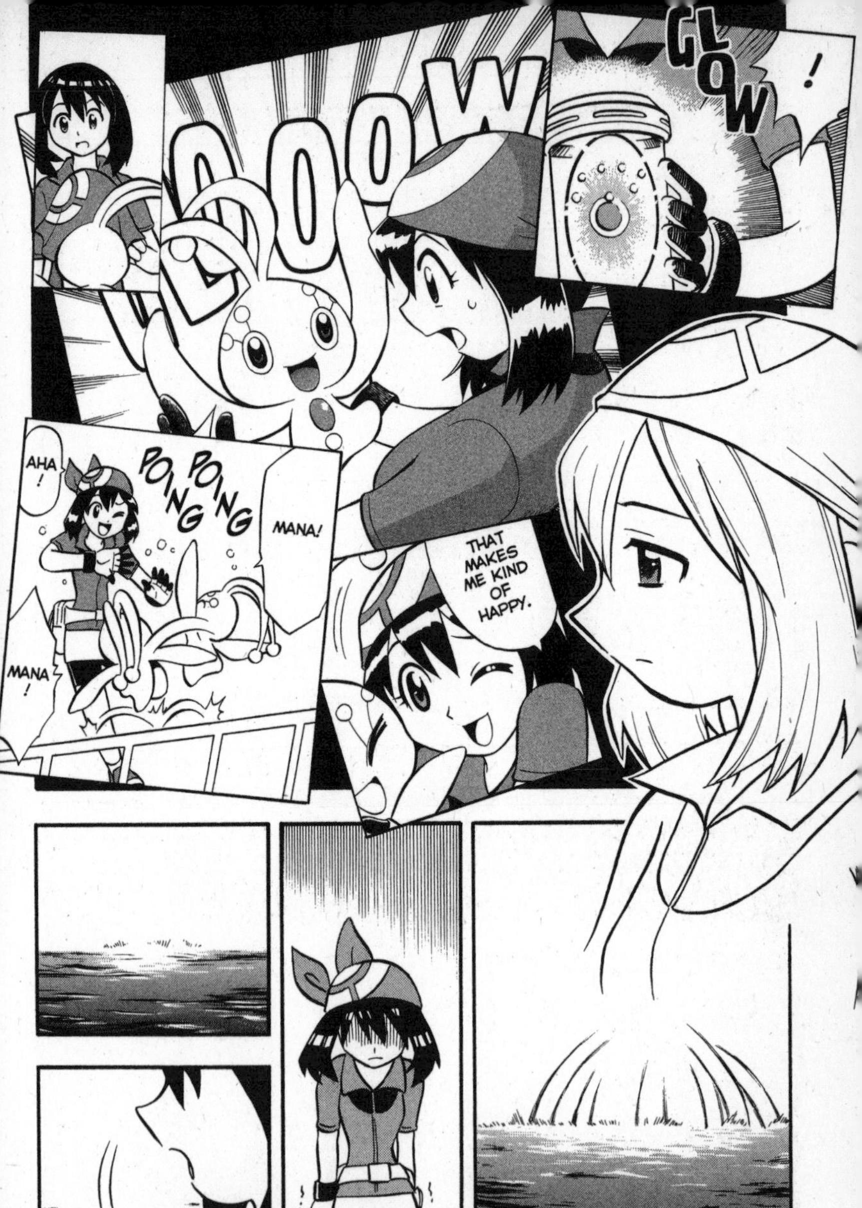

GLOW!
LOOOOW
THAT MAKES ME KIND OF HAPPY.
MANA!
POING POING
AHA!
MANA!

READ THIS WAY

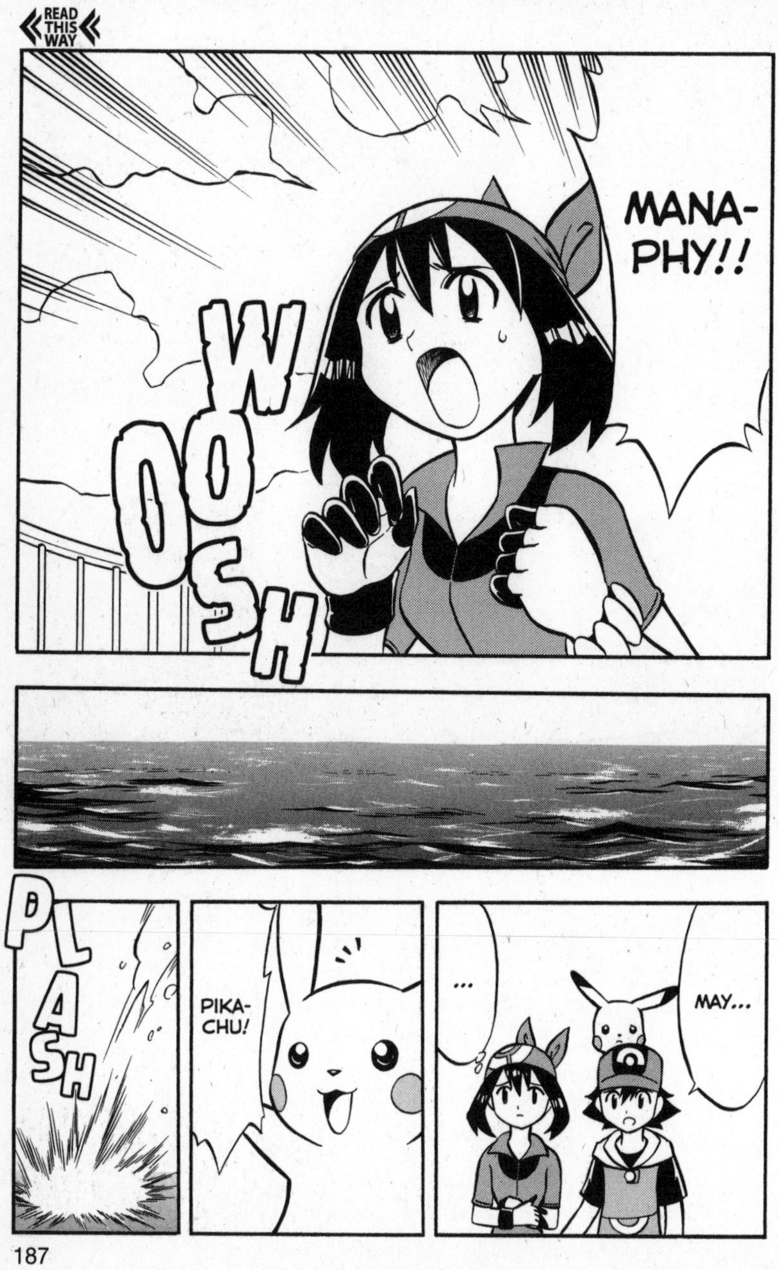
MANA-PHY!!
WOOSH
MAY...
...
PIKA-CHU!
PLASH

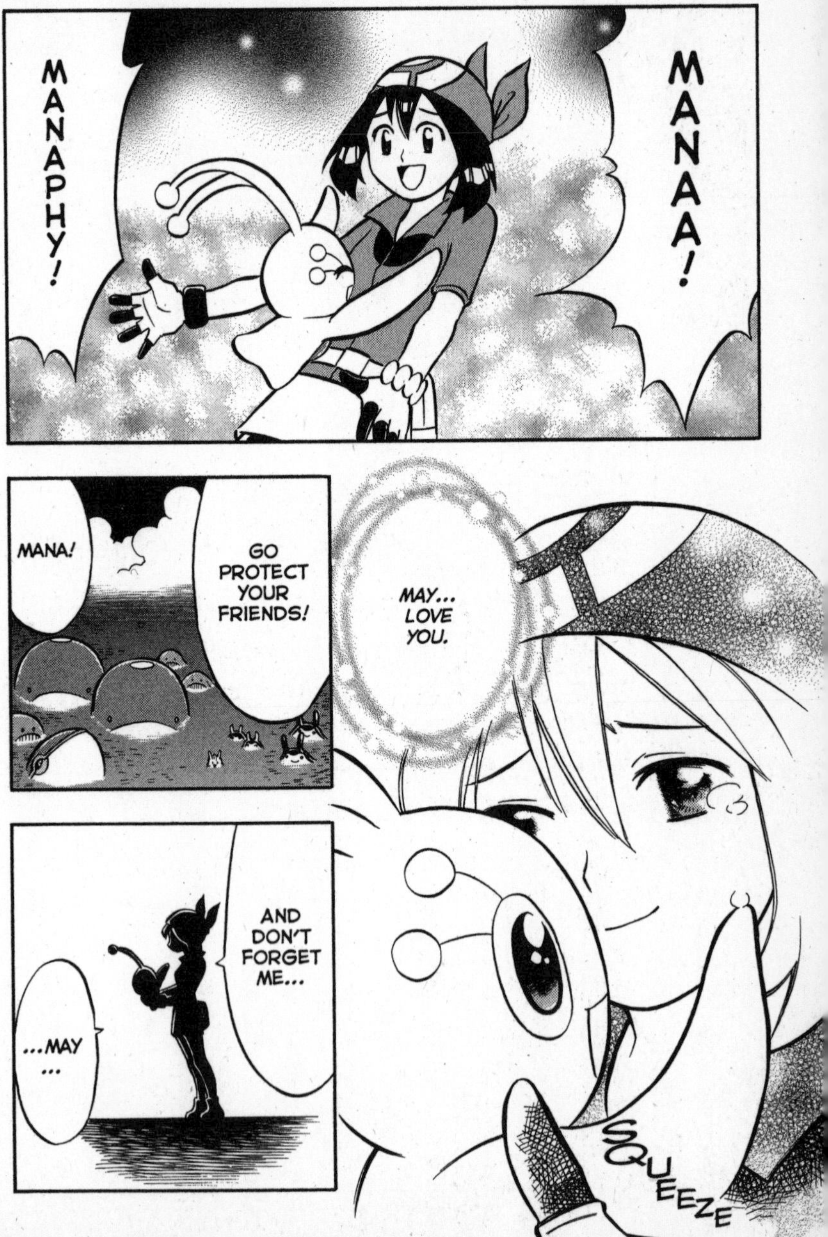
MANAAA!
MANAPHY!
MAY... LOVE YOU.
SQUEEZE
GO PROTECT YOUR FRIENDS!
MANA!
AND DON'T FORGET ME...
...MAY ...

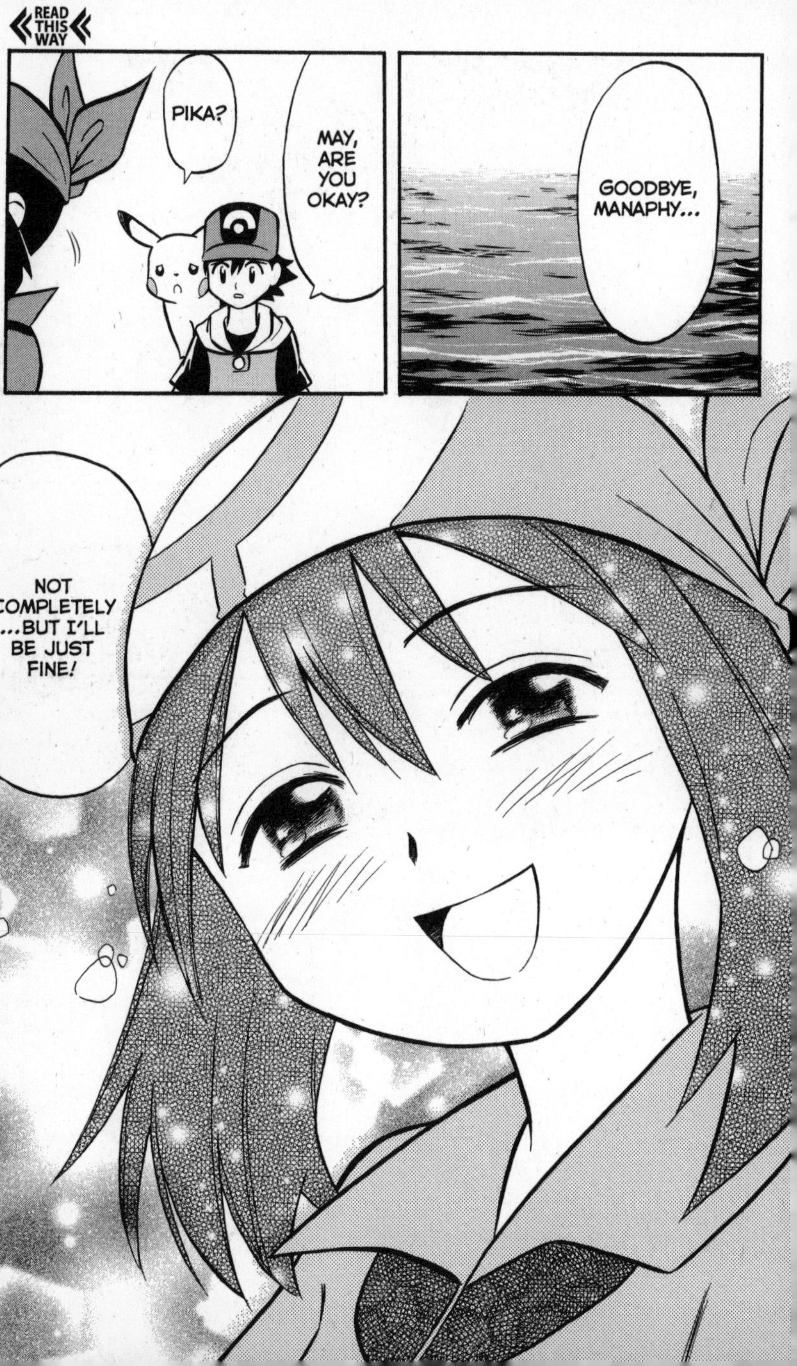
READ THIS WAY
GOODBYE, MANAPHY...
MAY, ARE YOU OKAY?
PIKA?
NOT COMPLETELY ...BUT I'LL BE JUST FINE!

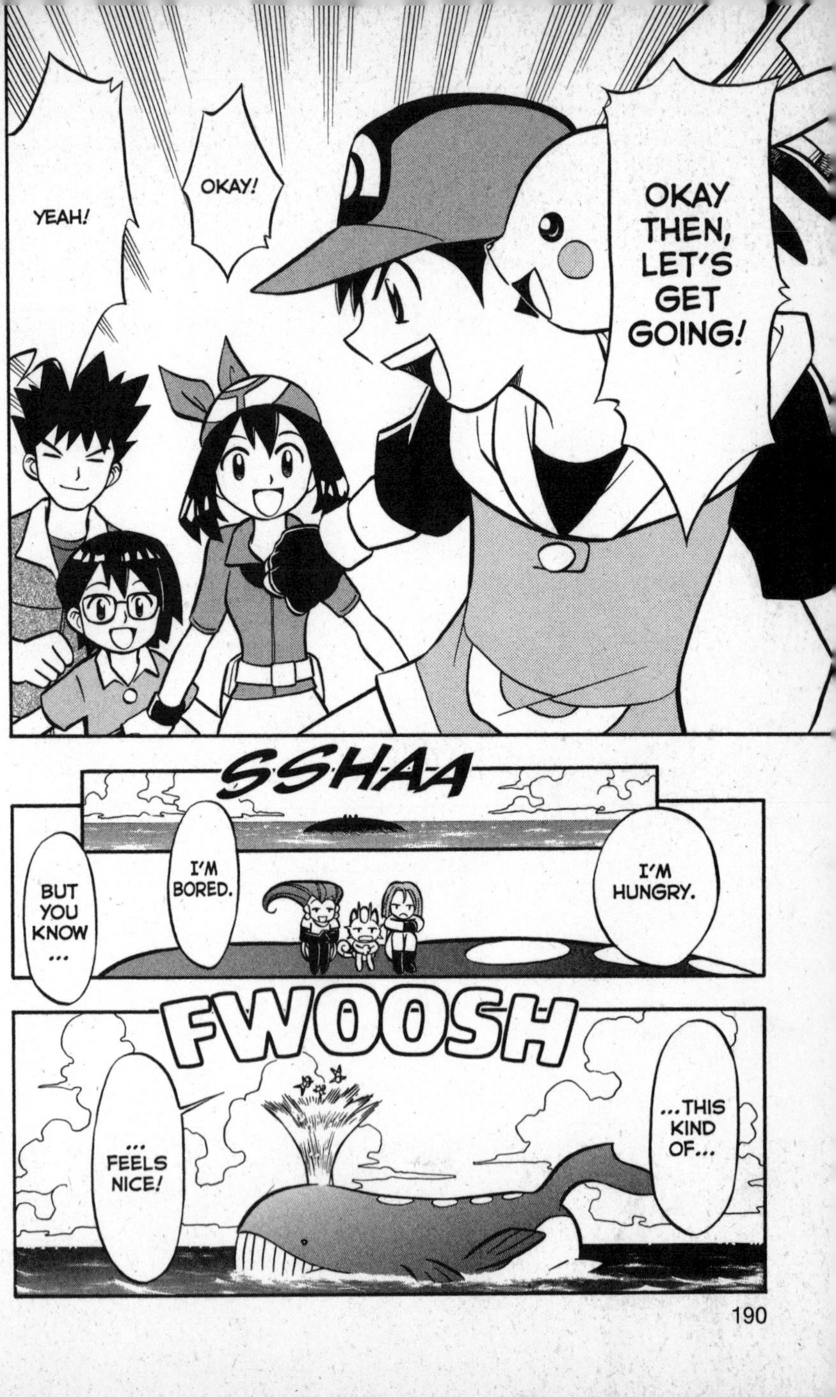

OKAY THEN, LET'S GET GOING!
OKAY!
YEAH!
SSHAA
I'M HUNGRY.
I'M BORED.
BUT YOU KNOW ...
FWOOSH
...THIS KIND OF...
... FEELS NICE!

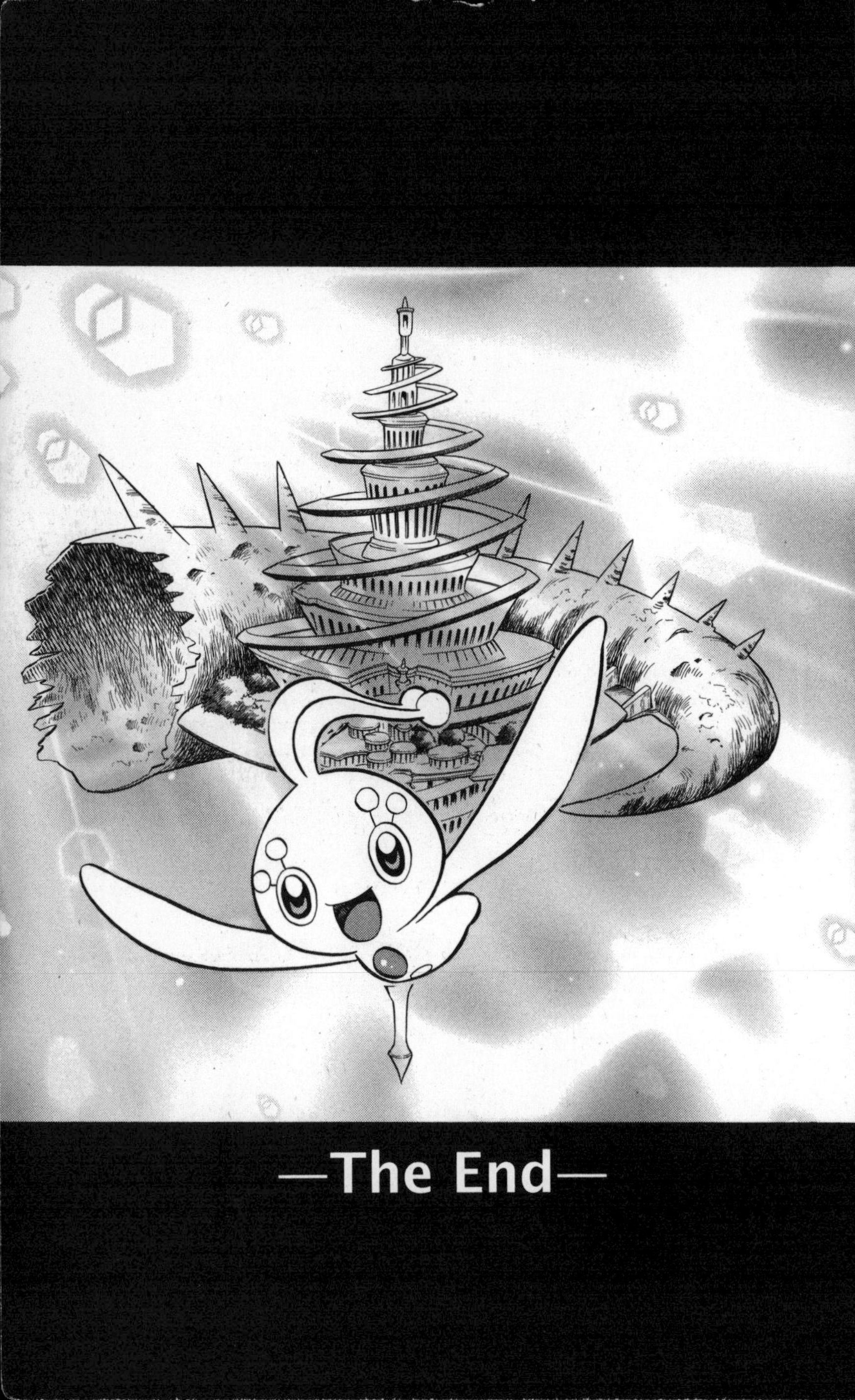

—The End—

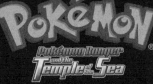

POKéMON®

Pokémon Ranger and the Temple of the Sea

VIZ Kids Editio

Story & Art by MAKOTO MIZOBUCH

Translation/Kaori Inoue
Touch-up Art & Lettering/John Clar
Graphics & Cover Design/Hitomi Yokoyama Ros
Editor/Leyla Ake

First published by Shogakukan Inc. in Japan as
"Pokémon Ranger to Umi no Ouji Manafi."

Printed in the U.S.A

Published by VIZ Media, LL
P.O. Box 7706
San Francisco, CA 9410

VIZ Kids Editio
10 9 8 7 6 5 4 3
First printing, August 200
Second printing, August 200

vizkids

store.viz.com

VIZ MEDIA
www.viz.com

RATED A FOR ALL AGES

PARENTAL ADVISORY
POKÉMON RANGER AND THE TEMPLE OF THE SEA is rated A and is suitable for readers of all ages.
ratings.viz.com

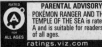

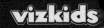

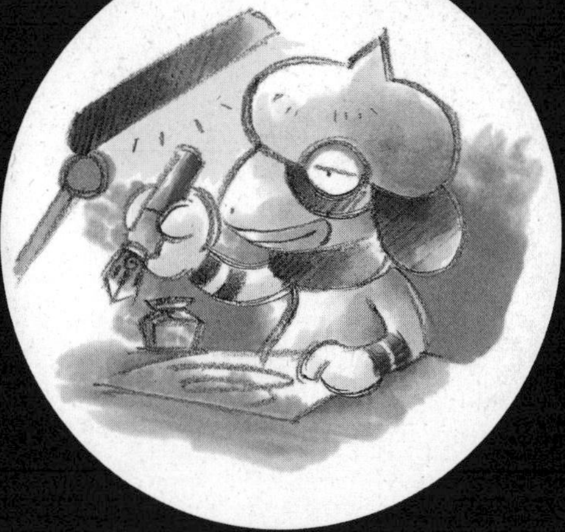

A lot of different friends helped me on this manga. We had a great time, and I thought, "This must be what being a Pokémon Ranger feels like." Everyone, thank you! It was a wonderful feeling, all of us working together as one. Making manga really is the best!

– Makoto Mizobuchi

Makoto Mizobuchi has been the artist for many series running in *CoroCoro*, one of Japan's most popular children's manga magazines. In addition to *Pokémon Mystery Dungeon* and *Pokémon Ranger and the Temple of the Sea*, Mizobuchi has also drawn for *ZOIDS* and *Hidemaru the Soccer Boy*. A movie version of *Pokémon Ranger and the Temple of the Sea* was released in theaters in 2006 in Japan and on DVD in 2007 in the U.S.

It's Tournament Time!

POKÉMON ®

Join Ash and his friends as he completes his first Kanto journey and battles his way through the Indigo League tournament! Will he reach the finals?

The final 27 episodes on 3 DVDs! Over 9 hours of Pokémon fun!

POKÉMON
Indigo League

Episodes 53-79

Season **1**

Find out in *Indigo League*—episodes 53-79 now available in a collectible DVD box set!

Complete your collection with *Pokémon* books—available now
www.pokemon.com

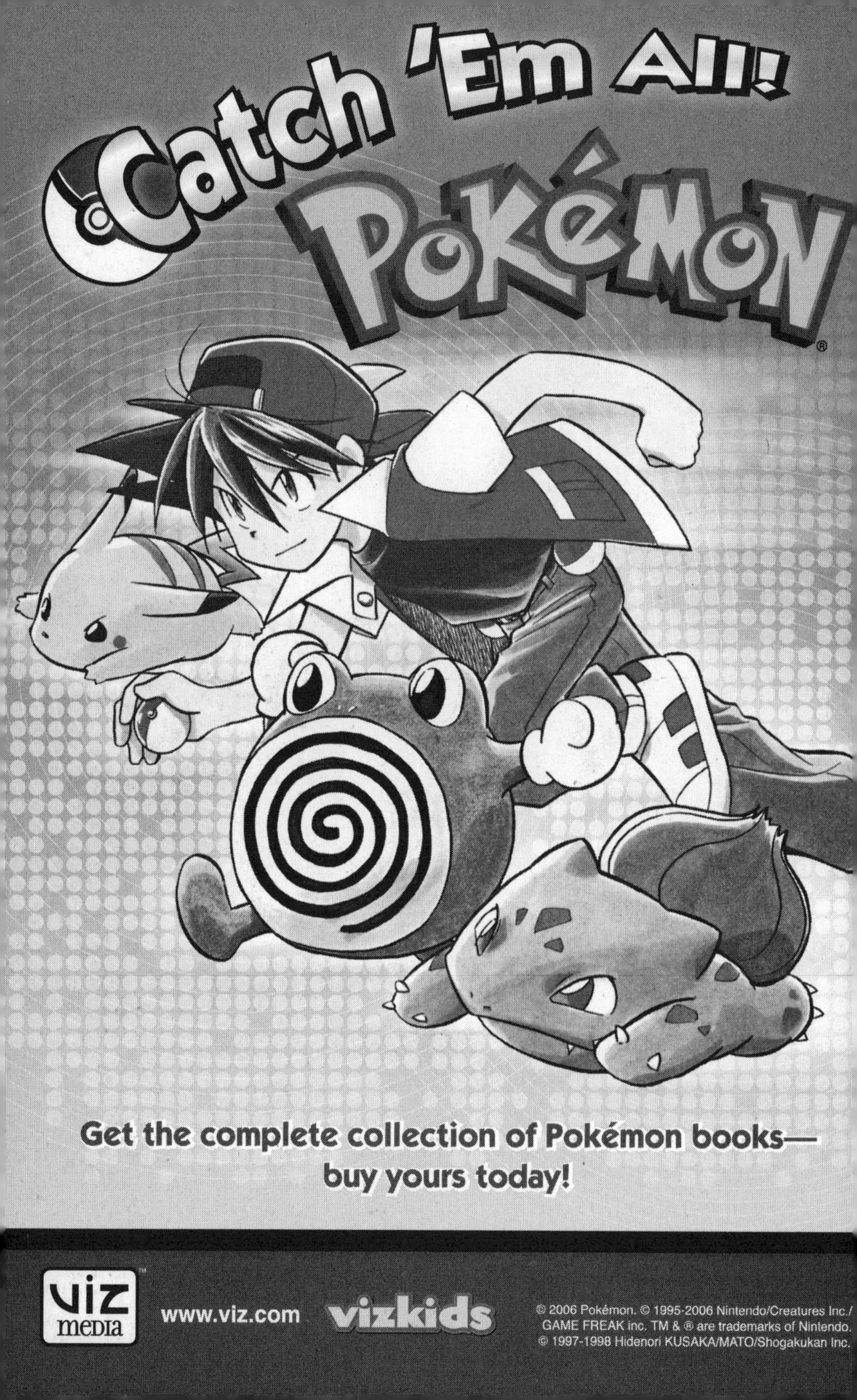
Catch 'Em All!
Pokémon®
Get the complete collection of Pokémon books—
buy yours today!
viz media™
www.viz.com
vizkids
© 2006 Pokémon. © 1995-2006 Nintendo/Creatures Inc./
GAME FREAK inc. TM & ® are trademarks of Nintendo.
© 1997-1998 Hidenori KUSAKA/MATO/Shogakukan Inc.

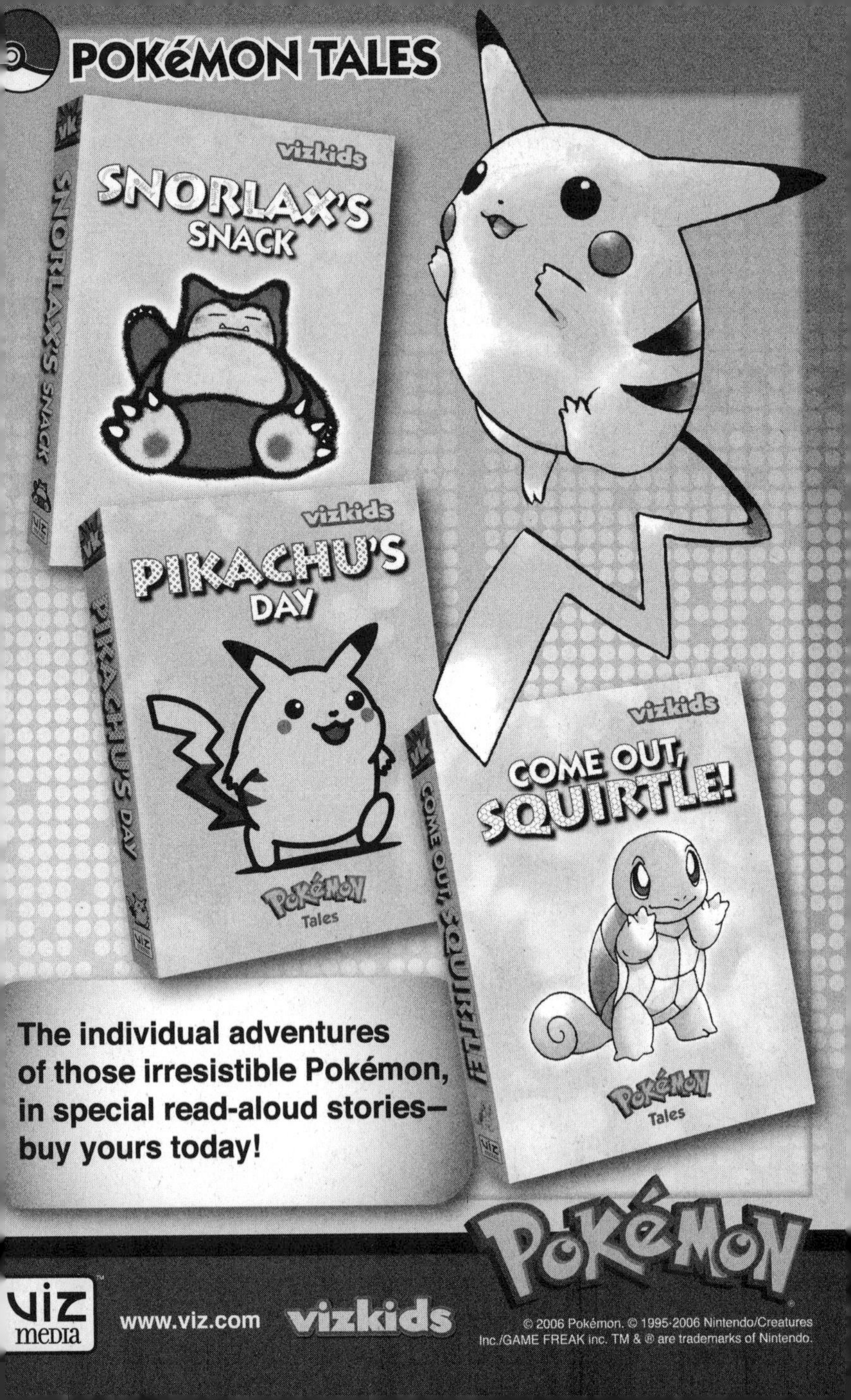

POKéMON TALES
vizkids
SNORLAX'S SNACK
vizkids
PIKACHU'S DAY
Pokémon Tales
vizkids
COME OUT, SQUIRTLE!
Pokémon Tales
The individual adventures of those irresistible Pokémon, in special read-aloud stories–buy yours today!
Pokémon
viz media
www.viz.com
vizkids
© 2006 Pokémon. © 1995-2006 Nintendo/Creatures Inc./GAME FREAK inc. TM & ® are trademarks of Nintendo.

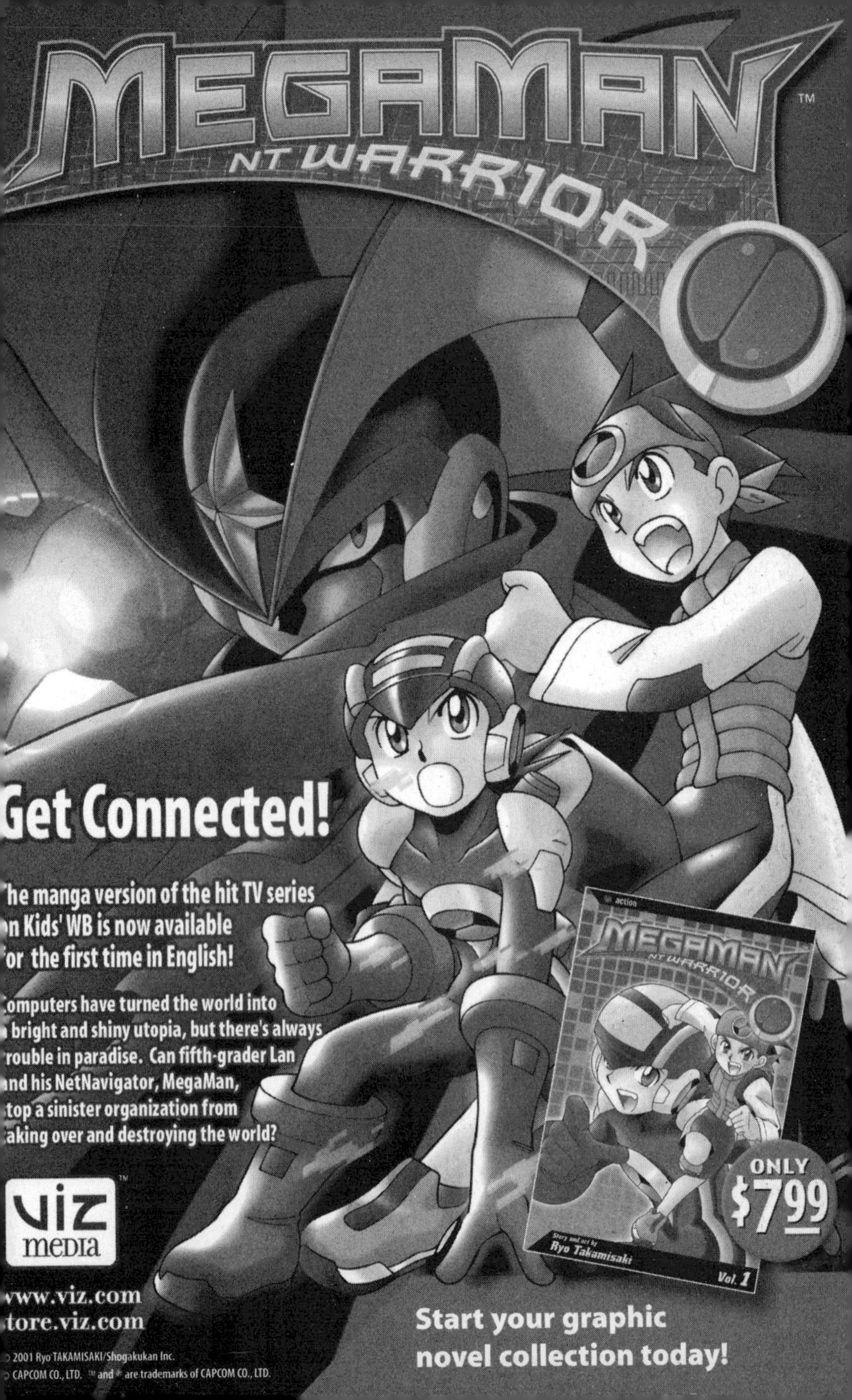
MEGAMAN™
NT WARRIOR
Get Connected!
he manga version of the hit TV series
n Kids' WB is now available
or the first time in English!
omputers have turned the world into
bright and shiny utopia, but there's always
rouble in paradise. Can fifth-grader Lan
nd his NetNavigator, MegaMan,
top a sinister organization from
aking over and destroying the world?
viz media™
www.viz.com
tore.viz.com
2001 Ryo TAKAMISAKI/Shogakukan Inc.
CAPCOM CO., LTD. ™ and ® are trademarks of CAPCOM CO., LTD.
action
MEGAMAN
NT WARRIOR
Story and art by
Ryo Takamisaki
Vol. 1
ONLY
$7.99
Start your graphic
novel collection today!